Praise for *The S*

"Marilyn Parker's debut novel, *The Struggle for Love: The Story of Leah* is an exquisite book that will break your heart and heal it again as you journey with Leah through her life of faith-testing trials. It's a beautifully written story and I'm happy to recommend it."

— C.S. LAKIN, award-winning author of more than thirty books, fiction and nonfiction. She teaches workshops and critiques at writing conferences around the country. Her blog Live Write Thrive has been listed in the top 10 blogs for writers.

"From the very first page, I absolutely fell in love with *The Struggle for Love: The Story of Leah* by Marilyn T. Parker. I honestly didn't want it to end! Marilyn expertly transports the reader to the world of ancient Israel to witness the bittersweet Old Testament story of Leah, Rachel, and their shared husband, Jacob. I found Leah's story of struggle and triumph as told by this author meticulously researched, beautifully portrayed, and absolutely unforgettable."

— DIANE MOODY, author of sixteen books, including Amazon Bestseller *Of Windmills & War*. She and her husband Ken are the founders of OBT Bookz.

"Never before have I seen the biblical character of Leah, the unchosen sister, as tangible and alive as in The Struggle for Love: The Story of Leah. Marilyn Parker's book brings life to a timeless story of family drama, deception, heartache, love, and loss with an epic story arc and a touching narrative. I highly recommend it.

— BETH LOTTIG, editor, book coach, and founder of Inspire Books

"There have been only a few biblically-based works of fiction that have impacted me as much or more than the scriptures they were gleaned from. *The Struggle for Love: The Story of Leah* is one of those. As I read, I kept going back to the Bible, comparing the novel with the Genesis account. While staying true to the Word, Marilyn fleshed out these Old Testament characters in such a powerful way I found myself reading parts of the book over and over. *The Struggle for Love* will move you to renewed faith in the purposes of God.

— SUZAN CARTAGENA, author of *The God Connection* and *Identity Theft*, which have been translated into a total of five languages. She and her husband Micky take the Gospel all over the world.

The
STRUGGLE
for LOVE

The Story of Leah

The STRUGGLE for LOVE

The Story of Leah

MARILYN T. PARKER

PW
PRESS

THE STRUGGLE FOR LOVE
© Marilyn T. Parker, 2021

Cover and interior by Roseanna White Designs
Cover images from Shutterstock

ISBN: 978-0-578-70246-9 (paperback)
      979-8-9857509-0-4 (hardcover)

DEDICATION

I couldn't even begin to name all of the people who have encouraged me in the writing of this book.

To my husband Peter who has shown the patience of Job as I've hidden myself away with Leah and Jacob and the rest of the family that was chosen to usher Christ into the world. On our wedding day Peter vowed to support me in all that God had called me to do. He has honored that vow in a way few men do. Thank you, my love.

To my wonderful children who have prodded me on with, "Mom, when are you ever going to finish that book?" Well, I did it, kids! Thank you for your encouragement.

To Marilee, the first person with real writing credentials to tell me, "You have the talent to write professionally." Those words meant more than she ever knew. I wish she were here to see Leah's story in print. May you rest in God's loving peace, Marilee.

To Lone Mountain Writers, the group Marilee led. You guys were tough on me! Thank you! It really was your brutally honest critiques that drove me to learn the craft.

And above all, thank you my wonderful Lord and Savior, Jesus Christ, for giving me the gift to tell Your stories. All praise and glory to You, always.

Above the mud-brick houses and the fields that lay around them.
Above the land between the rivers.
Above the brilliant expanse of stars, and planets, and galaxies,
moving with perfect precision along predesigned paths.
Above the universe and every other created thing.
The God of Abraham looked down—and wept with His beloved.

PART ONE

The Meeting

Jacob

The sky was gray the day I buried Leah, as though it had put off its bright garment and donned a dark robe for the occasion.

I stood at the entrance of the cave. Watching as the last of the mourners made their way back down the rocky slope to the verdant valley dotted with sprawling oaks and black tents.

In the distance, women were already crouching before campfires, baking bread on large, flat, cooking stones or stirring steaming pots of stew. A man skinned a rabbit for his supper. Living left so little time to mourn the dead. It ought not to be so. The dead deserved more.

Tears bit at the back of my eyelids. Leah had deserved more than my grief at her passing. She had deserved my love.

A gust of cold wind lifted the hem of my garment. I fisted my cloak to my chest, pressing against the chill—and the ache in my heart. It hindered neither.

I had sent the children and grandchildren back down the hill, asking to be alone in the cave with my wife—then couldn't find the courage to go in. But I could put it off no longer. With a long, shuddering breath I stooped to enter the tomb.

Torches saluting from niches in the wall cast somber light over the large recess where three stone crypts lay in solemn repose. Grandfather Abraham had purchased the cave and the valley below as a burial place for his beloved Sarah. His sons had brought him here to join her. Now their bones lay together, sheltered in one of the stone crypts, next to the crypt where my father lay peacefully with my mother. And the empty vault—where I would one day lie with Leah.

Using my staff to steady myself against the uneven limestone, I moved toward the shelf carved out of the wall of the cave.

Grief snatched my breath as I saw her there—taking her turn on the hard slab—waiting for the flesh to fall away from her narrow frame, leaving dry, brittle bones that her sons would gather and lay to rest in the empty crypt.

My fingers trembled as I touched the hollow of my wife's cold cheek. The woman I did not choose. Chosen of God.

Leah.

I laid my head on her still chest and wept.

CHAPTER ONE

Leah

Decades earlier

I blinked several times, trying to force my sister-in-law's pinched brow into focus as she removed the wrapping of sodden tea leaves from my eyes. She was shaking her head. Not something I'd hoped to see on this morning that could decide my future.

"I told you to get rest last night. Your eyes look like half-ripened pomegranates!" she said, tossing the soggy mess into a bowl.

"I tried, I just couldn't sleep, Olnah."

I wanted to tell her it was nerves that kept me tossing on my pallet, but when that scowl was fixed on my sister-in-law's forehead her ears ceased to function. My brother loved his pretty wife, but when she started to rant, he headed for the rooftop.

She handed me a rag to wipe the damp bits of tea leaves from my face. "Well, what am I supposed to do about your eyes now? You look like you haven't slept in days! I'm not a miracle worker, Leah."

The tight twist of Olnah's mouth did nothing to unwind the coil of nerves that moved in my stomach. She didn't have to say it. I knew I was no beauty like my younger sister Rachel. In addition to my red-veined, itchy eyes, my nose didn't quite fit my face. It was too long and too straight, like my hair, which hung limp unless I wound it in rags at night. And even then, the curls knew their way home and by noonday would successfully escape, leaving wilted strands of dull brown behind.

13

But it wasn't just Olnah whose impatient eyes were on me.

Rachel had not yet begun to bleed, but it would be soon, and our father had already received several generous offers for her hand in marriage—which, of course, he couldn't accept, since tradition demanded the elder daughter marry first.

Olnah and the other women of the family were looking to Rachel's flowering with great anticipation, each giving their advice on how to hasten its arrival.

"She should not be allowed to run."

"She should eat pomegranate seeds."

"She should sit by the creek and relax her mind."

"A suppository of warm olive oil will hasten the flow."

A long line of suitors awaited the blessed day. My blood had arrived without ceremony, and the only line awaiting me was the line of dear women giving unwanted advice.

"Leah, rub some oil on your face at night."

"Leah, your nails need cleaning."

"Leah, don't pull your hair back."

"Don't scowl. It makes you look old."

It wasn't as though I *wanted* to keep my sister from marrying. I loved Rachel deeply. I wished nothing but happiness for her, but what could I do? No one had come to inquire—until now.

The rough-wood door burst open and a servant girl motioned frantically for us to come. "Hurry! They're waiting for you!" The coil in my stomach wound tighter. No one was sparing my nerves this morning.

Olnah pulled a few curls over my shoulders and stood back for a better look. For a moment, I thought I saw a small glint of satisfaction in her eyes. But it was quickly doused.

"That will have to do, I guess. May the gods be merciful," she said, dipping her knee to the carved images sitting portentously on the stone altar in the corner.

It was obvious she thought it would take a deity to get this man to marry me. I breathed a prayer to the God of Abraham. She may be right.

I followed Olnah and the servant through the courtyard surrounded by mud-brick dwellings, a hive-shaped communal oven squatting at its center, and to the house Rachel and I shared with our father. Rachel had been sent to graze the sheep, to keep her out of sight, so the man wouldn't ask for her instead of me.

The servant opened the door. Olnah led me across the hard-packed-dirt floor, bowed to her father-in-law and his guest, and turned to go, giving me a sideways glance that said not to humiliate myself.

Father and the man were sitting at the table, an array of half-empty plates between them. I dipped my head. One of my father's bushy brows moved upward, a silent message that I'd taken my time getting there. Thin, tight lips split his heavy beard as he wiped his hands with a linen rag and leaned back in his chair.

"Anasa—my daughter Leah," Father said.

Anasa stood. "I'm very pleased to see you again, Leah."

The man was looking at me as though he actually saw me standing there, unlike most men with whom I had any interaction. I forced myself not to wipe my damp hands on my tunic.

Anasa could not be called handsome, but he was tall and square-shouldered. His eyes were the color of loamy soil, a touch of sorrow in their depths.

I'd only met him once. He'd come in the spring to purchase some milking goats. His wife had died not long before. He had two young children with him, a boy and a girl. The girl's eyes were big and full of sadness, and I was reminded of Rachel, who had been about the same age when our mother died in childbirth.

I'd held the girl on my lap and told her and her brother stories and fed them raisin cakes while the men perused the flocks. Their father had seemed grateful when he returned, but he'd gathered his children and left with nothing more than a nod. But now he was here—to talk to my father. About me. Perhaps, just perhaps, beauty wasn't what the man valued most. In spite of my effort to contain it, hope was breaking through my reserve like a chick pecking its way out of its shell.

"I apologize," Anasa said to Father, "for not mentioning it before . . . but would you allow me to speak to Leah alone? Within your sight, of course."

Surprise peaked my father's brows. To speak with a prospective bride at all was not the normal way of things. Usually the girl would be brought in, put on display, and then dismissed while the men haggled over an acceptable bride price and an ample dowry.

With the appropriate tenor of reluctance, Father agreed.

"It is unusual, but I suppose I will allow it. However, you will remain in my sight at all times."

"Certainly. And that is acceptable to you, Leah?"

My jaw went limp. No man had ever asked if *anything* was acceptable to me. I nodded, forcing my gaping mouth closed.

Anasa bade me sit across from him on one of the wooden chairs that had been arranged a good way from the cluster of houses but close enough to see if he made an untoward advance. Not that anyone thought it likely, but the appearance of propriety had been stretched and must not be breached entirely. I was thankful he had requested a private meeting. I was nervous enough without critical ears measuring every fumbling word I said.

Anasa smiled. "You look lovely today, Leah."

Lovely? Heat crept up my neck. I could almost feel the curls unwind and stretch in protest to their unnatural state.

"Thank you."

His eyes went to my father and brothers, a knot of folded arms against the brick wall.

"I hope you don't think it improper of me to speak to you alone. I mean no disrespect by it. But I wished for you to speak unhindered by"—he looked toward the wall again—"by anything."

He drew a deep breath, his gaze focused somewhere between the milking shed and the sheepfold. "My wife died in the winter." His voice trailed off. He swallowed and shook his head.

"I'm sorry."

A pinch of tears collected behind my eyes. I forced them back.

"I have children—two sons and a daughter who is only four. You met two of them." He looked to see if I remembered, as if it were important that I did.

"Yes. I remember them."

"I must ask you directly, Leah. Would you find it difficult to love another woman's children?"

Would I find it difficult? I tried to give his question the consideration it deserved. But no, I would not find it difficult. I would thrill at the opportunity to pour love and comfort on these little ones. I had been both mother and sister to Rachel since our mother's death. But I understood his concern. Women often died in childbirth, their successors happy enough to take their place and care for children not their own . . . until they gave birth themselves, and their affection shifted to their own offspring, causing jealousy and contention. But I would never do that! I was certain of it. I had suffered too much myself to inflict pain on a little one.

"No, my lord. I don't think I would find it difficult to love any child."

"Anasa—call me Anasa," he said, the tension easing around his eyes.

"Zerah was very young when we married, and frail. She was a wonderful mother. She loved our sons and daughter beyond all bounds, but with each birth . . . she grew weaker. She took a fever last winter and just didn't have the strength to recover." His eyes filled with moisture.

"I'm sorry," I said. "For the loss of your wife." I knew loss and grief, and I could feel the man's pain in my own chest. He had loved his wife. Perhaps there was no place left for love in him. The thought stabbed at my heart. But he was kind. He would be a gentle husband. And maybe—

"Thank you." A faint smile lifted the corners of Anasa's mouth. He ran a long-fingered hand through his thick hair.

"I am a merchant, away from home too much. I need a woman—a wife—with a strong yet gentle hand to take over my household."

My heart took a little leap. For a long moment, the words hung in awkward silence between us. Then Anasa reached into his pocket and drew something out.

"I brought gifts for your father and brothers—and this for you."

I stared at his open palm, eyes transfixed on an intricately carved bull sitting on its hoofed feet. Its horned head faced forward in an unnatural manner. It was shaped from an exquisite carnelian with a hole where a fine braided cord was threaded through it.

Anasa smiled, holding out the charm.

My hands didn't reach for it. They were clenched in my lap. I felt suddenly faint.

"Leah? It's an amulet, to protect you and bring you favor with the gods."

He looked confused, and then the smile on his face flattened into a thin line.

"It was crafted by an artisan in the temple at Ur and blessed by the Enzi."

The air felt thick, making it difficult to breathe. He withdrew his hand and leaned back on the chair, anger gathering in his eyes. "It is a fine gift. The only one of its kind."

I couldn't speak. I simply stared at the spot where his hand had been. A man was offering me a gift, signifying his intent to take me as his wife. A good man. I would have a husband who was gentle and kind, and children. But at what price?

My mother had taught me not to bow a knee to gods of wood and stone. What would she say if she knew I wore a symbol of a false god for protection? And could I dishonor the Living God and fear no consequence? Would I want to, even if there were none?

Anasa stood, the carnelian locked in his fist.

I forced myself out of my stupor and looked up at him. "Forgive me, Anasa. I meant no disrespect. Please—let me explain." He hesitated, then sat, his face a mottled red, his hand still tight around the amulet.

Just take it. You're going to ruin everything, Leah.

I exhaled a halting breath. "Please believe me when I say I am greatly honored by your generosity. It's beautiful . . . a gracious gift."

My lips twitched. *Just take it. You can put it away with your private things and never look at it again.*

But that would not be possible. Anasa would expect me to wear it. My eyes began to itch, the good effect of the tea leaves worn off. I pressed them closed, trying to force some moisture into them. When I opened my eyes again, Anasa's brow was still furrowed and angry. My shoulders fell with a slow sigh.

"I just . . . can't accept it."

Anasa blinked. He appeared stunned for a long moment, the anger contracting into confusion.

"And why is that, Leah? Don't be afraid to speak the truth. I want to know."

But I *was* afraid. The truth was not the accepted practice of the day. And how could I make this man comprehend something I barely understood myself?

I tried to compose myself. To gather what little courage I had.

"I worship but one God, Anasa—the God of Abraham. And to seek the favor of another would dishonor Him."

Anasa appeared baffled as he regarded me. "I know of Abraham," he said. "Everyone knows of Abraham. I know he worshiped an invisible god, but don't you think it wise to honor the other gods as well, in the event this god does not hear or finds you insolent?"

My father's argument exactly. How many times had I heard my mother dispute it? When Father planted the barley he prayed to Ninkilim, the god of vermin, and Ashnan the goddess of grain, *and* he prayed to the God of his uncle Abraham, which left my mother in a hot temper. She stood to her full height, her beautiful eyes fierce on his, and told him the God of Abraham would not be entreated in the company of idols. My mother was fearless in her defense of her God.

But I was not my mother.

"I am often given to fear, Anasa. I fear many things. But I do not fear gods made by men's hands. They have no life—no power to harm or to help."

He leaned forward, his brow creased with what looked more like concern than confrontation. He seemed afraid for me—that I placed myself in danger by my stand.

"And how can you be so sure, Leah? You can't even see this god of yours."

I hadn't thought to engage Anasa so directly, but there seemed no way out of it now. I would just have to face whatever my imprudence brought. "You're right, Anasa. I can't see Him . . . but does the wind not exist because I cannot see it?"

He shrugged. "Of course the wind exists. We can feel it on our face. We can see the leaves moving with its power. That is a different thing altogether."

"Is it?"

"You think not?"

"I can't see God, but I sense His presence. Not always. Like the wind, sometimes He's still, and I wonder where He is and if He will ever come again. But I cannot believe he leaves His children alone. Would you? Would you leave your children to fend for themselves?"

A flicker of comprehension crossed Anasa's eyes.

"And where did this invisible god of yours come from, Leah?" he said, waving his hand toward the heavens. "Who created him? Another god?"

"There was no god before Him, and there will be no god after. A true god must be without beginning or end, otherwise he is not a god at all."

"Not a god?" Anasa said, the line between his dark brows deepening. "You are saying that Enki and Enlil are not gods? Believing in this invisible god of yours is one thing, but denying the very existence of the gods of our ancestors . . . is quite another."

Twinges of apprehension tracked up and down my spine. The man could cause me much trouble with my father and brothers, and, if he chose, with the priests, who did not look kindly on those who spoke ill of their deities. Beor would be happy enough to see me at their mercy. My oldest brother had always resented that I followed my mother's example and spurned my father's gods. *Lord, give me wisdom.*

"Consider this, Anasa. A craftsman goes into the forest and cuts down a tree. From part of the tree, he carves a god and worships it. The rest he cuts into firewood." I leaned toward him. "Think of it. Did a god made by a craftsman's adze and awl create the world? Does the wood we warm our hands by have power to answer prayer? I could not believe in such a god, Anasa. To do so would be folly."

Anasa sank back on the chair, clearly shaken. He closed his eyes and pressed his fingers to his forehead.

I felt spent—and afraid. I flicked my eyes to where my brothers and father had been leaning against the wall. They were standing straight, their arms uncrossed. They could not hear our conversation, but it was obvious they knew something was amiss. I could see the curl of Beor's fists from where I sat. I could suffer more than a reprimand for this.

Anasa straightened and pulled a long breath. "I fear you speak the truth, Leah. But I am a merchant. I sell my goods in the temple square, both in Haran and in Ur. My rugs cover the temple floors. The priests drink from my cups. My carved pedestals hold household gods across the countryside. If I were to believe what you say, how could I continue to make my living off such goods? My livelihood would be in jeopardy."

For a long moment his eyes searched mine, as though looking for an answer—or absolution. I could offer neither.

Anasa stood, his shoulders sagging beneath his robe. I stood as well, knowing that my hopes were about to be shattered.

"I could never be as strong and brave as you have been this day. You are a woman of virtue, worthy of any man, certainly one better than I."

Anasa thought me brave? I wasn't. Not as I should be. So how could I fault this good man for his lack of courage? It would not be easy to give up everything. To trust God would bless him and provide another way to make his living.

His throat moved as he looked at me, sadness seeping into his eyes.

"I wish that I could make you my wife. But I am certain you would convince me of the things you have said today—and that would cost me everything. I am a coward at my heart, Leah. I would that I were not."

He crossed the distance between us and took my hands in his. They were big and rough, and I already mourned their absence.

"I'm sorry, Leah."

I watched Anasa's broad back as he walked away, passing my father and brothers with a few words, moving toward his servant, who held the reins of a restive camel.

It was just a stone, the amulet. What would be the harm? I bit my lips to keep from calling his name.

CHAPTER TWO

Jacob

I hunkered in the dooryard of my tent and stirred the blackened pot of lentil stew simmering on the open fire. The pungent smells of cumin, sumac, and a hint of hyssop made my mouth water. I was hungry, but the plumping grains refused to be hurried, luxuriating in their spicy bath.

I looked around for my brother, happy he had not yet returned. He must still be in the open country, doggedly tracking some animal, unable to let it best him.

I knew how the poor beast felt.

Esau always had to win—especially over me. Through the years I had learned not to give him the opportunity, if I could help it. To keep as much distance between us as I could. I hoped to finish my supper and retreat to my tent before he returned.

Most of the cook fires in the camp were out. The baking stones cooling. Women wrapped in shawls went about their afternoon tasks. I had come in from the hillside, soaked to the skin by the winter rains. But the rain had stopped now. The air was bright and brisk. The warmth wafting up from the coals felt good.

I sighed. My stew had taken too long. Esau was coming into the camp. I went back to my stirring, hoping he hadn't noticed me.

I watched my brother from beneath my lashes. He was empty-handed. No gutted deer over his brawny shoulders. Not even a wiry rabbit hanging from his belt.

Hmm. Bad day for hunting, I assumed, because if there had been a deer within bowshot, it would be bleeding over my brother's back.

I sighed and gave the stew another stir. He was coming toward me, his damp clothes clinging to his muscled chest, his unruly hair frizzed around his face.

"That smells wonderful, little brother. Give me some. I'm famished."

It wasn't a request but a demand, as it always was when Esau wanted something. And he knew how much I hated to be called "little brother," as though being a few minutes older made him the better man. He only said it to irritate me, and it always did.

We were twins, but no two brothers were less alike. I was tall, but Esau was taller by a handbreadth, thick-limbed and muscular, a wild bush of a man with a wind-whipped ruddy complexion, where I was lean and mostly smooth-faced, with barely a stubble of beard.

Father would deny it if asked, but Esau was his favorite. I'd known that since we were boys. Father's eyes always lit with pride when other men spoke of Esau's strength or skill or rugged good looks. I would stand beside my brother, embarrassed and hurt. Father would sometimes notice and pull me forward, telling the men I could already read some cuneiform and wasn't that an accomplishment for one so young? Which it was. They would nod their heads then continue touting Esau's latest feat, and Father would join them, leaving me standing alone, watching my brother bask in my father's praise. Occasionally Esau would slide a smug glance my way, and take a step closer to my father, just to emphasize that he was the favored son.

"Well?" Esau said, gesturing at the steaming pot.

"What? The great hunter has found no prey?" I said, unable to resist goading him a little. "You must be losing your aim, Esau."

Esau plopped down in front of the fire and stretched his hands toward the coals. "Me? I wouldn't speak of aim if I were you, Jacob. Especially since yours is so poor. I said I was hungry. Are you going to give me some stew or not?"

His voice made the muscles tighten in my neck. Arrogance swirled in the very air around my brother.

I poked at the graying embers and watched sparks spit into the air.

The coals flared, then settled into a warm glow—like Esau's face, which was washing red with aggravation. I had to swallow the smile tugging at the corners of my mouth.

"Maybe one of your wives has a meal prepared," I said, knowing that neither Judith nor Basemath spent much time laboring over a pot.

"I didn't marry them for their cooking skills," he said with a smirk.

That was true. Esau's Hittite wives were as beautiful as they were haughty. I wondered what Esau would say if he knew Judith had as much as offered me a taste of my brother's goods. I ached for a wife, but I didn't want one like that. I wanted a virtuous woman who served the God of my grandfather Abraham. Esau's foreign wives and their false gods were a constant source of grief to our father and mother.

"Stop this, Jacob! I'm serious. Give me some stew!"

"I'll give it to you, if you give me something in return."

"Well, name it, then. Would you let a man starve to death in front of your own tent?" Esau loved to exaggerate. As though he would die from going to bed hungry one night in his life.

There was only one thing I wanted from Esau. I wanted the birthright. Not for the greater portion of land and livestock. I wanted to be the spiritual heir of Abraham. I wanted my name to be joined to God's: The God of Abraham. The God of Isaac. The God of Jacob. But, as things stood, it would be the God of Esau, an honor my brother neither valued nor deserved in my opinion.

I raised baiting brows. "Give me your birthright, and the stew is yours." I was only taunting Esau. I didn't expect him to take me seriously, let alone agree.

He shrugged. "Well, the birthright will do me no good if I die of hunger. It's yours. You can have it," he said, as though it were of no more value than the pelts hanging in the door of his tent.

What?

"Swear it to me," I said, thinking he would laugh and mock me for believing him a fool.

"I swear the birthright is yours. Now give me the stew."

It was all I could do to keep my jaw hinged. I stood and gestured at the simmering cauldron and marveled that a man could be so senseless.

For a moment my conscience pricked me. I could have told him not to be so rash.

But I didn't.

If he wanted to be reckless with his gift, who was I to stop him?

CHAPTER THREE

Leah

Rachel and I followed the donkey and cart and the tethered goat through the splayed gates of Haran. Father shouldered through the jostling crowd while my eldest brother tugged the skittish ass along, an effort the animal resisted with locked knees.

Father had insisted I come to the city with him and Beor, and Rachel had begged her way into the bargain. I was glad she'd been allowed. I hadn't been looking forward to the long walk on such a beautiful spring morning with only my father and Beor for company. The donkey and the goat would have been more pleasant companions.

And something scratched at the back of my mind. My father didn't usually want to be bothered with women when he came to the city, any more than women wanted to be bothered with him. He was not a patient man, and I needed scarce herbs for poultices and tinctures. Michal, the local healer and midwife, had sent me with money. I usually came to market with my brothers' wives. My father would have no tolerance for such perusing, and since, for some time, Michal had been training me in her craft, I didn't want to let her down.

I chewed my bottom lip. There must have been a reason for Father's insistence that I come with him and Beor. But as things had been more uneasy than usual between us since Anasa's visit, I was quite certain it was not the pleasure of his daughter's company. And the smirk that played on my brother's mouth when he looked my way sent a prickle of apprehension through my thoughts.

It had been several weeks since Anasa walked away. He had given no reason to my father for his decision, no doubt thinking I would suffer for my refusal to take his gift. But Father had asked, and I couldn't lie to him.

"You think you're too good for a man like Anasa?" he'd said, his fists balled at his sides. "I'll never find a husband for you! All you had to do was take the wretched charm! How hard was that?"

Even Rachel had been angry. "How selfish of you, Leah! You should have thought of me! I'll never be betrothed if you don't find a husband." Her words had pierced my heart. I wanted nothing more than her happiness.

No one understood how difficult it had been for me to refuse Anasa's gift. I had agonized day and night since, asking myself if it had really been necessary. I didn't know. Perhaps Anasa would have understood if I'd explained it in the beginning. If I'd simply said I couldn't wear the amulet and not tried to convince him of the futility of worshiping idols. But I *had* tried to convince him—and hadn't that been the right thing to do? Right or not, there was nothing to be done about it now. Anasa had chosen not to marry me, and it was useless to think of what might have been.

The fragrance of the fresh spring air gave way to the odor of pressing bodies and beasts and the reek of not-so-fresh fish and chamber pots coming from the mud-brick houses with common walls that lined the narrow street. I held my hand over my nose until it numbed to the stench.

I heaved a sigh of relief when the narrow street emptied into the teeming marketplace that skirted the great temple of Haran. At least I could breathe again. But my stomach always churned at the sight of the massive structure, knowing what passed for worship within its walls. The mid-morning sun glistened off the surface, forcing me to close my eyes against the brightness for a moment. The edifice, scaled by two seemingly endless staircases, rose terrace by terrace to the *temenos*, the walled platform bedchamber of the moon god.

It seemed even the gods needed their rest. But the priests used the temple mats for more than sleep.

In the House of Great Plenty, nestled between the staircases, the harem of the moon god performed its service to the priests and worshipers who had the shekels to spare, a service my father and brother would, no doubt, require before we headed home.

"Close your mouth, you old fool!" a voice clucked from somewhere behind Rachel and me. I turned to see a round-bellied woman manning a booth draped with deep cerulean cloth, fists planted on her ample hips, glaring at her husband—who was looking at Rachel—his mouth hanging loose. The man's face reddened, and he busied himself straightening a perfectly straight fold of cloth. The woman turned toward us, her heavy chin jutting towards the street, a not-so-subtle suggestion that we move on. I took my sister by the elbow and lead her away from the booth.

"What a rude woman," Rachel said. "It wasn't my fault her husband was staring at me."

Perhaps not, but what woman wants her husband ogling another woman? Especially one as beautiful as you, Sister. I wondered if Rachel wasn't enjoying the effect she had on men—and their wives.

Rachel's blood had come the day after my meeting with Anasa. The news had spread like ants on bread and honey. A line of men had come to visit Father, each reminding him that they had been the first to offer.

But they would have to wait, since I still didn't have a prospect, and no one ogled me on the street. Sometimes I wished my father would breach tradition and offer Rachel first. It would be a relief to all, and I wouldn't be standing in the way of my sister's happiness.

A young scraggly-haired boy standing at a covered booth tested a carved-wood whistle. The donkey bolted, and the goat tethered to the cart gave a strangled bleat as the rope jerked tight around its neck.

Red-faced, Beor cursed and lashed the donkey with a narrow stick. The *thwack* of the rod made me flinch. The goat was still hacking choking gasps. I rushed to the animal, pulled the rope off and knelt before it, holding its face in my hands. It had recovered its breath. "Are you better now, my friend?" I said, rubbing my hand over the coarse hairs of its neck.

"What are you doing?"

I jerked my head towards the angry voice.

Beor's eyes were bright. His chest still heaving.

"Why are you setting my goat loose!" he said, the stick still raised in his clamped fist. I gasped, frozen in my place, afraid to move for fear my brother would unleash a blow on me in his fit of temper. I hated when Beor and Father led these animals to be slaughtered as sacrifices to their gods, but I would never think of letting the animal go! I wasn't that dull of mind!

"I wasn't . . . I was just seeing if the goat was hurt. The lead was tight around its neck." I watched my brother for what seemed like a long time, barely able to breathe.

Beor's lips were still pressed together, his nostrils spread wide, but he lowered the stick. I let the pent-up air out of my lungs, feeling that I had narrowly escaped harm.

With one last bellow, the ass began to move at a measured pace. I took Rachel's hand and followed from as far back as I dared.

The goat quickened its steps behind the rattling cart, as though it knew to keep the lead around its neck loose, lest the donkey misbehave again. I was sorry for the animal. It would face a worse fate than a tight tether before the day was done.

⬦⬦⬦⬦⬦⬦⬦⬦⬦⬦⬦

"That's the last one," Father said to the thick-waisted priest dressed in nothing but sandals and a fringed skirt that rode beneath his protruding navel. Beor laid the basket of barley grain beside the tax booth and stepped back. He glanced in my direction. I looked toward Father and the priest, but I could still feel his eyes on me.

"Ten biltu of barley? A poor crop this year?" The priest looked at Father through narrowed eyes. The cart had held the required portion of the barley harvest to be offered at the temple—provision for the gods who were thought to be celestial landlords of the farms and shops, and guardians of the wealth of the people.

Well, almost the required portion.

My father always skimmed a few baskets off the top—maybe more than a few this time.

"Not as good as last year. Better than the year before," Father said with a shrug.

I waited uneasily for the priest's response. Failure to make full offerings to the gods could bring the temple authorities to the farmer's door, demanding payment and threatening expulsion, though the lands had been held in families for generations, and no one had ever been evicted. But the priests could seize the farmer's crops, and that could mean a winter with little food, so the priests were to be taken seriously.

The man gave a knowing look and with two long fingers pushed the soft clay tablet forward. Father took the seal from his sash and rolled it across the bottom. The tablet would be stored in the temple archives, a record of taxes paid.

I sighed my relief. The temple authorities would probably not pursue the theft of such a small amount. It was hardly worth their while to make a trip to the countryside to inspect the granaries of a single farmer. But my father's intrigues always left my nerves on edge.

As we walked away, he lifted one shaggy brow.

"So I held back a few mana of grain. The gods don't have a family to feed!"

I thought to ask him how gods of wood and stone could eat grain anyway, and why the priests were all so fat, but thought better of it. My unfettered words had a way of getting me in trouble. And I didn't need any more of that today.

"May Rachel and I visit the booths while you make the sacrifice?" I needed those herbs.

"No," he said, the angles of his bearded face taut. "You are going with us. You will stand beside your brother and me during the ritual."

What? Why would he do that? Father had never made me witness the offering up close! Some small concession to my mother's memory, I'd assumed. I had only seen the horror from a distance, when the pitiful bleat of the animals demanded my attention. I didn't want to see a goat's throat slit or its chest laid open to the priest's inspection! Especially this goat!

Beor's eyes sparked with dark satisfaction. It brought him pleasure to see my color fade from one bloodless shade to the next. I imagined Father had told him of his plans and Beor had reveled in them, hence the knowing looks as we traveled through the city. Or perhaps it was Beor who had goaded Father into this. I wouldn't be surprised.

"You have no respect for the gods," Father said. "I can thank your dead mother for that."

His words were a slap across my face. It was all I could do to keep from crying.

"You think the gods don't notice my daughter ignores them? They notice, Leah. And they think me a poor father for allowing such neglect all these years. How can I expect their favor if my family disregards its duty?"

A poor father, indeed, who would force his daughter to go against her conscience. And how could gods without eyes notice anything at all?

I knew better than to argue. It would only bring trouble. I would observe the grisly sacrifice. But he couldn't make me like it.

The day had turned warm. I wiped my forehead with the sleeve of my tunic as we stood near the head of the long line of worshipers and agitated animals. The mordant smell of blood fouled the air. Too soon, it was our turn. I held Rachel's hand as we watched two priests heft the animal onto the bloody stone altar. The goat kicked as they secured its legs to the horn-shaped cornerstones. I could barely force the air into my lungs. I tightened my grip on Rachel's fingers.

The goat was staring at me. I could swear it. As though he expected me to rescue him as I had earlier.

"Sorry, friend," I said beneath my breath.

It wasn't that I hadn't slaughtered animals. I did it all the time, but this was different. It was a useless sacrifice to gods who couldn't see or hear or help in any way. Forget the herbs—I just wanted to go home.

Father handed me a cup of water. I looked up, startled. What did he want me to do? His black eyes dared me to defy him.

"Throw the water in the goat's face."

What?

I didn't want to have any part in this, and why would he ask such a thing? This couldn't be happening! I wished that I had feigned sickness and stayed home. I was sick now. I thought the cup would break for the grip I had on it, but I finally took a deep breath and tossed the water in the goat's face, sorry for insult added to impending injury. The goat's head jerked.

"The sacrifice has given its consent," the priest said through plump lips.

They thought a jerk of the head showed the goat a willing participant to his own slaughter? Well, the terror in his eyes said no such thing!

I wanted to weep for the animal. It was all so absurd. How could my father believe any of this?

"Put out your hand," Father said.

"Why?"

The word escaped before my mind knew what my tongue had done. A daughter never asked her father why. I braced myself, expecting to be cuffed, but he leaned into me, his eyes igniting with fury.

"Put. Out. Your. Hand."

This was some sort of trickery to get me to compromise myself. I was certain of that.

Spittle pooled in the corners of Father's mouth. I was reminded of the long-fanged dog Beor kept fenced behind the tool shed. Thinking of Beor made my blood run cold again. I kept my gaze away from his, and despite my trepidation, I stretched forth my trembling hand. My father gathered grain from his pocket and poured it into my cupped hand, jerking his chin toward the altar. "Do it."

I knew of this ritual. The worshiper sprinkled grain on the animal to show himself a party to the sacrifice. It would be like offering *myself* to the goddess of grain, in hope she would grant a plentiful harvest.

I couldn't do this! This would be worse than taking Anasa's amulet!

My heart raced. I could see the scarlet creeping up Beor's neck and thought of the donkey and the stick. Father was looking at me, his anger evident in his throbbing temples.

I turned toward the goat. He was calmer now, his seemingly resigned eyes still on me.

Go ahead, woman. They're going to kill me anyway.

They were. I knew that. But I couldn't participate in it. I wouldn't! Father could do whatever he wanted to me!

"Do it, Leah," Rachel whispered in my ear. "You're going to get a beating if you don't."

My stomach sickened. Father and Beor were glaring at me, their patience running out.

"Do it. It's nothing, Leah. Just do it."

"It's not *nothing*," I whispered back through tight lips. I drew a stuttering breath. I wasn't going to take part in this—beating or not!

"I'm not going to do it!"

Before I knew what was happening, Rachel grabbed my hand,

raked the grain out of it, and tossed it on the sacrifice. The air caught in my lungs.

Rachel! What have you done?

Not waiting for license, the priest slid his knife across the goat's throat. Shock surged through me. And then sorrow. I watched the blood gush in spurts, then drain slowly into the shallow clay bowl, the goat's eyes suddenly gone blank. Tears wet my eyes as I looked at the gash, gaping wide and red in the animal's neck. It was just a goat, but I grieved for the loss of its life.

The priest worked quickly, slicing the goat's abdomen, and after a cursory examination of the entrails, retrieved the liver.

My stomach lurched.

The priest held the bloody organ in his hands, turning it over to examine all sides. His countenance sobered.

"There's a flaw in the liver," he said. "This is an unacceptable sacrifice."

Father looked stricken.

The gods would not be appeased by this poor animal's death. The goat had its revenge, and I was glad.

The priest threw the liver on a bloody pile, and with the help of the other priest tossed the carcass after it, to be disposed of by temple slaves.

Father huffed a breath and looked at me. "The gods are fickle, Leah. And don't think your mother's god is any different."

The words were a deftly aimed sword. I had prayed for my mother, and she had died despite my prayers. *Was* God fickle? Maybe. Sometimes it seemed so. But He was not made of wood or stone, and He was always watching His creation. Of this, I was certain.

Father shook his head and walked toward the House of Great Plenty. Beor stayed, his black eyes fast upon me as he tossed several coins from one hand to the other. He handed one to me, ignoring Rachel altogether.

"Do you know the history of the shekel, Leah?"

He knew I did. Centuries ago, the shekel, which bore the image of the goddess Ishtar, had been coined as a token specifically to grant access to the services of the temple prostitutes. The shekel had since become common currency.

"It used to cost just one shekel to purchase pleasure in the temple. Now it takes three. Do you know why, Leah?"

The sneer on his lips broadened. I wasn't about to answer and help him trap me with my words.

"It's because the priests have to pay the fathers who sell their daughters into temple service."

He tucked the shekels into his bag and nodded at the one still resting in my open hand.

"Keep it."

I watched him go, knowing that someday my brother would act on his hatred toward me. It was only a matter of time.

CHAPTER FOUR

Jacob

How had it come to this? My mother's dry lips were pressed tight, her fingers fluttering over the goat skin she was using to make my smooth neck feel hairy like my brother's. "Mother—"

"It will be all right, Jacob." The small smile she offered wavered and her face fell into a solemn mask as she pulled the goat-skin gloves she'd hastily constructed onto my hands and up past my elbows.

My father's sight had been dimming for years. Only recently had he lost the last of it. He was completely blind now. But he wouldn't have to see me to know I was trying to deceive him. I was going to pose as my brother. Esau was a hairy man, and as soon as Father touched my arm, he would know that it didn't belong to his oldest son. Would the hair of a young goat fool him? My father was old and blind, but he wasn't stupid!

My mother handed me a robe Esau had left with her to mend. Of course, his wives had no skill with a needle. The robe smelled of the fields, and dead animals, and Esau's sweat.

I slipped my arms through the sleeves. It was too big. She folded the sleeves up twice and straightened the edges of the robe and patted my chest with her two small hands.

"Don't worry," she said. Her face was drawn, her cheeks almost colorless against her black hair. She was still a strikingly beautiful woman, but she looked to have aged ten years in the space of a morning.

How could I not worry? This was madness. But something had to be done. And quickly. My mother had stood outside my father's tent earlier and heard him tell Esau to go and find prey. To cook it the way Father loved and bring it to his tent and they would eat and he would give Esau the blessing that accompanied the birthright.

Of course, Father didn't know Esau had sold the birthright to me for a bowl of soup.

Esau wouldn't tell him, thinking no witness could attest to it. I felt the veins at my temples swell and heard the blood pound against my skull. God had witnessed it! And to God, a man was only as good as his word, which made my brother worth a great deal of nothing!

Father would have to honor our transaction, if I told him, and the birthright would remain mine—but he wouldn't have to give me the blessing that took the birthright from the realm of land and flocks to a place beside my forefathers as Abraham's heir.

I didn't care about the rest! Esau could have it! But if my father gave Esau the blessing—land and flocks would be *all* I'd have, and my father's ire besides. Esau was doing it again! Imposing himself between me and any favor that might come my way. And he was probably going to get away with it!

I wanted the blessing, but I wanted my father to choose to give it to me. I didn't want to deceive him. But here I was. Preparing to do just that.

Something else occurred to me—something that made my heart rise to my throat. "Mother, if he realizes I've deceived him" —I swallowed with difficulty—"he may curse me rather than bless me."

She reached up as though to touch my cheek, then drew her hand back. She knew the power of a father's words over his son. She had already thought of it. I could see it in the press of her lips and the fear hiding behind her eyes. If my father cursed me, his word would stand, even if he did it in a moment of anger. It couldn't be reversed.

She took my hand in both of hers. They were dry and chapped. My mother had always taken care with her appearance, but my father's weakening condition had worn on her. And now this. Esau shouldn't be adding to our mother's burdens!

"Jacob, before you and Esau were born, before either of you did anything—good or evil, God chose you over your brother. I know this, Jacob. I heard His voice in the night. I wasn't asleep," she said, shaking her head. "I heard it with my own ears, just as I heard your voice a moment ago. He said there were two nations in my womb. And from birth they would be two rival peoples—and the *older* would serve the *younger.*" She paused. "Do you understand what I'm saying, my son? The birthright was always meant to be yours."

It took a moment for the words to find their place in my consciousness. So that is why I'd longed so for the birthright! They say no one remembers his mother's womb, but I'd always thought I could remember the tangle of limbs as Esau and I fought for position—the desperation to hold him back—to be born first—the despair as he slipped past me. The midwife said I came out of my mother's belly grasping my brother's heel. So perhaps I did remember, and even before I was born, knew the eternal significance of the birthright. In a sense, the birthright was already mine, and Esau had stolen it from *me* when he slid around me in the womb!

"I don't understand it Jacob, how He chooses—or why. I don't know if what I ask of you is right or wrong, but I cannot take the chance that your father will give the blessing to Esau when I know it belongs to you. If there is a price to be paid for this, Jacob, I will pay it. Not you. Let your curse be upon me."

My body rang as though it had been struck with lightning.

<hr>

I pushed the flap open with my shoulder and carried the tray into my father's tent. Pricks of sunshine peeked through the panels where narrow cords laced them together. My eyes adjusted slowly to the dim light. The musk of goat hair and lamp oil, and a strong scent of urine, stung my nostrils. I swallowed hard.

I should just leave. This isn't going to work.

I was about to turn, when Father spoke.

"Rebekah?"

The blood rushed to my head. I wanted to drop the bread and meat and run from the tent, but I couldn't move. Then, with a few words I crossed the point of no return.

"It's me, Father. Esau."

"Esau?"

"Yes." My face was on fire, my head ready to burst.

My father said nothing. Sweat flooded my forehead.

"You are back? How did you find your prey so soon?"

"The Lord brought it to me, Father."

I winced. *Now I have made God, Himself, part of my deception. Why did I say that?*

"Come closer."

I set the tray on the small table next to a flask of wine and moved closer. The goat-hair coverings on my arms and neck itched like a plague of lice feasting on my cursed flesh. I wanted to rip them off—throw them as far as I could. I was fighting for breath.

Deep folds of skin draped my father's unfocused eyes, which seemed to search, straining but unable to see past their milky coats. He reached out and found my arm, felt of it, saying nothing. He was going to curse me, and I deserved it.

"Jacob?"

Everything stilled within me, slowed to a stuttering stop.

"The voice is the voice of Jacob, but the arms are the arms of Esau."

I needed to end this deception, before my father spoke words he could not take back. I could fall on his chest—maybe he would yet forgive me—but I didn't. Instead I chose my path, knowing it might lead to destruction.

"It's me, Father. Your firstborn."

We ate in silence. When we finished, he spoke.

"Come near and kiss me, Son."

I leaned over and kissed him on one cheek and then the other, and knelt beside the bed. Isaac, son of Abraham, laid his hand on my head and smelled Esau's clothing.

"The scent of my son is as the odor of a field that God has blessed. May God give you the dew of the heavens and the fatness of the earth and abundance of grain and new wine. Let peoples serve you and nations bow before you; be master over your brothers, and let your mother's sons bow down to you. Let everyone be cursed who curses you, and favored with blessings who blesses you."

I wept into the straw-filled mattress.

I had not long left my father when Esau came with a bowl of venison. The whole camp could hear him cry and curse from Father's tent.

My mother heard my brother had threatened to kill me. She feared for my life, so she took me to my father's tent, where he already sat in the doorway, the traditional seat of judgment. She said it would be the death of her if I took a wife of the sons of Heath like Esau had, and asked if he would send me to her brother Laban's in Haran, to choose a wife of his daughters.

I wished she had simply come with the truth. I was tired of lying.

"Rebekah, do not count me a fool," my father said, sorrow in his voice. "I know why you want to send Jacob away." He drew a breath that quivered on his lips. "I know my firstborn. He's not used to being set aside. He'll seek some sort of vengeance for this act."

Some sort of *vengeance* was severely understating the situation. My father knew my brother was just as apt as not to put one of his well-aimed arrows through my heart. I wondered for a moment if Father wouldn't welcome that—then Esau could take my place, and Father would have his favorite son at his side. Tears collected in my eyes. I was glad he couldn't see them.

He couldn't see my mother's tears, either, as they spilled down her cheeks and dampened the neck of her tunic. I knew it hurt her to betray my father. She loved him. But I knew she did not regret what she had done.

But I regretted it.

Was it worth it? To have an honor given unintended? And if I left and escaped my brother's bow, what good would the birthright and blessing do me? Would Esau's anger abate? Would I be able to return and claim my place? And what price would my mother pay for her part in this deception? I would give it back if it would free her from the consequences. But I couldn't change what was already done.

"Jacob, the words I spoke for your brother are yours. None of this can be undone. But I fear for you, my son. Your heart yearns for a God you do not trust. I cannot blame you for not trusting me. I have not earned it, although, it was owed me anyway. But could God not have intervened, even against my will? Could he not have spoken so loudly I would have to hear His voice?"

My mother's eyes dropped at my father's words. She had said she could not take the chance that my father would give the blessing to Esau. She had chosen to take matters into her own hands instead of leaving them in God's—as had I. And she had done it knowing what it might cost her.

"Give me your hand, Jacob."

I put my hand in my father's and remembered the skins I'd used to cover my deceit. I felt naked and ashamed.

"You will not escape difficulties at Laban's house. Do not expect to. He's a conniving man who seeks only his own advantage. I know your mother's asking me to send you for a wife is a ruse to save you from your brother. But I ask this of you, Jacob. Do not do as your brother has done. Seek a wife among the daughters of Laban. One who loves and serves the God of Abraham."

Father's hands trembled, and his voice quavered as he spoke. "May God Almighty bless you and make you fruitful and multiply you, that you may be an assembly of peoples; And give you the blessing of Abraham. To you and your descendants with you. That you may inherit the land in which you are a stranger, which God gave to my father."

The tears I'd been holding back burst forth like water behind a collapsing dam.

Father turned toward my mother, who was standing near, her head down.

"Rebekah. My love. I leave your judgment in the hands of God."

CHAPTER FIVE

Leah

I'd rather drink the beer than wear it," the man said, a sloppy grin lolling on his face as he reached for the skin. His breath implied he'd already emptied at least one.

I pushed the man back on his pillow. "I'm afraid you're going to have to wear it. You've had quite enough to drink." I removed the vessel from his reach and poured a bit more of the thick brew into the mixture of tamarisk root and fir turpentine and stirred it into the proper consistency for a poultice.

Michal had sent me to care for the farmer, who had an angry gash on his jaw, courtesy of his own donkey. I'd found the man to be thoroughly inebriated.

"I've a mind to bring the beast in here and let her finish the job," his wife ranted, her face a furious red knot. "Best donkey I ever had. Think I'll give her some extra fodder!"

The woman stomped out and slammed the door, which bounced once on its leather hinges and flew open, sending several pecking chickens into a squawking frenzy.

I had never seen such an angry woman. Was this what I was missing?

It had been months since Anasa's visit. I still thought of him daily, but that door was firmly closed, and I had come to peace with it. I had decided that I didn't want marriage anymore. I hadn't seen much to commend it to me. I wanted to pursue my craft. Michal said I had a gift as she had never seen in one so young. I loved coaxing babies into the world and tending to the ill and injured. It was exciting and fulfilling. And I felt some sense of worth at last.

The problem would be convincing Father. It was shameful to have an unmarried daughter in your house after a certain age. I wasn't there quite yet, but it would not be long before men began to look at father as less a man for siring a girl no one would take to wife.

My hope was Father's greed would work to my benefit. He already waited at the gate to claim the coins Michal shared with me. If I could convince him that there would be much more coming as my abilities grew, and Michal was already saying she was getting old, and maybe I could take her place one day so she could play with her grandchildren and sleep the night in her bed instead of squatting before the birthing bricks.

And he could betroth Rachel if it were known I was not going to marry. Going against tradition would be difficult. It was seldom done, and frowned upon by most. I hoped to broach the subject with him soon. I just had to wait for the right moment.

I spread the soggy mixture on the wound and wrapped a woolen band around the man's chin, and seeing no other way to secure it, tied it at the top of his head. He opened his mouth wide, straining against the bandage, fouling the air with the odor of stale beer and rotten teeth.

This wasn't going to work.

"You have to keep your mouth closed, or the bandage will loosen and fall off," I said, not adding that he was making the air around him unbreathable.

The man mumbled and reached toward the beer. "I need a drink."

I tightened my lips and shook my head. He looked toward the door. "You'd drink, too, if you had to live with the likes of that woman. Please?" he begged.

"No," I said with what must have sounded like the final word.

He sank back into the bed, thin-bodied and disheveled, his hair looking like the hackles of a narrow-stemmed thistle poking out around the bandage.

I dabbed at the bits of poultice on his face with a clean rag and patted his hand, feeling a bit of sympathy for his condition, both marital and physical. "It can't be that bad."

"So you say," he muttered. "I wish I'd married a girl like you, even if you're not so pretty. At least you're nice. A nice woman is a good thing to have."

Was that supposed to be a compliment?

"Maybe if you stayed away from drink and treated your wife with more consideration, you might find she's not so bad after all."

"Humph!" he snorted. "The ass has got more kindness in her than that woman."

I shook my head and started to gather my medicines, wondering who was to be pitied here. Neither, it seemed.

Cursing and braying caused me to jerk towards the door. The man's wife was pulling the donkey through the narrow opening, the beast's lip snarled over a gaping mouth of pink gums and large yellowed teeth. I could hardly believe the sight. When the donkey refused to go further, the woman slipped behind her and pushed the animal toward the bed.

"Do it again, beast! Do it again!"

The husband cursed at his wife, calling her something that reddened my cheeks. The woman yelled at the animal to do its duty if it ever wanted to see another stem of hay. The donkey had enough. Its hoof met with the woman's leg, causing her to lose balance and spill to the floor, legs splayed above her head. Her husband held his jaw against the pain as he guffawed. I struggled to keep from joining him, but the absurdity of the sight gave way to aggravation.

"Stop it!"

Even the donkey obeyed my shrill voice, unsnarling its lip and closing its long jaws in uncertain anticipation. I looked at the pair. They were staring at me as though it was I who was behaving strangely.

"Stop it, right now!" I said again. "You should be ashamed of yourselves!" The man gawked and the woman stared at me from the floor as though she couldn't understand to what I was referring.

"I'm sorry to say it, but you deserve each other," I said as I gathered my things, "so I will leave you to it." I pushed past man, woman, and donkey and out into the street.

I needed to talk to Father soon. Before I ended up in a marriage like this.

The specter of the woman's splayed legs and her husband's pained laughter was still running through my mind as I knocked on the door of my brother Beor's home. I had come to look in on Beulah, who was a few weeks from delivering what I was certain were twins.

Beor wouldn't be home at this hour. I rarely visited when he was. My brother made no effort to hide his contempt for me. And, if truth were known, I had felt nervous in his presence since the incident at the temple.

But I was worried about my sister-in-law. She had not seemed herself lately. And she did not look well.

Neba, their oldest daughter, a beauty at eleven years, let me in with a hug and a kiss. I couldn't help but wonder how such a lovely girl had come from my brother's loins.

The room was stuffy and warm with the scent of illness and sweaty children. Ruel, the youngest, rode on his mother's hip, plump body pressed against the swell of her bulging stomach, his round face damp and flushed.

"Ruel's not well?" I asked.

"No. I've given him barley tea with honey, but he's no better for it," Beulah said as she bounced the crying boy.

"Poor baby. Let me look at him." He went into my arms and thumped his dimpled hands against my cheek, as though to tell his favorite aunty of his plight.

A sigh strained against my lungs as I kissed his sweaty forehead. If I didn't marry, I would never have children of my own. Would I be happy to live my life without them? I knew it would be difficult. But I would have my nieces and nephews. And I would be bringing babies into the world. I believed it would be enough. I may never be betrothed anyway, so I had no guarantee of motherhood.

Beulah laid her hands on her bulging middle, thankful to be relieved of the boy's weight, I was certain. My sister-in-law had six children already, and what might be two more under her swollen breast. The three older children were boys, old enough to work in the fields, but they ate like men. And there was my brother, Beor, who expected to be waited on hand and foot, never tempering his demands, regardless of his wife's condition.

Thinking of my brother strengthened my resolve. No husband would be better by far than a husband like Beor.

"Are you well?" I asked. Beulah's normally rounded cheeks looked sunken in her pretty face.

She averted her eyes. "I'm tired. That's all."

Something was wrong.

"You look more than tired, Beulah. You look exhausted. Are you certain that you're not ill?"

"No. I'm fine. I promise."

Maybe she wasn't sick, but something was wrong. I'd seen it for a few weeks now. She seemed withdrawn, and it made her look small and vulnerable.

Ruel moved in my arms and started to whine. I studied his face. "Now what's the matter with my good boy?"

With some maneuvering involving honey and the handle of a spoon, I was able to see that white pustules dotted the back of his inflamed throat, which was engorged but not yet closed.

He gagged, and I lifted his warm weight, bouncing him and rubbing his back. He wailed, then seemed to decide it hurt too much to cry and reached for his mother with a whimper. I handed him back to Beulah. She sat on the bench and put Ruel to suckle.

"A bit of salt with the honey and tea will help." I prepared fresh tea, and after letting it cool watched Beulah as she held the cup to her son's mouth, wondering what it was that weighed so heavily on my sister-in-law. Soothed, the child gave in to exhaustion and slumped in Beulah's arms.

"While I'm here, why don't I make a sling to support your stomach? It will take the pressure off your back. It looks like you can hardly carry yourself around."

Beulah's face grayed. "No. It's . . . it's all right."

What was going on? Why this reluctance?

"It will make you more comfortable, Beulah."

Something in my sister-in-law's face said what I already suspected. She was hiding something. "Beulah. I don't know what's wrong, but you're like a sister, and I'm going to make you a sling," I said, accepting no argument.

I lifted the sweaty load out of her arms and laid him on the pallet by her bed, smoothing a strand of damp hair from his forehead. Neba had the little ones in control.

A goat-hair curtain provided privacy. I helped Beulah take off her shift. She was slight to be so heavy in the middle. Definitely twins.

I cut the appropriate length of broad wool binding and centered it under the bulk of Beulah's belly, threading it under her arms and crossing it over her back and shoulders. I attached it to the band in front and turned her around to tuck some tufts of wool where the bandage might cut into her skin. I started at the marks on her buttocks—bruises, a deep blue tinged with a sickly yellow in the recognizable shape of fingers and thumbs. I was an unmarried woman, but it didn't take experience to see the prints were perfectly positioned where a man might grip a woman in violent coupling.

"Beulah . . ."

Beulah heaved a sigh. "Is it bad?"

My stomach churned. "Yes, it's bad." Most men didn't touch their wives when they were with child, finding alternative ways to sate their lust. I imagined my brother was not so patient. But this late? And with force enough to leave marks like these? Anger rose from my gut.

Beulah pulled her shift over her head and tugged it down over her stomach. She wouldn't meet my eyes. *She* was embarrassed? My brother should be wallowing in guilt like the pig he was!

"It's not good for the child at this point," I whispered, not wanting Neba to hear, "or for you."

She shook her head. "What can I do? You don't understand, Leah. A man wants what he wants."

Anger tightened my chest and thinned my lips. The look in Beulah's eyes said what I already knew—there was no saying *no* to Beor, and he was not careful about any concern but his own.

"Perhaps Michal could talk to him . . . as a midwife . . . explain . . ." Even as I spoke, I knew that to do so would only make matters worse for Beulah.

Her eyes widened with alarm. "No. Please. It's almost time. They'll be all right."

"Perhaps, but what about you? This is—" I shook my head. How could my brother do this to a pregnant woman?

"I will be all right too. I've had worse."

Her words lay like small stones in my stomach. My heart ached for my sister-in-law.

"There's nothing for a woman to do, Leah. You'll find that out some day."

Nothing for a woman to do? No. I would *not* find that out! Not if I had my way. If I had any doubt about not wanting to marry, it fled from the room like a frightened mouse.

I put my arms around her, the precious mound stirring between us. *Dear God, have mercy.* "This can't continue, Beulah. Maybe you should tell Father. He's the only person that has any sway over Beor."

Beulah barked a little laugh. "And what would he tell me? That it was my duty to take care of my husband. I'd rather suffer a beating than talk to him."

I knew she was right. Father would never take Beulah's part over Beor's.

What *was* there for her to do? Nothing. The thought of it sickened me. Her husband could abuse her in her condition without consequence. This was not right!

I held the curtain back for Beulah and saw her face turn the color of day-old porridge.

Beor stared at us from across the room. My heart stopped still. Had he heard?

"What are you doing here?" he said, no doubt seeing something in our faces.

I wanted to say that I was caring for the wife he found such pleasure in abusing, but fear swallowed my bluster. I didn't want my words to bring worse upon Beulah.

"Caring for Ruel . . . and . . . making a brace for Beulah." The words sounded small and weak. I hated them, but fear for Beulah skittered down my back. I touched her arm, not wanting to leave her alone with him, and waited for a sign he had heard our conversation.

Beor's gaze locked with mine. His thick brows dipped like the wings of a vulture over his black eyes. My heart pounded against my chest. What would he do to Beulah if he'd heard? The taut line of his shoulders finally eased, and his body seemed to loosen, though his eyes still questioned.

I squeezed Beulah's arm and gathered my things. Beor looked at me with narrow eyes as I moved around him and out the door. I released the breath I had been holding but worried that my brother would not readily let go of his suspicions.

CHAPTER SIX

Beor

I didn't like whatever it was my wife and sister were talking about. Their bulged eyes looked as if they were about to pop out of their pale faces when they saw me. And now that Beulah was without Leah to hide behind, she looked like a child caught pilfering the honey jar.

"What were you and Leah talking about behind the curtain?" I knew she was hiding something by the way she was gripping her elbows, as if trying to cover her guilt.

"Nothing. Just about the brace Leah made for me," she said, pulling her arms closer to her body.

No. Why would Beulah be behaving like a scared rabbit if she had done nothing wrong?

Leah was a bad influence on Beulah. She shouldn't be allowed to traipse around the countryside with that midwife. It was disgraceful for an unmarried girl to be in a birthing room, seeing things only married women ought to see. I imagined Father only allowed it because the midwife paid Leah, and Father helped himself to what she brought home, and maybe because he knew he'd never get her married off anyway. Not only was she ugly but she ignored Father's gods and was always saying something out of turn.

Ruel let out a wail that clawed at the back of my neck. Neba rushed to get him from his pallet. Now there was a girl who knew her place. She jumped when something needed to be done, and she kept her mouth

50

closed. And she was pretty. Not like her aunt. Like her mother was, before she started bearing: delicate, like a slender flower in the wind.

"Neba, take the children outside," I said. She collected them like a hen gathering her chicks and went out the door, her head down. I watched until the door closed, then turned my attention to Beulah again, who was headed to the hearth.

"I'll warm some bread. There's cheese on the table, and I'll get some onions."

"I don't believe you. You two were up to something."

She stayed facing the hearth, the line of her shoulders strained. She may as well admit it. It was obvious. But enough of that. I'd deal with it later. I didn't come home in the middle of the afternoon for this.

"And I don't want food. Take off your tunic."

Her shoulders fell. "Please, Beor. It's not good this close to my time."

Beulah was still a pretty woman, with her fall of thick hair the color of burnished brick in the sunlight.

"Who told you that? Leah? She thinks she knows so much just because she works with that old woman. She's never been married. What does she know?"

Beulah turned around. Her face was pinched and pale. "Please." She was making me look like a beast. All I wanted was what was mine to take. What good was a woman who couldn't give her husband pleasure? It was her duty, and I'd see to it she honored her obligation.

"Take your tunic off. Now!"

She sighed, then turned her back and pulled the garment slowly over her head. White strips of wool crossed at the center of her knobby back and ran over her shoulders, with fluffs of the fiber peeking out from points of pressure. And what was that? Bruises? I hadn't realized I'd bruised her. So that's what Leah saw.

"Take that thing off. It's ugly."

"But Leah just put it on, and it helps support my stomach," she said, turning toward me. I took a step, and she quickly untied the ends. She acted as if she was terrified of me. I hadn't meant to hurt her.

"I didn't intend to mark you. If you wouldn't resist me, I wouldn't have to be so rough." I pulled her into my arms and kissed her. She tried to pull away. How dare she? I had my rights, and I would have them whenever I pleased.

I leaned into her ear. "You're my wife, and if you ever talk to Leah about our private lives again, you'll regret it and so will she."

She nodded, her head down.

"Lie on the bed. Now!"

I'd deal with my sister later. Now I had better things to do.

Jacob

I was weary from my long journey, and I thought I might be lost. Mother had tried to explain where to find my uncle Laban's home outside the city. Traveling for weeks alone, with nothing but my thoughts and my camel to keep me company, had made me anxious to get there.

My mother had given me some landmarks to go by—a small stream winding by a rock formation that looked like a man's head. Every rock I'd seen looked like a man's head, and I'd crossed several streams. I feared her childhood memories had been skewed, or the landscape had changed through the years. I saw something ahead, and a vague anticipation stirred in me. She had mentioned a well sitting on the gentle slope of a hill. There was one ahead, with patches of fleecy white strewn around it.

The shepherds nodded as I slipped off my camel. The animal stuck his nose in a thatch of grass and masticated it noisily.

"Greetings, brothers."

"Greetings," they welcomed, curiosity obvious in their sun-dried faces.

I asked them if they knew Laban, nephew of Nahor, and if they could direct me to where he lived. A boy with teeth too big for his mouth and a swath of white cloth wrapped around his head spoke up, saying Laban lived just down the hill. The others looked at him with raised eyebrows, no doubt wanting to see who the stranger was before divulging such information.

"I'm his nephew, son of Isaac and Rebekah." Their eyes lit, and they bowed in greeting.

"I knew your mother well," one of the older men with a pocked face said, a wistful look in his eye. "She was a real beauty. Every man around wanted her for a wife, but—"

Another man who seemed a little older smacked him on the side of the head.

The first man flushed and nodded toward Jacob. "Your mother was missed when she left."

I imagined she was.

"And why have you come now to visit your uncle?" he asked, trying to redeem the situation.

I stumbled for a moment. What could I say to them? I'm running from my brother and hope Laban can help make me rich so I can return and reclaim the blessing I stole?

"I come with greetings from my mother and father."

They seemed satisfied with my answer.

The sound of the bleating sheep drew my attention to the large flat stone covering the mouth of the well. I thought it strange that the sheep were not yet at the troughs.

"We're waiting for another shepherd." The young man pointed to the flock making its way up the hillside, "Laban's daughter, Rachel. She can't remove the stone from the well, so we wait for her."

My heart stopped mid-beat when I saw the young woman in the distance, guiding her charges up the hillside. I stepped in front of the shepherds and with all the strength I could summon rolled the heavy stone from the mouth of the well and began drawing water for my uncle Laban's sheep.

The shepherds looked at each other. "It takes two of us to move it," they said, seeming thoroughly impressed.

I didn't know where the strength had come from. But I had much to prove to my uncle. Taking care of his sheep and his daughter seemed a good beginning.

When the sheep reached the well, I guided the thirsty animals toward the troughs, then went back to draw again and again, until the last lamb had drunk its fill. Only then did I look closely into the more-than-curious gaze of my cousin Rachel.

The girl was beautiful. No. More than beautiful. She was . . . breathtaking. I felt myself beginning to tremble. A wave of unsolicited, incomprehensible emotion swept over me. Rachel was the most beautiful girl I had ever seen.

Perhaps it was weariness from my journey that stripped me of my good sense. But I couldn't help myself. I walked quickly to her, cupped her head in my hands, pressed my lips against hers, and wept.

Her eyes opened wide in shock.

What have I done? She thinks me a madman. My face felt on fire with mortification.

"I am your father's kinsman, his sister Rebekah's son," I said in haste, hoping to pass my outburst off as familial affection, but Rachel took a step backward.

"I've come to visit. I bring your father greetings from his sister."

"I . . . I'll hurry home and tell him that you've come," she said, still backing up. She turned and ran toward the settlement at the bottom of the hill.

"I'll bring the sheep," I shouted after her, thinking myself a fool for frightening the girl. I looked back at the shepherds. It was obvious they agreed.

CHAPTER SEVEN

Leah

Father was sitting at the table, that one shaggy eyebrow raised, as it always was when he was impatient or angry. "I've been waiting. Where's my dinner?"

I dished a bowl of barely-warm stew and placed it on the table before him, then set a loaf of bread on the hearth and flipped it from side to side. The aroma of roasted grain filled the room. The warm comfort of it soothed the nerves that had been knotted in my back. My brother had always been boorish, but now I knew him for the brute he was, and if not for Beulah, I would tell him to his face regardless of the price I'd have to pay!

I'd hoped to talk to Father at dinner about my desire to avoid marriage, but the soup had been cold and he was in no mood for conversation. It would have to be another day. Soon I hoped.

The door flew open with a rush of air and slammed against the earthen wall. I jumped, dropping the hot bread onto the dirt floor.

"Rachel!" I stooped to retrieve the bread. *What now?* I'd had too much to stretch my nerves already.

Father opened his mouth, ready to give Rachel a railing, but she cut him off.

"Our cousin has come! Your sister's son! He was at the well, and he—"

She caught whatever word skidded to a stop on the edge of her tongue. Father wouldn't notice such a thing, but I knew my sister.

"He's come to visit. He's bringing the sheep down the hill. I ran ahead to tell you."

"My sister's son?" Father seemed stunned "Which one?"

"Jacob. He'll be here any moment."

A cousin come to visit? I looked around the chamber. Plenty of bread. Beer. Plenty of stew? I could add some water. It would be enough. I hoped.

Father started for the door. Rachel grabbed my arm and pulled me aside. She held me until the door filled its wooden frame with a solid thud, then whispered, her words a mush of excitement and aversion.

"He kissed me, Leah," she said, her nose crinkling beneath her narrowed eyes.

"Kissed you?"

"Yes. He just kissed me and started to cry. I think there's something very strange about him."

He kissed her? A kiss could be many things. It didn't make the man strange. "It's not unusual for a kinsman to kiss a child, Rachel." I knew I had said the wrong thing before the words were out of my mouth.

"How old is he? I just meant . . . if he's a grown man."

Rachel had that look about her that warned I was about to get an earful.

"I'm not a child. And, yes, he is a grown man, practically ancient. Just the right age for you."

"I know you're not a child, Rachel." *Even if you do act like one sometimes.*

Having defended herself ably, the annoyance left her eyes, and she grinned.

"Really, Leah. That must be why he's come. Why else? There's no one with him. You need a husband. And he is a kinsman, though a strange one."

I really must talk to Father soon! It would be a relief to be free of my family's constant preoccupation with my marital status.

"So, he's too strange for you but not for me? Thank you for your high opinion of your sister," I said, kissing her on the cheek and shoving her toward the door. "Now go. I need to prepare." I couldn't tell anyone about my plans until I convinced my father to rid me of this burden.

The thought clanged about in my mind as I wiped the table and straightened chairs, but I pushed it out. All I could do was pray. It wouldn't be up to me. Such things were not in the purview of women.

◇◇◇◇◇◇◇◇◇◇◇◇◇

Jacob

I started the camel and my uncle's sheep down the gentle slope. Rachel was running toward the group of earthen houses, her black hair floating behind her. What had made me act so foolishly? I would be fortunate if my uncle didn't bar the door.

From partway down the hillside, I could see a small cluster of people gathering outside the courtyard. Excitement and apprehension collided in my mind. What would Laban think of his beggarly nephew? And, worse yet, would I be forced to tell why I had come all this way? That would not serve my ends well, which were to find a way to prosper and return to my home as soon as possible in something less than shame.

My father had told me Laban was a greedy man who sought his own advantage in every situation. The unwritten law of hospitality ensured my uncle's welcome, but if Laban knew what I had done, he might find occasion to disregard it, and I was going to need him if I was to return home with more than the crooked staff and a scraggly camel with which I'd come.

As I reached the bottom of the hill a man came toward me, followed by a younger man and three youths and a small group of curious women and children several paces behind. I bowed low at the waist before the older man as he approached. *This must be my uncle Laban.*

Laban was thick-boned, with a square and heavily bearded jaw. His smile seemed misplaced beneath his rutted brow.

"Nephew."

He took me by the shoulders and kissed me on one cheek and then the other. His breath smelled of strong onion. I tried not to breathe it in. No doubt Laban did the same. My road-soiled clothes and sweat-drenched hair clung to me, and I was quite sure the smell of my beast did as well, although I had long since been unable to detect it. I should have washed at the well. What was I thinking? This was not the way

57

I would have hoped to meet my uncle or a daughter of my mother's brother, especially one as beautiful as Rachel.

"This is my eldest son, Beor," he said over his shoulder to a tall man with Laban's jaw, which stiffened at the introduction.

Friendly greeting. Did Beor's diffidence extend to all visitors or just dirty cousins coming unannounced?

"My other sons are in the fields." Laban waved a hand. "And these are my sons' wives and children—some of them. And you have met Rachel, my younger daughter."

Rachel dropped her head. Modesty I hoped and not aversion at the sight of me. I forced my eyes back to my uncle a moment too late. Laban's gaze flicked to Rachel and back to me. Heat crept up my neck. *Stupid!* I scolded myself.

Laban nodded at a girl at the rear of the group. "My older daughter will prepare food. Simi will take care of your beast and show you to a basin where you can wash."

Laban gripped my arms and gave them a small shake. "You are the image of your mother. I will be glad to hear how my sister fares when you have refreshed yourself."

After I had washed and combed my hair and smelled better—I hoped—I followed Simi, who offered that he was Beor's oldest son. The boy seemed of better nature than his father and asked about my travels with wide-eyed interest, having never been farther than the neighbor's farthest pasturelands.

I ordered my countenance and took in a long breath as Simi opened the door. The mingled scents of well-seasoned meat and hot bread wafted over me as I entered the living chamber. My mouth watered in anticipation.

The room was simple: bare plastered walls, a few shelves, pots, a rough-hewn table at the center. And, of course, the shrine in the corner that supported the household gods. Not unexpected—but disappointing.

"Welcome, Nephew. Sit, please," Laban said through a mouthful of food, then gestured to a chair across the table.

"Forgive me for not waiting." He took a long drink from a clay cup and wiped his mouth on a rag. "I had already begun my supper before your arrival."

The offending onion lay half eaten on the table beside a bowl of some sort of meaty stew that looked delicious.

Laban was welcoming enough, but I felt my nerves abuzz beneath my skin.

"Thank you, Uncle." I took the seat across from him. I didn't tell Laban I had eaten the last of my provisions the previous evening and was hungrier than I remembered being in my lifetime. I had already made a poor showing of myself. I certainly didn't look like the heir to one of the richest men in Canaan, for all the good it did me in a foreign land.

I noticed Rachel's absence with disappointment. A young woman bent at the hearth and dished a plate of food. I assumed her to be Laban's oldest daughter.

"This is my daughter Leah." Laban gestured with a tilt of his chin and took another drink.

Leah gave a timorous smile. She looked nothing like Rachel other than being of the same moderate height. Her eyes were well shaped and a soft honeyed brown, but the whites were red-veined and irritated, which made her look tired. I would never have thought the two to be sisters.

"I'm happy to meet you, Leah," I said.

She nodded politely and placed a bowl of steaming stew and a loaf of bread before me.

I smiled my thanks, tore a piece from the loaf, and sopped it in the thick stew. It was as delicious as it smelled.

"This is wonderful, Leah. Thank you." I swallowed the too-big bite of bread and reached for my cup.

"Simple fare for the son of my sister," Laban said. "If we had known to expect you, Leah would have prepared some lamb in pomegranate sauce. She's a skilled cook—has been since she was a little girl."

Leah's face reddened, and I saw an odd discomfort in her eyes.

"It sounds delicious, but the stew is food for a king. I've never tasted better, Leah." And I hadn't. It was equal to my mother's.

I took a long drink of the thick beer. It tasted of grain and malt and something delicious I did not recognize.

"The beer . . . excellent."

Laban nodded as he drained his cup. He wiped his frothy mouth and settled back in his chair, his fingers tracing the rough grain of the table.

"Now, what brings you to a place so far from home? A desire to meet your eminent uncle, I presume?"

I laughed with Laban—a nervous laugh. *Maybe I should just tell him, "I stole my brother's blessing, so he threatened to kill me, and here I am. And by the way, I need your help to make myself rich, so I can return home with at least a shred of honor."*

I didn't think that would go over well, so I decided to keep it quiet for now, until I could prove myself useful.

"My mother wanted me to meet her family. The time seemed right."

Laban's expression did not change, but a faint sense of suspicion hung in the air between us.

"And she didn't send a message by way of a trader," Laban stated more than questioned. "It would have been good to make grander preparations for a visit from my family."

Laban's black eyes held me in my place. I had the strange sensation my uncle could read my mind, or perhaps it was the guilt on my face he read.

Laban relaxed and waved an arm. "No matter. We are honored by your presence. My sister was right to send you our way. You are welcome here as long as you wish to stay."

I was relieved not to be pressed into further discussion but under no illusion that my uncle's curiosity was sated.

We talked about my mother and father, and I longed for home.

"Some more bread?" Leah's voice was hesitant but almost melodic in its timbre. It didn't seem to match the rest of her.

I put my hand on my stomach.

"No. Thank you, Leah. Your father was right. You are a wonderful cook."

Her mouth hinted a smile, and her cheeks colored. I found myself watching her as she took the basket of bread back to the hearth. There was a certain grace about the girl.

"I find I am tired from my journey, Uncle. If you'll excuse me, I'll rest now."

Laban rose. "Yes, of course. Rest well. We will talk again tomorrow."

I kissed my uncle and nodded toward Leah.

Simi was waiting outside the door to show me where I would sleep. I pulled back the goat-hair mat that served as a door to the outbuilding of tall woven reeds, which were bent and tied at the top to form a roof. I was thankful for this humble privacy. Another mat and a thick wool blanket had been spread on a bed of straw, alongside a stand with basin and pitcher and an oil lamp that burned low, casting fragmented light over the stem walls.

I extinguished the flame, wrapped myself in my cloak, and lay down, thankful to have a bed to rest upon. But I was apprehensive about my uncle, no matter his offer of hospitality. And Beor. What was it about the man that bothered me so?

Depression settled over me. When would I be able to return to my homeland? Never, if my brother had his way.

I worried for my mother, who had said she'd take my curse, if my father gave one. He hadn't, but had God taken offense at my mother's lack of trust and cursed her for it? And had my father cursed me in his heart despite the words of blessings from his mouth?

Maybe he knew it was curse enough that I would be so far from home, since Esau would, no doubt, take over in my absence. Someone had to. And maybe my mother's curse was that she had watched me leave, promising that my brother's wrath would soon abate, and she would send word with a trader that it was safe for me to return. But it would not be soon at all, and she knew it.

I turned on my pallet and tugged the cloak tighter around me. The thought of Esau always left me cold.

I had the birthright I had longed for, and now I lay on a borrowed bed, with nothing to my name. I'd had a dream the first night away from my home. Heard a voice saying God would be with me where I went and see me safely back to my home again.

It had seemed real at the time, and I'd been comforted by it. But now I wondered—why would God speak to a man who had stolen his brother's birthright and brought a curse on his own mother? I wasn't sure any more.

But I wanted to go home. And if I was to return home with my head up, I would have to build wealth and prosper, and I'd have to be in my uncle Laban's good graces to do it. I would offer my services the next morning. I'd tell Laban I wanted to work for my keep, then offer to take over the breeding of his animals.

I had greatly increased my father's stock, and perhaps I could ingratiate myself with my uncle and secure my own future.

My uncle was cunning, but he had met his match in me.

CHAPTER EIGHT

Jacob

I squatted beside a bearded goat, which looked at me through slit-shaped pupils set in amber, as if I was a favorite relative—a warmer greeting than I'd gotten from Beor, who stood on the other side with arms folded against his chest.

Laban had seemed unimpressed when I told him how I'd increased my father's livestock but told me if I preferred the flocks, he'd have his sons show me around the pastures.

My uncle's holdings were modest, a few flocks of sheep and goats and fields of grain, enough to sustain his family and barter at market for needed goods, but he was by no measure a wealthy man.

After a few days of inspecting Laban's animals, I'd asked him and his sons to accompany me to one of the pastures.

"Look at his neck and shoulders. They're wide and well fleshed out."

I ran my hand over the buck's back and down his hind leg. "His back is broad and long, his rump almost level. His hindquarters have good extension. His thigh is round and well-muscled and extends far down his back leg."

Laban pinched his lips, nodding for me to go on.

The brothers aren't going to like this.

"Most of your goats are swaybacked, with steep rumps, their loins narrow—a sign of weakness in the line. A buck like this, bred with a similar doe, will strengthen the flock."

I stroked the animal between the ears, which looked like wings poised to lift in flight, and stood, waiting for my uncle's reply.

"Of course, we would have to build an enclosure for the females, so the feeble bucks can't get to them," I added, "but it won't take long for the stronger stock to multiply and eventually become a line for which men will pay far more than the going price."

The brothers stood tight-mouthed at my disparaging of their flocks, but a rapacious flicker lit in Laban's eyes. Just what I had hoped to see.

Laban raised one disheveled brow. "And you think it will make that much difference?"

"I know it will," I said without hesitation. "I increased my father's flocks many times over by the same means."

Had I been too brash? I waited for my uncle's response with an eye on my cousins. Their faces revealed their preference in the matter: I could take my ideas and go back from whence I'd come.

Laban nodded and ran his hand over the buck, which skittered toward a brown doe with a low-hanging udder. The goat didn't seem taken with his master. *Smart animal.*

"All right then. Beor will see that you have all you need."

Beor started to open his mouth, then pressed it shut. I tried to stifle the smile twitching on my lips.

Laban slapped me on the back. "We will see if your predictions are accurate, but I can see no reason not to believe it so. It was my good fortune that you left your home and came our way."

Beor's neck reddened, but Laban's demeanor had changed. I was now more than a beggarly relative imposing on a kinsman's good graces. But Laban's good will would be short-lived should I fail, and it was not just method that had brought me success in Canaan; it was God's blessing. But was God's blessing still upon me?

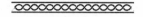

Leah

I placed a clay pot of lentils beside the bread and boiled fish. The men had been to the pastures at the rising of the sun and had returned for a fresh-cooked meal, which was usually served by their wives, in their own homes. But today, Father said the family would eat their mid-morning meal together. Jacob and Beor had just completed the enclosures that would separate Jacob's pick of goats for his new venture, and they would celebrate.

From the look of Beor's clenched jaw, he had been forced into the partnership. None of my brothers looked especially happy at their father's sudden admiration of Jacob or boasting of deeds not yet done. It remained to be seen what would come of Jacob's methods, but my father showed no lack of confidence. Jacob smiled under Father's praises. I thought I saw him look surreptitiously at Beor, a glint of victory in his gaze. I hoped Jacob knew what he was getting into, if he chose a battle with my brother.

I moved away from the table, trying to blend into the group of women waiting to refresh plates and cups and warming bread and cakes on the hearth of the communal oven at the center of the courtyard.

Olnah looked my way and headed toward the table with warm cakes. I felt a twinge of apprehension. *No.*

"Try some barley cakes, Jacob," Olnah said, nodding toward me. "Leah baked them. Her dough is so much softer than mine."

Olnah! Everyone's gaze followed Jacob's as he took a cake and looked toward me with a nod of appreciation and then back to my father, who was still touting Jacob's plan.

I caught Olnah's gaze as she returned the cakes to the hearth. I expected the anger that was raising my temperature showed on my face. She lifted her chin, letting me know that someone had to do something, and I should be grateful for her efforts.

And it was just beginning.

"Another drink?" said Paltith, the wife of my youngest brother, Chorash. "It's Leah's own recipe. She brews the richest beer."

Even dear Beulah. "If you need another blanket, Jacob, I have one to spare. Leah wove it. She spins the finest thread."

My face was hot with humiliation. And Jacob's discomfort was evident by the flush of his skin. My family's motives were obvious. I wanted to shout that all of this was unnecessary! I wasn't going to marry! They could leave Jacob to seek Rachel's affection. Couldn't they all see that Jacob was in love with her? It was plain on his face. A face that turned toward my sister when he thought no one was looking.

As though drawn by my thoughts, Rachel came alongside me. And just as I had noticed, Jacob's eyes darted toward her when my father's gaze was diverted for a moment.

"Take him some more beer, Leah," Rachel said in my ear.

Not Rachel too.

"He has a full cup, Rachel," I whispered back.

"Some lentils then," she said. "Talk to him."

"Stop it, Rachel." Jacob was watching our conversation, and I knew he didn't have to hear the words to know what was being said. I wanted to disappear. Why did my family put me through this mortification? I was going to talk to Father today! Did my family think I would want a man who was so obviously in love with my sister?

Rachel gave me a small shove toward our cousin.

"Rachel, I said stop it!" I spoke louder than I'd meant to. I turned and walked away, feeling every eye on me. Especially Jacob's.

<hr />

I sat beneath the terebinth tree that stood as sentinel over my mother's grave and pulled my knees into my chest. A round-eared mongoose stood a short way off, staring at me with wide unblinking eyes, a gold-brown scorpion hanging precariously from the animal's mouth. Did the mongoose even have eyelids? My mother had kept one in the house for years, guardian against creatures like the one that was now crunchy bits between the animal's small sharp teeth.

The mongoose finished the scorpion, then stood upright, thin front legs dangling like a crippled beggar's, looking straight at me.

"You've had your lunch," I said.

It waited another moment, and deciding I had nothing to offer, left, its long brindled tail trailing behind it.

It had been months since I'd been here. I didn't come often. Only when my need for solace outweighed the specter of difficult memories. My face still burned with humiliation. I hoped never to see Jacob's face again, I was so embarrassed. But there was no chance of that.

At the moment, my hope of convincing Father was waning. What made me think he would ever agree? My feelings mattered little to him—or to anyone except Zilpah, who was a servant and my dearest friend, and Beulah, of course. And other than Zilpah, who was considered homely by everyone but me, the women of my household were all beautiful. How could they possibly understand the need to feel of some worth in the world?

There was little doubt that Jacob had come to his mother's brother for a wife. Abraham had sent his servant here for a bride for Isaac, Jacob's father. It stood to reason that Isaac would send his son to seek a wife from Laban's household.

There were only two daughters in that household—Rachel and me. If Father insisted the older marry first, which I feared he would do, Jacob would be left with no choice but to take me as his wife. I did not want to be forced to marry a man who didn't love me, let alone a man who loved my sister! I did not want to marry at all!

As always, I found myself longing for my mother, who would never have allowed my family to do what they had done to me today.

I looked at the pile of rocks that marked where my mother and my stillborn brother lay and remembered the day Beor and Alib brought them here. They had wrapped her in a reed mat, her son in her arms, and laid her in the stone-lined pit.

The wind was cold that day, whipping my hair around my face. I'd held Rachel as she wept, her arms tight around my waist. I mourned my mother's touch, her soft voice that comforted me in my childish fears and sorrows. I had never felt more lost or alone.

We slept on the roof that night, Rachel tucked into my chest, a woolen blanket tight around us to ward off the chill. The stars hid behind the clouds, and the skies were a muted black.

I remembered looking up, knowing that God was above the gray-black sky. The Living God. The God of Abraham. I knew, without doubt, He had watched as my mother struggled on her bed. He had not been absent from her suffering. He had not turned a blind eye, and I wondered how He could do it—watch his children suffer when it was within His power to stop it.

I had buried my face in Rachel's hair, dampening it with my tears. I was aware that God was watching me but thought that if He could look on while my mother died, I could look away for just one night.

I still struggled to understand why God sometimes stood by when we seemed to need Him most, but I had given up being angry at Him. There had to be a reason behind our suffering. I just didn't know what it was.

I heard footfalls behind me and knew it was Zilpah before I saw her. She always smelled of sesame oil and garlic, her own treatment for an unremitting scaly patch on her forearm. I wondered if it did any good at all, since the patch never went away, but she swore by the concoction, and I hadn't the heart to challenge her.

"I thought I would find you here."

We sat in silence for several minutes. Zilpah always had a sense of when and when not to speak. She was much more than a servant. She was my dearest friend, and I appreciated her love and loyalty.

"Your father is looking for you."

"Why?" *To expose me to more ridicule?*

"He wants you to take the sheep to the well."

Take the sheep to the well? That was my sister's job. Was he trying to punish me now for making a fool of myself at breakfast? Not that it truly mattered. I'd rather be with the sheep than chance seeing Jacob again today.

"Where's Rachel?"

Zilpah shrugged. "Probably looking at her reflection in the polished brass."

I laughed. "Don't be unkind, Zilpah."

The girl's brown eyes glistened with mischief.

"Or perhaps parading before the servant boys, so she can see their mouths agape."

"You really are a wicked girl, Zilpah. I should tell my father."

"I won't worry much for that," she said, her mouth in a twisted smile. "Oh, you think you know me so well, do you?"

Her thin brows arched over her narrow face.

"Yes, I do. I only wish your cousin did, and he wouldn't be gawping at your sister. She doesn't compare to you, Leah."

"No, she doesn't. She's beautiful, and I'm—"

Zilpah made a derisive noise in her throat that sounded something like a sheep hacking bitter grass. "You're beautiful too. And not just on the outside. He would do well to look more closely." She paused and cocked her head to one side. "But then again—he might deserve Rachel."

I tried to quell the laugh that tickled its way up my throat, but I couldn't contain it.

"I know you mean well, Zilpah, but I will hear no more of this," I said through lips twitching at the corners. I wanted to tell Zilpah of my plan to pursue the healing craft and forget about marriage, but there was no point. It would probably not happen anyway.

I rose and straightened my tunic, looking again at the stones that marked my mother's grave. *I miss you so much, Mother.*

"Well, I may as well be about my sister's work," I said to Zilpah, who made the hacking noise again and took my arm.

CHAPTER NINE

Jacob

Laban had asked me to inspect the well, to see if more troughs were needed to accommodate the expected increase of the flocks. There had been a certain air about him that made me think there was more to his request than met the eye, but I wouldn't complain, since Rachel would be watering the sheep, and I might have an opportunity to speak to her and make myself look less a fool than I had at our first meeting.

It was warm. I tugged open the neck of my garment to let in some cooling air. Frowning yellow flowers dotted the sparse grass, wilted by the hot summer winds. I wondered if the level of the water dropped significantly in the dry season, and if the well had been dug deep enough.

Two servant boys were tussling on the hillside. They stopped short their cavorting, ordering more appropriate behavior in the presence of a member of the family. I waved them off. My position was more tenuous than theirs, since I had yet to prove my worth. They had nothing to fear from me.

I was almost to the flock, when I realized it was Leah sitting on the ground, her back against the crumbling stone well, stroking a lamb on her lap. At that very moment she looked up, and I knew she saw the flash of disappointment on my face. I cursed Laban under my breath for putting Leah in such a position and managed what I hoped was a convincing smile as I approached.

"Leah." I nodded my greeting.

"Jacob."

The humiliation in her cheeks saddened me. I had no desire to embarrass the girl. Her family had done enough of that earlier.

"Your father—he wanted me to check the well—to see if we could add a trough, since we expect an increase in the flocks."

She flushed again and drew the lamb closer, her narrow fingers stroking its nubby wool. The color in her cheeks suited her. Leah wasn't an uncomely girl—just not a beauty like her sister, something that she was made aware of often, I imagined.

I leaned over the edge of the well. The water level was high, indicating the depth more than sufficient, but, like the well itself, the long stone trough was crumbling about the edges from years of weathering. It had been patched many times, by the look of it.

"How long has this well been standing?" I asked.

Leah hesitated. She probably wished I'd turn and leave. But I wanted to break through this discomfort and set her at ease if I could.

"Decades. Perhaps a century or more."

Something occurred to me as I assayed the leather bucket hanging from a crossbeam supported by two stone pillars.

"Then my mother would have drawn from this well." I looked down at her. "And my grandfather?"

Another beat of silence before she spoke. "I believe Abraham helped dig it—with your great-grandfather, Terah."

My heart warmed. I peered into the dark well again, the damp air cooling my face.

"It's difficult to fathom that he may have stood in this very spot."

"Did . . . you know your grandfather?"

"Yes. But he died when I was a youth," I said as I pushed damp hair off my forehead. I suddenly remembered my grandfather holding me on his lap, his course beard tickling my cheek. His hands had fascinated me, with their swollen knuckles and raised veins meandering across loose wizened skin. I would trace the blue ridges, pressing them under my small fingers, intrigued by how they felt and how they filled again when I released them.

"My mother used to tell me stories of him when I was a little girl," she said, in little more than a whisper.

"What stories? I'd like to hear one."

She looked up, sorry, I was sure, for mentioning it. I was intrigued by the prospect of hearing about my grandfather, though, and would not let the opportunity pass.

"Please, Leah."

She shifted her weight, allowing the lamb to nuzzle into the crook of her arm. "What could I tell that you have not heard?"

"I'm sure there are many stories from his homeland I've never heard, and I won't stop asking, so you may as well begin."

I settled on the ground in front of her.

"I will have my story or beg till the sun sets on us," I said with as straight a face as I could hold.

"I'd rather not. I don't remember the stories well, and I'm sure you'd be bored."

"It's my grandfather. I won't be bored."

"Please, I—"

"It would mean a great deal to me, Leah."

She hesitated another moment then raised her shoulders. "I suppose I could tell you a short one. But I can't tell it as my mother did. You'll be disappointed I fear."

"I won't be disappointed. I'm certain of it." And I *was* certain. Somehow, I sensed Leah to be a woman of many talents.

She nodded and pulled a long breath. When she spoke her voice was touched with sadness. "We used to sleep on the roof at night, when the weather allowed.

"My mother would motion to the stars and say that they declared the glory of the Living God, and it was the stars that caused Abraham, as a young boy, to turn from his father's gods and believe in the Creator, since no lifeless deity could have formed something so magnificent."

She raised her eyes to mine. They were not so irritated today. They looked like pools of dark honey. I'd never seen eyes quite that color.

"You know that your great-grandfather, Terah, was a priest in the temple of Ur and had a shop where he sold images?"

"Yes. I know." My great-grandfather had been a priest in the temple of the moon god and yet claimed belief in the Living God as well. It had grieved Grandfather Abraham.

She was quiet for a long moment. I wondered if she thought of her own father, who seemed to be of two irreconcilable opinions when it came to deity. And perhaps Rachel? Where did she settle on the subject?

"Go on, Leah. I'm not going to let you stop until I've heard it all."

A small smile touched her lips. I was amazed how it brightened her face. She had a lovely smile, and I'd seen but a shadow of it since I'd met her.

She began again. "The story goes your grandfather was often left to mind his father's shop, which was filled with all sorts and sizes of idols. It grieved his heart to sell such abominations, but his father brooked no excuses from his son.

"Every day people left the shop with carved images of the moon god, Sin, a crescent atop his headpiece, or of Innana with her bulbous thighs." Her cheeks pinked. "I'm sorry, I shouldn't have—"

I laughed, "Go on Leah. I must hear the rest now."

Her cheeks went from pink to crimson, but she continued,

"One day there were two finely dressed men in the shop, and it occurred to Abraham there was a way to make them think about what they sought to purchase. The two men came to the front, their purses in their hands. Your grandfather greeted them cheerily.

"'How do you do today, my lords? What do you think of the weather as of late?'

"'Too hot for my tastes,' one said, wiping his brow.

"'And you, lord?' he said to the second man, who seemed in a hurry to pay the price and leave.

"'Tolerable,' the man said, fisting the coin purse in his hand.

"'May I ask how old you are, my lords?'

"The men looked puzzled that a boy would ask such a question, but one shrugged. 'Seventy, just last week.'"

I was completely mesmerized by Leah's voice as it lilted across the words like she had witnessed the scene herself, and remembered every twitch of a lip or raise of an eyebrow. She was a woman of many talents, indeed.

"'And you, my lord?'

"'Fifty and four. Now may I make my purchase? I'm rather in a hurry.'

"'Just one more thing,' said Abraham.

"He looked from one man to the other, gathering their attention before he spoke. 'How is it that men of such years would worship a god made only yesterday?'

"The man of seventy stood in shock at the boy's words. In sudden recognition of the truth, he laid down his planned purchase and left the store. The other, angry at Abraham's insolence, put down the idol that was in his hand, swearing he would never buy another image from that shop and would tell all his friends, who would follow his example.

"Abraham repeated this ploy on numerous occasions. And Terah never knew why his business had fallen off."

I burst out laughing, huge bellows I could not control.

"I told you I could not tell it as my mother did," Leah said apologetically.

"I'm certain that's not true, and since I haven't met your mother, you can't convince me otherwise. I'm not laughing at you, Leah. You told the story well. You're gifted with words, once someone can pull them out of you. It's just that the old man of my youth does not match this precocious boy. Thank you for showing me something of my grandfather I had not seen before."

The lines of Leah's face eased, seeing I didn't find her foolish. I did not. Not at all. In fact, there was something about the girl that I found intriguing, like inimitable layers of rock, each revealing something made more unique by pressure.

"I see there is division in your family. How did you come to trust in the God of Abraham?"

She was slow to reply. I liked that about her—that she thought before she spoke.

"I was just a child. We were sleeping on the roof. I had always been terrified of the dark. My fear took form in the shadows, and not even my mother's nearness could calm me when it came. I had sidled closer to her, seeking comfort in the familiar smell of raisin cakes on her shift and the steady rising of her chest.

"The stars hid behind the clouds that night, and the skies were a muted black."

Fine lines appeared in her forehead.

"My fear was a malevolent, paralyzing thing," she said, looking ashamed. "It was beyond reasoning away. I prayed toward the heavens, as I often did, to be kept from harm and evil. I had no thought to make an offering to my father's gods. I would have been too frightened to leave my mother's bed even if the thought had come."

She paused again.

"And then, with a certainty I cannot explain, I was aware that God was above the gray-black sky and that He was watching me. The Living God. The God of Abraham. He was there, as surely as my mother lay beside me.

"I was startled with the knowing—frightened, even. He was there, in the heavens, but who was He? And what was He like? And could one so great be concerned with the foolish fears of children?"

She looked at me, tears behind her gold-brown eyes. "I have no doubt that He is there, Jacob, but I must admit I've struggled to understand Him. Especially when my mother and brother died. I'm not to be commended for believing He exists. The devils believe the same. I've yet to truly know Him as I desire. To trust Him. For that I am ashamed."

Before I could stop myself, I reached for Leah's hand, tears threatening my own eyes. "It is no shame, Leah. And if it is, I share it. We are just dust, as was our father, Adam." Saying such to Leah was a comfort to me as well. Surely God knew I was just flesh, with no strength of my own. Perhaps He would use such an unworthy vessel after all.

We talked for a good while. I told her about my brother, Esau, and how my father favored my twin.

"I don't think my father means to favor one above another, but he does," I said.

Leah didn't say it aloud, but the drop of her gaze told me we shared the struggle of being seen at all when in the presence of our siblings.

She told me more about her mother, and I told her how much I missed my own.

"I fear I will not see her again," I said, and saw in her eyes she understood and grieved with me.

When the sheep had begun to wander, full of drink and grass, I helped her gather them and walked with her as she led them home and put them in the round stone sheepfold. She turned and thanked me for my help. I watched her walk toward the house, and something stirred within me. When she closed the door, I felt a loneliness I could not understand.

Leah

I was in the house, grinding long grains of cumin with the mortar and pestle, thinking of Jacob and how he had sought me out after our meeting at the well. He loved to talk about his grandfather and had by now heard every story my mother had ever told me.

He seemed to enjoy my company, even when the conversation turned to other things. I had laughed more in the last few weeks than in the whole of the year before. I had begun to wonder if . . . I could be wrong about marriage, and maybe—

Zilpah entered the house. I smiled and greeted her, but she didn't return my smile.

"What's wrong, Zilpah?" I asked, concerned by the sober look on my friend's face.

She swallowed visibly. I could see her throat move and her face cloud with sadness.

"What is it? Tell me now."

"It's Jacob. He just asked your father for Rachel's hand."

The words ripped their way through my mind, leaving my thoughts fractured.

"Your father agreed without even a mention of you."

I stared at Zilpah for a long moment—until the sharp edge of pain in my chest allowed me to breathe, then put my hand on her arm and thanked her.

"Don't hurt for me, Zilpah. I knew Jacob wanted Rachel from the beginning. I'm glad for him."

Zilpah's face said she didn't believe me. I could never fool her.

But I *was* glad that it was over—final. I had allowed my resolve to weaken. Entertained the thought that perhaps happiness with Jacob was a possibility. That marriage and children might yet be part of my life. I had begun to feel . . . something. And now I would pay the price for it.

Jacob.

Tears filled my eyes.

PART TWO

The Betrayal

CHAPTER TEN

Laban

Seven years later

"What do you hear from your sisters about my charmed nephew, Alib?" I said, pushing the plate of goat cheese and hot barley bread across the table.

His body stiffened. Alib hated spying on Jacob, especially through Rachel and Leah. Sometimes I wondered where the boy's allegiance lay.

Jacob's breeding practices had proven to be everything he'd promised and more. How I had persuaded him to serve seven years as a bride price was a mystery, even to me. I had meant it as a starting place to negotiate, a bid so high even half would be an exorbitant price, but he had accepted outright. And who was I to tell him he'd paid too much?

The seven years had certainly been to my benefit, as my own fortunes had grown considerably in the time. Which was why I was concerned that his departure could affect those fortunes and leave me in the meager circumstances I'd been in when he arrived.

Jacob would marry Rachel in two days. He kept his plans to himself, but with his debt to me paid and Rachel in his bed, there would be nothing to keep him in Haran. He would probably leave as soon as his preparations were complete. There were questions needing answers, and I hadn't long to get them.

Alib tore off a piece of the proffered bread but didn't raise it to his mouth. The subject of our conversation seemed to have stolen his appetite. The pinch of his lips and the flare of his nostrils said he'd rather not be sitting at my table discussing his brother-in-law's business.

"He continues, as always, tending your flocks and his own."

"Do you think Jacob has some special gift from the gods, Alib?" I was often frustrated with my middle son's disregard for the deities. It didn't speak well of me. A man who could not control his own household would not likely gain the gods' favor, fickle-minded as they were.

"I think he knows a great deal about breeding."

"You would give no credit to celestial sources?"

"Does it matter?" He shrugged and laid the bread on the table. "Jacob has increased your flocks and herds many times over. If it is by his methods, or some divine ability, your wealth still grows."

"Is there a brain in that head of yours?" I rubbed my forehead in frustration, wondering how the fruit of my own loins could be so dense. "Yes, Alib. It does matter. You can learn a man's methods and practice them in his absence—but a gift from the gods? It matters very much. I'm taking one of Jacob's goats to the temple tomorrow. I'll soon know if he gains advantage by being a favorite of the deities or if he is just shrewd. If it is the former, as I suspect, we will have to keep Jacob from returning to Canaan."

Alib's brows flew together, carving a deep line between them. "How? How do you hope to do that? You know he wants to leave. He's anxious to return to his home. Nothing will make him stay. I am certain of that."

I sighed. Had my sons learned nothing from their father? "And that is the problem, Alib. You are too certain of too much with too little to substantiate it. There is, indeed, something that would keep Jacob in Haran.

And I will use it if I must.

Leah

I pulled Rachel's hair off her shoulders and began tugging the wooden comb through the ends, working my way up, so as not to make a knot. Others would do the intricate braiding and weaving appropriate for the occasion. I would gladly leave it to them, since I had no knack for it myself. But on this last day of Rachel's childhood, I would untangle the mass of dark waves as I had every morning since our mother's death.

A gust of wind blew through the open shutters, sending my own hair flitting around my face. I raked the spidery strands out of my eyes and tucked them behind my ears and wondered about the canopy on the hilltop and the tent where the men would feast for seven days. It wouldn't do to have the tent come down on the roast lamb in pomegranate molasses I'd spent so long preparing.

My eyes burned with unshed tears. I left off combing and pressed thumb and forefinger against them, glad I was at Rachel's back. I couldn't let her see me cry. I didn't want to spoil this time for her. Today, my sister would marry, and in a few weeks she would leave for Canaan with her husband, and I would probably never see her again.

Rachel often frustrated me. She was insensitive and demanding, but I loved her dearly, and the thought of her going so far away imbued me with sadness.

A few mutinous tears made it over the berm of lashes. I wiped at them with the back of my hand.

"Do you think it will hurt terribly, Leah?"

I started to comb again, blinking hard to keep the flood at bay.

"Do you?" Rachel said again.

"Do I what?"

"Are you listening to me, Leah?" Rachel tried to turn her head, but I forced it back with two quick hands.

"Hold still. I can't comb your hair if you don't hold still."

"I said, do you think it will hurt terribly?"

Heat flared in my cheeks. "How would I know, Rachel?" Of course, I did know. I was a midwife and knew far more than most about such things. The first time was sometimes very painful, but I wasn't going to tell Rachel that.

"You have no reason to worry. If it were that bad, we wouldn't have so many nieces and nephews."

I separated another section of hair and worked at the snarls. Rachel tended to sleep all over the pallet, leaving me half on bare ground. In the morning, the girl's hair always looked like it had been fighting for its life all night. I supposed I should be happy to soon have a bed to myself, but I wasn't. I'd slept with my sister since she left our mother's breast. I would miss the sound of her breathing and her warmth.

And I would miss this every-morning ritual: the weight of the thick tresses in my hand, something I'd envied of my sister since we were children, when it took our mother twice as long to comb Rachel's hair as it did mine. The scoring and tugging. The way the comb slid through the black mane without resistance when I finished, leaving little hairs standing on their ends. There were so many things I would miss.

Rachel shifted on her stool. "I suppose you're right. But it is a noisy business, isn't it?" She sniggered, and I couldn't help but laugh. Sleeping on the roof afforded a cool breeze but not much privacy. We often heard our brothers with their wives. When we were young we used to bury our heads in our pillows to smother our giggling.

"Beor is the worst," she said. "He sounds like a hog at the trough."

I held my hand over my mouth, not wanting to encourage such conversation, but soon we were holding our sides with the pain of our laughter. At least it was an excuse for tears, which were streaming down both our faces. When we were somewhat composed again, I let out a slow, quiet breath. We had been *together*, separate from that society of women with their secrets and knowing looks, and now Rachel would be a part of it, and I would be alone.

At Jacob's insistence, the wedding was to be a simple one, with no obeisance to my father's gods, and only family, a few neighbors, and longtime servants in attendance. At least I would not have to stand among so many as they whispered behind their hands, "There she is—Laban's elder daughter. Poor thing."

Maybe Jacob had thought of that when he made the choice, sorry for my humiliation, and maybe my father had acquiesced because he thought it better not to flaunt his transgression of custom in giving the younger first. Whatever the reason, I was glad for it.

"You could go for me, you know. Just for tonight," Rachel said, laughing. "No one would be the wiser, and you could tell me all about it in the morning."

I didn't find the prospect funny. "Rachel. Stop it! Jacob loves you. He will be gentle. I am sure your fears will have been in vain. Now let me look at you."

I lifted the hair off her back and laid it over one slim shoulder. She was so beautiful. A lump rose in my throat. "You look so much like Mother, Rachel." She had our mother's shapely brows and long, thick lashes, shading eyes as black as onyx. And the same peak at the middle of her forehead. "I wish she were here with you today."

"I can't remember what she looks like anymore, Leah." Her eyes dampened. "But when I try to picture her . . . I see you. And you're here, so I'm content with that."

A fresh stream of tears spilled down my cheeks. We held each other, and I wondered how I would endure her absence. I was happy for her—I truly was—but I would miss her so very much.

At that moment our brothers' wives came through the door with a rush of wind, their skirts whipping about their ankles in the stiff breeze. They were carrying oil and water for Rachel's cleansing, and a mix of aloe, myrrh, and egg white that they would apply to her bare skin, let sit, and then wash away with warm rose oil and cooling wine. The concoction filled the room with a woody floral fragrance. Olnah shut the door with a solid thud and cursed the wind on such a day as this.

Rachel squealed and pulled out of my embrace. I stepped back, watching the room gush with laughter and sighs and puckered lips on pink cheeks, and I wondered if Rachel would really miss me, or if a husband and children, and the long distance would replace any thought of me at all.

Zilpah entered the room and touched my shoulder. "Beor's outside," she whispered in my ear. "He wants to speak with you."

"Beor?"

She shrugged.

What could he possibly want? Beor seldom spoke a word to me or to any of the women in the camp, unless it was to make a demand or a complaint. And since I'd seen the marks he left on Beulah before the twins were born, I felt he looked even harder for an excuse to put me in my place. A place I was sure I would not find comfortable.

I looked back at Rachel laughing as the women gathered around to begin their ritual and felt that deep sadness pressing against my heart again.

Unnoticed, I stepped out of the mud-brick house. Beor was wearing more than his customary scowl. He was never a pleasant man, but his countenance was several shades darker than usual.

"Father wants to see you, in my house," he said through tight lips.

Unease nipped at me as I started across the courtyard, holding my fluttering shawl tightly to my chest. It seemed strange that my father would want to talk now, knowing we were tending to Rachel. And strange that Beor was escorting me. I knew the way.

I did not like this.

When the door closed behind me, I ran my fingers through my windblown hair, smoothing the errant strands off my face again. Alib and Chorash were standing against the whitewashed wall, a certain sign that something was afoot. Alib looked at me through apologetic eyes, silently speaking his regret at being part of whatever had brought me here.

Alib was the only brother who treated me with kindness. Being the youngest, Chorash echoed Beor without a thought of his own. Even if he had one, he wouldn't dare to voice it in Beor's presence. Something twisted in my stomach.

My father pulled himself up from the rough-hewn table and straightened the edges of his woolen robe, his jaw set under his graying beard.

"Leah." He squared his shoulders like a man facing an unpleasant task, ready to be done with it. "There has been a change of plans that involves you. I believe you will find it to your liking." I stood in silence for a long moment, wondering what plans were being changed, since I had no plans at all other than to witness my sister's wedding and clean up the mess when it was done. The air began to still in my lungs. I could not imagine what my father planned, but whatever it was, I was quite certain it was *not* going to be to my liking.

"Wh-what plans?"

"Wedding plans."

Wedding plans? From the corner of my eye, I saw Alib rub his fingers over the crease in his forehead. That did not bode well. What wedding plans could change that would require all this intrigue?

With an upward thrust of his chin my father said, "You are going to marry Jacob today."

I heard the words, but they made no sense, like sounds drifting in the air with no tether to reality. My mind struggled to sort them into some rational order.

I felt a small burst of excitement. Jacob had changed his mind? After working for seven years for Rachel? At one time I had thought Jacob might ask for me. We had held so much in common, and he'd seemed to be drawn to me.

But he hadn't changed his mind. Of that I was certain. Jacob loved Rachel. He most certainly did not love me, and if he had changed his mind about who he'd marry, he hadn't come to the decision on his own.

I searched my father's face for some sign of levity, but there was none. It was a fool's pursuit, since I had no memory at all of humor in my father's dark features. The blood drained from my head, and I thought I might faint.

"What are you talking about?"

"You're the oldest. You have to marry first. It's our custom."

I stared at him, confused. He had known the custom seven years ago. He hadn't given it a thought then.

"I've come to see it was a mistake to promise Rachel to Jacob. You must marry first. I'm your father, and I must defend your honor."

Defend my honor? I felt my eyebrows stretch toward my hairline. I was quite certain my honor had nothing to do with this abhorrent act, but what his true motive was, I had no idea. Panic thickened in my chest.

"This is for your good, Leah. Surely, you want a husband, a family. You are not a pretty woman. You may not have an offer of marriage. You should take this and be glad for it."

My eyes found the floor. A familiar ache jabbed at my heart like a wood bird pecking holes in his favorite tree. *I should take this and be glad for it.* That's what my father thought of me—too ugly or too inept for any man to desire. Forget that I had run his household, washed his filthy clothes, baked his bread, and brewed his beer since I was little more than a child.

And there *had* been offers in the years since Rachel was betrothed. It was his greed or pride or both that had caused him to refuse them. And I'd been happy that he did. I'd continued working with Michal and was now a midwife and healer of some renown. He'd reaped the rewards of my skills, since he still claimed most of the coin. And this was no real offer of marriage. I was certain of that.

"Jacob doesn't want me."

My father huffed a breath and pointed a long finger at me. "You don't know what Jacob wants."

"Did he offer willingly?" I asked, knowing that he had not.

The line in my father's forehead sank so deep, it looked like it might swallow up his face. "It will be done, Leah. It would be best for you to accept it."

The tone of his voice said there was nothing more to be considered. He had made up his mind, and accepting it was not a suggestion.

"And how do you plan to make Jacob go through with it?" I said, my voice rising despite my effort to keep it level. "I know he has not agreed to this, and he will not! He loves Rachel."

The room was getting warm, and I felt a glaze of sweat on my forehead.

"He will do it."

"He won't! I know he won't. You would have to sneak me into the bridal chamber under cover of darkness to get him to marry me instead of Rachel."

My father's jaw twitched.

No! I froze in my place—then staggered, the dirt-packed floor threatening to give way beneath me as I realized his intention. I knew my father was always about some scheme, but I wouldn't have thought it possible for him to do such a thing as this to his own daughters. And why? What good could come of it?

"I won't do it!"

I turned on my heel and met the blur of Beor's hand. My head whipped violently to the side. The room swirled in an eddy of whitewashed walls, and I hit the floor with a force that left me in a thick pulsing silence. I could see angry mouths moving—my father's, Alib's, Beor's. Father's long finger in Beor's face. Beor was practically convulsing.

"Can a daughter refuse to obey her father? She could be drowned for such insolence!" The words suddenly stabbed at my ears, and I pressed my hands over them.

"You are not yet head of this household. I will deal with the insolence of my children. All of them!" My father's face was flaming red, like the area around an open sore.

He leaned down and lifted me up by my arm. The room began to move again, and I struggled to stay on my feet.

"Are you all right?" His eyes were not as kind as his words. His hand was too tight on my arm.

Of course, I wasn't all right. How could he expect me to be?

"You will do as I say, Leah, and you will not reveal yourself to Jacob until morning. If you do, you will be bringing more trouble upon his head than you can imagine, and don't think I don't know how you feel about him."

Heat climbed my neck. My hopes had been crushed when Jacob chose Rachel. I had been so certain he would ask Father for me. But he hadn't. And it was too late now. It didn't matter how I felt about him. He was in love with my sister!

My father told Alib to stay with me until Zilpah came to help me dress. He said to let the women stay occupied with Rachel for now, that he would deal with her when the time came.

He locked eyes with Beor. "You! Come with me!"

I groped for the sleeve of his robe. "Please, Father! Don't do this. I will work harder at my craft, and you can have all the coin. All of it! My life will be ruined if you make me do this evil thing."

For a moment the stiffness seeped out of his shoulders, and I saw a hint of indecision drift across his face, but then it was gone, and so was he.

I heard Alib's voice as he guided me to a chair and told me how sorry he was. I closed my eyes, unable to summon the strength to respond. This couldn't be real. My father couldn't expect me to go to the bed of a man who didn't love me, who didn't choose me when he'd had the chance—and pretend to be another woman.

Jacob would hate me. Rachel would hate me. Everyone would hate me. Leah—the woman so desperate for a husband she stole her sister's.

But what trouble would come to Jacob if I refused? I would put nothing past my father or my brother now.

God, why? Why would you allow this? What but grief can come from it? I longed for my mother. But she was gone. It seemed God had ripped everything from me. And I didn't understand why.

CHAPTER ELEVEN

Leah

I convinced Alib I wanted to be alone until Zilpah came. He was more than willing to leave me, sorrowful for my situation but hardly able to comfort me. As soon as he was out of sight I ran to the cowshed and burrowed deep between stacks of musty hay.

I could have thought it a dream, if my cheek wasn't still pulsing with the pain of my brother's blow. It was a dream of sorts, a night terror in the broad light of day.

Sneak into the bed of my sister's betrothed? How can you expect me to do such a wicked thing, Father?

I pushed stems of hay out of my eyes and spit them out of my mouth. The air scratched at my throat. I should have brought some water. As if I'd have taken the time to dip from the clay crock and fill a leather skin or make a quick trip to the well before I left. No. Thirst was the least of my problems.

The shed wasn't much of a hiding place. It was little more than a large stick-covered lean-to with a few stalls to secure the cows so they could be milked. But it would have to do until I could think of something else.

I couldn't just run away. I wouldn't know where to go, and the rolling hills would give little cover, since there were few trees other than the occasional small terebinths, some stray seedlings grown up as orphans from their kin along the rivers and the creek banks.

The wind had eased, and the servants were raising the wedding canopy on the hilltop and would see me whatever way I went. My brothers would ask, and the servants would not know to conceal my whereabouts.

I had considered lowering myself into the midden but couldn't bring myself to do it, although, it might yet come to that. I only needed to elude my father and brothers until time for the wedding. If Father couldn't find me, he would be forced to send Rachel to Jacob. He couldn't leave the groom standing without a bride while bewildered wedding guests looked on.

I felt like a naughty child evading a whipping. I would gladly take the rod if it would end this, but there would be a bigger price to pay. I was certain of that.

A long lowing sound from one of the cows startled me. Someone would come to do the milking soon. From my childhood, I had loved to milk the cows, which I considered proper mothers and better behaved than the goats, who seemed to want to dance around the milk bucket rather than deposit their frothy treasure in it. There was familiar comfort in the pungent smell of the large sweat-drenched animals, cow dung, and moldy hay. I still did much of the milking, but because of the wedding, one of the servants would do it today. Amos? Perhaps young Johanna? If either of them found me, they would keep my secret, but what if it were Eli? He would run to Beor in an instant, happy to ingratiate himself with his master, fawner that he was.

I would have to leave my hiding place before milking time. I wiped my face again and leaned back against the hay, trying to calm myself. My head felt light from the pace of my pounding heart.

What am I doing?

Why should I put myself through so much for Rachel's feelings? She never worried much for mine.

If the truth were told, Rachel had not been thrilled with Father's choice—and most certainly not happy for the seven years of waiting.

"I'll be an old woman!" she had protested, as angry at Jacob as at Father.

She had come to care for Jacob, but she could have married anyone, and it wasn't as though there would be no one else to ask for her if I did this thing. The line would form the moment word was out that Rachel's sister had snuck into her betrothed's bed. Father might have to take less bride price, since she was older now and had such scandalous relatives. But everyone would blame me anyway, so why should I not do my father's bidding and save myself this trouble?

I feared I would have to do it in the end, no matter how I fought it.

Rachel had never wanted for anything at all. Let her be the one put out this time. And why should I care if trouble came on Jacob like my father had predicted? He was a man. He could care for himself. I was a woman, nothing more than chattel.

I shook the wicked thoughts from my mind. I loved Rachel, and I didn't want to do this because it would hurt her—and Jacob. But what of my hopes and dreams? In the past seven years, I had become a midwife and healer of some renown. Would Jacob allow me to continue? And how could I live with him, loving him as I did, as I had from the moment I saw him, knowing he would never love me in return?

Tears filled my eyes. I rose from my place in the hay and wiped my nose with the sleeve of my tunic. I would find a way out of this. I would go through with the wedding ritual. It would be null anyway, since it would not be consummated. I would reveal myself to Jacob in the bridal chamber, where there would be no one to stop me.

Jacob would confront my father, and Father would be forced to give him his true wife. I would leave myself at Jacob's mercy. If he decided to shame me publicly, at least I would not be shamed in my own heart—and I would not betray my sister. Relief flooded my mind, but it was short-lived. Alib was standing at the first milking stall, his face angrier than I had ever seen it.

"There you are! What are you doing, Leah?"

Alib pulled me along by the arm, my feet stumbling to his long strides. He closed the door behind us. Zilpah was standing in the corner, eyes wide. My brother jerked me around to face him.

"Why did you leave?" He was barely containing his fury. For a moment, I thought he might hit me himself, something I would never have thought of Alib.

"I knew I shouldn't have left you alone. I'm sorry for all of this, Leah. You know that I am, but there's no getting out of it."

I shook loose of my brother's hand. "Why? Why would Father do such a thing? And why would you help him?"

Alib pressed his hand to his forehead as though trying to keep his head from bursting open. He looked at me with love and pity in his dark eyes.

"There's more going on than you know, Leah. Father was telling the truth about the threat to Jacob, and if you think you're safe from Beor, you should think again."

I was tired of all these ambiguities. I raised my voice, demanding an answer. "What is the purpose of this, Alib? I want to know!"

He pulled his hand through his hair and looked at me for a long moment, his face an equal mix of aggravation and regret.

"I may as well tell you. Father is going to offer Rachel to Jacob for another seven years' work."

"In my place? Thank God. He has come to his senses!"

"No."

"But . . ."

And then I understood. My father was going to give both his daughters to the same man. I was his excuse for holding Rachel back, his justification for breaking his word to Jacob. My father was determined to keep him here. He rather liked his newfound wealth and was concerned it might not be sustained without Jacob's skill. He couldn't simply tell Jacob he had decided to raise the bride price by another seven years. I was the piece of dry bread, offered to stave off hunger until supper could be served.

Beor would probably just as soon see Jacob go, but I understood now that he would not let Jacob take so much as a lamb, and that would not end well for one of them.

Jacob would be too stubborn to leave what he knew was rightly his, and Beor would think it his familial duty to keep him from it. My father would likely not do Jacob physical harm, but if he chose to leave, Father would not go out of his way to protect him either.

I found my way to a chair and sat. There was no hope. No chance of stopping this. I was going to lose my sister, and in marrying Jacob I would spend the rest of my life with a man who did not love me, and possibly lose the one thing that gave me a sense of satisfaction and worth, my craft. I felt like my essence was seeping out of me, leaving nothing but a dull ache behind.

"I'm sorry, Leah. You don't deserve this."

Alib's face was filled with sorrow. I knew he cared for me, and it pained him to have any part in this travesty. I gave him a weak smile. "I'll be all right, Alib. It's not your fault. Don't worry for me."

I promised Alib that I would not run again, so he left me to ready myself for my wedding. *My wedding.* Tears welled in my eyes.

Zilpah set about picking hay out of my hair and putting out water for me to wash. There would be no rose oil and cooling wine for my skin. No excited sisters-in-law to fuss with my hair and kiss my cheeks and tell me what a beautiful bride I was.

When I was clean and my hair was brushed, I pulled on a simple linen tunic that Zilpah had taken from my father's house for me to wear. Not even a special gown for the occasion. It felt like a shroud over my thin shift

"Alib brought this for you. That's how he knew you were gone."

I looked at the wool-wrapped package sitting on the table with no enthusiasm until a memory congealed in the back of my mind.

"As the older daughter, you will wear it on your wedding day, Leah. And I will look on, proud to be the mother of such a lovely bride," Mother had said as she kissed my forehead.

I had been afraid to touch the smooth softness of the strange material, fearing I might snag or stain it with my young hands. It was my mother's *mitpahath*, a veil of such fine color and weave and broidered design that it was given as part of her dowry.

She had worn it on her wedding day, as her mother had before her.

Mother. I cried again as I touched the pale-blue cloth, glad my mother couldn't see this farce.

CHAPTER TWELVE

Jacob

The wedding canopy had swelled and sighed and settled into a gentle flutter as the men and women parted ways. I had been taken to the tent where the men would celebrate the way men do when not in the company of women. The tent smelled of roast lamb in pomegranate sauce. The warm, sweet scent made my mouth water, but I picked at my plate without appetite, knowing Leah had made it. I had hurt her deeply when I chose Rachel, and the thought of it broke my heart.

The ceremony had been short since I had refused the wedding rites of Laban's gods, and my father wasn't here to play his part. I was glad, though, that he wasn't here. I think he might be disappointed in me again, and I didn't think I could stand up to it. There had been a peculiar tension in the air. Laban wore his usual dour face above his finest cloak, Rachel at his side, covered from head to ankle in a beautiful blue linen *mitpahath* embroidered with fine white thread. But there was a stiffness in his stance. And the brothers stood tight-faced, hands at their wives' elbows, something I found odd, since these men seldom touched their wives in public. The few neighbors who were invited seemed the only ones of a mind to celebrate.

Then something had occurred to me.

Where was Leah?

I looked at each face in the small group, then looked again. She wasn't here? Why? Was she preparing food? Surely not during her sister's wedding. The thought that Laban would allow it made me clench my fists.

Or had she been so humiliated to be passed over that she had been unable to witness the affair that evidenced her inferiority to her sister? It wasn't true. She wasn't inferior—not at all.

I had been drawn to Leah like a moth to light. There was no guile in her. No artifice. She was kind and good, and honest about her struggles with her faith. She worshiped the God of my fathers with unfeigned devotion, and isn't that what my father had asked of me?—to take a woman who worshiped the God of Abraham? Leah's presence had comforted me, like a stream of warmth in the marrow of my bones.

But I loved Rachel.

I had loved her from the moment I saw her leading her father's sheep to the well. She was beautiful and well formed, and there was a playful, childlike quality about her that made me feel younger than I was. She had entered my heart, and I had swept out the dust of reason to make room for her.

Without mirth, I smiled and laughed at the ribald jokes and drank the beer and wine. A man with slick black hair tied with a cord at the nape of his neck sat in a corner trying to play a lyre while swatting at a fly that seemed bent on stopping the discordant rendition. My new father-in-law hadn't put out much on entertainment.

"Have another drink, Son," Laban said, patting me on the back. "You have much to celebrate." Laban had never called me Son. I wasn't certain I liked the sound of it.

Beor kept my goblet full long into the evening, until I had to say, in no uncertain words, I'd had enough. "I don't want to be sick in my marriage bed, Beor," I told him as I pushed away the cup. A strange look passed between the men that made me wonder if something was afoot. I'd seen that look before.

"Just one more," Beor had said with uncharacteristic jocularity.

And it was one more after that, until I really did feel I might lose the contents of my stomach.

I steadied myself on the shoulder of one of the guests as I made my way from the tent to the mud-brick house I had built for Rachel and decorated as a bridal chamber.

"May you delight your wife with your ardor, and may your seed settle in her womb and grow into a healthy son," the man said through crooked teeth blackened at the gums. I fought to keep from gagging as his foul breath crept up my nose.

"So be it!" said a chorus of slurred voices.

"And may your wife's ardor match your own!" said another guest as he winked one glassy eye.

Hands slapped my back as I pushed open the coarse door of the bridal chamber, where I would wait for Laban to bring my wife to me. I closed the door and leaned against it.

The smoke of freshly lit castor twines burning in the clay lamp pricked my eyes, and the flame sent shadows skipping across the colorful tapestries covering the lime-washed walls.

I had lived for years in this house I had built for Rachel, longing for the day she would join me. I had spared no effort in readying it for her, though we would return to Canaan soon. Seven years was time enough to scour the markets for tapestries, clay pots, and broidered coverlets. A rug—not as grand as the one Abraham had purchased for Sarah but far better than a discarded goat-hair tent curtain.

We would take it all with us to Canaan, where we would live in a tent, as our family had done for generations. When my mother and father passed, we would live in my grandmother's tent, if my father hadn't promised it to Esau. I hoped not. It would seem a shame for women like Basemath and Judith to live where my grandmother and my mother had lived.

I worried for our return. How would Esau receive me? My mother had sent word that my brother had taken a wife from the daughters of my uncle, Ishmael, obviously to appease Mother and Father, since his Hivite wives had been such a grief to them. Did that mean that he had changed through the years—given up his anger? I hoped so. It seemed unlike Esau, though. But God had told me He would bring me safely back to my homeland. *I will just have to deal with my brother when I get there.*

I sat on the raised bed and felt the crush of barley hulls beneath me. I had built it with my own hands and stuffed the woolen ticking while dreaming of this night.

Watching Rachel grow from a beautiful girl to a ravishing woman had been torturous. My flesh had burned until I was tempted to find a woman of the night to sate my desire. But I couldn't do it. I had never lain with a woman. I had feared to, lest the seed of Abraham be defiled and the promised blessing be made null.

Tonight I would lie in this bed with Rachel. Feel her soft flesh against mine. All my hopes and dreams would be fulfilled. This was meant to be the happiest occasion of my life, so why was I filled with angst? Had I chosen the right woman?

The knock startled me out of my reverie. I rose from the bed in haste, only to see a sudden burst of studded black. I sat down, took a deep breath, and rose again with more consideration of my inebriated state.

Laban appeared in the doorway, his long fingers encircling his daughter's forearm. The soft blue of her veil caught the lamplight, and for a moment it seemed she was clothed with the blue sky itself.

I had questioned myself until my mind was a mush of misgiving. If I had wrongly chosen there was nothing to be done about it now, and I knew one thing for certain; I loved Rachel with all within me. However spoiled and self-centered she was, I loved her and she was mine now.

The merriment of the night was gone from Laban's visage, and he seemed to gather himself at the doorway before entering. He drew Rachel across the chamber and stood before me for a long moment. Then he placed her hand in mine, nodded, and turned toward the door, pausing to snuff the fluttering flame. *Strange.*

The room darkened but for the pale apparition of Rachel's veil. Her hand trembled in mine, but with her touch, the rock in my chest was gone and peace was in its place. How could I have doubted? This was the woman I loved. This was the woman that God had given me. I would trust Him with the rest.

I gently lifted the veil from her head and let it pool around her on the floor. She covered her face with her hands and turned her back to me. This was not what I had expected at all.

For a moment I stood disappointed and bewildered. But, of course, she would be frightened of the marriage bed. What I had dreamed of was most likely terrifying to her. She had no mother to ease her fears, and I wasn't sure if her brothers' wives had done their duty properly.

"Beloved?" I placed my hands on her shoulders, and she quailed beneath them. I didn't want her to be afraid. I wanted her to come to me with delight, in celebration of our love. I pulled her to me gently, leaning down to whisper in her ear.

"You don't need to be afraid, Rachel. I'm your husband. I will be gentle. I promise. I love you."

The warmth of her back against my chest set my heart pounding. In seven years, I'd never felt more than the touch of Rachel's hand. I was shaking. I waited for another moment, then buried my face in the nape of her neck. Her smooth skin rippled, and she let out a small gasp. I turned her slowly toward me and, in the dark, found her lips and touched mine to hers, breathing in her honeyed breath. She stiffened, but I kissed her again, a long and gentle kiss. When I kissed her once more, she kissed me back, and my heart swelled with joy.

I lifted her into my arms and laid her on the marriage bed. The scent of aloes and cinnamon and years of longing wafted through the air.

I knew the wonder Adam must have felt when he first knew the woman God had made for him alone. Flesh of my flesh, bone of my bone—and in an ecstasy akin to worship, the seed of the patriarchs burst forth and flowed into the fertile field that God had prepared to receive it.

Jacob

My eyes fluttered open, then closed against the light filtering in from the shuttered window. It couldn't be morning. My body felt like a sack of grain held it to the bed. An incipient pain in the center of my forehead threatened a pounding headache, and my mouth felt like I'd been eating sand. Why did I feel so terrible? I lay still for several long moments, trying to gather my nebulous thoughts.

I forced my heavy lids open enough to see dizzy bits of dust swirling in the narrow streams of light. How much had I drunk? Whatever the amount, it was taking its vengeance.

As the fog in my head thinned, I remembered the feast. Beor and Laban putting one cup and then another in my hand. Me wanting to be done with it, so I could have my wife. The knock on the door. Rachel's warm flesh pressed to mine.

I turned to touch my bride, to pull her into my arms again, but the bed was empty. I rose up on one elbow, forcing my eyes into focus. She was across the room—huddled in the corner—wrapped in one of the covers I had tossed aside the night before.

What? I slid out of the bed and walked to where she sat. Why was she on the floor? And why was she shrouded from head to foot like a corpse awaiting burial? I knelt beside her, the hard-packed earth cold against my bare legs.

"Rachel, what is it?"

She buried her head in her knees, pulling the cover closer around her.

My mind jerked from thought to thought. Had I hurt her in my drunken state? Did she despise the marriage bed? I didn't think it was that. She had melted into me last night.

I touched her shoulder. She was shaking. "Rachel. Please tell me what's wrong. You're frightening me."

Her shoulders continued to shake. I tried to hold her, but she turned her head toward the wall.

I began to panic. My voice turned ragged as I said her name again. "Rachel. I'm so sorry. Did I . . . did I do something wrong? Did I hurt you some way? I'm sorry, my love."

I took her by the shoulders and brought her to her feet, holding her until the struggling stopped and she leaned against my chest and wept. "Rachel, what is it? I pulled the cover from her hair.

Eyes squeezed shut, she tried to turn away, but my fingers tilted her face to mine. Her eyelids were swollen from the strain of her tears, her face flushed. There was a tinge of blue on her cheek that made me shudder. *Where did that come from?*

"Beloved?"

My eyes sorted through pieces of a puzzle, arranging, rearranging, waiting for a whole to emerge from the parts. Then weakness spread through my muscles. The arm pressing her to my chest slipped to my side. I took a step backward, my feet struggling to find purchase.

I stood, staring at the woman standing before me, who was clutching the cover tight around her body, disheveled, weeping. Was this the woman to whom I had whispered intimate words of love? The woman whose body had trembled under my touch. I could feel myself begin to faint.

Leah?

My mind could not accept what my eyes clearly saw. How did she get here? Where was Rachel? It couldn't have been . . . No! I would have known. What was happening? I couldn't believe my eyes.

Rage seized at my gut and surged through my body like the roll of the earth when it quaked. I shook violently with it for several long moments. I took the step toward her and ripped the blanket from her body, then hurled it across the room. Wide-eyed, she crossed her arms over her chest. I picked up the garment I had so gently removed the night before and flung it at her.

"Put it on!" I said, then slipped the linen wedding tunic over my head, half-fastening the sandals onto my feet.

"Jacob . . . I didn't. It wasn't . . ."

"Be quiet!" I said, fighting the urge to hit her. Then I had her by the arm, yanking her out the door of the bridal chamber into the eye-piercing morning light. I pulled her to the tent outside the courtyard, where Laban and Beor had deliberately gotten me drunk.

Men were lying on pallets and cushions spread over the packed earth, passed out from too much wedding drink. Bowls of dates and figs and half-eaten pieces of lamb and fish stained pink with pomegranate lay scattered over the serving tables. The men who still teetered at the edge of consciousness gawped through drink-dulled eyes as we stepped over fallen revelers.

Laban reclined at a small table with Beor and Chorash. I headed toward him, Leah in tow. The brothers rose and flanked the table where Laban was leaning back in his chair dabbing his mouth with a linen napkin. I flung Leah at Chorash and slammed my open palms on the table.

"What have you done to me? Where is my wife!"

Laban looked up, his lips puckered like a fish as he ran his tongue over his teeth.

"Your wife?"

"Yes. My wife!"

He nodded toward Leah. "Your wife stands where you have put her."

"She's not my wife! Where is Rachel?"

"Not your wife? Hmm." He raised an eyebrow. "I think the law would differ with you on that point." He took one of the plump dates from the bowl beside him and tossed it into his mouth.

I should shove that bowl down your throat!

"Where. Is. Rachel?"

"Rachel's whereabouts is none of your concern," he said around the sticky fruit.

"None of my concern? What about our contract? You're a thief!" My voice pounded in my own ears. Laban glanced narrow-eyed around the tent, then back at me, then spit the seed into his napkin.

"Contract? Maybe you should read what you sign, Jacob. You contracted with me for seven years' labor for my daughter's hand in marriage. Our custom does not allow the younger to marry before the elder. I have fulfilled my part of the contract, and I assume you have already enjoyed the fruits of your labor?"

Heat stung my cheeks. The thought of Leah listening to me call her sister's name sent another surge of fury through me.

"You deceived me! Both of you! I worked for seven years for Rachel. Now, where is she?" I lunged toward Laban with every intention of ripping his throat out of his thick neck, when someone grasped my arm from behind and jerked me backward.

Alib shoved a hard hand into my chest, fury in his black eyes.

"Calm yourself, Jacob! Now!"

Calm myself?

Laban's eyes blazed, and he snorted a laugh. "Deceived you? You accuse me of deception? I'm not a stupid man, Jacob. It's easy enough to make inquiries from traders. Your brother didn't give you his birthright out of the goodness of his heart. Your very name speaks of who you are."

Laban's taunt found its mark, but I would not let him turn this on me. I looked over my shoulder at the glassy-eyed men looking with curiosity toward us, cups in hand, beer dribbling down their chins, then turned back to my father-in-law.

"Your guests might not understand why for seven years I've planned to marry your younger daughter—and suddenly I choose the older? You are not a well-loved man, Laban. Some of them might be willing to bear witness with me before the priest as to your duplicity."

Laban took a fig from the plate.

I have had enough of this. The man will regret what he has done.

I spun on my heel.

"Jacob!"

I turned back, brows lifted in challenge.

Laban composed himself. A humorless smile appeared at the corners of his mouth.

"Jacob, there's no need to get overwrought. Perhaps we can work something out."

Overwrought? I will show you overwrought!

"If you are bent on having Rachel for your wife, we may be able to come to an agreement."

I spread my feet and folded my arms over my chest. I trusted Laban as much as a coiled snake.

"Maybe"—his black eyes feigned geniality—"if you were willing to work for me for, let's say, another seven years, at the end of that time I would be willing to give you my younger daughter."

Does the man think me a complete fool?

Now I understood.

"You have not fooled me, Laban. I see what you're doing. You and your daughter have devised a plan to keep me in Haran and get her a husband at the same time. I've already worked for seven years for Rachel! I would gladly work another seven, but then you would want seven more and seven more after that, and I would be an old man before you gave her to me. I want my wife, now!" Furious, I struck the table with my fist. He wasn't going to get away with this!

Laban laid the fig back in the bowl and raised an open hand. "All right, Jacob, all right! You win!" He shrugged and reclined against his chair. "If you agree to work another seven years for Rachel, I will give her to you as soon as you complete Leah's week."

Leah's week? He wanted me to *keep* this woman who had defiled my bed with her treachery?

"I don't want her! Give her to someone else." My gaze flitted to Leah. Her eyes were closed, and she seemed unable to stand on her own.

No! I won't feel pity for her!

She had robbed me of something that could not be restored, and I would never forgive her for it.

Laban leaned forward, hands splayed on the table, his face darkening like a gathering storm. Something in his eyes stilled me, and I swallowed the words that strained against my throat.

"You will fulfill Leah's week, and you will be a husband to her, or you will have neither of them and you will find yourself somewhere lying in a ditch! Do you understand?"

I clamped my jaw shut, grinding my teeth until they hurt. I understood exactly what he meant.

CHAPTER THIRTEEN

Leah

C horash was holding me up. I could hear Jacob and my father—voices bent and distorted, like listening from under the waters of the canal where Rachel and I swam as children.

"I don't want her. Give her to someone else!"

Alib moving toward Jacob—Beor holding him back. Eyes everywhere. My father's, black and cold. Jacob's—hot, full of hate. The guests', embarrassed, ashamed.

So this is what it feels like to drown.

Everything turned dark.

∞∞∞∞∞∞∞∞∞∞

Something made me stir. I must have fallen asleep leaning against the wall. My neck was stiff where it had bowed toward my chest, and my head felt too heavy to hold up.

Chorash had brought me here. To the bridal chamber. He had tried to lay me on the bed, but I refused, settling myself on the floor. I had told him that I had recovered, and he could leave. I didn't have to say it again.

I straightened and stretched my shoulder, pressed my fingers to the back of my neck just below the hairline, and tried to knead the knot of pain away.

A movement caught my eye. Jacob was sitting against the opposite

103

wall. His eyes darted to the floor when he saw me. His eyebrows bristled over a face of solid stone. I sat, the force of the silence pressing the air out of my lungs. I had to say something. Try to explain.

"Jacob, I—"

His head jerked up. "Don't!"

He pulled himself up and raked his hand through his hair. I lowered my head. I didn't want to look at him. I could hear the long hiss of his breath as he let it out.

"Don't say a word unless I tell you to!"

His sandals scraped against the hard-packed dirt as he paced back and forth.

"Why, Leah?" His voice sliced through the air like a knife.

I blinked, looking up at him.

"Answer me!"

I tried to open my mouth, but now that he demanded an answer, my mouth wouldn't comply.

"I said answer me, woman!—and don't tell me your father made you do it!"

I looked at him. His countenance broke my heart. It was utter hatred. Jacob hated me. I tried to tell my father this would happen. Oh, why did I not just put a knife to my own throat? That would have solved it all.

"I . . . I'm sorry, Jacob, I . . ." I wanted to tell him that I hadn't wanted to do this, that I did it to save him from my brother's wrath, and to save myself from it as well. But I knew the words would not ring true. It would do no good to speak them. And I wasn't sure I believed them myself. Maybe I had used my father's threat as an excuse. I didn't know anymore.

He snorted. "You're sorry." He threw back his head and laughed. Then his face changed, and he looked as though he was on the verge of tears.

"I revered you, Leah. I thought you a better woman than any I had ever met, better than your sister." He shook his head. "I thought you were a woman of integrity and good sense."

He pulled in a long breath and squared his shoulders. His mouth was tight, his jaw determined, his eyes fixed hard on me.

"You're my wife. There's nothing I can do about that now. I will provide for you. I will do the things a husband must do, but you will never have my love, Leah. Never."

He pulled a cover off of the bed and lay on the floor, his face to the wall.

I sat, staring at his back, knowing that every hope I'd held for my future was destroyed. I would live the rest of my life with a man who couldn't stand the sight of me.

Neither of us spoke a word during the seven days. We didn't participate in the reveling, and from the sounds, the normally raucous seven days of celebration had ended long before the appointed time.

A servant brought food and drink and water to wash with and took away the scraps and waste. Jacob slept during the day. Then, in the night, he slipped out of the chamber and returned just before the dawn, turning his face to the wall and his back to me.

On the seventh day he gathered his things and walked toward the door. His hand was on the latch when he turned and looked at me standing in the corner.

Say something! Make him understand! I knew if he walked out that door, thinking the worst of me, I wouldn't be able to convince him otherwise. I needed to explain it to him. Surely he would see why I had had no choice. But I didn't. It was no use.

He opened the door and left. I don't know how long I stood, staring at the closed door before I lay down on the bed, pulled a blanket over me and curled into a tight ball—and finally began to cry.

Leah

The moon had waxed and waned and waxed again since my wedding night.

I had removed the colorful draperies hiding the spidery cracks in the lime-washed walls of the house that had been my bridal chamber.

105

All signs of celebration were gone. A simple woolen blanket lay over the bed where the embroidered coverlets had been. The bed Jacob had built for Rachel.

I felt like an interloper. This house was not meant for me. I saw Jacob's love for my sister in every detail: the shelf he had built into the earthen wall that held the mortar and pestle, the clay bowls and iron pots he had gathered in preparation for his bride—abandoned now—to the wife he never wanted.

My sisters-in-law had turned their heads when I emerged the eighth day after my wedding. Only Beulah had conversed with me about more than whose turn it was to bake loaves of round flatbread on the oven at the center of the courtyard.

"It wasn't your fault, Leah. I know that, and so do the others," Beulah had said with sympathy. But I was beginning to wonder if it was my fault after all. No one had put a knife to my throat.

The women had eventually restored me to my place on the edge of their society, but it was still all that I could do to move about under the weight of the humiliation and loneliness I carried.

I had seen Rachel from a distance the day she emerged from the reed outbuilding on the other side of the flax field where she had spent her wedding week. I grieved that she had had no special place on her wedding night. I hoped for a chance to tell her how sorry I was for it all, but the moment our eyes met, she turned her head. It felt like a knife cut through my chest.

The next day Father sent Jacob to care for some flocks in distant pastures, providing a tent for Rachel and him to live in while Jacob's hired men built a house on the other side of the courtyard.

I had watched them from my shuttered window as they pressed damp clay mixed with fine straw into molds and baked them in the sun, then laid them in plumbed rows with bitumen, leaving space for a small window and a door.

This morning, from the same window, I had watched Jacob and Rachel enter their new home, Jacob's hand resting on the small of Rachel's back as he guided her through the narrow doorway and stooped to follow.

There was something about that simple act that pierced my heart—

the familiarity of it—the intimacy of the newly wed. I was a bride, but I had no groom. It would have been better to have spent my life alone.

I balanced a bowl of dough on my hip and stepped out into the courtyard. Baking bread had been one of my favorite tasks. But Rachel and I had always done it together, and I'd found no joy in doing it alone. Perhaps it would be bread that would bridge the breach between us.

I would talk to Rachel at the oven, where she couldn't walk away. I would make her understand how this travesty had come about, and how much I wanted all to be well between us.

The sight of her at the oven, hair pulled back and wound at the nape of her neck to keep it free of flour, sent a heave of dread through me. I almost turned to go back inside but changed my mind. I had to do this, and there was nothing to be gained by putting it off.

"Rachel."

Rachel turned toward my voice, her face seemingly caught in shock that I would try to speak to her.

"Can . . . I help you with the bread?" I nodded toward the bowl of dough on the brick hearth.

She stared until her wide eyes finally blinked and her face colored. She turned back to the oven and stirred the fire with a long stick.

"I don't need your help." Her words were short and sharp, her jaw stiff.

Rachel.

I took a deep breath and held it to stay the tears gathering in my eyes.

"I know you don't, but . . . we've always done it together."

Her head jerked toward me. "That was before you connived to steal my husband."

"Rachel, that's not true." I said, shaking my head. "Do you really think I would do such a thing? Surely, you realize I acted under the most severe pressure. It was not my plan, Rachel. I fought against it. You know I would never deliberately hurt you. You're my sister, and I love you."

"Well, you did hurt me, Leah," she said, her small hands pulling at the ball of dough, forming a circle and slapping it on the surface of the oven.

"I'm sorry, Rachel. I truly am."

Her dark eyebrows flew toward her hairline, and her face turned an angry red. "Sorry? You're sorry?" She pursed her lips and took another ball of dough from the bowl. "You did this because you were jealous that Jacob chose me instead of you. You may be sorry, Leah, but I don't have a sister anymore, so let me finish my baking, please."

The words hit me as though she had lobbed a rock. She didn't have a sister?

My hands were shaking. How could she turn on me as though I were not the sister who had brushed her hair and washed her face and seen that she went to bed with clean feet? The sister who had held her when she cried for her mother in the night. Who had attended her first blood. I hadn't expected her to embrace the situation with cheer, but to think I would have concocted such an abhorrent act just to hurt her?

I snatched up the basket of dough I had set on the ground and stumbled into my house, closing the door with a resounding thud. My entire body was quivering, my breath coming so hard my head began to swim. I threw the basket across the room, aiming for the wall. It fell short and dumped the dough on the dirt floor, a glob of misshapen balls.

I had feared that Rachel would blame me, but hearing it from her mouth made me realize how unfair it was. How wrong to blame me for what I had been forced to do. What would have happened to me if I'd refused? Would Rachel have rather seen me beaten or sold? And what would have happened to Jacob? Would she have cared? She didn't want him in the first place. She wanted a husband who was young and dashing and with a home in the city where she could be as far away from goats and sheep as possible. Maybe she loved him now, but the person she loved most of all was herself!

I sat on the bench that lined the earthen wall, trying to calm myself. Surely this would pass. Rachel would apologize, and all would be as before. But I knew it was just beginning. If she was behaving like this now, what would she do when she learned what only I knew?

CHAPTER FOURTEEN

Jacob

I had found some comfort walking behind the oxen—the rhythmic sway of their massive bodies plodding in tandem through the open field, the tang of freshly turned soil and sweat, the sun baking my back were all somehow soothing.

The oxen stood still, eyes drooping and dull. A servant and I unfastened the plow and loosened the lines stretching over the notched beam that joined the massive creatures. We lifted the yoke and placed it over the hooks fastened to a long pole the length of the milking shed.

The oxen didn't move from their place. I wondered sometimes why they didn't bolt the moment the heavy beam was lifted from their necks. No one would be foolish enough to stand in their way if they did. Would I become like these dumb beasts?—too burdened to remove myself from Laban's yoke?

At least I had Rachel, and Laban could do nothing about that. There had been no canopy on a hilltop, no celebration of the men, and I'd missed none of it. It had been spoiled, and to relive it would have brought more grief.

The rites were held in Laban's house with only him and his sons and their wives. I wouldn't have let Rachel wear her mother's *mitpahath* if she had so desired, and she didn't. I had insisted she be uncovered, allowing me to veil her myself, a practice I would instill as tradition with my sons. This would not happen again, if I could help it.

My mind had been a roiling cauldron of emotion. I railed at the play for sympathy it made for Leah. She deserved none, and she would get none from me! She had taken so much from her sister.

I wanted nothing more than to leave this place behind, but Laban had me in his grip. If I didn't do something, I'd spend the rest of my life under my father-in-law's thumb.

I longed for Canaan. My father was still living. At least he was when my mother sent word by a merchant following the trade route from Beersheba to Haran. I hated the disappointment I'd seen in his lined face. I wanted to return in a fashion that would make him take notice. I'd accumulated a good amount of wealth since I'd entered my uncle's employ, but he was always finding ways to reverse it and get the larger share.

"Jacob."

A cold voice pulled me from my thoughts.

I huffed a breath and turned around.

"Alib."

My three brothers-in-law had hardly spoken a word to me since the morning in the tent. But I wasn't surprised to see Alib's stony face before me now. I had been expecting this.

"I need to talk to you." Alib shot a glance at the servant.

I nodded toward the man. He looked between us and scurried away.

I folded my arms over my chest. This was not going to be a pleasant conversation.

"I'm listening."

Alib's hands were fisted at his sides, the line of his mouth taut in his dark beard. "You have a wife. Her name is Leah, or don't you remember that?"

My eyebrows shot up. I could feel my temperature rising. "Oh, yes, I remember. How could I forget?"

Alib's chilly eyes narrowed. "Well, I hope you have not forgotten something else."

So there it was. I had not forgotten. A threat from my father-in-law. "You will be a husband to her, or you will find yourself somewhere lying in a ditch."

I had not doubted Laban's words then, and I did not doubt them now. I had sent meat and other goods to Leah by a servant, but almost three months had passed, and I had not visited my first wife's bed. I couldn't bring myself to do it. How could I lie with a woman who had deceived me in such a way? I doubted my body would even oblige me if I tried.

I ran my hand through my hair and stared at my sandals for a long moment. For some reason, I wanted Alib to understand my pain.

"You know I held your sister in high regard—more than high regard. I revered her."

I closed my eyes to compose myself. Something in me grieved the loss of the Leah I had known. The girl who told me stories of my grandfather and who held to her faith in the living God, even when she suffered for it.

"But to stoop to this—to trick me into marrying her—what did she think would happen? How did she think I would react? Did she think she could deceive me, that she could intrude into my most intimate moments, and I would just shrug and let it pass?"

My body stung as if an unseen horde of insects had taken a thousand little bites from it. I resisted the urge to dig at my flesh. I wanted to scream.

"I've tried to understand, Alib. But there is just no logic to this madness. How could she—why would she do such a thing?"

Alib clenched his fists. "You can't believe she did this of her own accord."

"Oh, I'm sure it wasn't her idea, but Laban didn't drag her into the bridal chamber, and he wasn't standing over the bed when I called her by her sister's name. She could have stopped it, Alib. She could have told me who she was."

"And what would have become of her then?" Alib leveled his shoulders. "I came to warn you—that's all. What you do with it is up to you. Personally, I couldn't care less if you end up in that ditch. My sisters are all I care about."

Alib started to walk away, then turned back to face me again. "If you had married Rachel first, you would have taken all you own and left, true?"

"Immediately," I said, firming my jaw.

"That may not have been as easy as it sounds, and you may owe your first wife a debt you don't realize."

I watched Alib's back as he crossed the plowed field, heading toward

111

the goat pens. What debt did I owe Leah? Was he insinuating that Leah had done this deed for *my* welfare? For a moment I wanted to believe it. Believe she was the woman I thought she was. And I believed Alib told the truth about his father's threat. His words weighed on me like the beam on the oxen's back. This yoke was not easily put off. I would have to be careful. I would have to plan.

But he was wrong. I owed Leah no debt but a husband's duty, which I would have to meet if I was ever going to get away from here.

Jacob

I pushed open the door to Leah's chamber. She was standing at the washstand in a thin night shift, a damp rag in her hand. Her eyes went wide with surprise. I stood in the doorway for a long moment, then closed the door behind me. The silence was heavy and uncomfortable, like winter wool on a summer day.

Leah seemed frozen in place, the rag still dripping in her hand. I scrubbed the line dividing my forehead. *How do I do this?* Exhaling, I shrugged off my cloak.

"You don't have to, Jacob," Leah said, as if she had heard my thoughts—or had I said it aloud without realizing?

"Oh, it seems I do." The words were sharper than I had meant them. I saw her flinch as they found their mark. I didn't enjoy hurting Leah. I just couldn't control the eruption of anger when confronted with what she'd done.

She laid down the rag. Her eyes sparked pain and anger as she spoke.

"No—you don't—not tonight."

"Leah," I opened my mouth to soften the words I'd said. My mind was a jumble of conflicting emotion. I had once cared for Leah enough to consider asking for her hand. Was there nothing of that left in me?

"I'm pregnant."

Pregnant? My eyebrows shot up.

"That's not possible."

Her brow furrowed, as though she questioned if I'd heard her.

112

"One time? It can't be so."

I had made love to Rachel every day, sometimes twice, and with each cycle of the moon her blood had come. My mother and my grandmother had been barren for years before they bore children. And Leah pregnant the first time?

Some force sucked the air out of my lungs. Why had the thought that she could be pregnant not even entered my mind?

But I could see it, as she stood there in her thin shift, the subtle rounding of her form. It was growing inside of her—my seed. The seed she had stolen from her sister by deceit. And if that seed produced a boy child, her son would be the heir. Her son would get the birthright and the blessing. She would hold an honored place above her sister.

Rachel.

I looked at Leah for a long moment. I could see the question in her eyes. Would I rejoice at the prospect of a child—a son, as any man should?

"You've robbed your sister again," I said. I could see the tiny spark of hope on her face flicker, and with my next words I saw it drown.

"If you think this changes anything, Leah, you are mistaken."

I left Leah where she stood and walked out into the courtyard. I walked past the bleating sheepfold, hearing nothing but the hammer of my heart. Then I began to run; the tall plants in the flax field pulled at me—slowing me like a bad dream, but I didn't stop until I was on one of the rolling hills overlooking the settlement below.

I put my hands on my knees and dragging in deep breaths of the night air, I looked around for something to crush. I wanted to pulverize something, grind it to powder.

I unearthed a large stone from the dark earth and threw it as far as I could, cursing as it fell to the ground only a few paces away.

I sat down hard on the damp hillside and buried my head in my hands. One time, and Leah was with child. What would this do to Rachel? I saw the worry on her face each time her blood flowed. And I wanted my first son to be born from the woman I loved. Not from a deceiver!

"Jacob."

113

My head flew up. I looked around, but I was alone on the hillside. And yet I had heard my name. I had heard it spoken thousands of times, but this time it fell on me as if the heavy rock I'd thrown in frustration had fallen on the hard ground—the name I had been given when I grasped my brother's heel, trying to be first: supplanter, deceiver, Jacob. I knew this voice. I'd heard it in a dream on my journey from Canaan to Haran.

Jacob. Deceiver.

Leah wasn't the only one.

Grief poured through me. I would reap what I had sown.

I let the male goats into the enclosure Beor and I had built to keep the weaker bucks from the prized females. I smiled at the memory of Beor's sulking face as he worked beside me, furious that his father had chosen him for the task. Laban was a shrewd man, and I imagined he wanted to keep his oldest son in his place and saw a way to humiliate him a bit and took it.

I didn't like my uncle much, but I liked Beor even less. There was an arrogance about him that scratched at my nerves, and I imagined someday Beor and I would find ourselves at odds, and who knew what would happen? But for now I needed to keep the peace. I wanted only to increase my wealth and leave this place as soon as my debt was paid. A flash of heat flamed in my chest. My debt had already been paid! And now I was paying through the nose again.

The female goats pranced back and forth, wagging their tails vigorously, bleating at the bucks. Life was simple if you were a goat. Nothing was simple for a man with two wives. Leah was pregnant, and Rachel was devastated. And I feared my life was going to be a battlefield.

Simi approached the goat pen with a man I had never seen. He wasn't a farmer or a shepherd, I was certain of that. His clothes were dusty from the road but of fine material. He wore a green-and-red striped sash around his waist and a white turban on his head. His face was serious. He was a trader.

My heart began to flutter against my chest. It was Father. He was dead, and my mother had sent a trader to inform me.

"You are Jacob, son of Isaac of Hebron?" he asked, his eyes steady on mine. I nodded, unable to speak.

"I regret to inform you that your mother has died."

The words hit me like a fist to my gut. *Mother?*

I felt the blood run from my head and thought that I might faint. My mother was dead? A cold sensation rose from a hidden place in my consciousness—the feeling I had when I left my home in haste that I would never see my mother again. I had fought against it. Shoved it back when it wrenched free, but it was always there, a feeling in my bones that I couldn't escape.

Was this God's judgment? The curse she'd said she would take for me? No! I couldn't believe it was that. She was only trying to see me in my rightful place. Wouldn't any mother have done the same? But she would gladly take it if it were a curse. She would give her life for mine without a second thought. My stomach turned, and bile rose in my throat.

"I'm sorry for the loss of your mother, but I must be going. I've merchandise to deliver to the market."

But he didn't go. He was waiting to be paid.

I was certain my father or Esau had paid him handsomely before he left, but he seemed to expect payment on both ends. I didn't care. He could charge whatever he wished.

"Simi, could you take the man to Rachel and tell her to give him whatever he requires."

The boy nodded, his face filled with sadness. "And Simi, say nothing of this to anyone, please." I wanted to grieve in private for a time.

The trader gave a short bow and followed the boy toward the group of earthen houses.

I sat on the ground, shocked and brokenhearted. My mother was gone. I had walked away and left her. If I had stayed, given up the thought of gaining the blessing, would she be alive?

I felt alone in a way I had never felt before—and, strangely, the person I wanted to comfort me in my pain was Leah. She would understand.

I shook the thought from my mind and leaned against the goat pen and began to weep.

Mother.

PART THREE

The Dream

CHAPTER FIFTEEN

Leah

No! If I have twenty children, they'll all be girls, and my husband will take another wife!" the woman said, then resumed her mournful yowl.

The delivery had not been long or difficult, and the babes were the image of health, which could not have been assumed by the plaintive wailing of the mother.

Salah was a wide-hipped, sturdy sort who bore her children with enviable ease. The births of my own three sons had been easy enough, but this woman made giving birth look like a minor indisposition.

The source of her dismay was that she had just birthed twin girls, bringing the number of her children to seven—and not a male among them.

"Surely next time you'll have a son," I said, comforting her, thinking it safe enough to say, since eight girls in a row seemed unlikely at least. Well, not in a row, as most children come, months or years after the other. The oldest daughters were twins, as identical as two siblings could be. Two sets of twin girls—I had never seen it. But Salah had insisted she would never have a son, and her husband would be looking for another wife.

Her husband, a pleasantly homely man, had seemed devoted, holding her hand and brushing tendrils of damp hair from her forehead before I sent him from the room. But Salah's fears were not without merit, since having sons was the measure of a man—and the measure of a woman in her ability to provide them, which made it all the more painful that I had given Jacob three and still did not have his favor.

I'd named my firstborn Reuben, meaning *see, a son* because God saw my affliction, that I was not loved and opened my womb, while my sister remained barren. Even at birth, Reuben was the image of his father, with wet curls plastered to his head. If shown a hundred infants, I could have picked him as his father's child. I'd thought, *surely now my husband will love me*, but he didn't.

When the second son was born, I called him Simeon, which meant *God hears,* because the Lord had heard my cry and given me this son also . . . but, again, my husband's heart did not change.

When I became with child the third time, I knew I carried a boy when I first missed my flow. It's strange that I could be so certain, but I was. I was having another son. Three in almost as many years.

Other than our wedding night, when Jacob thought I was my sister, he had never spent an entire night in my bed. Surely, after I had given him not one but three sons, he would take pleasure in my company and lie with me through the night, our limbs entwined as we slept in each other's arms, so I named my third son Levi—*joined*—but nothing changed, and, still, I slept alone.

Salah had said if she had twenty children they would all be girls. If I had twenty boys, would it be enough to win my husband's affection? I was beginning to doubt it.

One of the twins brought the valerian tea I had requested for her mother.

"The tea will help you to relax," I said, lifting the woman's head.

Spluttering like a chastened child, she calmed herself enough to take a sip and settled down to quiet sobs as I dipped a cloth into the basin of warm water and began to wash away the slick stains between her thighs.

There were many reasons men were barred from the birthing room, but I thought, more than privacy and the fear that they might faint, it was their inability to abide the odors that accompanied childbirth: sweat and vacated bowels and blood—not the metallic tang of the blood of wounds but that thick, sweet smell of woman's blood.

The older sisters were leaning over the babes lying in a small bed, their sprawling smiles revealing the same overlapping teeth.

"Can we help?" they begged as Zilpah crushed shards of salt

between her fingers and mixed it with fenugreek juice to cleanse the newborns.

"You can help me swaddle the babes when I've cleansed and oiled them."

Michal had died some time ago, and I had taken her place as local midwife. Zilpah had taken my place as assistant, and I thanked God for it. She had the makings of a fine midwife, and she was a wonderful friend. Rachel's rejection was made a little more bearable by Zilpah's care of me. But I missed Rachel. The chasm between us was a constant source of pain.

Zilpah dipped the cloth into the emulsion and began washing the newborns, who submitted with all good grace, considering their mother was still bemoaning their gender.

"There you are, lovelies," Zilpah said to the little puckered faces.

Excitement blossomed in identical brown eyes as the girls skillfully wrapped the babes in woolen strips, a task they had obviously done many times before.

I wondered if I'd rather have a daughter next time than another son, a girl to teach and guide and with whom to share the world of women. Soon enough my sons would follow their father into that emotionless realm of males, and I would be alone again, but a daughter would never outgrow the need for her mother's comfort and guidance. I knew that only too well, since I still longed for my own mother.

Zilpah strapped my bags to Lily, the donkey a grateful mother had given me some time ago. I had named the animal after the benefactor, a gentle woman, reminding myself not to use the donkey's name if I should attend her again, which was not likely since she had politely served her husband notice that she was too old for his attentions and would not be receiving them again.

But Lily had proven not to have the sweet disposition of her namesake and was loudly braying her discontent, making me wonder if she was daughter of the last beast we'd owned.

People milling through the narrow streets scowled as they looked at the donkey and at Zilpah, who shrugged apologetic shoulders and cuffed the beast with the back of her hand.

"Be quiet, you fiend, or I'll have you skinned and make myself new sandals from your stubborn hide."

Lily brayed one more time and quieted like a child who must always have the final word.

I smiled at my two ladies, thinking how much alike they were and how much I would hate to part with either of them, despite their stubborn streaks.

"Could I speak to you for a moment?" Salah's husband asked with a hesitant voice. His narrow face was drawn below pained black eyes, making him look a bit like Lily.

He guided me a few strides away.

"This is a subject of . . . some delicacy, and I . . . uh . . . I assume you to be a woman of discretion."

I wasn't sure whether it was a statement or a question, but I was feeling a bit uncomfortable about whatever was coming.

"Er . . . uh . . . you have three children?" he stuttered.

"Yes," I answered, wondering why he would ask.

"And they are sons, I am told?"

"Yes, they are sons."

The man was turning pink about the ears, which was quite a sight since they were sizable and seemed to bend attentively foreword from the sides of his long face.

"Please, feel free to ask your question," I said, looking at Zilpah, who was holding Lily's rein with a look that brooked no nonsense from the animal.

"I . . . was wondering if you have an unmarried sister by any chance."

When the words had settled in my mind, anger swelled in me. I wanted to slap the homely face, and I clenched my fists to keep from doing so. I pursed my lips against the unpleasant words behind them.

"I have only one sister. She is married and has no children at all."

"Oh,"

His throat bobbed as if there were a small animal trapped in it—a rat, no doubt.

"Perhaps a niece?"

I did have three nieces of marriageable age, but I wasn't about to tell him so. I didn't want my nieces to be the second choice of any man.

Despite my attempt to keep rage focused at the timid man before me, I could not entirely do it. The world about him placed great value on a male heir, a son to carry on the name and blood, and he had waited through seven girls before seeking a second spouse.

But my heart was saddened for the wife of his youth as well as the wife he might take, who would be the object of the other's jealousy. I knew too much of such things.

"Do you love your wife, my lord?"

He seemed taken back by the question.

"Yes. Of course. I love her very much."

"Is that not enough?"

The man looked puzzled. "Enough?"

"To have a woman you love, who loves you, and seven beautiful daughters?"

His shoulders drooped into a forlorn slump, and I felt pity for him, but I would not be party to his wife's grief.

"I'm sorry, but I cannot help you," I said as I joined Zilpah, sorry for both father and mother of the newborns.

Rachel was in the courtyard when I returned, sitting on the brick bench playing a hand game with Simeon.

"How has your day been, Rachel?" I asked, trying to make conversation.

She looked up, barely acknowledging my salutation. Rachel had long since realized that to live across the courtyard and never speak or interact with me was not only impractical but impossible. Women worked together. It was just the way of things, and there was nothing for her to do about it. But the upward tilt of her chin was meant to remind me that she let me in only at her pleasure. And apparently, she was not pleased to do so today.

Simeon fled the bench and found a firm grip around my leg. I heaved the two-and-a-half-year-old onto my hip and kissed his gritty face. His fingers went straight for my mouth. They tasted of salt and dirt, and I dared not think what else.

"Have you been a good boy for your aunties today?"

"Good boy!" The child smiled widely, revealing a mouthful of nubby teeth.

Reuben jumped up and down in front of me, exclaiming with shrill delight that his cousin Simi had taken him to the field, and he had ridden the ox as it plowed, something I had already suspected from the smell of him. I ran my hand through his curly hair and pinched his cheek. He was such a beautiful boy.

I looked back to the place where Rachel and Simeon had been sitting. Rachel was up, her back to me, walking to her house. Not one of her warmer days. But my fertile days never were. It was the sixth day from my courses, and Jacob would come to me tonight. I sighed. Rachel resented every time Jacob came to my bed. But if she worried that Jacob enjoyed my company, she needn't. My husband did not come to my bed with love but out of obligation. His visits left me empty and full of longing.

Unlike Rachel, my status with the women at the well was much improved. They no longer whispered behind their hands when I passed but said, loud enough for me to hear, "That Leah. Three sons, and not four years have gone by!" then in whispered tones, "Poor Rachel. No children yet? The gods must see something is amiss."

I had to admit it seemed pleasant to be on the other side of their sharp tongues for once, but I still could not find pleasure in their disparaging of my sister. I loved Rachel, and I missed her companionship so very much. The loss of her love was a deep hole in my heart. But my sister and I were more alike than I cared to acknowledge. We both wanted what we did not have: Rachel, sons, and me, the love of my husband, something I doubted would ever be mine.

"Thank you, Olnah," I said, setting Simeon down and lifting Levi from her arms. He was heavier by far than his brothers had been. He opened sleepy eyes, then let them flutter to a close.

My heart swelled with love for my boys. I had to remember how truly blessed I was, even as I grieved for my sister's companionship and my husband's love.

I shifted Levi's warm weight to my hip. Reaching into the folds of my sash, I pulled out a lovely linen scarf the mother of the twins had given me in payment and handed it to Olnah, along with a few coins.

"Thank you. I hope the boys gave you no problem?"

"Oh," she said, her normally almond-shaped eyes round as she tucked the coins in her sash and pulled the scarf over her shoulders. "No, they were no problem at all."

Olnah no longer looked down her pretty nose at me. I was a woman with a measure of independence she would never know. Before I married, Father had met me in the courtyard with his hand out, taking all my coin and anything easily sold in the market, leaving me only trinkets for my hard work. Jacob took nothing from me. I almost wished he would. It would be better to be robbed than to be ignored.

"If it's ever too much trouble, I'm happy to hire a wet nurse, Olnah."

"No. No. It's fine," she said.

My sisters-in-law were a fertile lot, usually with a nursing child or two and milk enough to spare. Olnah and Paltith were always eager to come to my aid and sometimes argued between themselves for the opportunity. I chose not to concern myself with their motives. I was sure they would have helped me without payment, if perhaps not quite so cheerfully.

Beulah couldn't help me often. Beor was demanding, and there was a dear price to pay for any chore undone. I worried what Beulah might still be suffering from my brother's abuse behind closed doors. I had broached the subject with her once or twice, but she always refused to talk about it. I was certain Beor had told her to not tell me anything. And, no doubt, there was a threat behind the words—to me and to my sister-in-law. I didn't take threats from my brother lightly. But when Beor was away shearing sheep or occupied for a considerable time, Beulah would help the others or take one of the boys to her house to nurse and nap, and I would always pay her more than necessary.

I missed my sons dreadfully when I was gone. But I loved my work. I was seen as having special skills and was called upon in increasingly difficult cases. It was exhilarating, since most of my life I had not been seen at all, other than as Rachel's homely sister.

But my children were my heart, and I worried I was away from them more than I should be.

Reuben pushed the door open and held it. I set the boys on the rug covering the earthen floor, kissed Reuben's soft curls, and sat in the wooden chair at the table, glad for a moment's rest.

The thick mud-brick walls kept out the heat so effectively I found myself rubbing my arms against the chill of the room. I looked at the cold fire pit, dug into the ground beneath three stone sides and a flat slab of rock across the top, and wished it was lit, but a fire was for cooking. I would have to put on a heavier garment or bake, so I got up and took my extra shawl from its peg.

I tore bread from the round loaf I'd retrieved from the bread basket and spread it with goat cheese and gave it to Reuben and Simeon to eat while I nursed Levi. Jacob would come when it was dark. The thought sent my feelings flying every which way.

When the boys were sleeping soundly on their pallets, I washed at the basin and took my hair down and brushed it several times. Not that my husband would notice or be pleased if he did. He had said from the beginning he wanted no pretense of love between us. And there was none—from him. I hid my emotions as best I could, but I knew Jacob sensed my feelings for him, which served only to make him angry.

I heard the scrape of the door. The sight of Jacob made my heart quicken. He was a handsome man with his hair teasing the nape of his neck in the same soft wave as his eldest son's.

Jacob looked at the boys asleep on their pallets, his eyes full of tenderness. He loved his sons, though he seldom held them or gave them much attention. I knew Rachel was at the root of it. She couldn't bear to see him dote on them, though she often did herself. I hurt for my little ones and worried that Jacob would regret his neglect someday. They wouldn't be young forever.

My husband looked at me for a long moment. I could see the lines of his face clearly in the lamplight. He seemed drawn and tired, and full of something vulnerable and sad. I had never seen him this way.

"Leah—" He looked at the floor, his back bent under an invisible weight.

What was this? "Is everything well, Jacob?"

I wanted to go to him and comfort him, and for a moment, I thought he might welcome my embrace, but he stiffened and his face closed. He shook his head.

"Yes. Everything is well."

The moment was gone. Whatever was bothering him, he didn't want to share with me. Why would he when he could talk to the wife he loved?

He removed his cloak and sat on a chair to unfasten his sandals. I pulled the goat hair curtain that gave a measure of privacy and lay on the bed, my heart aching, waiting for my husband to do his duty toward me, praying tears would not betray me.

After, when I heard the door close, I stared at the ceiling, praying. God had opened my womb three times, and I was grateful, but it seemed even He couldn't open my husband's heart.

I have to accept things as they are and stop hoping for more.

I vowed to accept the situation. I wouldn't cry another tear. I turned on my side and tucked the cover under my chin.

<hr />

In my dream I felt light, as if my feet only touched the ground out of habit. I looked before and behind and realized that I was in a line—a long line of women. The line stretched far into the distance, but in my dream I somehow knew that it was not distance I saw but time—a long line of women through time.

There was no discernible commonality among the women. Some were beautiful and some were plain. Some wore fine garments and some humble attire. One appeared to be a woman of the night, her face painted and the bodice of her dress cut low. She held a long scarlet cord.

As is only possible in dreams, I did not move from my place but could see where the line ended. The last woman stood on a hill looking up, her eyes deadened with grief. She was looking at a man—bloodied and beaten, hanging on a tall pole planted in a hole in the ground, his arms stretched across a shorter crossbeam.

Nails held his wrists to the rough wood. A wreath of thorns pierced his head. His face was red and tight with swelling where large tufts of his beard appeared to have been pulled out by the roots.

He was naked. His suffering eyes settled on me. I began to weep.

Then I was in the line again. I turned to the woman behind me. It was my mother. She looked as I remembered her—young, beautiful. I thought to raise my hand and touch my mother's precious face, but my arms were suddenly filled with warmth; I held a child, a son.

I awoke with a start and sat up in my bed, my heart thrashing. This was like no dream I had ever had. Most of my dreams hovered over my mind in distorted waves, like the hope of water in the desert heat, but this dream was sharp and clear. I remembered every detail: the line of women, the woman who stood on the hilltop, the man who suffered on the pole—and his eyes, which seemed tortured beyond the worst of deaths. His gaze had felt like knives dividing body and soul. And the son in my arms. I ran my hand over the hollow of my middle.

CHAPTER SIXTEEN

Leah

A knock sounded through the door. I pulled myself from my bed and slipped a tunic over my shift. Judging from the light filtering through the window slats, I'd slept long past the rising of the sun, something I never did. And the boys were still sleeping soundly on their pallets. A rare morning, indeed. The dream of the man on the pole came back to me, and I felt a strange tingle moving up my spine.

Zilpah was at the door. "Leah. There is someone here. He says he needs to speak with you."

I followed Zilpah into the courtyard. A gentle rain drizzled. A young man with wide eyes and damp hair held the reins of a small donkey.

"My master has requested that you come quickly. His wife has been in labor for a day and a night and is suffering terribly."

"Where is the woman?" I knew of no neighbor close to her time.

"In the city. Near the temple. Please. We must hurry."

"Are there not midwives in Haran? Or a physician? Why come to the countryside?" I attended women in Haran, but they were known to me. To come outside the city for a midwife when the woman was already laboring was unusual, and I had delivered the twins just yesterday and was hoping for some time with my boys today.

"Two physicians were called but were busy with other patients. There is a midwife in attendance, but my master wants you to attend his wife."

A midwife in attendance? Then why another? And why me?

Maybe Tesup, a physician I sometimes assisted, had referred me. But the servant would have said so.

I let out a sigh. "Zilpah, would you ask Paltith if she can care for the boys? Hurry, please. We need to leave right away."

She nodded and hurried to my brother's house. I gathered a cloak and my things and told a servant to tell my husband where I was going.

"I brought the donkey for you to ride, mistress," the young man said.

"I can walk faster, but I'll take my own beast. Her saddle pack is fitted for my bags. Leave the donkey here. You can collect her later."

Zilpah and I followed the servant through the back entrance of the two-storied house and down a wide hallway into an open courtyard with a fountain at its center and several flowering plants in clay pots peppered about. A drain was set in the sloped stone floor. Another servant took my cloak, which was drenched. The rain was not heavy, but the hour-long walk had been enough to soak it. I took off my muddy shoes and wished for a towel to dry my feet, but the servant who had brought us motioned to follow him. A carved railing meandered up the stairs and around the upper story lined with arched doorways. We followed the servant to one of the tall doors. My bare feet were cold on the stone floor.

An old woman with tufts of white hair hovering about her wizened face let us enter the large bedchamber. The sickening odor of incense assaulted my nostrils. I discreetly closed my mouth and huffed the tainted air out through my nose.

"Thank the gods you are here. I don't know if she can take much more."

Another woman with a terse mouth rose from the bedside and walked toward me, looking me over with angry eyes. *The other midwife.*

"I don't know why they called you. I've done all that can be done. But I'm glad you're here. She's going to die, and when she does, you can take the blame. I'll send for my things."

She pushed past me, nearly knocking Zilpah over as she left the room.

What have I gotten myself into? Something that felt like rocks rattled around in my gut, and it wasn't my morning meal, since I'd taken no time to eat. I knew the tendency of the rich to blame healers when things went awry. I wanted to call the midwife back and leave, but a deep moan drew my eyes to the birthing bed.

"Please. Do something." The old woman wrung her hands.

I put my hand on the young woman's shoulder. Her tortured green eyes opened in a sweet round face; fresh tears followed the rivulets flowing into her matted hair. Her breath came in short spasms.

"Please . . . make it stop."

I was worried. What could I do that the other midwife could not? I took the woman's hand.

"What's your name?" Her hand was clammy. I resisted the impulse to wipe my own hand on my tunic.

"Padi."

"Padi, I'm Leah. I'm a midwife." I tried to steady my voice. The girl was flushed, her pillow wet from her sweat-soaked hair. She moaned again, her face contorted with pain.

I spoke over my shoulder to the servant. "Please, warm some olive oil. I need to examine her."

I nodded toward the small alcove built into the wall. "And would you please remove the incense and open the shutter. The air is stifling."

"But the incense burns to the goddess Nintu, who watches over women in childbirth. If we remove it—"

"I'm sure the goddess can smell it from another room. Your mistress needs fresh air." *The goddess could have smelled it from the next city.*

"Yes, mistress." She scurried to the alcove and out the door.

I pulled a tendril of damp hair off the young woman's forehead. Zilpah took a clean cloth from the stand beside the bed, dipped it into a cup of water, and handed it to me.

"Open your mouth, please." I squeezed some water from the cloth into her mouth—just a bit so she wouldn't choke—and then dampened her parched lips and wiped her face.

"You're going to be all right, Padi," I said with what I hoped sounded like conviction. I had no idea if the young woman was going to be all right.

The deep orange and red of a carnelian strung on a tightly woven cord around the woman's neck caught my eye. It was an intricately carved bull sitting on its hoofed feet. Unique. *The only one of its kind.* My heart stopped.

"Leah."

I turned toward the husky voice behind me.

"Anasa?"

A tall worry-eyed man looked back at me.

Anasa.

He was older but with the same kind rugged face. I stood, and he took my hand in both of his.

"Thank you for coming, Leah. This is her first child. If anyone can help her, I know you can."

I was without words. It had been years. I had never thought to see Anasa again. My mind was tangled with questions. My heart was pounding.

I shook my head. "I will try, Anasa, but the other midwife . . ."

The fear on his face deepened, and I thought better of what I was about to say.

"I'll do my best." I removed my hand from his and turned away. He caught my shoulder. A guilty wave of emotion poured through me. I prayed he couldn't feel my trembling.

"Leah, I sent for you for more than your skill as a midwife—and from what I have heard through the years, your skill is great." His eyes held mine like a man in mire grasping at a rope. "I called because of the faith you have in your god. Maybe if you pray to him, he will spare my wife and child. I can't lose another loved one, Leah. Please."

He had followed my vocation through the years? Asked about me? I was more than a little shocked. And that he thought my prayers of any worth. I wondered myself.

"Anasa." My heart drew down with the weight of his words. "I . . . It's not up to me."

"Please, Leah. Just ask him, please."

The old woman entered the room again. "Let the midwife do her work, master. Please. This is no place for a man."

He took my hand again and held it for a long moment, his eyes shimmering with tears, then turned to leave.

My hands were trembling. I tried to pull my thoughts together. I couldn't think about the past now. I had a job to do. *Dear God, please help me.*

The servant laid the bowl on the bedside table and cracked open the shutter.

"Help me raise her legs, Zilpah," I said in what I hoped was a steady voice. Zilpah kindly kept her eyes from mine, knowing I was affected by seeing Anasa again.

"I'm going to see how far you have opened, Padi," I said, forcing my mind away from her husband. I dipped my hand in the warm oil and slipped my tapered fingers through the damp flesh.

"Ahhhhh."

"Shhhh . . . It's all right." I soothed while rubbing my fingers gently around the orifice. It had softened and was open enough. *What's holding the child back?*

Zilpah handed me a clean rag, and I wiped my hands. We had worked together so long, she anticipated what I needed.

I rubbed some of the oil onto the woman's stomach and slid my hands over it, probing gently. It was difficult to tell the child's exact position, but something was not right.

"Oh, oh, ohhhhhhhh. It's coming again." Padi's abdomen hardened under my hand.

God, help me to trust in you. For this woman and her child. For Anasa. Give me wisdom to do what must be done.

I placed two fingers at the woman's neck. Her heart beat too fast.

"Zilpah, the mallow, please."

Zilpah poured some oil from the clay bowl into the thick jell and stirred it vigorously.

The old woman stood at the foot of the bed, worrying her hands. I wished she would leave the room.

"I'm going to need some hot water and clean rags. And if you could fetch some salt and another bowl of warm oil." I had salt and rags in my bag, but I hoped to keep the servant occupied for a few moments.

"Padi." I touched her cheek. "I'm going to have to put my hand inside you and move the child."

Her chest rose and didn't fall for a long moment, as though fear had thickened the air in her lungs and she couldn't force it out. I could hardly breathe myself. My head was feeling light. I shook my thoughts back into motion.

"It will hurt, but, hopefully, when I'm finished, the babe will come quickly."

I dipped my hand into the bowl and nodded at Zilpah, who took her place, ready to hold the woman's shoulders to the bed if necessary, her narrow face longer with concern. I hoped I hid my fear better than my patient and my assistant, but I doubted it.

I waited for another pang, and then massaged the orifice with the thick jell, stretching it carefully until I could force my hand through. Padi's mouth opened wide with a strangled cry.

I felt something I did not expect. A hand? One arm was stretched forward!

My heart hammered so hard, I could barely hear my own thoughts. I traced the arm to the child's shoulder.

What do I do?

Sweat was stinging my eyes. I wiped my brow with my sleeve and placed my fingers underneath the shoulder, lifting the babe up and back into the cavity. With one hand to the woman's belly and one hand inside, I turned the little body in line and bent the elbow, straightening the arm along the side and thigh, praying I wouldn't break a bone. I eased my hand out of the wet womb.

Padi caught her breath and began to push, and in a short time the little boy slipped from his mother's body.

Thank you. Thank you. Relief unwound my taut muscles. The lusty howl brought the old woman running through the door.

"Oh! Thank the gods!" She enfolded me in a fleshy embrace. The sharp smell of days-old perspiration stung my nostrils.

I delivered the afterbirth and cut the cord with an iron blade. Zilpah cleaned and swaddled the babe and put him to his mother's breast. Padi winced as the eager boy latched on, her damp face glistening with joy.

The door flung open and Anasa hurried to his wife's side. I stood at the wall watching the couple—tears flooding their eyes as they watched the babe suckle.

The orange-red of the amulet caught the light from the window. I stared at its fiery beauty and thought of all that it had cost me.

I slipped down the stairs, holding to the rail leading to the courtyard, which was profuse with color. The rain had stopped. The fountain glistened. My shoes, clean and dry, were where I'd left them.

I sat on a cushioned chair of fine wood and closed my eyes. Anasa was a man of means, but everything in the courtyard, and what I had seen of the house, spoke of quiet beauty meant for comfort and not for exhibition, much like the man himself. But for that amulet, I might have been mistress of this house, the wife of the good man who owned it.

A small, narrow-faced woman brought a basin of water and a rag and towel and knelt to wash my feet.

"I'll do that." I looked up to see Anasa, his eyes damp and full of joy. The servant rose, bowed, handed her master the cloth, and left. Anasa took the servant's place, washing my feet gently and drying them with the towel.

I was shocked and mortified. But no argument would come out of my mouth. It was an honor I dared not belittle through protest. He slipped my sandals on my feet and looked up with tears flowing down his cheeks.

"Thank you, Leah. Thank you for what you did."

I shook my head, still rattled by his humble gesture. "I'm not the one to thank, Anasa. It was in God's hands—as all things are."

His smile widened. "Yes. Thank you for praying to your god. May I sit with you for a moment?"

I nodded. He stood and took the chair next to me. His head tilted toward the ground.

"Leah, I must ask your forgiveness. I was a foolish man not to take you as my wife. I married a woman I thought would do, but she was no mother and left within the first year. I found Padi just a year ago, and she has brought me back to life again."

He took my hand.

"I thought about you and all you told me, for years. I wanted to come back and ask your father for your hand, but . . ." He shook his head.

"I could not get the courage to face him—or you. And I didn't have the courage to lose business from those who held the gods in such high regard." Shame and regret pulled on his rugged features.

"I hurt you, Leah. I am profoundly sorry. But I hope you realize what an impact you have had on my life. I never forgot you. Your god has used you for my good. And now my wife and child live because of you and your god. I believe I am finally ready to worship only him, no matter the cost."

A huge lump rose in my throat. I was moved by Anasa's words. Something I had said had stayed with him. Had made a difference. My pain had a purpose. It had not been for no reason.

"Anasa."

I tried to swallow so I could speak the words churning in my mind.

"I am so thankful that you are beginning to believe, but if you come to the God of Abraham and choose to worship Him, it can't be for what He has done here today. Your wife and child live, but what if they had not? Would you worship Him in spite of your loss?"

He didn't speak.

"You must worship God for who He is, not for what He does, for if calamity strikes again, you will blame Him and turn from worshiping Him."

Tears pooled in his eyes again—and in mine. I was speaking to myself.

"I've been angry at God, Anasa."

I lowered my head.

"For circumstances in my life I would rather not discuss. I am deeply ashamed for that, but in all things we must believe God has a purpose. Today, after seeing your wife and son alive, I can believe that all things work for good, but tomorrow when I face disappointment and pain, I will forget these words and wonder *why?* And I will have to be reminded again."

Anasa said nothing for a long moment, his eyes thoughtful.

"Again you challenge me with your words, Leah." He took my hand. "This time I will consider them carefully."

And so will I.

I watched his retreating back as he walked up the stairs to his wife and child, as I had watched it so many years ago. I could have had the love of a good man had I been willing to compromise in just the smallest thing.

But life is full of small things.

I knew I would never have the love of my husband, but I had my children and my work. I would try to be content with that.

Help me, God.

CHAPTER SEVENTEEN

Jacob

The hinges groaned as I pushed open the door to the house I shared with Rachel. She was lying on the bed, her face to the earthen wall, crying—again. A knot of pain formed in my chest. I sighed, my shoulders sagging with my spirit. I was still grieving my mother's death. I needed my wife to console *me,* but her own sorrows left little room for the burdens of others.

"Rachel." I sat on the bed and gently touched her shoulder. She pulled away.

I let my hand rest on the woolen blanket and stared into the ebony waves spread across the cover. Leah was pregnant again, and there were no words that would comfort Rachel. I had tried them all. A crushing ache swelled in my rib cage, pressed against my heart. I had watched Rachel wither with every passing menses. In the beginning she would look to her time with hopeful anticipation, but in the last year or two, she would set about cleaning or working the fields frenetically so no one would guess her blood was upon her. I worried for her, since she had always had difficulty with her flow and needed to rest, but she didn't want to look weak to the other women.

"Jacob." Rachel spoke in a hoarse whisper, looking up at me, her eyelids swollen, her lovely face mottled and tear-dampened. "How could you not have realized that it was Leah? How could you not have known that it was her instead of me?"

I puffed out a breath and studied the blanket's coarse wool fibers, rubbed my fingers across the weft and the warp of it, opposite threads weaving in and out becoming one fabric, wishing it was so easy to bind two lives together into one.

I had asked myself that question hundreds of times. I had been drinking. It was dark. But still—how could I not have known?

"Please, Rachel. Don't."

I didn't want to go over this again. I was tired and just wanted to eat and go to bed.

"Why not, Jacob? Does my question not deserve an answer?" She blinked, fresh tears springing to her eyes. "Did you know it was Leah? Did you want my sister more than you wanted me?"

The words gouged at my nerves. It never helped to talk about this. Rachel knew I hadn't wanted Leah, but she continued with this accusation.

"You know I didn't, Rachel."

"But you must have. You continue to be a husband to her! Have sons by her!"

"Rachel, you know I have no choice in the matter! I did not choose Leah, but she is my wife. I have an obligation. I didn't ask for it, but I have to fulfill it. I owe her the opportunity to bear children." *Children you haven't been able to give me.*

I wanted Rachel to be the mother of my children, but it was Leah that was a fertile field. The irony of it. That Leah could conceive so readily, when all the women of my ancestors had struggled for years before bearing children. If it was meant to be a sign, I refused to accept it.

Every time I went to Leah's bed, I felt the sting of her deception. The loss of something only given once. Something I had guarded when my brother's wife had tried to seduce me. When I'd passed women of the night and was tempted to the point of pain. Something I'd reserved for my wife. For Rachel.

I remembered the warmth of Leah's body that night. The depth of emotion I had felt as we became one flesh. Joined by a lie. I had told myself many times that it wasn't her fault. That Laban was to blame. And perhaps he was. But Leah had responded to my love as though it belonged to her. She had taken what I had not offered, and *that* I could not forgive.

I knew my continued rancor toward Leah was not helping Rachel, but I could not let it go. I had let this animosity burrow into my soul, the way an asp slithers in a hole beneath the earth. I feared it would surface and strike some day and be the death of me, but still I clung to it. Even when I'd longed for Leah at my mother's death, I hadn't been able to reach out to her.

Rachel pulled herself off the bed, her damp eyes flashing, her face warped with emotion.

"And what do you owe me, Jacob?" Her mouth quivered. "I want sons! Is that too much to ask? Give me sons, Jacob!"

Her words tore through the air like a whip. In a twist of Rachel's mind, she blamed me. It was my fault she had not conceived, when I would give all I had to have it so. I would take the blame, if it would do any good. But it wouldn't. I loved this woman as much as a man could love, but I sometimes wondered if that love was returned, if Rachel had ever loved me.

"I'm not God, Rachel! I am not the one withholding children from you!"

I didn't realize what I'd said until I heard the words in my own ears. I would have given anything to snatch them from the air.

Tears exploded from her eyes, and she folded into herself, looking impossibly small.

"God is withholding children from me? I knew you believed it, and now you've said it plainly." She pressed her hand over her heart, as though trying to keep it inside her chest.

"Jacob. Give me children or I die."

Oh, God. What have I done?

"Rachel." I reached for her, tried to pull her into my arms, but she struggled against me, and I let her go, helpless to comfort her.

"Maybe I've offended Inanna," she said, weeping. "Maybe it's she who is closing my womb. Maybe I should make an offering to her, Jacob."

Waves of anger and fear broke against me. "How can you offend a piece of wood, Rachel? That's all they are, these gods you worship— wood and stone." When would Rachel give up these lifeless deities? How could she continue to hold to such foolishness? *Was* God withholding children from her?

"I don't worship them. It's just . . ." She closed her mouth, finding no words with which to justify herself.

139

I pressed my fingers against my forehead, trying to clear my thoughts, weary down to my soul. "I will speak no more of this tonight. I'm tired. I'm going to bed." I lay down on the bed and pulled the cover tight around me.

∞∞∞∞∞∞∞∞∞∞∞

When I awoke at dawn, Rachel was sleeping at my side. I slipped from the bed, not wanting to wake her, not wanting more harsh words between us. A suffocating sadness filled my chest. I loved Rachel with all that was within me. I just had no idea how to please her.

I took Reuben with me to the pasture. The boy didn't walk; he jumped like a frog or ran, his long curls bouncing about his head. My heart ached as I watched him. What kind of father was I to my sons? Not a good one. I knew that. Rachel's jealousy and my animosity toward Leah kept me from showing the love I felt for my boys. I didn't want them to grow up feeling isolated, on the edge of their father's affection, as I had. My father never said an unkind word to me. He never raised a hand to me that I did not deserve. I knew my father loved me, but he had never seemed to *see* me standing in the shadow of my brother. I didn't want that for my sons.

Reuben bounced at my side. I reached down and picked him up. He put his arms around me, and I couldn't hold the tears.

God, I don't want to fail my children, but I fear I will do just that.

∞∞∞∞∞∞∞∞∞∞∞

I didn't know what I would find in the evening. I took Reuben back to the courtyard and told him to find his mother. With trepidation I opened the door of my house—to the smell of raisin cakes?

Rachel was standing beside a table set with my favorite foods: succulent roast lamb seasoned with cardamom and thyme, leeks, and thick dark barley beer. She was dressed in her best tunic. Her hair hung in dark waves over her shoulders. She was so beautiful it hurt my chest to look at her. She had poured water into the basin, for me to wash.

This was strange behavior at any time but especially under the present circumstances. I washed my hands without words and set the

140

basin on the goat-hair rug, then sat on a stool to wash my field-soiled feet, wondering at the sudden change in my wife and worrying if the gesture was only the prelude to another argument.

Rachel took the rag from my hand and knelt. "Let me do it."

What? I watched as she washed the day's dirt from my feet and dried them with a gentle hand, and my heart moved with compassion for her. I tipped her face to mine. I had loved Rachel from the moment I saw her leading her father's sheep to the well.

"I love you, Rachel. You know I do."

She nodded, tears slipping down her cheeks. I pulled her to her feet and kissed her, then lifted her in my arms and laid her on the bed.

After we made love, we lay enfolded in each other's arms. I stroked her hair and held her close to my heart. I hated the discord between us. If Rachel could only wait and pray, as my mother had, surely she would someday bear a child.

"Jacob."

"Yes, my love." I touched my lips to her forehead. It was a long moment before she spoke.

"Would you do something for me if I asked it of you?"

My heart plunged, the peaceful moment gone. I would do almost anything for Rachel, but I knew this elaborate manipulation meant I was not going to like it.

"And what would that be, Rachel?" I said, barely covering my rising anger. There was another long moment of silence.

"I want you to take Bilhah and have a child by her."

I shot up in the bed and stared down at her. "No! How can you even think of such a thing?"

She pleaded with me. "The child would be mine, and I would have a son to give you. Please, Jacob. I want to do this for you."

I stood, found my tunic, and pulled it over my head, looking down at my wife in disbelief.

It was an accepted practice for a barren woman to offer her maid to her husband and claim the child as her own. I knew it only too well. My grandmother had offered Hagar, her Egyptian slave, to Grandfather Abraham. And although she had meant it for good, it had brought nothing but trouble to their lives.

Sarah had later conceived, by a miracle, after her blood had long ceased to flow, but her impatience had brought enmity between my father and his half-brother, Ishmael—rifts that would probably endure for generations to come.

My father wanted nothing to do with such practices, seeing what they did to the children born of them, and prayed for twenty years for my mother to conceive. There was trouble enough between my wives without putting another in the mix.

"Don't pretend this is for me, Rachel. It's for you!"

She pulled herself off the bed. "I have to have sons, Jacob."

"You want a child so badly that you would sell your own husband to have one?" I shook my head. "You hate it when I have to be with your sister, and you want me to take another woman? I don't want to be with another woman, Rachel, and I can't believe you want that!"

"I don't want it, Jacob," she sobbed, "but I can't live without children."

"Why? Because your sister has them? Is this all about envy, Rachel? You have to have children because Leah has them?"

I choked, barely able to speak. This obsession. It had blinded Rachel to all that was good in her life. It had blinded her to me. To my love. She couldn't see what was before her very eyes.

"Leah has my children, but you have my love, Rachel. Is that not enough for you?"

She sat on the bed and buried her head in her hands. Her silence said it all. It was not enough. Had never been enough.

She could cry all she wanted; I would feel no pity for her tonight.

I took my cloak from its peg and wrapped it around me and lay on the floor, my thoughts crashing one upon another, angrier at Rachel than I had ever been. It was some time before I spoke.

"Make the arrangements. I will do as you have asked. But you will regret this day, Rachel. I promise you that."

I pulled my cloak tighter around me and hoped for sleep.

Leah

I wiped my brow with my sleeve. The day was warm, made warmer by the repetitive motion of carding wool in the courtyard with the women. I didn't mind the sweat. I enjoyed carding. The whisper of wool as I pulled it through my wooden carders always gave me a sense of satisfaction. The journey of the white fluff from the sheep's back to the backs of those I loved was born of artful skill learned at the skirts of women from the time Mother Eve was told to stop walking naked through the garden.

Little ones laughed and some cried for their mothers, who shushed them with a cluck of their tongues, not wanting to break the rhythm of their spindles.

Rachel rolled the carded wool into small tufts and placed them in the basket beside Zilpah, who was designated spinner because she spun such a steady thread.

Rachel's pursed lips were a pale line in her sun-warmed face, which was not surprising since we always seemed to lose what little ground we'd gained at first word that I was with child.

But Rachel's countenance showed something more today. Her gaze was sad and bleak in the morning light, and with good cause, I supposed, since Jacob had gone to Bilhah's tent the night before. Rachel laid down the wool and went to her house without a word.

Zilpah leaned into my ear. "Jacob didn't return to Rachel's bed last night. In fact, he hasn't yet come out of the tent."

I hadn't realized, thinking he had gone to the pastures at the break of dawn.

My stomach wrenched at the gloat in Zilpah's voice—though I knew any word she spoke against Rachel was meant in my defense—and again at the unwelcome sting of my emotions. I still could not bring myself to rejoice when my sister suffered, no matter how angry I was at her, which was often quite a lot. And I was aggravated with myself for feeling anything approximating jealousy of Bilhah.

Zilpah snorted the hacking-sheep sound that signaled she had something censorious to say. "I'd wager Rachel regrets sending her husband to another woman's bed, especially one like Bilhah."

"What do you mean, one like Bilhah?"

She laughed. "You know."

"No. I don't know."

"Well—there's something about her. Men can't keep their eyes off her."

"They can't?"

"Don't tell me you have never noticed Jacob gawping at her . . ." Zilpah's face colored. "I'm sorry, Leah. I didn't mean to—"

I waved the comment off. "It's all right. It brings me no pain."

I was not telling the whole truth, but it *was* true that I hadn't noticed my husband looking at Bilhah. Rachel had always been the standard of beauty in my mind, and Bilhah looked nothing like my sister. The sharp edges of Zilpah's shoulders could be seen under her tunic. Everything about her seemed long: her arms, her legs, her almost flat torso.

There was a fragility about her that made one worry she might break. Her huge eyes made her look like a startled deer.

My father had bought her in the city. I didn't know the entire story, since Bilhah was not one to talk and I not one to ask, but I had been told she'd been an orphan, raised by relatives who had tired of supporting her and sold her to a man who then sold her in the marketplace like a goat or a pig.

Father gave her to Rachel on the eve of her wedding, as he had given me Zilpah. I had always felt I got the better of the bargain, although there was something about Bilhah that stirred my sympathy.

I looked at the small black tent beyond the flax field and breathed a sigh of resignation. I had given up on the prospect of Jacob's love, and I had to school my emotions to the fact. What difference did it make? One more woman in my husband's bed? But it wasn't just one more. There was another to come, and this time I couldn't blame Rachel.

CHAPTER EIGHTEEN

Leah

All of the women of my family were bent over, working in the field, removing tares, their babes strapped to their breasts or backs and older children at their sides or running through the fields. Judah, my youngest, was bouncing behind them, his little legs trying to keep up.

I straightened, rubbing that place in the small of my back that always ached when my blood was close at hand, and looked out over the rippling waves of wheat. My itching eyes were on fire with the chaff borne on the gentle breeze. I pressed my fingers to my eyelids, trying to sooth the scratchy orbs. Working in the fields was a miserable task for me.

Tares were the wheat-like weeds that hid in full view until the harvest. Other weeds showed themselves early on and could be expunged from the crowded soil before the crop matured, but tares were so like the wheat, one didn't dare disturb them until they showed themselves the imposters that they were.

When the wheat was bowed with the weight of precious grain, the tares stood straight and conspicuous in their barrenness, no longer able to evade their fate. I was not barren in the common sense; I had four sons already, but I felt like an imposter nonetheless. My soul was as dry as the weeds awaiting their imminent demise. Sometimes I wondered if God would pluck me like a tare and throw me into a pile of nothingness.

The older children were making a game of the weeding, seeing who could find the most invaders, or the biggest, and trampling no small amount of wheat in the process. I knew I should correct them, but the memories of my father angrily stalking the fields behind me when I was a child made me soft. I had longed for my father's approval and worked so hard, my mother had to bathe my hands in aloe and wrap them in linen cloths at night, but my efforts were always met with some complaint.

Little Judah came toward me, pushing the rustling wheat out of his way, winding his arms around my legs. The three-year-old could never be long from my side. I picked him up and kissed his straight nose, so much like mine but better-looking on a boy. He put his arms around me, then wriggled out of my embrace and ran away as fast as he had come, satisfied that I was still close by.

Judah was overly attached to me. Almost as though he feared I might disappear if he didn't keep me in his sight. I wondered if he could somehow sense how close I'd come to dying at his birth.

My other sons had been born with ease. But Judah's birth was different. My labor had been hard. I had seen the panic in Zilpah's eyes. In my semiconscious state, I'd seen dark figures hovering around me and above me, ominous and threatening. I knew they wanted to destroy my son. To destroy me, so he'd die in my womb.

I saw the man on the pole that I'd seen the night Judah was conceived, the same dark entities laughing and congratulating one another as they watched him suffer on the tree. I'd called to him, knowing that some way his fate and my unborn child's were intertwined—but he was dead. The earth shook. And the demons stopped laughing. His death terrified me. I would die too! And my baby.

But we didn't.

I knew Judah was a special boy, and something great would come from him. And I had praised the Lord, despite my fears and failings.

Rachel was working by herself, tugging the tares out of the ground, her movements stiff as Bilhah moved beyond her, one son at her breast and the other playing with one of Beulah's boys.

Rachel ignored them, as she always did. She had sent Jacob to Bilhah, saying her maid's sons would be hers, but then she couldn't seem to stand the sight of them. No doubt, reminded by their faces that her husband had lain with Bilhah—and judging by his persistence in the act—had enjoyed it. My heart went out to my sister, though. For the first time, I knew a bit of how she felt. Jacob had been to me many times since I'd borne Judah, and still I was not with child.

I rubbed my lower back again. I knew this pain. My flow would begin before supper. I'd conceived so readily in the past, and to cease bearing children was a bitter wound. Could it be a result of Judah's difficult birth? Or was God angry at me for my attitude toward my sister? Rachel had two sons by Bilhah, and I had four from my own womb. But sons were the only thing that set me apart from my sister. I hated this jealousy that ate at me.

Leah

We were sitting in my house, resting from our day in the field, talking about the circumstance of my uncooperative womb, which had just presented its mutinous scarlet stain when Zilpah said, "You could send me, like Rachel did Bilhah," her face flushed as bright as a ripe pomegranate.

I was so shocked at Zilpah's words my mouth gaped like it had lost a hinge.

I couldn't discern if she was serious or jesting. But the look on her face did not reflect levity.

She caught her bottom lip behind crooked teeth, watching my reaction.

"I will never have a husband, Leah. I probably would not have had one if I were free. I will never have a child of my own, but to bear one for you would be the greatest honor."

Her gaze dropped. "And . . . I want to know what it is like to lie with a man, if just one time."

She looked at my face, which must have been the color of curdled milk.

"I'm sorry. I should never have said such a thing. I have offended you. Forgive me, mistress." She hadn't used the title "mistress" for years. She fell on her knees in front of me as though pleading for her life.

"Get up, Zilpah."

She pulled herself up, still blubbering her apology. Thoughts flew in circles inside my brain, colliding and bumping against my skull, until

I was certain I would have a headache to deal with soon. It was several long moments before I spoke.

"You really want to do such a thing?"

"No. I'm sorry. I didn't mean it," she said, her cheeks so red, I could almost feel the heat of them.

"Zilpah! Stop sniveling. You act like I'm going to beat you."

Her countenance began to return to something slightly less like a terrified child.

"Answer me. You would be willing to do this? You would want to go to Jacob's bed?"

"Only if it served you, mistress."

"If you call me mistress one more time, I *will* take the strap to you."

She took a deep breath. "Er . . . yes, I mean . . . I just want to . . ."

I raised a hand. "You don't need to say more. You are my friend, Zilpah, much more than a servant. I will have to think about it. If you open this door—coupling—it becomes difficult to live without it."

We said no more about it for several weeks. Zilpah seemed embarrassed to even look me in the face. But as months went by and my blood continued to flow as if it had found the road to freedom and refused to give it up, I began to seriously consider Zilpah's offer and finally proposed it to Jacob.

He could hardly refuse me what he had done for Rachel. And apparently Rachel didn't protest too loudly, since Zilpah was a homely girl and not likely to keep Jacob's attention over the necessary time to plant his seed. And I suppose Rachel thought it better to keep Jacob occupied with Zilpah than have him look with longing at Bilhah.

When Zilpah came from the reed outbuilding where Jacob had taken her, she couldn't face my gaze, and I feared I had lost another sister, but by evening we became comfortable again.

"It really wasn't what I thought at all," she whispered. "Is that what all the fuss is about?"

I laughed, but I remembered the first time I had lain with Jacob and wished now I *didn't* know what all the fuss was about.

Zilpah spent four more nights in Jacob's bed, and when her courses didn't come, we both rejoiced at God's blessing. We named the boy Gad, and the next year Zilpah bore another son we called Asher. Together, we loved and doted on the boys, but I soon learned that a child can't have two mothers. One must be mother and the other a doting aunt or some other term of endearment. So I gladly became Aunty Leah. A role I was happy to fill.

My womb finally gave up its protest and opened again. I first bore a beautiful boy whom I named Issachar, meaning *hired*. Rachel had taken to keeping Jacob from my bed every chance she got. I'd purchased my husband's body for the price my sister set—some mandrakes, dug from the dirt by Reuben. They were used as a charm worn around the neck or placed under the bed to ensure fertility. Or by those less superstitious, they could be cut up and eaten—in small portions, since they were poisonous—to increase desire and perhaps increase the likelihood of conception. They didn't work. Rachel was still barren. I conceived again and gave birth to Zebulon, meaning *gift,* a handsome boy with bright eyes and a sweet disposition.

And then something happened that had made me forget the pain of my husband's rejection. The next child was a girl.

PART FOUR

The Swindle

CHAPTER NINETEEN

The flock of sheep looked like a lumpy white cloud taking its rest on the grassy hillside. Father had called me to a far pasture, where shepherds grazed some of Jacob's sheep. The flock seemed to have doubled under Jacob's care. And the goats even more. The man's wealth was increasing rapidly, in spite of my father's best efforts to stop it.

Father looked out over the hillside where the flock was feeding. "What do you see of Jacob's movements, Alib? Anything different?

How many times have I answered this question? "He continues as always, tending your flocks and his own."

That one unruly brow rose in question as Father studied me. The crooked gaze was always unnerving, as if the man could see my bones beneath my skin.

"And there is no mention of returning to Canaan soon?"

"Not before his debt is paid. At least, not that I have heard."

"And, of course, you would tell me if you did hear such talk." The brow edged higher.

"Of course." I endeavored to relax the muscles in my face. My father's suspicions always made me feel guilty, even when I'd done nothing wrong. And I hated being used as his spy.

"Jacob's flocks will soon be larger than my own, and I'm not sure how that is so."

"You think he's stealing from you?"

"I didn't say I think he's stealing, Alib. That would be easy enough

153

to address if I spotted it. But his flocks increase faster than mine by far, and a man richer than his master could be difficult to control."

My father was not Jacob's master, and I hoped not to be nearby if he inferred such to my sisters' husband.

"I want you to go through Jacob's flocks and cut out all the goats you can find that are kidding and remove them to my furthest pastures."

A nerve jerked in my jaw. I despised Jacob for the way he treated Leah, but the man had certainly done what he had promised, and I didn't want to rob my sisters of what belonged to them. And why was I the one my father always chose to do his dirty deeds? Why not Beor—who enjoyed getting the better of his brother-in-law? Chorash could help him, since he trotted at Beor's side like a gangly pup.

"Why me? Let my brothers deal with Jacob this time."

The brow eased upward, and I knew I had said enough. This was one of Father's tests of loyalty and to fail it would bring a wrath I had seen on several occasions, and I had no desire to see it again.

"Yes, of course," I said, trying not to roll my eyes. "I'll start in the morning." I turned and walked away, cursing my father's controlling ways beneath my breath.

<hr />

The doe bleated as I pressed my fingers firmly in front of her udder, checking for the tautness that would indicate the goat was with kid.

"This one," I said to the servant, who placed a lead over her head and tugged the unwilling mother toward the group of yammering animals.

I didn't want to do this. Why couldn't Father just leave Jacob alone and be thankful for the increase the man had brought him?

I looked up to see my brother-in-law coming toward me.

Curses.

The servants and I had been working all day, separating the flocks on the hillsides. I had hoped to finish before Jacob returned from the furthest field.

So much for that plan.

"What do you think you're doing?" Jacob's eyes were on fire.

I debated what to say and then decided that there was nothing that would make this palatable to my brother-in-law. I had been caught in the act.

"I'm recovering what belongs to my father," I said, standing as tall as I could but still forced to look up at my brother-in-law's angry face. We were close to the same height, but Jacob and my father both had a way of expanding when they were angry, making everyone around them feel smaller for it.

"No! You're stealing my flock. None of these animals belong to Laban. They are my wage, and far less than I am due, at that."

I bristled at Jacob's accusation, however true it may have been. "These goats are my father's, and I act on his orders."

Jacob let out a puff of breath.

"Of course you do. He's doing it again, and you're helping him!"

I hated defending my father. He had not been fair to Jacob. "I'm doing what I was told, Jacob. If you don't like it, take it up with your father-in-law."

"And I am supposed to believe that would do any good? Do you always do what you're told, Alib? Even if it means stealing what doesn't belong to you?"

I flinched. The words stung, but Jacob had a point. Why did I let Father put me in this position? And I wondered about my brother-in-law. Would this kind of treatment make him even more likely to leave?

Father, you may be causing the very thing you fear.

Laban

I was more nervous about meeting with Jacob than I would have liked to admit. I knew the man would eventually notice the dearth of pregnant does in his flock, but if my bumbling son had not allowed himself to get caught in the act, I could have denied culpability. Now I would have to take another tack.

Alib was sitting on the bench along the wall, looking like a child waiting for a whipping. Good! He *should* be embarrassed. I'd demanded he come. He'd made this mess; he could watch me clean it up. Maybe he'd learn something, but I doubted it.

The servant set two clay cups of beer before Jacob and me and a plate of cheese and bread. Alib could go without.

I pulled off a piece of the warm bread and passed it to Jacob, then took another for myself and settled back in my chair, assessing the situation as I chewed.

"So. How may I help you, Jacob?" I said and took a long drink.

Jacob seemed calm enough, a concealment of his true emotions, I knew. The man wasn't known for his patience.

Jacob took a long drink in turn.

"There was some sort of misunderstanding in the pasture today," Jacob said with barely a twitch in his lip.

Hmmm. No blistering accusation? What was my son-in-law up to?

"Yes, Alib told me. A misunderstanding, indeed," I said, looking at my pink-cheeked son. *I misunderstood Alib's ability to do anything right.*

"Your son was . . . taking my goats."

"*Taking* your goats?"

"Yes."

"And you were sure they were *your* animals and not mine? The flocks are often mixed, you know."

"You are correct; it is impossible for me to care for your flocks and mine and keep them completely separate, especially since the little you had before I came has swollen into a great multitude—but I number yours as they are born, and the rest are mine.

My body stiffened. My son-in-law liked to think he'd made me rich, but he didn't take into account that, without me, he wouldn't have an animal to his name. He'd come here, running from his brother, with nothing. He thought he'd hidden that small bit of information, but I'd learned the details of his treachery from a trader for a few coins. I'd extended hospitality and given Jacob a decent wage, when I could have just let him work off his bride price with no extra compensation at all. No. I didn't owe Jacob anything. He owed me!

"So what proof have I that your numbering is correct?" I raised a palm. "Not that I would accuse you of deliberately misrepresenting the situation, but mistakes can be made, and it seems your flocks have grown at an astounding rate."

"It is true," Jacob said, still calm. "Mistakes can be made, although, when there has been a question in my mind, I have always settled it in your favor. And when wild beasts have killed the animals, I have counted them mine and taken the loss upon myself, no matter which flock they came from."

I doubted that he spoke the truth. Why would anyone take a loss they knew wasn't theirs?

Here it comes. Jacob was leaning forward, that wily look on his face. He, most certainly, had come with a plan of his own, one that would bear watching.

"I think I have a solution that will make it obvious to all which beasts belong to whom. Would you agree that there are far less brindled among the goats, and black and brown among the sheep?"

I took another bite of bread. The question seemed straightforward enough, but there was something beneath Jacob's simple observation that smelled of a trap, one Jacob was trying to lay for me.

"I suppose that could be said. And what is your point, Jacob?"

"Let the brindled and the black and brown be my wage. Then when you do an accounting, there can be no question which are yours and which are mine. All in my flocks that are not multicolored among the goats or black or brown among the sheep will be counted as yours, and I will return them, with payment for your trouble.

Hmmm. Yes, there were far fewer of the marked animals, and that would be a positive for me, but it would also be obvious if I decided our shares needed . . . realigning.

"And what of the animals you possess now? How would I know if they were yours or mine?"

"By the next accounting, when the sheep are sheared, it will be as I have said. Any goats not speckled or spotted, any sheep not black or brown, are yours."

So you are going to give me what you have now and take only those animals? Why? What are you up to, Jacob?

I would surely come out the better for it, since the animals in question were a small part of the whole of the flocks. But would I come out the better? Why would Jacob agree to something that would put him in poorer stead than he was now? I didn't trust Jacob as far as

I could toss him. Jacob was no fool. But neither was I—and I enjoyed besting the man just for the entertainment of it.

"And when would you begin this endeavor, Jacob?"

"I will prepare fenced areas in the lower pastures to segregate the flocks we agree upon. I will not mix them with your flocks at all. Since there are so few, it shouldn't take more than two days, perhaps three."

Two or three days. That should be long enough. I tried to hide the satisfaction on my face.

"Well, if this is what you want, I see no reason to refuse you. We have an agreement, Jacob."

I walked my son-in-law to the door, patting him on the back as if he were a beloved son.

Thank you, Jacob.

I stood when Jacob walked out the door, still furious that Father had humiliated me in such a way.

Jacob's plan was ingenious. Not even my father could claim that speckled animals were plain or that brown and black were white. But why would he agree to something that would make him keep honest dealings with Jacob? He turned to me, a smile cracking the corners of his mouth. I was about to find out.

"You heard," he said. "Jacob will be building a fenced area to house his new acquisitions. Beginning immediately, you and your brothers are to separate every brindled, black, or brown animal from the flocks and take them to my Uncle Nahor's pastures."

The pastures were part of my father's inheritance but lay fallow except for the land he let out to the neighbors. But I must have heard wrong. What was he saying? That he wanted to move Jacob that far away? And then I realized it was just Jacob's sheep he wanted to move. He wanted me and my brothers to filch all of Jacob's breeding stock.

The look of triumph on Father's face confirmed my suspicions.

Jacob would have no speckled animals to breed, meaning my father would reduce the man to nothing, and Jacob would be forced to stay in Haran.

My stomach churned until I thought my bowels might loosen on the spot. I was sick—in every way. I said not a word in response to my father's command.

I left the room and found the midden, and when I had relieved myself I went over to a grassy spot and sat hard on the ground. He had gone too far this time.

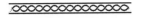

The servants and I had separated the animals Jacob had been promised from the flocks in a short time. There were not that many— less than a hundred. Father, Beor and Chorash were already two days into moving the animals to their new pastures. Of course, my father had left me to face Jacob, saying he was going to settle in his uncle's old home for a time—to do business. More to stay out of Jacob's path. I wasn't looking forward to Jacob's return, but I wouldn't have to wait any longer. He was coming down the hillside with his men.

"The enclosure is ready. We will move the animals tomorrow," my brother-in-law said to a small group of servants speaking quietly among themselves. There was a sudden stillness of the men, a dropping of the eyes. I saw realization dawn on Jacob's face in widening waves. His color drained then rose again as he grabbed one of my father's men by the robe.

"Tell me!"

The man hung his head. Jacob turned his gaze to me.

Jacob

By the time I crawled into my bed, Rachel was making that rumbling sound in her throat that said she was sleeping soundly. I was glad she wasn't awake to question my dour mood. I could only think of Laban and what I wanted to do to him. My body itched as if I'd lain in a bed of ants. I dug at my arms, knowing I was probably drawing blood, but the pain was a relief.

Since I had no goats or sheep to breed, I had nothing for my bargain with Laban. I couldn't even continue as I had, since once a deal is struck, there is no recourse but to honor it. Not that my father-in-law honored any deal he made. Laban had done many devious things in the years I'd been working for him, but nothing that came close to this.

And Alib—who'd been left behind to face my fury. Maybe I should have bloodied Laban's son. He was a sickly shade of gray when I confronted him, probably expecting that I would do just that. But his own father had left him to take the brunt of my anger. I would have my vengeance on Laban, not his son—as soon as I found a means of meting it.

As I lay in the darkness, I thought about slaughtering all Laban's animals to see if the stench would reach him where he was hiding. Or perhaps burn his fields, hoping he would see the smoke from such a distance. I lay awake for hours, rehearsing the day's events over and over and longing for sleep—and for an answer to my dilemma.

In my sleep I was watching myself soak rods of poplar, almond, and plane tree in the water channel. I saw myself peeling them, revealing sap-soaked stripes of white beneath the dark bark, and standing them upright in the troughs, opposite where the flocks of goats came to drink and mate. I set the sheep that were in heat to water across from the goats.

I watched the bucks as they sated their thirst then mounted the one-color does, and the sheep found their mates. And even in my dream, I wondered why I was doing this and how striped logs could reverse my situation.

When I brought Laban's herds to drink and mate, I did not place the rods, and I matched the weaker animals for breeding.

I awoke confused, not certain what the dream meant but certain it had been more than a fancy of my mind. What did I have to lose? I had no other option, so I determined to do what I had seen in the night.

CHAPTER TWENTY

Leah

I tucked the small bundle inside my sash and entered Rachel's house, concerned about the task for which I'd come. Rachel wasn't going to like it. But Rachel seldom liked anything I did. Joseph lay sleeping in his small bed, his thumb in his mouth, his chest rising and falling in a soothing rhythm. Much had changed in the last few years. Most shocking that Rachel had given birth to a son.

The whole camp had erupted in celebration when she announced that she was with child. The women danced, their hair flying about their heads. The men slapped Jacob on the back, as if it was his first son. I forced a smile, but it sat on my mouth as if it had been tacked there with a wooden nail.

I loved my sister, and I was appalled that I struggled with anger at her good fortune. Not only anger with Rachel but with God, as though He'd betrayed and abandoned me by granting my sister a child—chosen Rachel over me, just as Jacob had. I was full of shame for my feelings. I was a well-known healer, and I now had six sons to Rachel's one. And a daughter who grew more beautiful each day. How could I be so selfish? God had blessed me, and I should be grateful for so much. And why did Jacob's affection matter now? I had set my heart to let go of any hope of my husband's love. I wouldn't wait for it or long for it. I wasn't certain I even wanted it anymore. It was too painful to live with hope of something that was never going to happen. And I had my work. And Dinah.

Dinah was the most beautiful child I had ever seen. Her skin was so delicate and flawless, one was drawn to touch it. When she was born, her eyes were already long-lashed and cast feathery shadows on her soft cheeks as she slept. She rarely cried, and when she did it was a gentle mewling. Her first smile, her first toddling steps, filled me with joy I had never imagined.

When I took her to the market, people stopped so often to pat her dark curls or touch her cheeks, I had difficulty moving down the street. I swelled with pride when women turned to me with praises for my daughter's beauty.

But I determined Dinah would be as kind as she was beautiful. Even at six years old she was thoughtful of others and the delight of her brothers, especially Reuben, who could never refuse her a ride on his shoulders or a sweet treat when she begged.

But I'd determined she wouldn't be spoiled like Rachel. Her beauty would be mixed with grace, and she would marry a man who loved her and treated her with respect. Dinah would never suffer as I had. I would see to it.

"How are you feeling?" I said to Rachel. "Have you been drinking the honeyed wine I brought for you?" She nodded, not willing to acknowledge that she was unwell. But she wasn't fooling me. Her face was pale, a stark contrast to the dark circles under her eyes. I didn't like what I saw. I was worried for my sister. For all that had passed between us, I still saw Rachel as the little girl I had held to my chest at our mother's grave.

Rachel had always had a difficult and painful flux. When she was young I would rub her lower back with an emulsion of fenugreek and linseed and fill animal bladders with warm grain and lay them at her sides or on her back to give her comfort.

When Joseph's birthing had gone on too long, I'd sent for Tesup, a physician I sometimes worked with, fearing my emotions would override my judgment. Joseph—though he was now a gentle child, had ripped his way into the world. Rachel had barely lived through the birth and the bleeding afterward. Tesup had warned that another child might be the death of her. Which was why I stood in my sister's house, dreading the coming conversation.

"Rachel, I need to talk to you about something." I touched my sash where the mixture of ground unripe oak galls, ginger, and the inside of pomegranate peels lay wrapped in a piece of cloth. "Your milk is gone."

Rachel pursed her lips. I knew she hated to be reminded that she'd had to get a wet nurse after only a few months. She didn't want to face that she was weaker than other women, especially me. I was sorry she hadn't been able to suckle Joseph to his weaning. I truly was. But now that she was no longer nursing, she might get pregnant again, and that could cost her her life.

I pulled the small bundle out and watched Rachel's eyes as they settled on it. She knew what was coming. "I've brought something for you," I said, watching her reaction. "Mold this with wine into the size of a vetch pea and place it inside before you . . ." I didn't finish the sentence. It was difficult to speak of such intimate things with a woman who shared my husband.

Rachel stiffened, and her color changed like kindling smoking slowly into flames.

"I'm not going to use that!"

"Rachel, you heard what Tesup said." I had hoped that Rachel would be sobered by the physician's words of warning, but apparently that was only a wishful thought.

Her nostrils flared over her tight lips. "I don't care. You're just trying to keep me from having another child because you're jealous."

A pang of guilt pricked at me. Rachel was right. I *was* jealous. But that wasn't why I was doing this.

"You have to use it, Rachel. It would be too dangerous for you to be with child again so soon. At least until you've regained your strength." I only gave her hope to soothe her, thinking that if she would be put off, Jacob might convince her of the risk of ever having another child. But I could see she wasn't going to consider anything but her obsession with having sons.

Rachel's eyes had a sharp edge as the next words came out of her mouth, as though her tongue were a knife, and she was coldly deciding where to thrust it to cause the most damage. She found her mark.

"You have children, Leah, but Jacob doesn't love you. He never will. I've always had his love, and now I have given him a son—so I have both—a child *and* the love of my husband, something you will never have!"

Anger boiled up in me like an unwatched pot, but I kept it at the rim, not allowing myself to boil over. This was too important. I was once again amazed at how thoughtless and cruel my sister could be.

But if Rachel had a knife, I had a sword.

I dropped the bundle onto the table and looked Rachel in the eye, not flinching. "If you don't use this, you will die. And I will have everything. I'll be Jacob's only wife and Joseph's mother. So do what you will."

Rachel's face froze with shock. It was several long moments before she snatched the parcel, her mouth pinched closed. I straightened, turned, and walked out the door, not a bit sorry for what I'd said.

CHAPTER TWENTY-ONE

Laban

I looked out at the multitude of brindled goats, unbelieving. I had just come from the sheepfolds and the pastures where droves of black and brown sheep nibbled on the lush grass.

How could this be? It was impossible! I had been almost a year away, staying in my uncle Nahor's abandoned house, attending to business with the neighbors, trying to make the land bring a profit, when Beor had come with the tale that Jacob had, by some trickery, acquired a horde of spotted goats. He hadn't mentioned the many flocks of dark-haired sheep.

I had speculated that Jacob may have acquired a few breeding animals from a local shepherd and had the start of a flock, but the marked goats and dark sheep were not common among us, and there was no way the handful of animals he may have purchased could have produced, in such a short time, what I saw before me.

I queried the servants, who told some tale about peeled logs in the watering channel, but that didn't make sense. I didn't know what Jacob had done, but I was going to find out. And I was going to find out why my own flocks were all so puny.

I slammed my fist on the table. "What have you done, Jacob! I know you've cheated me some way. I will figure it out, and then I'll have my due—and your hide, as well."

He leaned back and gave a silly smirk. "Please, feel free to go among my flocks and recover any white goat or sheep you find. It's possible some of your stock has mixed with mine. You may take them with my apologies, and I'll pay you for your trouble."

"Believe me, I will look. But there is no way all those marked animals . . . What did you use to breed? Goats don't just appear in the air!"

"Breed?" he said, the silly grin sliding off his face. "But didn't you leave me the brindled as we discussed? That was our agreement, wasn't it? So if you did as you said you would, there is no question where my breeding stock came from."

He thought he was smart, tricking me into admitting I'd taken what I'd promised him, but I didn't care what he knew. I only cared that he had by some machination put himself in a position above my own.

"And what of my stock, Jacob? I've never seen such a sorry lot of animals!"

He flipped a hand. "I graze your animals on the same grass. They drink the same water and are tended to by the same shepherds. I cannot be held accountable for more than that."

I leaned in and locked gazes with my son-in-law. I didn't care how he'd done it—by his own act or the act of a god. He would not make a fool of me. "If you think you've gotten the best of me, Jacob, think again. I've been at this longer than you. And I will not rest until I've regained all that's mine. You can be sure of that." *And if you think you're going to leave me with this sorry lot of animals and return to your homeland, you're not. You can be sure of that also.*

CHAPTER TWENTY-TWO

Leah

Dinah ran to me as I opened the door to Beulah's house and threw her arms around me. She was getting taller by the day.

"I missed you, Mother," she said, reaching up to kiss me on the mouth.

"I missed you too, my sweet."

I had always missed my boys when I was away from home, as I still did. But I missed Dinah in an almost painful way. I didn't want to miss any part of her growing up. I had worried that before she talked, I might not hear her first word and before she walked that I might not see her first step. She was getting more beautiful each day, and I was getting more prideful.

Adinah, my mother's namesake, was at the table grinding herbs with the mortar and pestle. Sometimes it pained me to look at my niece. She was the image of her grandmother, beautiful and kindhearted, and with a gentle spirit. It was as if I were looking back in time to what my mother must have been at that age. But Adinah wasn't smiling—something so unusual, it made my shoulders tense.

Beulah's normally high-colored cheeks were a dull gray. I saw her eyes move to her daughter. Something was wrong. I wondered what had cast such a pall over these ladies that I loved.

"Thank you, Beulah" I said, handing her a few coins.

"It's not necessary, Leah," she said, with a smile that did not make it to her eyes. "I'm always happy to help with the children."

"I know." I pressed the coins into her hand. I paid all my sisters-in-law when they helped me. Beulah didn't get the opportunity often, but Beor was away with Father, so she'd volunteered. "But I insist. I'm comforted to know they're in such good hands."

I looked around. "Where are the boys?"

Beulah pushed a piece of hair off her forehead. "The older boys are with Jacob and the twins in the far pastures. The young ones went to milk the goats with Olnah and Paltith."

Beulah's twin boys were nearly men now, and my older sons were not far behind. It seemed impossible that our children had grown from babes so quickly.

I watched Beulah as she tucked the coins into a little purse she kept hidden in a clay pot. I didn't like that she hid the pay I gave her. She shouldn't have to, but I understood how difficult my brother could be. And he'd probably take her small earnings for himself and use it for services at the temple, and I certainly didn't want my money going for that. But it bothered me that she didn't tell him. If he found it, it would not be a pleasant thing.

But that was not my only concern at the moment. I needed to talk to Beulah. Alone.

"Dinah, would you like to show Adinah the baby goat I said you could have for a pet?"

"Yes," Dinah said, her eyes bright with excitement. "I haven't chosen a name yet. You can help me, Adinah!"

Adinah didn't look me in the eye when Dinah took her by the hand and headed out the door. Something was very wrong, indeed.

"What is it, Beulah?" I said, allowing no evasion. It seemed I'd been in this position before.

"Nothing. I don't know what you mean."

She didn't want to talk to me. I knew it was because of Beor, but I wasn't going to let this go.

"Yes, you do. Something is wrong with Adinah, and it's not a small thing."

Beulah sighed and sat at the table. "How do you always see what I try to hide, Leah?"

"It's not difficult."

She closed her eyes and took a long breath. "The truth is, Beor took the rod to her. That's nothing new. But he seemed overly agitated and called her terrible names and accused her of impossible things. He said he would never be able to get her betrothed."

Never get her betrothed? Beor could have betrothed Adinah long ago. She had been a woman for more than a year. And there certainly had been interest. I'd been relieved that Beor hadn't put her up for the highest bid, but I couldn't know his motives in holding out. And now to say this terrible thing. If he was implying that Adinah was immoral, that was impossible. She was never around anyone but family, and never alone at that—except, perhaps, with Beor himself on occasion? I wasn't certain about that.

My heart clenched. I didn't want to say to Beulah what went through my mind. It was too horrible. But I had to. "Beulah, do you think . . . Beor has . . . done something to Adinah?"

Small circles of red bloomed in Beulah's face. "No. No. I would know it if he had, and I never leave her with him. But I worry some imaginary offense could put him in a rage. In his . . . frustration, he could beat her too hard, Leah. He could make up some story, and no man would hold him guilty, even if he killed her.

I believed Beulah was right about that. And no girl should be forced to hear her father accuse her of unspeakable acts, when it was his own evil imagination producing them. And who knew what else Beor might do if the circumstances were right?

My thoughts went to my mother and how she would feel about the child who looked so much like her living under threat of harm. She wouldn't let it happen. My mother was courageous in the way she faced the men in her life. She hadn't been afraid to stand between me and my father's whip, if such punishment was unwarranted. And she would never have allowed a man to hurt me in other ways. She would have done something. But what?

I carried Beulah's words and Adinah's downcast eyes in my heart for several days. Then one day, when I was in the countryside, I decided to make a visit to one of my patients.

"The older twins married a few years ago," Salah said over a cup of beer. "Their father found them good husbands." One is a merchant and the other a woodworker."

The twins I had delivered several years ago were images of each other, as their older sisters had been. And I had delivered the eighth daughter the year after. I had come to believe Salah's words that if she had twenty children they would all be girls.

"Your daughters are beautiful," I said as I watched the pair through the open shutters. They were chasing a frightened chicken—their supper, I assumed, by the axe leaning against the block.

"Yes. That is some consolation at least."

Salah's eyes were wet. What did she mean?

"Consolation?"

She sniffled, then ran the back of her work-roughened hand across her nose and wiped it on her skirt.

"I should have let my husband take another wife. We seldom come together any more. He is loyal, and I know he loves me, but I was selfish to keep him from marrying another. He is the object of unkind humor among the men. Sometimes I see him look at other men's sons with a longing that breaks my heart. And he has no brothers and no heir, and his father's name will die because of my pride. I am a wicked woman."

Her nose was streaming now. I handed her a cloth from my sash.

"Thank you," she said, and blew into it with a force.

I put my hand on her shoulder. "You are not a wicked woman, Salah. It is not natural for any woman to want to share her husband, especially one with which there is such great love."

I knew the difficulties of sharing a husband. But I wasn't the one my husband loved. Would it be even worse if Jacob did love me? Would I be like my sister if the circumstances were reversed? I didn't know how much Rachel loved Jacob. Sometimes I wondered if she loved him at all, or if what truly bothered her was that she didn't have him to herself. But Jacob loved my sister. There was no doubt about that. And he didn't love me. There was no doubt about that either. He had made it as plain as a matter can be. And I was beginning to accept it.

My heart hurt for Salah, and I didn't know if what I was going to propose would give her comfort or increase her pain. I didn't want to see this woman suffer.

I struggled with the words before I spoke them.

"I think I may have a solution."

Beor

I sat across the table from the man, nibbling on the bread and cheese Beulah had placed before us, wondering why he was back. I'd refused his offer for Adinah just last week, saying it wasn't nearly enough for a girl of Adinah's capabilities, not to mention her beauty. He'd protested that it was far above what he could afford since he had another wife and eight children. But here he was again. I took a drink from my cup and leaned back in my chair.

"I've brought the price you set," he said, his narrow chin lifted.

What? I thought I'd set the price so far above his means, there would be no way he could come up with it. It was a great deal of money.

"You have?"

"Yes. I have."

There was something odd about this situation. Where did he get such a sum in such a short time? I shifted in my chair, looking for a hint of what was behind the man's sudden good fortune. Had he been holding back last time, hoping for a better bargain? I didn't think so. He had been so dejected when he left, I almost felt sorry for him. Almost.

But his ears and his long face were reason enough to refuse him. A man that ugly should not have a wife as beautiful as Adinah. I couldn't let her live her life with such a homely man. It wouldn't be fair to the girl.

I shook my head. "I'm sorry, but I've reconsidered the price I previously stated. Adinah is worth much more. In fact, I've decided to double it."

The man's mouth fell open, making his face look even longer. He stared at me for a few moments, then snapped it shut.

"You know you can't do that. You set a price. I've met it," he said, the nostrils of his sharp nose flaring. "I have a reputation as an honest man, Beor. I'm not sure you or your father can say the same. If I take it to the priests for judgment, I am quite certain they would believe me over you. And what would be the consequence for your reneging? You would be forced to take my original offer plus a penalty. Probably a heavy one. I wouldn't take the chance if I were you."

What? I could feel the blood rushing to my head, pounding through the veins in my temples. Who did this fool think he was, threatening me? I wouldn't give Adinah to him for any price!

The man leaned in, his hot breath on my face. I could smell the goat cheese I'd just served him. "Speaking of priests, Beor. I wonder how honest you and your father are with your taxes." He raised his shoulders. "A word from a neighboring farmer that he suspects you're not paying your due might cause them to keep a careful eye on you both—making you give an account, checking your granaries every year. That could be quite an aggravation. One I'm sure your father would blame on you."

"You have no proof I cheat on my tax!"

"No, I don't. But I suspect a man who would renege on an agreement would cheat on anything. And I wouldn't *have* to prove it. Just the word of an honest man in the priests' ears would be enough."

I could see my father's face, purple with rage, if the priests checked our granaries. But I didn't want to give Adinah to this man! I didn't want to give her to anyone! I took a drink of beer to stall the conversation and leaned back in my chair, trying to figure how this timid farmer had become such a shrewd manipulator.

"Where did you get the additional money?"

A shadow flitted across the man's eyes. *Ahh.* He had not been holding out last time. Someone gave him the money. A relative?

"That's none of your business. I have it. Now what do you say, Beor? Do we have an agreement, or am I on my way to the temple?"

When the agreement was completed, I watched the homely man walk out the door, swearing that I would find out where he got that money, and when I did, I'd look for a way to make the person wish they hadn't given it to him.

CHAPTER TWENTY-THREE

Leah

The panels had been unfastened and removed from the tent, allowing the summer breeze to drift through and cool the guests. Salah and Adinah sat on either side of their husband, behind a table heavy-laden with roast lamb and every sort of delicious treat.

His name was Eli, shortened from Eliezer, something I had only recently learned. I had thought of him only as Salah's husband, but now he would be Adinah's husband as well. I sighed a deep shuddering sigh, hoping I'd done the right thing.

Eli was beaming, his homely face almost handsome in his joy. My niece looked nervous sitting beside her new husband, but she seemed happy. I knew it was not the marriage a girl would dream of. But Eli was a good man and kind. And if she'd stayed any longer in her father's house . . . I didn't like to think what might have happened. It had cost most of the coin I'd saved through the years, but it was worth it.

I studied Salah's face, wondering how she was holding up. There was pain behind her eyes as she smiled at the women congratulating her and her husband, as though her husband taking another wife was something Salah would be ecstatic about. My heart ached for her. She was braving the situation as best she could. Seeing her husband take a bride as beautiful as my niece had to hurt.

Salah had probably been pretty as a girl, but she looked older than her husband, and her sash rode high over her waist, her stomach having swollen with time and two sets of twins. I was worried she might not be able to hold back tears, then something happened that brought tears to my own eyes. Her husband took her hand and leaned toward her, eyes full of love, and smiled and kissed her palm.

I wanted to weep at the sight. Why did this have to be? Why were sons better than daughters? There was something wrong with a world that saw it so. But Salah smiled back at him, her lip quivering, and I knew she would find a way to live with it. And that she would be kind to Adinah. Salah was a better woman than I could ever be.

"Thank you," Beulah said as she came beside me. The lines had eased in her forehead, and she looked at peace. For months after the betrothal it had seemed she was holding her breath, taking in just enough air to keep her alive, but she appeared loosened from the terrible weight that had ridden on her shoulders for so long. I hoped it was not just a temporary reprieve.

Beulah had been listening from behind the curtain when the two men were negotiating. She'd told me Salah's husband had shed his docile demeanor and faced Beor down, like a mongoose grappling with a snake. I couldn't imagine the nervous man who had first approached me about a wife facing down anything. I looked back at him as he held Salah's hand and spoke in Adinah's ear. If there was no avoiding this situation, I thanked God Eli seemed to be a man who would not neglect one wife for the other, and he would find a way to make both of them feel loved.

Beulah squeezed my arm. "I don't know what would have happened if you had not intervened, Leah. I am deeply indebted to you. I'm sorry for the cost. It was far too much for you to pay."

I waved her off. "No price would have been too much, Beulah. I'm only grateful I was able to help."

I nodded toward Beor, who looked more like he attended a funeral than a wedding, although he was making a show of it to the men who were standing about him, pounding his back and congratulating him for his shrewd negotiating.

"Do you think he suspects where the money came from?"

Beulah's face sobered. "I hope not. He probably has no idea you had that amount of money. I certainly didn't. But it would not go well for you if he found out. That is the only regret I have—that you have put yourself at risk for us."

"It's no risk, Beulah. The worst he could do would be to give me a tongue lashing," I said, not believing my own words. I'd been hit by my brother before, something I did not wish to experience again. But it would be worth it—if this was the right thing to do. I only hoped it was.

Everyone clapped as Adinah's husband stood and took her by the hand, his eyes full of adoration. The men laughed and hollered, and the women sighed and sang, as he led his new wife out of the tent toward the house where they would consummate their marriage and place the bloody sheet outside the door as proof of Adinah's purity.

Salah watched them as they went, unable to stop the tears. I prayed that I would not give in to them myself. If I did, I wouldn't be able to stop either.

I turned away from the bride and groom and saw Jacob looking at me. Rachel's eyes were intent upon the celebration, but Jacob's gaze was fixed on me. His face was drawn and he seemed sad. I turned back. I couldn't let myself think about Jacob, and weddings, and men who loved their wives.

Leah

I was kneeling in the damp soil, pulling weeds that threatened my herb garden, when a small cloth bag, tied with a wool string, clinked on the ground in front of me. I looked up to see Beor's glowering eyes. I caught a breath. He'd found it. After all this time.

My stomach soured, and my heart sped up. I was afraid of this. Had he beaten Beulah? Would he beat his wife over a few coins? Of course he would. I should never have allowed Beulah to care for my children. I'd hurt her more than helping. And did he know about the money I'd given Eli?

"Next time you give Beulah money, I will shove it down your throat!" he said with a look that indicated he would like to do it now. "And you think you can spread your poison to my wife?"

Poison?

I rose and wiped my soiled hands on my skirt. Was he referring to

Beulah's service while I worked, or did he think I'd convinced his wife he had evil designs on his daughter?

"What poison? What are you talking about, Beor? I simply shared some coin with Beulah for helping with the children."

"You have poisoned her mind! She thinks there is no fault to be found in a woman neglecting her duties."

Neglecting duties? I should have left it alone and been happy enough if that's all he thought I'd done. But Beor neglected every duty of a father and a husband. Who was he to accuse me?

"You say I'm neglecting my duties? What duties am I neglecting, Beor?"

"You are not doing your share of fieldwork or grinding the barley or weaving your own wool! And before they were weaned, you even paid someone to nurse your children!"

"I hire others to do what I have no time for. What work has gone undone?" I'd grappled with guilt on my own, but I wasn't going to allow Beor to put it on me.

"It's not a matter of the work going undone. It's a matter of *you* not doing it. You think it is acceptable to hire someone to do what you should be doing yourself?"

It seemed I had avoided discovery for paying the bride price, and I should have averted my eyes and not challenged my brother, but my own anger was getting the best of me, and I didn't want to let this issue go unanswered.

"The work is done, Beor. Whether I do it with my own hands or pay another makes no difference. I'm not trying to escape my duties," I said. And I wasn't. I never had. I worked as hard as any woman in the camp. Harder.

"What I do when I am away is important. I am helping women who are in need of my services. It is an honorable vocation. What do you expect women to do? Die in childbirth or see their children dead?" My voice was rising "What I do is for the good of women and children, and I do not have to answer to you."

I shouldn't have said that.

The red in Beor's face was turning deep shades of purple. I was nervous. I was already familiar with the force of his hand.

"Your own husband is too weak to look after his wife's impropriety.

Or doesn't care enough to put a stop to it. Who could blame him? But I will not have you defiling my family! And don't think I don't know how you've meddled in my affairs!"

I was certain my face flushed with guilt. I could feel my cheeks hot with it. So he *did* know I'd given Eli the money. And he accused *me* of defiling his family?

I knew I shouldn't, but I met his gaze straight on. Someone had to stand up to Beor, and I concluded it may as well be me. "It is not I who has defiled your family, Beor. I spent almost every coin I had to keep *you* from doing it."

Confusion seemed to pull his brows together, then they unknotted and rose high over his wide eyes. He hadn't known! But he did now. I should have kept my mouth closed!

Beor was shaking. He looked as if the veins in his temples might actually burst or his eyes pop out of his head. "It was you! You're the one who gave that fool the money!"

My brazen show of courage was suddenly gone. What had I done?

"I should have known it was you. You've always had your fingers where they didn't belong. I should have sold you to the priests when our father didn't do it. He was too much of a coward! The priests wouldn't have you now, but there's more than one way to rid yourself of an ugly dog." His face was so contorted with anger, it was almost unrecognizable.

I didn't see it coming. Beor grabbed my arm and jerked me forward. Pain seared through my shoulder. What? He was pulling me along, cursing as he went. My arm hurt. I stumbled alongside him, trying to keep my feet beneath me.

"Stop! What are you doing?" He didn't answer. Where was he taking me? I looked around for someone to call out to. How could it be that there was not one person in sight? He would take me somewhere and beat me. I needed help!

And then I saw it. The stone trough where we watered the oxen, with its crumbling edges and green slime growing over much of the surface.

My brother was going to drown me. He had threatened it before, and now he was going to do it.

I pulled back, desperate to get away from him, but I fell. He didn't even slow down. He dragged me across the dirt. Small stones dug into my flesh. My arm screamed with pain, but my mouth was uncannily silent.

177

He lifted me up, threw me into the trough, and slammed my forehead to the bottom.

I finally thought to scream, but it was too late.

I closed my mouth tight against the dirty water, but it pressed against me, rushing up my nose. I flailed my arms, struggling against my brother's large hands. My effort was useless. Panic spread through me as I tried to push up from the stony bottom. My lungs were going to explode! My body told me to open my mouth and pull in a breath of saving air. *It will be all right. You will feel better if you do.* But my mind knew there was no air—just water—over, under, around me. Teasing my pursed lips with a promise it would not keep. Tempting me like the serpent tempted Mother Eve to bite the fruit.

"Open your mouth."

"Take it in."

"You won't surely die."

My body won, and my mouth opened and swallowed the water, and I knew I was, indeed, going to die in this dirty trough where the oxen's frothy spittle floated at the top. Someone would find me here, facedown, limp and lifeless. My children would have no mother. My boys would live in the impassive world of men, without a feminine influence to pull them to the middle. Dinah would grow up as I had, a hole in her heart, missing her mother every day for the rest of her life. Was it possible for tears to flow while one was submerged in water? If it was, I was weeping for their loss.

Then the weight of my brother's hands was gone, and someone was holding me as I threw up the water I had swallowed and gasped for a precious breath. My chest was aching, not wanting to take the air in. I panicked again, pulling short, stuttering breaths until the air flowed freely to my lungs. My head felt hollow. The arms lifted me and set me on the hay.

"Are you all right?"

I looked through my dripping hair and saw Jacob, his eyes on fire. I looked around for Beor. He was standing a ways off, a dazed look on his face.

I didn't know. Was I all right? I was breathing. I touched my head where I'd hit the stone bottom. My fingers came back bloody, and I felt a trickle of liquid meandering down my face. It stung. The bite of small sharp rocks my brother had dragged me over stung also. My shoulder hurt the worst, but it wasn't out of socket. No lasting harm, it seemed.

But my brother had tried to kill me. No. I wasn't all right. Not at all.

Zilpah was suddenly beside me, her arm around my back. "Stay with her," Jacob said, then turned toward my brother.

Jacob ran and jumped on Beor, knocked him to the ground, and pounded him with his fists. There was commotion as people were running to the scene—my brothers, servants, Olnah and Bilhah. I saw Rachel, her hand over her mouth.

Now they come.

Alib and Chorash pulled Jacob off of Beor, who stayed on the ground moaning, his nose spurting blood like a wine skin that had blown its stopper.

I started to shiver.

"Here, take this," Zilpah said, and slipped her shawl around my shoulders.

Jacob was struggling against my brothers as they tried to hold him back. Father was running toward us, huffing like a sow in labor.

"What's going on here?" he barked, gasping for air.

"Your son was trying to kill my wife!" Jacob yelled, straining against my brothers' grip. Father looked at me, then at Beor, who had pulled himself off the ground.

The words seared through me. My brother had tried to kill me. He would have held me under that water until my lungs collapsed for lack of air if Jacob hadn't come. He had threatened before, but I'd never really believed he would do it. I began to shiver again. Zilpah rubbed my arms to stop the tremors.

My father raised his palms to Jacob. "Just calm down, Jacob."

Jacob spat on the ground at my father's feet. "I won't calm down. I said the man tried to kill my wife. He would have done it if I hadn't seen him dragging her as I was coming down the hill."

Father turned toward me, his face white, and raised his hand to Jacob again. "I'll take care of it. Just calm down so my sons can let go of you."

Alib and Chorash let go of Jacob slowly, their hands at the ready in case he moved toward Beor again. Jacob's chest was heaving, his face still bright red.

"I know how you take care of things, Laban." He took a step and gathered the neck of my father's tunic in his hand. "If your son touches my wife again, I'll kill him. Do you understand?"

My father's eyes flashed. He removed Jacob's hand. "I said I'd take care of it." He nodded at Alib and Chorash. "Take your brother to my house. And don't leave him until I get there."

My thoughts were spinning. I still couldn't believe my brother had tried to kill me—and, even less, that my husband had come to my defense with such vehemence. My father looked at me again with something like an apology on his face, then turned to follow his sons as they steadied Beor, who was still moaning and holding his bloodied nose.

Jacob knelt before me, his face drenched with sweat. "Are you sure you're all right?"

I nodded. Tears seemed to be pooling in his eyes.

He took my face in his hands. "I don't know why Beor did this, Leah. But I want you to know that it will never happen again. I won't allow it."

The warmth of his hands made me want to weep. How many times had I seen my husband touch the small of my sister's back, or brush her cheek with his fingers when he thought no one was looking, and longed for such tenderness myself? I had stood by and watched him give to Rachel all he'd never given me. Never would give to me.

I drew back in a panic. Something passed through Jacob's eyes. Whatever it was, it was touched with sorrow. But I couldn't give in to my emotions. It had taken me too long to tame them.

Zilpah seemed to sense my thoughts and drew me up carefully by the shoulders.

"I need to tend her cuts."

"Let me carry you to the house," Jacob said.

"No," I said, "I can walk. Zilpah will help me." I couldn't let my heart stir for my husband. It had taken too long to harden it.

Jacob

I knocked on the door of Leah's house, then opened it cautiously. Leah was sitting at the table. The scrape on her forehead looked better since it had been cleaned. Zilpah was setting tea before her. The house was warm with the pungent smell of it.

The woman looked at me with grudging tolerance. I always thought of Zilpah more as Leah's handmaid than my concubine. The few times we'd been together had been awkward for us both, and I had the feeling Zilpah would rather not think of the means by which she'd gained her sons. But she was a good woman, and she was loyal to her mistress. I doubted there was anything Zilpah wouldn't do for Leah, and for that I was grateful. She took any mistreatment of Leah personally, so I had long been out of her favor. She was a better handmaid than I was a husband.

Leah still looked shaken. My heart sickened at what could have happened had I not seen Beor dragging Leah as I was coming down the hillside. I had run so hard I'd thought my chest would explode. When I threw Beor off her submerged form, I thought for certain she was dead, and I knew I was going to kill my brother-in-law. The crack of bone beneath my fist as I broke his nose sent a thrill up my arm and through my body, and I found a perverse pleasure in feeling his flesh give beneath my blows.

"May we have a word alone, Leah?"

She looked up at Zilpah. The servant made a guttural noise and headed toward the door.

"How are you feeling?" I asked.

Leah's half-dried hair hung in disheveled strands over her shoulders. Her eyes were red and irritated and still wide with shock. But it was strange; she had never been more beautiful to me. I wanted to hold her. To comfort her.

She inhaled, as though trying to get a sense of her own well-being. "No real damage done," she said in a shaky voice.

No damage? She'd been dragged and almost drowned. And worst of all, what damage comes from your own brother trying to kill you? My temper began to rise again, and I wanted to go find Beor and finish what I'd started.

Instead, I sat at the table and pushed the clay cup toward her. "Drink some tea." Leah picked up the cup, but her hands were trembling, and she set it back on the table. "Here." I pulled my chair closer and put the cup to her lips. She took a sip and nodded her thanks.

"I'm so sorry, Leah." I shook my head. "I can't believe he would do such a thing."

She caught her bottom lip. I knew she was fighting tears.

"Do you want to tell me what happened?"

She inhaled what looked like a painful breath. "It was money. I gave money to Beulah, and he found it." She looked at me as though I might disapprove of what she was going to say next. "And to Eli, for the bride price. He didn't have enough, and I had to get Adinah out of Beor's house."

The hairs on my arms began to rise. Why would Leah need to get Adinah out of Beor's house?

I waited for her to go on.

"He was beating Adinah, and . . . I thought he had evil intentions for her."

It was a moment before I realized what Leah was saying. My jaw clenched so tightly it hurt. I couldn't think of a name vile enough to call the man.

She shook her head. "I don't know that for certain, but Beulah was worried, and it seemed . . . likely. I didn't want to take a chance."

I reached for Leah's hand. "You did the right thing, Leah. I wish I'd killed him." And I wasn't simply saying it for Leah's sake. If I'd known it, I would have ripped out his bowels and fed them to the pigs.

She withdrew her hand. I leaned back, giving her the distance she seemed to want, but I was saddened by it.

Why had I been so angry with Leah for so long? I'd held her to a measure I could never meet myself. I'd seen her virtue and expected her to be clear of anything not pure or true.

As I looked at her, shivering beneath her shawl, I realized why I'd reacted so viscerally to what I perceived as Leah's betrayal. I hated what I saw in myself, and when I thought I saw the same in Leah, I hated her for it. I hadn't wanted her to be like me: deceitful and undeserving. And what had I offered her for the perfection I demanded? Nothing. I had chosen Rachel anyway. Demanded that Leah be perfect and left her standing by herself.

I did not deserve this woman.

A thought occurred to me: I had gotten what I deserved. I deserved Rachel.

I pulled the truth long-buried in my heart to the surface and exposed it to the light of day.

I loved Leah.

I had loved her since the day at the well when she had told me stories of my grandfather and impressed me with her faith. I'd seen something in her heart that had pulled at me for weeks. I'd thought of asking Laban for her. Felt it was what my father would want and what would most please the God of my grandfather.

But Rachel was so beautiful—and funny with her childlike wit. So I'd gone against the voice in my head and asked for Rachel.

I loved Leah.

But I loved Rachel too. In spite of her insane jealousy and conniving ways. I still loved her. And the saddest thing of all was Rachel wouldn't let me love them both.

As I watched my wife shiver, I knew the voice I'd been hearing in my mind by day and night was more than my imagination. It was the voice of God. It was time to leave.

"Leah, this incident only affirms what has been in my heart for some time. I've served your father well. I believe you know that." I waited for her acknowledgement. A shallow nod told me she agreed.

"I owe him nothing, but he finds one way after another to keep me here because he fears my absence will mean the hand of God will leave with me—and he's probably right in thinking so. God defended me against his wiles when he tried to steal all the marked animals. Now my brindled flocks cover his pastures." The look on Laban's face when he hammered his fist on the table and demanded to know how I'd done it still filled me with satisfaction. But his countenance had changed toward me since his wheedling was no longer effective, and he was unable to manipulate me with promises he had no intention to keep. I didn't need him anymore, and he knew it. Which made him a dangerous man.

"The old methods don't work on me anymore, and I fear he will resort to other means. I don't know what those might be, but . . ."

The thought of Beor's hand pushing Leah's head under water made me dizzy.

". . . considering your brother's instability and your father's growing animosity . . . I think it's time to leave."

Leah seemed a bit surprised, but did she disagree? It had always been my goal to return to Canaan; she knew that. But did she want to stay here? This had always been her home. To leave would mean never coming back. Perhaps escaping her father and Beor held some appeal, but what of Beulah and her nieces and nephews, and Alib? Would she want to make the long journey to a new home where uncertainty awaited? And I still had to face my brother. What would I be leading my family into?

"I shouldn't have brought this up now. We will talk more when you're feeling better." I stood, looking down on this woman who meant so much to me, wishing she knew it. I touched her shoulder. "I'm proud of what you did, Leah. You are brave. Braver than anyone I know." *Especially me.*

I left the room, my heart heavy with the words I couldn't say. *I love you, Leah.*

CHAPTER TWENTY-FOUR

Leah

Rachel and I folded the extra blankets we had woven and packed them into Lily's saddlebags. The beast opened her long snout and brayed her aggravation at having been removed from proximity to the hay barn. She was getting even more stubborn in her old age. I'd thought of leaving her behind but didn't have the heart to do it.

We had set about to work in secret, preparing the last two months for our departure. There had been some curiosity about the industry of the servants who seemed to go above the normal call of their duties these days. Jacob had told the overseers to be careful about their work of gathering grain and provisions for the animals and securing enough tents. And to keep things out of sight. Many of the herds were already well on their way to a gathering point where they would wait for word from a runner to proceed.

I had been discreetly overseeing the securing of foodstuffs for the journey and seeing that clothing was in repair and there were warm blankets enough for the family and servants as well.

It was quite an undertaking to be done in secret, and the final preparations had taken longer than we thought. We should have been gone two days by now.

Father and Beor had been at my uncle Nahor's old place for weeks, which had made it easier to evade their notice. I thought my father suspected Jacob might be planning something, but all we needed was a head start to avoid a confrontation here, where things could get out of hand. They had only recently returned for a short time and left again with herdsman to move the sheep for the shearing.

Father's herdsmen were to graze the flocks on the greener grasses of the upper pastures as they moved along, while he and Beor would go ahead to secure the best prices for their wool and to attend the celebrations, as well as spend some money on carnal pleasure, if the truth were told. For once, I was glad for their preoccupation. We needed every moment.

Father had kept Beor close by his side since he'd tried to drown me. He seemed shaken by my brother's act, but he never talked to me about it. I hadn't really expected him to, but somehow I longed to hear him say that he cared if I lived or died and would have grieved if my brother had succeeded in his attempt. Of course, he would never say such a thing. I had no memory of an affirming word from my father, and now that we were leaving, and I wouldn't see his face again, I felt the loss of it keenly.

"I don't know why we have to leave," Rachel said, her lips in that crooked pout.

We had talked about it at length—Jacob, Rachel, and I. Jacob had explained the situation to her, that God had promised that He would bring Jacob again to that place—the land God had promised his grandfather, Abraham. That His seed would be as the stars in the sky and the sands on the shore. And that he no more felt welcome in our father's house.

He said Beor could not be trusted. Rachel had agreed to go, but I thought it bothered her that Jacob seemed concerned for my welfare. Of course, she had been appalled by Beor's actions. She'd patted her chest and said how terrible it was and how glad she was he hadn't actually killed me. I didn't doubt her, but I saw a new strand of jealousy wrapping itself around my sister. It had always been about children, but now it seemed she worried my husband actually cared for me.

She need not have. I had thought I'd seen something in Jacob's eyes after Beor's attack that hinted such a possibility. But it was only concern he'd have for anyone in such a state. His long-held anger toward me had cooled, but my husband didn't love me. If he did, he'd say so.

"We have no choice but to leave, Rachel. Surely, you can see that."

"I suppose not, but to leave our home—"

186

"What home, Rachel? Our father makes us welcome? He treats us like beloved daughters?" The answer to my own questions stung me. We were not beloved daughters, and we had no home in our father's heart. He had spent the money from the bride price that was supposed to be kept for us in the event our husband put us aside or died. He had stolen from Jacob, which was the same as stealing from us and from our children.

"It's not easy for me either, Rachel."

Rachel had the comfort of her husband's love to lean upon. I had to find the strength through other means.

I trusted that God would fulfill His promise to Jacob. But I wasn't sure where I fit in.

Here, I was well known and well thought of for the work I'd done through the years. Mothers stopped me on the street, pulling their children in front of them, saying "This is the woman who coaxed you into the world when it seemed you'd not survive the passage." The very young would look up at me with curiosity. The older ones, having heard the stories since they were little, would smile their thanks, staring at me as if I were more than human. I would always blush with discomfort at such encounters, but if truth were told, it was only in such moments that I felt any worth at all. And I was leaving that behind.

And I felt responsibility for Rachel's health. She was better now, with some color in her face and more strength than I'd seen her have in a great while. I didn't want to jeopardize that gain. It would be a long, strenuous journey.

"We will have a *new* home, Rachel," I said, touching her arm. She looked at me with a measure of hope in her eyes and nodded—and for a moment I felt I had a sister again, that things were with us as they were when we were young. Maybe we could leave all our grievances here and walk away from them. I prayed that it was so.

Jacob

Alib and Chorash were walking toward me, their faces pinched. I had ordered the donkeys and camels loaded while the brothers were in the fields, but I knew there would be no leaving in their absence. My hope was that Alib would not hasten to ride to the wool market to alert his father, so we would could get farther away before Laban discovered we were gone. With our many flocks and maidservants and menservants and hired herdsmen, Laban would have less confidence he could turn us around and perhaps decide not to follow us at all.

"What are you doing?" Alib said. He and Chorash stood, legs spread and anger on their faces.

I sighed. "You know what I'm doing, Alib. Tell me you can blame me." Surely my brother-in-law could see the truth of the matter. He knew what his father had done to me these many years. I saw indecision playing at the edges of his taut lips.

"I am not the one to place blame. It's my father who must deal with you."

"But your father is gone. Will you ride to tell him? Or will you give us a chance to get away? You know he has wronged me, Alib."

Alib's face colored. "What I know or don't know has nothing to do with this! You put me in a predicament, Jacob. You know who will get blamed."

I had hoped for Alib's support, but it didn't seem forthcoming. I would just have to leave without it. Did he think a few words were going to stop me? I was going home. Nothing was going to keep me from leaving this place today.

"Please, Alib." Leah was suddenly by my side. "You know we have to go. Jacob needs to return to his father. He has done more than what was required of him. There is nothing here for us but trouble." Her eyes said what her mouth did not. To stay would put her in harm's way. The reminder made my stomach hurt. We couldn't stay here. I couldn't give Beor a chance to hurt Leah again.

The stiffness in Alib's posture eased a bit. I knew he didn't like me, but I had gained his grudging respect through the years. And he was well aware of his father's unjust ways.

"I can't stop you, Jacob. To tell you the truth, if you weren't taking my sisters, I'd be glad to see you gone. I'm not responsible for your actions, so don't look to me for permission to do what you're clearly going to do regardless."

I nodded, understanding that my brother-in-law was saying he would not go for his father. He was going to give us the lead we needed.

"Surely, you're not going to let him get away with this, Alib?" Chorash had come to life beside his brother. "It will be you and me who pay."

"And how can I stop them, Chorash?" Alib said, raising his hands. "Tie them up? There's nothing we can do."

"I can do something! I'm going to get Father. Now! I'm not going to take our father's wrath for the likes of him."

"Chorash!" Alib called for his brother, but he was rushing away.

I saw the wilt in Alib's shoulders. "You need to go now. One man on a camel could get there in less than three days. And at the pace you will have to move . . . I'll stop Chorash, or at least try to slow him down."

"Thank you, Alib."

Alib's face hardened. "Don't thank me. I'm not doing it for you." He looked at Leah, sadness in his eyes, and back at me. "You don't owe my father anything, Jacob. You've earned what you're taking. You deserve it all. The only thing you don't deserve is my sister."

"You're right, Alib," I answered.

Leah lowered her head.

"But I thank you anyway."

Beulah was sitting at the wooden table when I entered her house. Her face was flushed, her eyes red and damp.

"Is it time?" she said, her voice rough with emotion.

"Yes."

My heart ached. How could I leave Beulah here to face Beor's abuse alone?

"If you hurry, you could come with us. Bring the children and just go."

I knew it was not possible. If it were Beulah alone, I would insist.

But the children. And Beor would follow and find her, and life would be worse in the end.

She stood and wiped her tears with the sleeve of her tunic.

"Thank you for wanting that, Leah. But we both know it's impossible. And I would never leave Neba and Adinah and my grandchildren." Her voice cracked. "But I will miss you so much."

I went to my sister-in-law and held her in my arms.

"I will miss you too." And I meant it. Beulah had been my only ally among my family. "I will pray for you, Beulah. Every day."

"And I will pray for you, Leah. To the God of Abraham."

I kissed her cheek and walked away, my heart aching, praying that God would show mercy to her and protect her.

I had one more stop to make before I left.

Zilpah waited a ways off while I knelt at my mother's grave. The small stones beneath my legs reminded me of the ones Beor had dragged me over.

"I miss you so much, Mother. I need your wisdom to guide me." I thought how different my life might have been had my mother lived. She would not have allowed me to become bitter in my circumstances. She had always told me that God had a plan just for me. That He loved me more than she did, which seemed impossible, since she loved me without condition.

She would have challenged me to love my enemies, be they even of my own household, and to be strong in the power of God's might.

But all I felt was weakness.

I spread myself on the ground before the stones that marked her grave. I couldn't leave her here. I couldn't leave my mother behind.

"I don't understand, God. Why you let my mother die. Why you left me with no one to take my part." I lay there weeping for a long time before Zilpah knelt and put her hand on my shoulder. "We have to go, Leah."

I pulled myself up and shook the bits of dried grass and dirt from my garment, then looked again at the pitiful stones that marked my mother's grave.

"I love you, Mother."

I touched the thick trunk of the terebinth tree that marked this sacred spot. Its rough bark beneath my hand seemed to say it would

MARILYN T. PARKER

watch over my mother in my absence—that it wouldn't let her family forget her.

I looked up at the sky, a brilliant blue, and asked God to watch over me and my family.

Leah

As we expected, Father followed us. He caught up to us ten days into our journey, saying he only wanted to say good-bye to his children and his grandchildren, and seemed willing enough to let us go, which was a great surprise to Jacob as well as to me.

"He had a dream, mistress," One of my father's servants who favored me said while father was talking to Jacob in the tent.

"Cursed Jacob all the way from Haran, swearing he'd have his head in one of those baskets on the camel's hump. Had some plan of talking peace to Jacob then letting Beor at him if he wouldn't listen. But when he woke up this morning he was as pale as a nanny's milk.

Heard him telling Beor that he'd had a dream or heard some voice that said not to do that or your God would take Jacob's side. Beor was mad as a mess of bees. Said if Laban was too scared to deal with Jacob he'd be pleased to do it himself. Your father poked his finger in your brother's face and told him to take all the men but Rudi and me and go home, and if he didn't, he'd be losing his birthright for it and wouldn't have a pot to . . . well, you know what he meant."

The servant was grinning from one side of his pocked face to the other.

"It was a sight, mistress Leah. I thought Beor's head would bust open and his brains spill out on the ground. He's half way back to Haran by now. Won't be bothering you again. I'm sure of that."

I was comforted. My brother wouldn't hurt me again. But Beulah?

I didn't know if women could speak a curse as men could, but just in case, I asked God to let Beor's manhood shrivel up and fall off if he even thought of hurting his wife or children again. Just the thought of it made me feel better.

The one thing that Father chastised Jacob about was stealing the household gods. Jacob denied it and said anyone found with them would die. Fear knifed at me. Could Rachel have taken them? But Father searched every tent, including hers, and didn't find them. I was relieved. Rachel still clung to our father's beliefs, and I wouldn't be surprised if she had hidden the images away and brought them with her.

My father pulled beside me as he faced his camel toward Haran. His shoulders hung low beneath his robe.

"Leah . . . I . . ." His voice trailed off. He shook his head. "I'm sorry for what Beor did. And . . . I'm sorry for more than that."

He didn't say what "more than that" was. He couldn't say it. I knew that. I didn't reply. I just acknowledged his words with a slight nod and watched him as he rode away, and prayed God would help me to forgive him.

CHAPTER TWENTY-FIVE

Jacob

I was thankful to finally be free of Laban's foot upon my neck. But there was something very sad about the man as he rode away. He would never see his daughters or their children again. Perhaps he'd realized what he'd lost. Too late. I could empathize with him. I'd been slow to see what was right before my eyes also.

I didn't know if I could ever mend things with Leah. I loved her, but she didn't seem to want my love anymore. I couldn't blame her, and I wouldn't try to force it on her. I had no right. I would give anything to go back and undo the harm I'd done. To show Leah she was worthy of the greatest love. But maybe, like Laban, I would have to suffer the loss of her and live the rest of my life with my regrets.

We arrived within a short distance of the hills of Seir, where I'd learned my brother camped with his multitude of animals and men. He'd done well for himself in my absence, but I had no idea if he would receive me or come to take his vengeance. Knowing Esau, I feared it was the latter. Had I left Haran only to be killed by my brother's hand? I would soon know—a runner had brought the news that Esau was on his way to meet me—with four hundred men behind him.

I'd found Reuben among those watering the animals at a shallow place in the river Jabbock. He was a man now. As a child he had been eager to please me, doing all I asked and more to gain my favor. But now there was a wall between us I couldn't seem to breach. I loved Reuben, but I had held back the attention he needed. Was it because of Leah? Because Reuben was the result of her deception? Perhaps, in the beginning. Or because Rachel took it personally when I showed the boy the least bit of affection? But I couldn't blame either of my wives. I was to blame for neglecting the needs of my sons. I hoped that some way the damage could be mended, but it seemed to worsen rather than get better.

"I want you to gather your brothers and the servants and cross the river with the women and children. Then return and lead the livestock across. I will stay on this side of the river tonight."

Reuben was my heir. Someday he would take my place and lead this family. The birthright would be his. I wanted to give him every opportunity to lead while I was still here to see that his brothers followed.

Stony-faced, he turned towards the river. "Whatever you say, Father."

Reuben. A wave of sadness rolled over me. *My son.*

I pulled the saddle off my camel and led it to drink and feed on the grass that lined the water's edge. I sat on a rock jutting out from the earth and watched the last of the servants reach the other shore. The sun had set, but the stars and moon shone brightly in the sky, making it easy to see.

I was reminded of the first day after I'd left my home so many years ago, running from my brother. When night fell, I had settled beside a stream edged with tall grass where I could graze and water my beast and rinse the day's dust from my face.

The night sounds of the valley: the incessant summer drone of cicadas, the gentle gurgling of the stream—all comforting on an ordinary evening—had served only to intensify my desolation.

I had fallen asleep, using a slab of stone as a pillow.

It was a dream, I supposed. I was standing, but I could see myself sleeping slack-mouthed on the rock. I wondered if I had died in the night. But I could see my chest as it rose and fell in regular rhythm, and my mouth twitched from time to time.

A subtle change in the air had made me turn around. What I saw that night sucked the air from my lungs—a wide staircase—translucent, almost transparent, a crystalline sheen against the darkness of the night.

There were men ascending and descending on the crystal stairs. They were dressed in brilliant white, reflecting a shower of pearly iridescence. I had wanted to close my eyes against the brightness, but they wouldn't close. Panic threatened me. I took a deep breath. The air prickled on my tongue, tingling its way to my lungs.

The brilliant men were fearsome yet beautiful. My eyes traced the rise of the stairway from the ground to where it faded into the heavens.

Then a voice spoke from the top of the stairs.

The memory of it made my heart speed up. I looked across the river Jabbock to remind myself I was here, not beside that stream in Bethel.

The voice had called my name. My name was a source of shame to me. It meant "deceiver," and I had certainly lived up to it. But the voice had said He would give me and my descendants the land on which I was lying. That my seed would be as innumerable as the dust of the earth. All of the families of the earth would be blessed through it. That the voice was the voice of the God of Abraham and Isaac and that He would be with me and keep me wherever I went and bring me back to that holy land.

And here I am, a few days journey from my father's home. But why would God make such a promise to a man like me? And what was Esau's intent? I had sent messengers to my brother, saying I was sending gifts, and had learned at the men's return that Esau was coming to greet me. Greet me? With four hundred men? What kind of greeting would it be?

I sent before me two hundred female goats and twenty male goats, two hundred ewes and twenty rams, thirty milk camels with their colts, forty cows and ten bulls, twenty female donkeys and ten foals—all in separate droves, with instructions for the herdsmen to tell Esau they were a present from his brother, who had wronged him and would follow shortly. Would it be enough? Could anything be enough to assuage my brother's wrath?

"Why do you sit on that rock, Jacob?"

I jerked to my feet and spun around, my breath caught in my lungs. A man stood before me. Where had he come from? I hadn't seen him approach, and I could see clearly in the light of the moon. I didn't know him. He was a plain man, nothing of note in his appearance, but his steady gaze sent shivers down my spine—and he knew my name.

"Who are you? How do you know my name?" Perhaps he was a

shepherd who had heard that Jacob, son of Isaac, had returned to his father's land. We'd seen flocks along our way, but most of them had given us a wide berth. Or could he be someone sent from Esau to kill me quietly and avoid a broader confrontation?

A faint smile touched the man's wide mouth. "Doesn't everyone know the grandson of Abraham?"

I narrowed my gaze. "Where did you come from? I don't see your beast. How did you get here?" Did he have a sword? I didn't see one. I wasn't much of a swordsman. Should I engage him—or try to wade across the river before he caught up with me? The water was too shallow to swim.

The man ignored my query and gestured at the rock behind me. "Why were you sitting on that rock, Jacob?"

I scowled again. Why was he asking all these questions?

"I was resting," I said, still assaying the distance to the other side of the river. The moon had painted its rippled image on the water, and the tents, shadowed against the hillside, were mostly dark, with an occasional fire burning in a dooryard. No one would hear me over the rush of water.

"You've traveled far?"

My hand rested on my sword.

"Yes, I've traveled far."

"And for what reason are you traveling?"

"You ask many questions. Answer mine. Who are you? What is your name?"

"Why have you come so far?" he said, ignoring my question.

Who was this man? I wanted to tell him to leave me alone and be on his way, but I couldn't say the words. For some reason, I felt compelled to answer him.

"I'm going home."

"Home?" His brows rose in question.

"Yes, I'm going home, to the land of my grandfather, Abraham."

He nodded. "Abraham. Yes, I remember your grandfather."

Discomfort niggled at me again. The man's age was hard to discern, but Abraham had been dead for decades.

"You knew my grandfather?"

"Yes, I did," he said, a shallow curve of a smile on his lips.

"But . . ."

"You doubt me?" His thick brows arched over eyes bright with the reflection of the moonlight.

"No, it's just . . ." I couldn't seem to get a word out of my mouth! The man was having a strange effect upon me.

"Why did you decide to return to Canaan?" he said.

Why, indeed? At the moment, I questioned the sanity of such a decision. Life with Laban had been bad enough, but I was facing a brother who might kill me. And now this man I wasn't certain I could trust and certainly didn't understand.

"God spoke to me to return," I answered. *Why am I telling this stranger such a thing? He'll think I'm mad.*

"And why do you think God wanted you to return to your homeland? To let Esau take vengeance upon you?"

What? The man spoke of my brother. Perhaps Esau *had* sent him to destroy me. I put my hand full around the hilt of my sword. The man saw and chuckled softly, unaffected by my unveiled threat.

"You know of my brother? You spoke his name. I'm tired of these ambiguities. Who are you? Has my brother sent you to do me harm?"

"You worry too much, Jacob. Of course, I know of your brother. I know your entire family. I knew you and your brother when you were fighting in your mother's womb. I knew your father when he was nothing more than the prayer of a barren woman," he said, his eyes intent on mine. "Why do you fear your brother, Jacob? If God told you He would deal well with you, why are you afraid of a mere man?"

Why? His question drained me of strength, and I sat on the ground. Why *was* I afraid? The man was right. God had told me He would watch over me and bring me again to this land, and He had done what He had spoken. I had left with a camel and a staff and returned with a great multitude. When my father discovered I'd posed as my brother to obtain the blessing, he said I yearned for a God I did not trust. Why couldn't I simply trust the word that had been spoken to me? Why did I quake in fear of my brother when the voice had said He'd bring me back again and give me the land He'd promised Abraham?

The man sat across from me, his arms resting on his splayed knees. Why was I carrying on this conversation with a stranger who knew too much for it to be coincidence? I didn't know, but I felt compelled to continue.

"I stole my brother's birthright, and I fear he seeks vengeance. I can hardly blame him."

"You stole it?" the man said, raking his fingers in the dirt.

"Yes, I stole it." There was no sense in hiding it, and saying it aloud was a relief.

"And how did you manage to steal something of such import?" the man said, looking up at me. He shrugged and shook his head. "Was there a contract, a tablet that declared your brother the heir?"

"No." I was getting irritated. "I traded him a bowl of stew for it."

"Ahh, so, he sold it to you?" he said.

"Yes. I guess you could say that."

"For a bowl of stew?"

"Yes."

"It sounds as if your brother didn't place much value on such a gift. And what about you, Jacob? Do you esteem the birthright?"

I swallowed the emotion that rose in me. I had longed for the birthright all my life, and my mother had said it was mine from the beginning. God had spoken it to her while I was yet in the womb. But how could it be rightfully mine when I'd gained it by deceit? But I did value it. Enough to cheat to get it.

"Yes, I value it very much."

"Why? For the land? For your place as head of the family?"

"No. Because of the blessing that accompanies it."

"And what is this blessing?"

"The blessing is more than just place or power. It is the favor of God. It is to be called by His name. The God of Abraham, the God of Isaac, the God of . . ." The word caught in my throat.

"You wanted your name to be joined with God's?"

"Yes." I swallowed hard. "But I'm not worthy to have my name associated with Him. I'm a deceiver. A thief." My face was warm, but somehow I'd felt a compunction to tell this stranger something I'd never admit to another. I could barely admit it to myself.

"How so?" The man gathered soil in his hand and let it slip through his fingers back to the earth.

"I pretended to be my brother, and my father gave it to me in my brother's stead. But it wasn't my blessing. I stole it."

"You stole it?"

"Yes."

"From whom?"

"From my brother." Was he deaf? I'd just told him!

The man stood and dusted his hands on his garment and looked full in my face.

"From whence did the blessing come, Jacob?"

The hairs on my arms straightened. "It came from God."

"And you fooled God into giving it to you?"

"No. I fooled my father." All of the spirit went out of me with a long sigh. The man's questions were lying like huge stones on my back, weighing me down.

"Jacob, have you never considered that the blessing was always meant to be yours? That God chose you for that purpose before you were born?"

My mother had spoken those words. I looked into the man's face. It still betrayed no emotion. "But why would God choose me? I'm not worthy."

The man nodded his head. "That is true. You are not worthy. And it is true you are a deceiver. But God's blessings do not come because of worthiness. God chooses for His own reasons. No man can reprove Him for His choice. It is His and His alone. He needs no one's approval. How did your grandfather get his faith, Jacob?"

"I don't know. He always had it, I suppose."

"Always?"

I was becoming irritated now. "I don't know. You said you knew him. Do you know?"

The man said nothing.

"Who are you? I demand to know! What is your name?"

The man turned to walk away.

What? He was going to just turn away and leave after stirring up this pot of questions? I reached out and caught hold of his arm. "I want some answers, and I'm not going to let you leave until I get them!" I had no idea how I would stop him, but I could not let this man leave. I'd fight to my last breath to keep him here!

He didn't attempt to escape my grip. His gaze was palpable. I could feel it penetrating my pupils. It pricked as it went through my eyeballs into my head. I could feel it inside me, like some foreign object coursing through my body, searching out every part.

I let go of the man's arm and slapped my hands over my eyes. What was happening? The man turned to go, and I grabbed his arm again.

"Please, don't leave! I know who you are! You can't leave until you bless me."

"Why should I bless you, Jacob? You're not worthy. Isn't that what you said?"

The words pierced me, but I hung on to the man's arm. "I am not worthy. It is true. But I must have the blessing of God in my life."

The man shook loose and again turned as if to leave. I grasped his robe, holding so tightly it would have to rip from his body for him to escape.

"Bless me. Speak your favor upon me. I know who you are!"

"You know who I am, but you dare to command me?"

I tightened my grip. "I must have the blessing. I will not let go until it is mine!"

The man reached down and touched the hollow of my thigh. A hot flame burned in it and spread down through my leg into my foot. I let go and fell to the ground, moaning in agony.

The man watched until the pain eased, and I lay breathless upon the ground. Then he asked me the question I had been asking him. "What is your name?"

I pulled myself up and shook my head. My thigh still burned. What had happened? What had the man done to me? "You know my name," I said, rubbing the inside of my leg. "You called me by it."

"What is your name?"

The word fought to keep its place in my mouth. To speak my name in the man's presence was to claim all it meant. But I had to say it.

"My name is Jacob." *Deceiver. Supplanter.* I had been named truly. It was what I was and always would be. I closed my eyes against the shame.

The man placed his hand on my head. I felt the weight of it like any other hand, but a soothing warmth seeped from it through my head and down to my feet.

"Your name is no longer Jacob. You shall be called Israel for, as a prince, you have struggled with God and with man and have prevailed."

When I opened my eyes, the dawn was breaking and the man was gone. The sun had barely set when the others crossed the river. What had seemed like a few moments in time must have been hours. I pulled myself up and looked around. The man was nowhere to be seen. I took a step. My thigh throbbed. My muscles screamed in pain. I went to my knees and raised my hands towards the heavens. Tears burst from my eyes.

"I will call this place Peniel, meaning 'Face of God.' For I have seen His face and yet I live."

<hr />

Leah

My husband had gone to meet his brother Esau with dread, sending flocks and herds of his best stock before him. Whether it was Jacob's show of contrition or a change in Esau's heart wrought over the years, he fell upon Jacob's neck and wept.

I wept at the sight of it. Two brothers so long apart, joined again in peace. I wished for the same with Rachel.

In the dooryard of Jacob's tent, we served Esau and his closest men our best lamb smothered in pomegranate molasses. I had prepared some for the trip, not knowing if pomegranates even grew in Canaan. Esau couldn't get enough and complimented me over and over again. Rachel and I and our handmaids stood near the men as they ate, watching for a plate needing replenishing or a cup that needed to be refilled.

I saw Esau's gaze flit to Rachel and back to his plate several times. If Jacob saw it, he didn't let on. My sister was still a beauty, even past her first bloom. I was just glad to see him looking at someone besides my Dinah. I had told her to stay in my tent, so Esau might not see her and Jacob be compelled to offer her as another gift. Such things happened.

I was able to hear Jacob and Esau as they spoke—mostly of the past, about their mother's passing, and their father's health, which seemed to be better than when Jacob had left all those years ago.

"And what is the meaning of the droves I met along the way?" Esau asked, draining his cup.

"A gift to find grace in my brother's sight," Jacob said.

Esau waved his hand as they pulled themselves up from the cushions. "It is not necessary, Brother. I have all I need. More than I need. You keep what is yours."

Jacob bowed. "If I have found grace in your sight, Brother, please accept my gift. I have done well in my absence. I want you to have this token of my regret."

"That is quite a token, Brother," Esau said, raising his eyebrows. "I have no need, but if it will make you feel better, I will accept your gift."

Jacob smiled and gripped Esau by the shoulders. "I'm happy to give it."

I wasn't certain if Esau thought the gift to be a bribe, or Jacob's way of showing his prosperity, or something else, but I felt something was still not quite right between the brothers.

"Then let's be on our way. We will accompany you the rest of the journey. Provide protection and provision. My brother and his family will be well taken care of."

Jacob hesitated. The glaze of moisture on his forehead made me stop wiping the pomegranate sauce that had dribbled down the side of the clay bowl. I knew Esau saw it too.

"No, my brother. The journey will be too slow for you. The women. The children. The livestock. We must take our time, so as not to weary them. You go ahead. We will follow at a slower pace."

The smile remained, but a shadow crossed Esau's dark eyes. "If you insist, but I will leave a contingent of men to accompany you, Brother."

"Thank you, but there is no need. I have servants enough and men to move the herds." He patted Esau's forearm. "You go on ahead. We will follow."

Something wasn't right.

"And Father? Shall I tell him he will be seeing his son soon?"

Jacob rubbed the side of his nose. "Soon. Yes, I will see him soon." Esau nodded and with a shallow bow took his leave. I could see his taut mouth when he turned from Jacob. Esau knew his brother well.

When the cloud of Esau's dust had disappeared on the horizon, Jacob ordered the camp be readied to move. But we were not going to his father's home. My heart sank. Wasn't that what Jacob had longed for since the day he left Hebron? Why wouldn't he make haste to return? And he was breaking trust with Esau again. Jacob offered no explanation. Unease ate at my stomach. This couldn't be a good thing.

PART FIVE

The Prince

CHAPTER TWENTY-SIX

Leah

I was worried as I walked the hour-long journey to the city of Shechem, palace guards on either side of me. The men had assured me that all was well, that the governor's wife had requested I be brought to her on urgent business. Something to do with my standing as a midwife. Jacob had seemed satisfied that no harm was intended and encouraged me to go. He had purchased the land where our tents sat from her husband, Hamor, who was the sovereign of Shechem, a walled but small city in a beautiful valley between Mount Ebal and Mount Gerizim.

Something about Shechem had set my nerves on edge from the day we arrived, three years ago. Three years, and we had not returned to Jacob's home. Jacob had not yet seen his father. I couldn't understand it, no matter how I tried. We were only a few days' journey from Isaac. I had envisioned living among Jacob's people, where they worshiped the Living God, and not in a place where the stench of animals offered to false deities could reach my own tent if the wind blew in the right direction.

Jacob prospered here, as he always did, and somehow my reputation as a midwife and healer had preceded us, and I was busier than I had been at any time, but something churned in my gut. This is not where I wanted my family to root. My sons were young men seeking wives. The men of Shechem would be more than happy for the sons of Jacob to marry their daughters. This was the way trade alliances were made, but I wanted godly wives for my sons, not business partners.

My heart was heavy for my children. Reuben, still a kindhearted young man, seemed more withdrawn from his father than ever, which worried me, since I feared my own withdrawal set a poor example for him. Levi and Simeon spent far too much time in the city, and Judah, who I had felt held some special place in the plan of God, was practically living in the Canaanite city of Abdullah, in the house of Hirah, supposedly managing his flocks. But I feared there was a Canaanite girl who had caught my son's eye. It would break my heart if Judah married a woman who did not worship the God of his fathers. Issachar and Zebulon were younger and still innocent, but what would this place do to them?

My heart found some peace in Dinah, who was as sweet-natured as she was beautiful. But Dinah was of marriageable age too, and there was not a man in all of Shechem I would allow near my daughter. We needed to return to Hebron. For our children's sake. And for ours. It seemed our own morals were in decline.

The smell of incense came from the tents of our servants, and Jacob ignored it. He allowed them too much freedom to worship their own deities. As long as he didn't see it, he made no demands on the people to put their gods away. I wondered what the Living God thought of the idol worship in the camp of Abraham's descendant. Atop all this, like a sack of bricks on my back, was my concern for my sister. Rachel was pregnant again.

I had regularly provided the herbs to prevent it, but Rachel had gone against Tesup's warning and my constant admonition and stopped using them. And, as before, I was angry with Jacob, who should have seen to it Rachel used the preventives. And angry with Rachel, not because she flaunted her pregnancy in my face, which was bad enough, but because I feared she wouldn't survive another birth. And as much as she irritated me, I didn't know what I'd do if I lost her.

She seemed to be faring well, thus far. I saw to it that she ate, taking over the cooking when I wasn't delivering a baby or attending the sick. I gave her cream from atop the goat's milk, the fattest portions of meat, and berries when I could find them. I made her rest and insisted she let Bilhah grind the grain and get water from the well. For several years, Rachel had taken to doing as much of her own work as possible, to prove she was as strong as other women, and she could hardly stand the sight of her handmaid. But making life harder for her husband's concubine suited her, so she listened to me in that, at least.

<hr/>

The guards led me into a side entryway and turned me over to a young woman in a colorful tiered dress. The palace was elegant but small compared to the palace in Haran, which I had seen on occasion, since the entry rooms were open to public view.

My heart was heavy when I saw the walls covered with repeating carved panels depicting a hunter between two forward-facing bulls, similar to the amulet Anasa had offered me so many years ago. I still thought of Anasa from time to time. And when I did, it brought a dull pain. I wasn't sorry for refusing the amulet, but my mind would sometimes wander, and I would imagine life with Anasa as my husband, then wrestle the thought into captivity until it broke its bonds and spilled into my conscious thoughts again. I prayed that Anasa had found faith in the God of Abraham.

The servant girl took me to a larger room and told me to wait. "I'll tell the queen you are here," she said, then headed toward a door twice the height of the average man.

Queen? A pretentious title it seemed, since Hamor didn't refer to himself as king, though many rulers of city-states did. *King* might have been an improvement, since Hamor meant "ass," and the governor was rumored to be a stubborn man.

My leg was cramping by the time the queen floated into the room. I unconsciously smoothed my tunic as the woman appraised me through eyes heavily lined with kohl.

She was wearing a red dress made of something that looked uncomfortably like feathers. It was wrapped around her shapely body, leaving one shoulder bare and draping in long folds over the other. A thick beaded necklace encircled her long neck, and she wore a golden fretwork headpiece with three golden stars attached at the top. The headpiece looked rather like an upside-down latticed bowl perched on her head. It was obvious that under the thick coat of face paint Kishara was yet a beautiful woman.

"Hmmm. Not much to look at, are you?" she said, gesturing at my frumpy tunic.

I felt heat climbing up my neck. I hadn't thought to make myself more presentable. I was used to leaving in a hurry when someone came calling for a midwife.

"The messenger said I should come right away. I didn't change," I said, feeling the heat touch my cheeks.

She waved a bejeweled hand. "No need to apologize. I suppose it was rude of me to state the obvious. And I don't suppose it's necessary to be beautiful to be a proper midwife," she said, extending her negative opinion from my clothes to the rest of me.

First of all, I hadn't apologized, and I had no intention to do so. And I hadn't walked all this way to be insulted. And the "queen" was obviously not with child and in no need of a midwife, so I thought I may as well go home.

"Please, sit." The woman sat in a cushioned chair and motioned to the one opposite her. I hesitated for a long moment, considering excusing myself and leaving. "Please, Leah."

She knew my name? That was a surprise. I took the seat reluctantly.

"I suppose you are wondering how I came to know of you and why I have asked you here. Of course, your husband's father was known widely in Canaan."

I nodded.

"When Abraham's grandson came within our borders, it did not go unnoticed. Especially since he brought with him large herds of cattle and goats and flocks of sheep. Not to mention a multitude of menservants and maidservants.

"But I had already heard of his wife Leah. It seems you made quite a reputation for yourself in Haran. You attended Sinbalti, wife of Omari, did you not?"

I remembered the woman well. She was visiting relatives in Haran and had had some difficulties in her pregnancy so decided not to return to Canaan until after the child was born. Tesup had recommended me, being unable to attend the woman himself. She had a difficult birth and credited me with saving her and her child. I wasn't certain that was the case, but she insisted it was and rewarded me with many times my normal fee.

I nodded again.

"Well, I am in need of a midwife to serve the palace, and I would like you to take that position."

"Serve the palace solely?" I said. Did she think she could buy me like a slave? "I'm afraid I have already established a practice in the city and the surrounding countryside."

"Yes. I know that," she said, as if I was a bit simpleminded. "The palace would not require your services exclusively. I would only require you for family births. Of course, I would expect you to be available when my son's wives are near their time."

How much do I dare say to the imposing woman before me? "May I speak openly, Queen Kishara?"

She flipped her hand. "Yes, yes, of course."

"Why me? I am a stranger to your land and to your customs. Are there not midwives who have served the palace before now?"

She let out a long sigh. "Yes, but it is because you have *not* served the palace that I desire your ministrations."

I wasn't certain what the woman was getting at, and I had no desire to be at her beck and call.

"My oldest son, Prince Shechem, has been chosen to govern after his father. He has brothers, of other wives. Two are older and thus think the governance should fall to them, but my husband has honored my son above the sons of his other wives, even naming him after the city. Shechem has two wives presently. Both are with child. The older brothers have two male children already. If Shechem does not produce an heir, his place will fall to one of the other brothers."

The woman's face turned sharp. "I do not trust my husband's other wives. I believe there is nothing they would not do to secure their sons a place as Hamor's heir. I would rather have someone outside the palace, not affected by the politics of it all, in attendance should these pregnancies yield a male child.

"Midwives and servants, like anyone else, can be bought. I fear the wrong woman could kill a male child. A hand over the mouth and nose? Poison? I can't be expected to attend the births myself, and one is never certain who one can trust. But you would have no motivation for such an act, and, from my impression of you, would not be capable of it."

A midwife kill a child? I shuddered at the thought. Now, more than ever, I had no desire to become part of the intrigues of these people. But perhaps my presence would protect a boy child? I was torn by Kishara's appeal.

"How close to delivery are the women?"

"One is close. The other a few months away. Of course, you will be paid handsomely. Perhaps some new clothing would be in order. We wouldn't want people to think we do not adequately compensate those in our service."

I felt myself color. Queen or not, this woman would not denigrate me. I'd had enough of that in my lifetime.

"My husband is a wealthy man, and I have earned a great deal of money in my work, but I do not find it necessary to dress beyond that which is common among the people I serve. I would have to insist my attire be of my own choosing, *if* I choose to enter your employ."

The governor's wife bowed her head, a smile playing at her mouth. "I am aware of your husband's prosperity, and that your success has been well compensated, I am not surprised. Forgive my boldness. You are free to wear what you will."

"I would like to examine the women before I make up my mind. Would that be possible now?" I wanted to see for myself that the women were healthy. If something happened to one of them, or her offspring, I might be blamed. I was leaning toward not taking the position for that reason, but the picture of a child dying at a midwife's hand would not leave my mind.

The queen brightened. "Yes, certainly. Follow me, please."

I followed Kishara through a wide hallway. The stone walls were covered with intricately woven indigo and red tapestries depicting lines of little men in profile with eyes too big for their faces. The same wide eyes looked out from stone statues sitting on carved pedestals along the walls. The feeling of being watched was difficult to escape.

"Mara, this is Leah, wife of Lord Jacob. She has kindly agreed to be your midwife."

What? I had agreed to nothing of the sort! I gave Kishara a look that said as much.

"Well," she said, smiling at me, "not exactly agreed, but we are hopeful."

The young woman raised her eyebrows nonchalantly. "Whatever my mother-in-law desires."

A look passed between the two that spoke no fondness of either woman for the other. The queen led us to a chamber that had been set up for delivery. I took notice of the richly covered narrow bed and the fine birthing stool. The room was certainly well stocked and luxuriant.

"I will leave you to your work, Leah," Kishara said, without acknowledging her daughter-in-law.

I gestured to the bed. Mara took off her robe and lay down, aggravation emanating through every movement.

"How has your pregnancy been?" I asked as I pressed my hands around the girl's middle. "Have you had any cramping? Blood? Anything that caused you concern?"

"The only thing that has caused me concern is the loss of my fine figure," she said in an indignant tone. "I fear I will never regain it."

I tried not to show my opinion of her priorities, but it was difficult.

"With time your body will regain much of its former grace. I will give you some exercises that will help put things back in their proper place, but our bodies change with childbearing. It is part of becoming a mother."

The girl rolled her eyes at me without shame. "I just want to get it out of me. I'm tired of being confined, and I'm tired of looking like a fat kine!"

The girl obviously did not want to become a mother. I had a twinge of concern for the child that would soon be entering this world. "I would think bearing the child of a prince would be an honor most women in Shechem would aspire to."

"Of course, I want to bear Shechem's child. I just want to get it out and turn it over to a nurse, so I can try to regain some of my former beauty."

"You will turn your child over to others?" The girl looked at me as if I was a simple woman. "Children born in the palace are always given to the care of others. Who would want to be burdened with such drudgery?"

I swallowed my words and continued my examination. The girl appeared healthy, and all seemed as it should be. The child would be born soon—perhaps another week or two. I was saddened by the notion of a mother who did not wish to care for her own child. Then I felt a flash of heat in my cheeks. Hadn't Beor accused me of the same?

It wasn't true, of course. I had taken complete care of my children except when I was delivering or tending the sick. What I did helped women, and my children had not been the worse for it. Had they? Sometimes I wondered. Jealousy was rampant in my household.

But that seemed to be the way of Abraham's seed. It had been so with Jacob and his brother Esau, as well as with Isaac and his half-brother, Ishmael. Abraham's wives and concubines had wielded jealousy like a sword. It almost seemed as if the forces of evil paid special attention to the seed of Abraham, stirring discord wherever possible.

And the same had been true of Rachel and me, and I would not place all of the blame on my sister. Our father's actions had pitted us against each other, but I didn't have to reciprocate.

"That is all I need from you, Mara. If you lose water or start to bleed, let someone know right away." *Another midwife who might kill her child?* I was beginning to feel protective of this little one.

When the girl had exited the room with a flurry, another young woman entered behind Kishara.

"Leah, this is Sepha." This girl was not so far along as the first and decidedly less pretentious. Her gaze fluttered to the floor, and she appeared almost frightened.

"If you would please lie down on the bed, Sepha, we will see how you and your baby are doing." The queen was out the door before we reached the bed. She didn't bother feigning the fawning grandmother.

"If you could raise your legs for me, Sepha. I'm going to oil my hand and reach inside to see if everything is as it should be. It may hurt just a little. I will be as gentle as possible."

I dipped my hand in olive oil, ready to begin my examination.

The girl was trembling. She seemed terrified. Something about her reaction bothered me. Was the girl afraid of pain? Was she unduly modest?

I wiped my hand with a dry cloth. "It's all right, Sepha. We will do this next time. I just need to feel your stomach and ask you a few questions, if that is all right with you."

She nodded, her body beginning to ease from its tremors. I probed her stomach. The size of it led me to believe she was many weeks away from delivering her child.

"When did you have your last blood?"

The girl stuttered, "I, I think it was about four months ago. Maybe five."

"And before that, your courses had been regular, for the most part?"

"Yes." The girl nodded tentatively.

"Well, as far as I can see, Sepha, everything seems to be fine. You will, most likely, have a normal delivery and a healthy child. Are you excited about becoming a mother?"

The young woman did not answer my question, and I chose not to ask it again. What was it that bothered me about her? Something seemed off. I just didn't know what it was.

I helped her sit up on the side of the bed.

"May I ask you a question?" Sepha looked toward the door and back at me. "Could you tell the queen that it is unsafe for me to have . . ." she looked down. "To have intercourse with my husband while I am with child?"

I frowned. Many women did not enjoy sexual intimacy, but Sepha seemed terrified of it.

I shook my head. "I'm afraid that is not necessarily true, Sepha. When you are further along it is not recommended, but for now it is not imperative to cease intimacy with your husband. Of course, some men prefer not to." I thought of Jacob, who never came to my bed after I had conceived. Pregnancy had not stopped me from longing for my husband.

"It is, of course, an individual decision."

"Could you please just say that it might hurt the child? That I shouldn't do it?"

The girl seemed panicked.

My brows pinched. "And why would you ask such a thing, Sepha? Do you have pain?"

"Never mind," she said, shaking her head, a forced smile upon her lips. "I was just rambling. Please, do not say anything. Please."

I paused for several long moments. "I won't, but you can tell me if you are having a problem. I may be able to help. I've helped others.

Women who were so tense they caused themselves to contract and suffered pain. Or if it's something else that bothers you?"

"No. It is nothing. Truly. I am sometimes embarrassed, that is all."

I took her by the hand and smiled. "All right. But remember, I am here to help you, Sepha."

I huffed out a breath as I turned away. As much as I didn't want to do it, I had to take the position. There was too much going on with the prince's wives to ignore.

CHAPTER TWENTY-SEVEN

Reuben

W e need to have some enjoyment while we're in the city, Reuben," Simeon said as he took a huge bite of goat cheese we had purchased from the only hawker whose booth was not completely covered with flies.

We were in Shechem to deliver some wool to the market, and the shekels in Simeon's pocket were begging to be spent, it seemed. I probably shouldn't have given my brothers their shares while we were within the city walls. As the oldest, I needed to see that they made it out of the gates with at least a portion of their profits.

Simeon swallowed and wiped his mouth on his sleeve. His eyes were alight, and his mouth was spreading into a wide smile. I followed his gaze and saw the reason for that giddy grin on his face.

A woman in a bright garment with kohl-lined eyes was standing before a booth with a curtain for privacy, looking at Simeon with an invitation in her gaze.

"Don't do it, Simeon," I said, knowing my words were like dull arrows bouncing off their target.

"Don't tell me what to do, Brother. What I do is my business," he said as he followed the smiling woman into the booth and disappeared behind the curtain.

Being the oldest son, I would receive the birthright and lead the family when Father died, but it was easy to see my brothers would not make it easy for me—at least the older ones. Judah was more amiable than Simeon or Levi, but he was always away on business. The same sort of business as Simeon, I feared—however, with a somewhat more respectable partner.

It wasn't that I cared so much what Simeon did behind the curtain, but I did concern myself with the money in his pocket. Father would expect me to hold some sway over the funds he had put in my care. But I might as well talk to the dumb ox behind the plow, for all my brothers listened to me.

Jealousy was stamped upon the sons of Jacob, and for good reason. Simeon, Levi, Judah, and I—sons of Leah, were all close in age, with a few years separating the younger boys, Issachar and Zebulun. My father's concubines each had two: Bilhah's Dan and Naphtali, Zilpah's Gad and Ashur. And Rachel had Joseph, a boy of seven, who was already a major source of aggravation with his vivid imagination. He was obviously Father's favorite. It was all I could do sometimes to keep Simeon and Levi from tormenting the boy to death.

His mother had been frail for years, so my mother had taken over his care for the most part. Aunt Rachel was pregnant again, but Joseph was her only child thus far—unless you counted Dan and Naphtali, and no one did. They were supposed to be considered Aunt Rachel's children, since they were born of her handmaid, but ever since Joseph came, she treated the other boys with total disregard. She had hardly claimed them before.

Aunt Rachel had made Bilhah's life miserable, with all her animosity and anger. I learned through servants that Rachel had demanded Father not step foot in Bilhah's tent again—and he hadn't, as far as anyone knew. But even I could see the wistful look on his face when he saw his concubine walking like a slender willow swaying in the wind.

I could well understand why he longed for Bilhah. Who wouldn't? Bilhah was twelve years older than I, but I couldn't help the attraction I felt toward her. She was slight of build, but she moved with grace, like a long-legged fawn, eyes wide with wonder—and with sorrow. It seemed sad that she would never know another man. She was still bound to my father, and his death was the only thing that would release her, unless he put her away, and that was unlikely.

Simeon was back on the right side of the curtain in remarkable time, a sheen of dampness on his face.

218

"It doesn't seem you got your money's worth, Simeon. Maybe you should put your money to better use," I said. "And perhaps you should check your purse."

Simeon patted his bag. "My purse is where it should be, and I put my money to very good use, Brother. From the sour sounds coming out of your mouth, maybe you should get in line."

I could feel the color in my cheeks.

Simeon smirked. "If father doesn't find us wives soon, our manhood will cease to function. I may as well keep mine in working order until then."

I understood Simeon's frustration. Father had refused to allow us Hittite wives, and there would be no returning to our northern relatives to take a wife, as our father and grandfather had done.

Maybe Esau's daughters? Or a daughter of Ishmael, our uncle born of the bondservant?

I didn't know, but I didn't want to take my pleasure with a harlot. Well, I wanted to, but my better judgment held me back.

We walked on through the maze of booths. The voices of men and women hawking their goods competed with the bleat of goats and sheep and the yapping of dogs in the distance. I spotted the vendor who sold shawls and scarves. I'd buy a gift for Dinah. She seldom had opportunity to come to the city, and she always squealed with delight when I brought her something.

I picked a pretty white shawl, paid for it, and tucked it away in my satchel. I had loved to spoil Dinah since she was a baby. The only girl in a family of boys, she could have been obnoxious, but Dinah was a delight—full of energy and enthusiasm. She was beautiful, even more beautiful than Rachel, but she had none of her aunt's ways.

It was hard for me not to resent my Aunt Rachel. Mother had been at Rachel's heel all of her life. My mother was a pretty woman, not beautiful, but a woman of deep love and faith.

But even she had a limit, a point where she could or would take no more, and it seemed she had reached it some time ago. I knew my mother still felt pain, but she had covered it with a thick layer of self-protection. Sometimes I could see it red and raw beneath the surface. My mother's pain made me resent my father and my aunt, and sometimes it rose up in me with a great force.

I felt the weight of my position in the family, and I wanted to be a worthy leader. I just didn't know if this family could be led.

I picked up another shawl, felt of the fine thread. It would look beautiful draped over narrow shoulders.

"I'll take this one too," I said to the merchant, who raised an eyebrow and grinned.

Jacob

I walked out of the small tent I had erected temporarily on the ridge of the mountain and made my way down the narrow path to the pasture where Dan and Naphtali were grazing a flock of sheep.

Bilhah's boys didn't speak to me if they didn't have to. No doubt carrying their mother's grievances as well as their own. I'd stopped visiting Bilhah's tent years ago to keep peace with Rachel, and Rachel had ignored the boys she'd bargained so hard to get. I told her she would regret sending me to Bilhah, and she had.

Dan saw me coming. He hardly tried to cover his disdain. It started with a dip of his brow and spread down his face like the evening shadows swallowing the sunlit day. Naphtali caught his brother's look and mimicked it. He reminded me of Chorash, who had followed Beor like a faithful dog.

Not that Dan was anything like Beor, but there was a canniness about him that put me in mind of a snake lying in wait to snip at a horse's heel for the pleasure of watching the rider tumble off. It saddened me to see it.

"Where's Reuben?" I asked, looking around for my eldest son. I hadn't seen him for some time. I was trying to include Reuben in the daily decisions of managing so great a multitude of animals and men. He was the heir, and I wanted to establish him as such before his brothers. He was going to need all the help he could get.

The shadow on Dan's face darkened, and Naphtali's face matched it. What was going on between Reuben and Bilhah's sons?

Dan didn't answer. I looked at Naphtali, thinking I might get a response from him, but nothing was forthcoming.

"Well?" I asked Dan again. "Do you know where your brother is?"

"I'm not in charge of your oldest son, am I?" he said.

"I asked you a simple question, Dan. I require an answer. Do you know where Reuben is?"

The arrogance slipped from Dan's face, replaced with—what? Fear? What was going on?

"I . . . I think he's in the far pasture with Levi . . . yes, that's where he is . . . I'm sure of it."

Reuben wasn't with Levi. *I* was sure of that. Levi and Simeon had accompanied Reuben to the city, but they'd returned hours ago. They wouldn't be in the same place unless they had to be, and nothing required their mutual attention now. What was this? One moment Dan is displaying anger at Reuben and the next he seems to be covering for him?

CHAPTER TWENTY-EIGHT

Leah

I was greeted at the palace door by one of the servants, a dignified man with a stiff carriage.

"Welcome, Mistress Leah. The queen has asked me to see you to your room and to allow you to refresh yourself before you see to the princess."

I nodded. "Thank you."

I hadn't expected such a grand room. The bed was almost bigger than my tent. I washed my face and hands in the brass washbasin and dried them with a towel that hung on a peg beside a polished brass mirror. I looked at my reflection and sighed. When had those lines at the corners of my eyes appeared?

What was it about this place that made my blood creep cold in my veins? I shook my head at my image. "You are a foolish woman, Leah. You are allowing your trepidation to get the best of you."

A knock came on the door, and the queen walked in before I had a chance to answer.

"Thank you for coming, Leah. Mara is showing signs of impending labor. I thought it best to have you close at hand."

I wasn't certain what was expected of me, but I wasn't going to bow. "I think you acted wisely. When will I be able to see her?"

"As soon as possible would be best. I'll have a servant bring her to the birthing room so you can assess her condition."

"Thank you." I nodded, feeling relieved when the woman left the room. I would never adjust to the palace pomp. I went to the birthing room and waited. A short while later Mara came in on the arm of a servant, her lovely night robe straining over her middle.

"Please tell me this is going to be over soon. I'm feeling so uncomfortable!"

"Let me help you onto the bed," I said, taking her elbow. "I will take care of Mara now. Thank you." The servant bowed and backed out the door.

I probed the girl's stomach. The child was in position. An internal examination indicated it would be some time, however. "I don't think it will be tonight."

Mara sighed. "Surely you are wrong."

I gave her a sympathetic smile. "I have been doing this for some time. I'm sorry to tell you that I am seldom wrong about such things."

"Well, you must be wrong this time! There is nothing you can do to hurry it along?"

"Nothing that would be safe for the child."

"If that is the case, I want to rest in my own bed. This one is far too hard."

"It is meant to give support during labor, not comfort, I'm afraid."

"Oh, this whole business is just so . . . so vulgar! I will thank the gods when it is over and this thing is out of me."

I called for the servant to assist Mara back to her room. The queen must have been close by, for she entered as the two were leaving.

"You really should watch your tongue, Mara. It could be the prince's son you are calling a thing."

The girl blanched and bowed her head as she left. The queen turned to Leah—a look of disgust upon her painted face. "My son lacks taste in choosing his women."

I made no comment. Instead, I asked, "Would you like me to see Sepha now?"

"No. It can wait until morning. You do not expect Mara's delivery to be forthcoming?"

"No. Another day, most likely."

"Well, I will have food brought to you. One of the servant girls is sleeping on a mat in Mara's room. She will wake you if you are needed. Rest well, Leah."

I nodded. A servant brought roast pheasant and honeyed wine. The flavors were full and rich. I had not tasted anything quite so good in my memory, but I took only a few bites. A weight rested on my chest—something I did not understand and could not shake off.

The sound of a slap of the hand and a cry woke me from a light sleep. I sat up in bed, listening for the sound again. I heard a scraping of wood against wood and knew at once it was the sound of a bed as it moved under bodies. But this did not sound like the lovemaking I had heard from my perch on the roof of my childhood home. It sounded violent. I could hear whimpering and the sadistic sound of a mocking male voice. Fear trickled down my spine as I remembered Beulah and the bruises I had witnessed. I was quite certain I knew where the sound was coming from.

<hr />

I came out of my room at daylight. I was tired of being shut away, and more than curious as to the well-being of my patient. I looked for a servant to direct me to Mara's room, wondering how the girl had slept and if she was any closer to delivering her child.

A young man, handsome with dark hair that fell across thick brows and striking black eyes, stood in the doorway of Sepha's room. His sleeveless tunic hung unbelted over his strong frame, exposing the chiseled muscles of his upper arms. He barely glanced at me, then walked toward a room across the wide hall. The spittle stuck in my throat, and I could not swallow. What those muscles were capable of, I had no doubt. I would ask to see Sepha as soon as I checked on Mara.

Mara moaned when I entered the room. I had her removed to the birthing room for an examination.

"Yes. Your labor has begun, Mara." The young woman let loose of an oath and grabbed my hand. "How long will it take? How am I to bear this pain?"

I wanted to tell the girl she had only just begun to feel pain, and it would probably be some time before the child came, but thought better of it.

The labor was not difficult for a first birth, but Mara had screamed and moaned and cried until I wanted to scream myself. And then when the mother was told she had given birth to a girl child, she began to cry some more.

"Now I will have to do this again!" She moaned. When I tried to show Mara her daughter, she screamed and said to take it away. I wanted to slap the girl into realization of how fortunate she was to have a healthy child of either gender when so many were unable to conceive, but I bit back the words.

"A girl?" The queen glared at Mara as though she had *planned* to disgrace the prince. I was thankful there was no "royal" blood in my veins.

I walked into Sepha's room and found her lying on her bed. "How are you feeling, Sepha?"

The girl's gaze found the floor. She tried to speak, but her voice caught and tears began flowing down her face. My heart wrenched. Sepha reminded me of Dinah: lovely, of delicate frame and form, and with huge eyes fanned by thick dark lashes. I was sure that the child's husband abused her, probably regularly.

"I think we need to do that examination now."

Sepha pressed her lips together and gave a shallow nod.

I tried not to gasp as I helped Sepha out of her gown. There were bruises on her arms and her buttocks. The violence I heard in the night hours was painted in blue on the girl's body. I dreaded what the internal examination would reveal.

I looked toward the closed door and spoke in a quiet voice. "Sepha, does this happen often?"

Her cheeks reddened. "Yes, but it has not always been this way. Shechem was sometimes tender when we were first together. But it has been a long time since I've felt a gentle touch from him."

"What do you think has brought about this change?"

She shrugged. "I think it might be because he stands to lose his place if he doesn't have a son. I don't know. Maybe this . . . this was there before, and I didn't see it until he became violent."

"Do you think he does this to Mara?"

"I don't think so. I sometimes think I bring it on myself because Shechem can see in my eyes that I'm hurt—in my heart as well as my body—and it makes him feel guilty."

"It's not your fault, Sepha. No man has a right to do this." I was thinking of Beor and hoping God had honored my curse if he had tried to abuse Beulah again.

Sepha's face turned pale as she continued. "Sometimes I see something . . . evil in his eyes. It takes him over, and then he seems sorry. I fear someday it may take him over completely and they will find me dead."

A cold chill crept up my spine. What had I gotten myself into? And what would become of this poor child?

<hr>

A different servant opened the door and moved his shoulder toward the lavish entry hall. The other man had become somewhat friendly to me, but this man showed no sign of camaraderie at all.

"I will tell the queen you are here," he said in a drone and walked away. I watched him move across the stone tiles, thinking that if I hired someone to greet my guests, I would hope to find someone a bit more welcoming.

I was beginning to regret the time taken from my other patients. Zilpah was an able midwife now, and her knowledge of herbs equaled mine. But she wasn't able to care for all those in need, and I was forced to turn some to healers in whom I had less confidence.

The man returned, no friendlier than before. "The queen will see you now."

I gave a shallow bow when the queen stood from the fur-covered chair on which she sat, robed in an exquisite purple tunic.

"Leah. It is good to see you again."

"And you, Queen Kishara. How is your new granddaughter?"

The queen looked puzzled for a moment, as though she had forgotten she had a new grandchild.

"Oh. I suppose she is well enough. She has been sent to the country with a maid. She will not grace the palace again until she is some years older. I can't abide the whine of little ones. I might force myself for a boy child, but the girl will be better off in the country."

For once I agreed with Kishara. A boy might be better off also.

"And Sepha? She has seemed to be well?"

"How would I know?" The queen softened her countenance. "The girl hardly comes out of her room."

"And why is that, do you think?" I wondered if the queen would talk to me about the obvious brutality of the prince.

She stood. "Ask her, why don't you? I really have things to attend to. I believe she's in the garden." The woman swished out of the room.

I found Sepha sitting on a bench under a cypress tree. Her face was drawn, but her eyes brightened at seeing me.

"May I sit down?" I asked.

"Yes, of course."

I sat on the bench and looked about at the profusion of color. What a beautiful garden, with vines climbing the stone wall and more sorts of flowers than I knew existed.

Neither of us spoke for a moment.

"I'm afraid, Leah."

My heart clenched. "Afraid of what, Sepha?"

The girl pulled a long breath. "Everything. I'm afraid that if I have a girl, Shechem will become so angry . . . well, I just don't know. You never know with Shechem. And if I have a boy . . ."

The girl looked up at me with tears in her eyes. "I don't want my son to be raised in this house. I don't want him to be like Shechem. The strange thing is, sometimes I think I love my husband. Sometimes he is tender and kind to me, and I love that man, but when he rages, he is another man altogether. That man I fear."

My heart hurt for Sepha. How terrible to be so young and yet so hopeless.

A question crossed Sepha's eyes. I saw her struggle with it.

"Leah, you are trained in all aspects of childbirth, are you not?"

"Yes." What was she asking?

"In methods of contraception?"

"Yes."

"In abortive methods?"

"No!" I almost shouted, then stuttered. "Yes . . . I am aware of the methods, but I have never used them. Nor will I."

Sepha grasped my arm. "You could say that the child did not take hold in the womb." Tears flowed down her lovely face. I laid my hand on her shoulder.

"Why would you think to destroy your own child, Sepha?"

"It's not a child yet . . . is it? I mean, that's what I've always been told—that it's not alive until it breathes outside the womb."

"That is not true, Sepha. It is just an excuse people make so they won't feel guilty for destroying a life."

Sepha shook her head. "But to let a child be raised in a place such as this. Is that not destroying a life? Sometimes I wish I had never been born!" Tears exploded from her eyes.

"Look at me, Sepha." I took the girl's head in my hands. "To God this child is precious, and to take his or her life would break the heart of the Almighty. And you too are precious to Him. He loves you, and even though our lives are not always as we would wish, God does not abandon us. He sees your troubles, and He loves you."

My heart smote me as I spoke. Why did I not act on the words myself? I knew that God had not abandoned me. I knew that God loved me and wept over me, but I was letting myself slip into an abyss of bitterness and resentment.

Lord, help me, so I can help this girl. I held her while she wept, my heart breaking with her. I had to do something about my own faithlessness. God was worthy of more honor than I was giving Him.

I escorted Sepha to the birthing room. She slipped off her robe and lay on the table with just a shift covering her too-thin body. I was dismayed to see fresh bruises among the ones of sickly yellow.

"He continues to do this?"

The girl's lips pressed into a pale line and then parted as she looked past me, fear suddenly in her eyes.

"Is my wife well?"

I turned to the voice in the doorway. Anger surged through me at the sight of Shechem, tall and thick-shouldered and handsome in his rich robe.

"No, your wife is not well." I spoke sharply. Something that looked vaguely like concern flitted across his dark eyes.

"And the child?"

"The child seems to be well—at this time, but your wife has happened upon some bruising. Have you any idea what the cause might be?"

Oh, God. What am I doing? This might not end well for Sepha. But it was not well now, and I had to try to help her.

The prince's face flushed, first with what looked like shame, then more like anger.

I proceeded, not giving him time to respond.

"It would be a shame if rough treatment of the child's mother resulted in an early and unviable arrival. As a matter of fact, it is not in the child's best interest for her mother to have intercourse during her pregnancy."

The prince looked sharply at me, then narrowed his eyes at Sepha. "What have you been saying?"

The girl's mouth opened but nothing came out.

"She has said nothing. I'm not blind." I stood at my full height, my shoulders squared. "This ill-treatment of your wife must stop. Today!"

"I don't answer to a midwife," he said, glaring at me. "I don't answer to anyone!"

I tipped my chin. "That is obvious!"

Suddenly, darkness covered the man's eyes, and he reached out and took me by the arm. "I am the prince, and if you speak to my wife about such things, I will see to it that you regret it."

I pulled my arm away, suddenly emboldened. I looked him in the eyes, feeling power in my words. "And I am wife of Jacob the grandson of Abraham and daughter of the Most High God. And if you ever touch me in such a manner again, *you* shall regret it!"

Suddenly the prince's eyes seemed to change, and he looked almost frightened. He turned and walked away.

The power I had felt a moment ago left me, and I felt weak at the knees. *What have I done?* I had antagonized the source of Sepha's torment. Had I made things worse for her?

Foolish woman! God forgive me. Protect this girl.

I wasn't certain what I would do about coming back to the palace. I thought maybe I should send a message to the queen stating that I could no longer attend Sepha. I would have to think about it.

CHAPTER TWENTY-NINE

Reuben

I looked up from the fence I was mending and mopped at the sweat making its way in little rivers to the neck of my tunic. Dinah was running toward me, her feet barely touching the ground, her eyes wide with excitement.

"Reuben! You have to help me. You have to!"

"Wait!" I caught her before she slammed into me. "Take a breath! What is it that my sister wants so badly she would run her brother over for it?" Her hair was whipped to a frizz around her damp face. She looked like the little girl I loved to tease, more than the young woman she'd more recently become.

"I'm sorry, Reuben. I'm just so excited, and I need you to help me. Please, Reuben!"

"Dinah, what in the world are you talking about? I can't help you if I have no idea what you need."

"The festival. I want to go!"

My mouth twisted. Of all things she could request, I feared this was one beyond my ability to influence. There was to be a festival for the women of the city. A parade of entertainers, games, and vendors, but it was not likely Mother would allow Dinah to attend. She watched the girl with the eye of a hawk.

"I don't know, Dinah. Mother is not likely to approve."

"Please, Reuben. You can convince her!"

"I don't know that she would allow it. There will likely be rituals to the gods and who knows what else?" I wasn't at all sure I would like my little sister in such an atmosphere. The festival was innocuous in itself, but what happened on the fringes might be more offensive.

"It's meant to be a festival for women. It's not as though there will be fornication in the street."

What? "And just what would you know of fornication? You had better not use that word with Mother, or you will be seeing nothing but the inside of your tent until you're old and gray."

Dinah blushed. "We have servants. They talk. But I will not speak of it to Mother. All the other girls of the camp are going. I want to see what the daughters of the city are wearing. Their clothes are so bright and full of color. Not drab like mine."

I smiled. "It's what they're not wearing that concerns our parents."

"Please, Reuben. I'm not a child. I want to go. Please encourage them to allow it. They will trust your word. Please?"

∞∞∞∞∞∞∞∞∞∞∞

Mother looked up from her dough. The smile on her lips lost its curve as soon she saw Dinah and me. She knew something was astir—no doubt by the sheepish look on my face. How had I let Dinah talk me into this? Mother stood straight, her shoulders back, her eyebrows raised.

"Absolutely not," she said before I'd finished with the speech I'd carefully prepared.

"Please, Mother!" Dinah begged.

"No!" she said, her tone sharp.

"It's not fair for you to say no without even giving it a thought!"

Dinah had raised her voice to our mother. Something I'd never heard any of my siblings do. She was immediately sorry for it by the look in her eyes, but it didn't take the sting from the words or the stricken look from my mother's face. Fat tears ran down Dinah's cheeks, and she lowered her gaze. My sister had always been of such a sweet disposition. She had always tried to please our mother. But she was older now, and her interests were going beyond our mother's tent. But this was not a thing done in our home.

"I'm sorry, Mother. I didn't mean . . ."

Mother raised her trembling hand. My heart hurt for her. Dinah had become her life in the absence of a loving husband. I always felt Mother lived vicariously through her daughter, although she truly sought only the best of life for Dinah. For Dinah to show anything but love for her must break my mother's heart. Why had I let Dinah drag me into this collusion?

"Mother. Could I speak with you alone for a moment?" I asked.

Her eyes could not hide the wrench of pain in her heart. She nodded.

Dinah bowed her head and left the tent, tears still flowing. I knew she was torn between grief for how she'd hurt her mother and the longing to be part of what the other girls were going to enjoy.

"I'm sorry, Mother. I'm sure Dinah didn't mean to disrespect you. She's young and—"

She shook her head. "I shouldn't have raised my voice. I should have at least let you finish."

"It is no excuse. Dinah had no right." I was angry with my little sister for hurting our mother. I'd make that plain when I left the tent, although I was quite certain Dinah would have thoroughly reprimanded herself by then.

"Many of the girls of the camp are attending with their mothers. Perhaps . . . if you attended with her. If something untoward were to happen, you would be there to see her home."

"Something untoward is bound to happen, Reuben. It's the nature of the city. And I doubt your father would allow it anyway." She shook her head. "I wish we'd never come here."

I doubted Father would care. He allowed idols in his own camp as long as he didn't see them. That was how he handled everything: out of sight, out of mind. He was blind to everyone but Rachel. He didn't mind what she did to Mother or to Bilhah or Bilhah's sons. Rachel and Joseph were the only people he cared about.

"I doubt he would care what any of us did," I said, unable to hide the anger in my voice.

"That's not true, Reuben. Your father cares very much for all of you," she said, desperate for me to believe it. I know it hurt her to see any of us in pain. And pain was all I'd gotten from the man besides a crumb or two of affection when guilt ate at his conscience. He was too weak to stand up to Rachel and insist she treat my mother with the dignity she deserved. Sometimes my emotions ran almost to the point of hatred.

"I understand your reticence, Mother. Just think on it for a while, please?"

She pressed her lips between her teeth and nodded. "But don't encourage her, Reuben. Nothing is likely to change. And I will speak to your father. I would not allow her to go without his permission."

I bowed my head and kissed my mother's cheek, thinking that she hoped Father wouldn't allow it so that the decision would be taken out of her hands. But Dinah would know. And it wouldn't be Father that she blamed.

CHAPTER THIRTY

Leah

The tower was old, and as I drew close, I could see the crumbling rock, sloughed from the edifice by long years of wind and rain. But it seemed safe enough, and I had an urge to see it from the inside. It had been built more than a century ago, during a time of battles between the city-states, as an observation tower to spy out approaching enemies. More recently, it had been used by shepherds to keep a better eye on their flocks. It was abandoned now, as far as I knew.

I stepped over the debris scattered about the entrance and into a musty circular room with a stone floor and rough stone walls. The remnants of a fire, ashes, and the lingering scent of burned sheep dung, testified that others had sheltered here. There was a rock staircase that curved up the side of the wall to a second floor, where I'd seen a window from the outside. I wanted to look over the fields and flocks from it. To see the world from a higher vantage point.

There was no rail, and my head began to swim as I made my way up the narrow steps. I stopped to look down before I entered the opening and immediately regretted it. I leaned against the rough wall and closed my eyes, trying to stop the whirl within my head.

A noise came from within the upper chamber. An animal? Not a large one, I thought. Maybe a rat rummaging in a leftover bed of straw. I thought I should make my way back to the floor beneath me, but I'd braved the treacherous stairs, and I wanted a look out that window, so I entered the room quietly looking about for the source of what I'd heard.

Light from the window glazed a path across the gray stone, illuminating little bits of crystal held captive in the dull rock. Straw was strewn here and there about the chamber. I saw something in the shadows. When I realized it was a blanket moving in a recognizable rhythm, I froze. I had come across a couple making love in what they thought was a private place.

Before I could tell my feet to move, the man turned toward me, and the woman raised her head. Waves of shock rippled through my body.

"Mother?" Reuben's mouth dropped open. His eyes looked painfully wide in his stock-still face. I looked at the ashen pallor of my husband's concubine. Bilhah!

No one moved or spoke. It was as though we were looking at our own stone images from another place.

I sucked a breath into my air-starved lungs and spun around. I heard Reuben and Bilhah scramble up. Heard the wisp of fabric as they slipped their tunics over their heads.

Bilhah was the first to attempt to speak.

"Leah." Her small voice quavered. I turned to look at my sister's maid, her hair a tangle around her narrow face, color rushing into her cheeks.

A muscled arm shot out in front of her, pushing her back in a gesture of protection.

"Mother . . ."

I shook my head violently. How could they do this? A son and his father's concubine? A concubine was considered a secondary wife, without the status of a married woman but with all the obligations. Jacob could have both their lives for this. If he took Reuben and Bilhah to the city elders and they judged the pair guilty, they could bind them together and throw them in the river!

"Mother . . ." Reuben took a step toward me.

"Don't!" I held out my palm and took a step back, shaking my head several times. The raw edge of Reuben's tunic circled his neck. The tunic I had made with my own hands. He had put it on wrong-side out. The sight of the frayed threads reminded me of how many times he'd done the same as a child, in a hurry to catch up to his father or to roam the hills with his cousins. Of how I'd scolded him and sent him back to right his garment before he left my sight. I wanted to tell him to re-dress himself, but the thought of Bilhah seeing his nakedness one more time was unbearable.

"How could you do this, Reuben?" Tears sprang to my eyes. "And you, Bilhah. You've dishonored your husband and your mistress!"

Reuben clenched his fists. "Neither Father nor Rachel have earned Bilhah's honor."

I knew Reuben spoke from deep resentment of his father and aunt, primarily for their treatment of me. But he dishonored me, also, by this terrible deed!

"And you?" I said. "Are you an honorable man, Reuben? Are these honorable actions? You've taken your father's wife!"

"It's not the same! You know that. She's his concubine, and he hasn't been to her bed in years."

"So that gives you a right to bed her for him?" I said in a shrill voice I didn't recognize. "How long has this been going on?" I said, glaring at Bilhah. "You're almost old enough to be my son's mother! Have you preyed on him since he was old enough to perform such a vile act? It's not just Rachel and Jacob you've wronged. You've wronged me! You've both hurt me more than the two of them ever did."

Reuben looked wounded by my words. He seemed smaller, younger than he had a moment ago. "I didn't want to hurt you, Mother. That was not my intention."

"Your intention was to ease your lust. You cared not who it hurt." I drew a sickened breath. I couldn't believe it. Reuben. The gentlest of all my sons. The one who would carry on in his father's stead.

Dear God, what has become of my family?

Reuben squared his shoulders. "I'm going to ask Father to put her away. That way I can marry her."

An involuntary noise escaped my lungs. "And are you going to tell him that you've already had her? Or do you think he won't ask? He's not a dull man, Reuben!" I shook my head. Tears streamed down my face. "Why would you do such a foolish thing?"

"Please, don't blame him, Leah," Bilhah said. "It was my fault. Jacob awakened me. For two years I knew what it was to feel passion, and then Rachel made him quit my bed. You don't know how that feels, Leah."

She blanched. "I'm sorry, Leah. I didn't think."

"No, you didn't. But you have endangered yourself—and my son."

236

I looked at Reuben. "If you cared for Bilhah, why would you risk her life in such a careless way? I thought I'd raised a wise son, but I fear it's a fool who stands before me!"

"Please, don't tell him, Mother." Reuben was suddenly holding my arm, his face full of grief, his eyes bright with fear. What would become of my son? I couldn't hide this from Jacob. I had a duty to tell him.

"How can I keep such a thing secret? To do so would be to sin myself."

"I'm not asking for myself," he said, moisture gathering in the corners of his eyes. "I'm sorry, Mother. You're right. I'm a fool. I should have known better. I don't care what Father does to me, but he will kill her, Mother. Please."

Would it be so egregious to protect my own son from the possibility of death? I didn't know what Jacob would do. The relationship between the two was always strained. I knew Jacob loved his son and that he might not feel compelled to subject him to judgment from men who served false gods, but who would blame him if he rendered such judgment himself?

But even if I didn't tell Jacob, it would come out. Sin cannot be long hidden. And then Jacob would count me as a party to this betrayal, and he would be right to do so. And God knew about it. If He watched from the heavens as I had always thought He did, He'd seen what I saw and more. He'd seen the part of Reuben and Bilhah that I could never see, the depths of their hearts, and I feared what lay there would not evoke sympathy.

"I will pray that your father finds it in his heart to show mercy."

I turned and stumbled to the door. The winding stairs swam before my eyes. I kept my hand on the stone wall as I moved down the steps, not at all sure I would make it safely to the bottom.

When my feet touched the floor, I ran out into the warm air and down the hill, tripping and getting up to run again. I ran to a copse of trees and fell down in their shade and wept.

"God, please! Please! Have mercy on my son." I felt as if my heart would rip apart from the pain.

"Why, Lord? Why? Why can I have no peace? I love you. Why is my life in such disarray?"

The heavens were silent—and somehow I knew there was more trouble to come.

⬯⬯⬯⬯⬯⬯⬯⬯⬯⬯⬯⬯⬯

Dinah slipped the new shawl I had given her around her shoulders. It was a lovely blue, edged with delicate stitching. It reminded me of the veil I had worn on my wedding day, a memory I immediately pushed from my mind.

A wealthy patient had given it to me in gratitude for the care she had received. It was very expensive, and its beauty was only enhanced by the girl who wore it.

"You look beautiful, Dinah. Too beautiful, I fear." I always felt a burst of pride when eyes turned Dinah's way, but I also fumed when those eyes were anything but respectful of the beauty they beheld.

I was still sick to my soul for Reuben. It had been a week, and I'd not yet told Jacob. I'd decided to wait until after Dinah's outing. I didn't want to ruin it for her, since her heart was so set upon it. But the day was here, and tomorrow I'd have to do it, or I'd lose my courage. I'd beg on my knees if I had to. Surely, Jacob wouldn't require his own son's life. I didn't think so. But I didn't know, and whatever the punishment, it would not be a pleasant thing. My chest ached as though the pain, grown too large for the cavity, pushed from the inside, trying to crack it open and escape into fresher air.

I'd seen Bilhah once about the camp. Her face had turned the color of my hands after breaking pomegranates and scooping out the seeds for sauce. Reuben had avoided conversation, asking only with his eyes that I keep his secret. I'd avoided looking in his face as much as possible.

Dinah put her arms around me and held me close. She had tried to make up for her outburst, and I found comfort in the circle of her embrace. It would be difficult, but I had to take a step back from my daughter. I couldn't depend on Dinah for my own sense of self-worth. Someday soon she would marry, and I'd have to share her with another, whether I wanted to or not. Maybe a husband would take her to a place far from her family, as my husband had taken me. I needed to prepare myself for the future. I needed to give my daughter into God's care. To let Him be her comfort—and mine. But it was not an easy thing to do.

Dinah loosened her embrace and looked me in the eyes. Hers were glowing with excitement. "Thank you for coming with me, Mother. It means so much to me. We will have such a wonderful time together."

"Don't forget us," a voice came from outside the tent.

Adah and Nabaioth, daughters of Jeush, the head herdsman, and Rebi daughter of Timnah and Herman, the craftsman who fashioned our plows and other tools, were peeking through the open flap. "Are you ready?"

I drew a breath and smiled. The girls all looked lovely, but none were as lovely as my Dinah. The thought usually gave me comfort, but, for some reason, it bothered me today.

The other mothers and I walked behind our daughters as we started down the road toward Shechem. The small city sat arrogantly atop a little hill, its thick stone walls boasting against intruders who would dare to breech them. It rather reminded me of a short man who tries to proudly stretch his neck to the height of his fellows.

I wiped at my throat with the corner of my scarf. It was hot for a spring day. On either side of the dirt road, patches of yellow, white, and purplish-blue wild flowers peeked out from the sparse grass. There was no breeze, and the flowers seemed to be waiting in quiet anticipation of the spring rains.

The trail of women and children and the occasional man grew long as we left the outskirts of our encampment. The girls were getting farther and farther ahead of us, eager to begin their adventure in the city.

"Slow down!" one of the mothers cried. "We are not so young anymore."

The girls slowed their pace and continued laughing among themselves.

It was good that Dinah and I had come. It would be an enjoyable day. I'd been foolish to be so fearful. What could happen? I was here to watch over her. If something untoward took place on the city streets, I'd be there to steer her clear of it.

"Leah!"

I heard my name and then saw Eileon, servant in the household of Basmati, whose wife was nearing delivery. My heart dropped. *No. Not now.*

The servant bowed and with labored breath said, "My mistress is too soon in labor, and it is not going well. Please, come now!"

Dinah was walking toward me, her eyes moving between me and the servant, disappointment already flooding them.

I could send Zilpah, but she was attending a child with a fever, and I had no idea how it had gone with the boy or when Zilpah would return. Why today? Eileon's face was anxious. He was plainly wanting me to leave immediately. I had to go. There was nothing else to do. Dinah's countenance was already crumbling.

I let out a long sigh. "Dinah, I'm sorry."

Tears spilled over her lower lashes. "Mother, isn't there someone else?"

There was no one else. Not that could be dispatched quickly. "No, Dinah. There's no one, and the woman's labor is early and already with complications. If I had any other option, Dinah, I would take it."

She bit her bottom lip. I knew she was trying hard not to say something that would cause me pain, as she had before, but the hurt on her features made me want to cry myself.

"She can come with us," Timnah said. "I will watch her as my own."

Dinah's eyes lit with hope, silently pleading with me.

I shook my head. "I don't know. I'm not comfortable sending her into the city without me."

The woman took my hand in hers. "She will be fine. I promise."

"Please, Mother. Please. I've so looked forward to this." She nodded toward Rebi's mother. "Timnah will take responsibility for me, and I will be careful. Please?"

I didn't want to do it. I shouldn't do it. Jacob had given his permission if I went with her. But I hated to disappoint Dinah. The look on her face tore at my heart.

"All right." The words lay upon the warm air between us, as though waiting to be snatched back. "But you must stay with Timnah at all times."

Dinah squealed with delight. "I will. I promise, Mother. Thank you. Thank you." She hugged me, excitement lighting her lovely face.

"You will not let her out of your sight, even for a moment," I said to Timnah, a cautionary edge beneath the words.

"Not even for a moment. Go in peace, Leah. I will take care of her."

I stood for another moment, still not satisfied that I should allow this. The servant laid his hand on my shoulder. "We must hurry."

I gave a shallow nod. "I will have to return home to get my bag." It was on the way and would take only a moment. I hugged Dinah and held her chin in my hand. "You will stay with Timnah at all times. Not for one moment are you to be out of her sight."

Dinah hugged me again and darted back toward the girls.

Eileon and I started toward the encampment. We'd gone only a few paces when I turned and looked at my daughter as she moved toward Shechem with the group. I bit my lip to keep from calling her back.

CHAPTER THIRTY-ONE

Leah

The sun was just beginning to glow pink over the tops of the tents as Eileon and I approached the camp. The servant had seen me home because of the late hour. The delivery had been difficult, and the child had died in her mother's womb. I had known the babe was dead, as had the mother, which was why she had no spirit to deliver. She was long past her youth, pregnant for the first time after years of yearning for a child. The woman was inconsolable. I had tried to give her some valerian tea to help her sleep, but she would not give up her grief. Her pain rent my own heart so, I could hardly bear it. It seemed to me it would have been better for her not to have conceived at all than to have had the joy of expectation turn to such grief. But I was not God and could not answer such questions.

I had washed the babe as I would any newborn, and, although none was needed to stave off infection, had rubbed salt and oil into her small torso and limp limbs. But for the mottled blue around her eyes and the cool pallor of her skin, she looked like any sleeping newborn. Her mother had insisted the child be given to her and had lain with the baby girl tucked into her bosom until finally falling into an exhausted sleep. I'd slipped the cold bundle from her mother's arms and given her to a servant, who removed her from the room, my heart breaking as she took the child away.

Two figures stood in the dawning light: Jacob and Reuben, in front of my tent, their faces grave. I thanked Eileon for seeing me home and approached the men. Had Reuben confessed? *Dear God, help him.* But it wasn't that. It couldn't be. There was no anger directed from Jacob toward his son, and Reuben's face showed none of the resentment a confrontation with his father would have caused. It was something else. A look of dread crossed their eyes as they met mine, and my hands began to shake.

"What is it? Just tell me!" I said, my lungs stilled, waiting for what I knew was no good news.

"Leah," Jacob said, his face discerningly pale even in the dim light. "Dinah did not return from the city with Timnah."

My lungs refused to expand. I couldn't move. "Wh . . . what do you mean? Where is she?"

Jacob's throat moved as he swallowed. "She is still at the palace."

"At the palace?" My heart slammed against my chest. "What are you talking about? Why is she at the palace?" The ground began to rock beneath me. Dinah at the palace? She had promised me she would stay with Timnah. And Timnah had promised she would take charge of her! They were to have returned in the afternoon. It was already morning!

Jacob drew a deep breath, which made my own catch within me.

"The palace guards who stopped the women on the street said the queen extends an invitation to a commoner during each festival—to dine in the palace as her guest. Timnah said Dinah was in her care, but since you knew the queen, she thought you wouldn't mind. The palace guard said she would be returned before dark."

What? "Dine with the queen? But the queen is not in the palace! She told me last time I was there she was going to the countryside, that I was to confer with her about her daughter-in-law when she returned—two days hence!"

Jacob blanched.

"Did you send someone to fetch her home when she didn't return at the set time?" My chest was swelling like an overripe melon, ready to burst open.

"I did," he said, gesturing towards Reuben. "I sent Reuben, and he was refused entrance. When he demanded to see his sister, the steward said that she was unwell and would be a guest of the palace until she was better. When Reuben tried to push his way in, guards escorted him out and told him not to worry, that his sister would be well taken care of, and he should not return until notified."

Bile rose in my throat, and I felt like I did when Beor tried to drown me. Only worse. Much worse.

"Don't worry, Leah," Jacob said, his hands suddenly on my shoulders. "We will get her back. I will go. They will return her to her father. I will send Reuben for a physician to await our return. I'm sure that it is nothing of consequence that has befallen her."

How could he be so ignorant? I shook my head.

"You are wrong. Something of great consequence has befallen her, and I know exactly what it is." I took a step back. "I will go. I am known at the palace, but not as Dinah's mother. I would be going in two days anyway, to check on the prince's wife. I will see what has become of Dinah with my own eyes."

Jacob nodded. Something in me wanted him to insist that he accompany me. But he didn't. And I had no time to concern myself with my husband now. In the end it was Reuben who said he would not be left behind.

The spring rains had come. My hair was sodden strings about my damp face. Reuben stayed out of sight with the donkey we'd brought to carry Dinah home, while I knocked on the door, my breath suspended. My lovely daughter was here. I had seen firsthand the horrors of this place, the tortuous treatment of Shechem's wife.

I knew my daughter was not here as a guest of the queen. It was the prince that had been responsible for my Dinah's presence in the palace, and I already knew why. The faint hope that she had escaped the prince's pleasure was nothing more than wishful thinking, but I would hang on to it as long as I could. Perhaps, by some miracle . . .

The door swung open, and the old man who received guests looked at me from my damp head to my muddy sandals.

Act natural, Leah. He doesn't know you're Dinah's mother.

My heart jittered in its place. I was here. Where was my daughter?

"The queen is not in the palace, mistress."

244

"I know. She told me to check on Sepha in her absence." I lied, hoping it wasn't written on my face.

He hesitated a long moment, then opened the door wide and stepped back. "I'll get a servant to bring a towel and a basin for your feet."

"It is not necessary. I need to see the princess now. I'll see myself to Sepha's room," I said, walking past him.

"But, mistress, your feet," the servant said as I moved ahead, knowing I was leaving a muddy trail on the polished stone floor.

I walked down the long hall, wondering where Dinah might be and decided I would go to Sepha's room as I had stated. She would help me if she could.

Sepha's door was open. She was seated on a stool. Her handmaid was winding her hair into curls and pinning it on top of her head. Sepha's face lit when she saw me.

"Leah. I am surprised to see you. I didn't expect you for another day or two."

Her countenance shadowed as she regarded me more closely. She asked the maid to leave and close the door after her.

"You look . . . terrible. Is something wrong?"

Sepha again reminded me of Dinah, with her large gentle eyes and her tender spirit. The tears appeared without permission, streaming down my cheeks. "My daughter. She is here in the palace. The prince . . . I fear."

Sepha's face paled. "No! Your daughter? It is your daughter?"

My legs felt boneless, and I gripped the edge of the table by my side to stay on my feet, the last of my hope slipping away. "You have seen her?"

Sorrow filled the girl's eyes. I knew she struggled to speak.

"Yes, I saw her. I didn't know it was your daughter, Leah. I would have tried to stop it. I promise you. I would have tried."

"I know you would have, Sepha, but it would have done no good. You could have done nothing to help my Dinah. Do you know where she is? What happened to her?" I pushed back hard at the tears.

"All I know is that a beautiful girl was brought into the palace by my husband's guards. Something was said about her dining with the queen. It caught my attention, since the queen is not here and the guards know it. So, when my husband told her the queen had taken ill, and the girl would dine with him in the queen's stead . . . I was jealous." She shook her head. "How could I be jealous, Leah? He mistreats me, and I am jealous?"

"It is a reasonable reaction," I said as I touched her arm, thinking how I was jealous every time another woman was in my husband's bed, no matter how I'd sworn to put Jacob from my mind and heart. "What happened next?" I asked, fearing the answer.

"He took her to a table set in the garden. I watched from behind the foliage. His back was to me, and I could see the girl's face plainly. She seemed nervous, and after they had eaten she asked to be taken home. Shechem said he would see to it as soon as she had a tour of the palace. They were gone for a while . . . then I saw him take her to his room." Sepha began to cry. "I'm so sorry, Leah. I truly am."

My heart felt dead as I looked at Sepha and faced what I knew to be true the moment my husband told me my beautiful daughter was in the palace. Beautiful. Beautiful enough to attract the attention of a prince. He had probably been stalking the streets full of women behind the curtains of his conveyance. A festival of women. What better place to find his prey?

A voice came from the doorway as the tall door groaned open.

"Sepha, I want you to . . ."

The voice stopped in mid-sentence. I turned, knowing the face I would see. Shechem looked surprised, but I saw nothing in his visage that said he knew I was Dinah's mother.

"Where is my daughter?' I said. "What have you done to her?"

It took a long moment for realization to register on his face, which immediately lost every bit of color.

"Your daughter?"

He knew it now.

"Yes. Dinah. What have you done with her?" I said, with a voice only a bit less dangerous than a mountain cat's.

"You have to leave." His voice quavered. He had threatened me before, and I'd countered in the name of the Most High God. He was afraid of me. He should be. I would kill him with my own hands, though he towered over me.

"You have to leave. Your daughter is not harmed. She is well, and . . . and she wants to stay here with me."

Fury burst through my veins like hot melted rock. "No! She doesn't want to stay here with you! She is my daughter. I am taking her home with me." I walked toward the door. He stood in front of me, his tall frame filling the doorway.

"No. You are not taking her," he said, trying to sound calm. "Not now. No harm will come to her. I want to marry her. I will speak with your husband."

What blood still flowed in my head drained to my toes. Marry her? My Dinah, marry this monster? Since Dinah was a toddler I had dreamed of the day she would marry. How proud I would be to be the mother of the most beautiful bride in the land. What would happen to her now? What man would want a girl spoiled even though not by her own choice? And I knew it was not by her choice. My Dinah would never go willing to this beast's bed.

I looked into Shechem's black eyes, thinking mine must match those of the mountain cat that'd come to mind a moment ago. "You will never marry my daughter. I will see you dead first."

His patience was done. "We will see about that. Now I want you to leave." He nodded toward a servant who had appeared behind him. "Show her to the door."

"I demand to be allowed to see her—so I know she's all right. Then I will go."

He shook his head. "She is well, and you will see her soon enough. Now leave!"

I locked eyes with the prince, seeing fear hiding behind the black orbs. "You will regret the day you touched my daughter. That I promise you."

The servant took me by the elbow. "Dinah!" I shouted. "Dinah, we will come for you! I promise!"

Shechem's face hardened. "Get her out of here now!"

CHAPTER THIRTY-TWO

Jacob

I had been watching for Leah and Reuben from the dooryard of my tent. A damp curtain of drizzle had made it difficult to distinguish one traveler from another on the dirt road. But even before I saw the riderless donkey, I knew the stooped frames in the distance were my wife and my son, and I knew my daughter wasn't with them.

The sick-at-the-stomach feeling I'd had since Timnah had come home without Dinah—saying she was at the palace, and wasn't that an honor?—intensified, and I thought I should take a bite of bread to keep from heaving in my dooryard. But Leah and Reuben were close enough now for me to see the pain in their eyes, and my own roiling gut would have to wait.

I walked toward them. Leah's hair was straight and wet around her pallid face. She looked at me and said Shechem had raped our daughter and was holding her at the palace, then swayed once or twice like a boat listing in a storm. I caught her before she hit the ground and carried her into her tent.

I laid her on her pallet, pulled the damp cloak from her shoulders and the muddy sandals from her feet, took a woolen blanket from the pile in the corner, and lay behind her, pulling the warm wool over us and tucking her into my chest. Recovered from her faint, she began to weep, her shoulders and chest moving in concert with the small sounds coming from deep within her. I tucked the damp tendrils of hair that lay over her cheek behind her ear and held her as she wept herself to sleep, my heart breaking with her pain and my own. "I love you, Leah," I said, knowing she couldn't hear me.

If only she knew how sorry I was for all the grief I'd caused her through the years. I couldn't put the blame on Rachel, although she'd made it plain that I couldn't love both Leah and her without paying a price for it. I hadn't done Rachel a service by allowing her such an ultimatum. I was a coward, and I'd let my love for Rachel do harm to both my wives.

God forgive me. This was all my fault. I should have said no when I felt Leah's hesitation. She had needed me to make that decision for her. And if I hadn't come to Shechem at all—if I'd followed my brother home—this would never have happened. Why had I refused to go to my father's tent? Was it pride, my worry that Esau might yet seem the victor if he had led me home like a vanquished foe? Could I not forgive my father? Or did I fear he would not forgive me? Was it because my mother wasn't there?

What would happen to Dinah? And could Leah survive it?

I pulled her closer, comforted by the rise and fall of her chest. *Forgive me, my love.*

Leah

I awoke from a dream. A horrible dream that my daughter had been raped and held against her will. It was only a moment before the truth struck at my heart, like an ax to the trunk of a tree. *Oh, Dinah.*

Jacob was gone. I knew it by the absence of his warmth. I hadn't fought against his presence in my bed—his arms around me, holding me tightly. If he hadn't, my mind and body might have drifted off in different directions, never to be one again. But I knew I'd pay in pain for those moments of comfort when there was no crisis to hold him to me. To his honor, he'd been there in the moment I had needed him most in all our years of marriage. But he did it for compassion's sake, to ease a mother's broken heart. Jacob didn't love me, and holding hope of that was only more pain, and at the moment, I couldn't take another bit of it.

Jacob was gone, but Zilpah was sitting beside me. I could smell the concoction of sesame oil and garlic on her arm. I didn't open my eyes. She knew I was awake, but she let me gather myself before she broke the silence. I sat up, my muscles sore for the tension that had wound them like a braided cord, and looked in my servant's face. The grief in her eyes bespoke her constant love for me. I reached for her and wept in her arms like a child.

I wiped my nose on the sleeve of my disheveled garment.

"Rachel came while you slept," she said. "I sent her away. I don't think she liked it very well. I hope I didn't do wrong, but I thought she'd make it about her own sorrow for her niece and how distraught she was for the situation, and you'd end up trying to comfort her instead of her comforting you."

"No," I said, thankful to my friend. "You did well. She may, indeed, need comfort, but I've none to offer at the moment."

"Jacob sent for Simeon and Levi," she said. "They were coming down the hill a moment ago. I thought you'd want to know."

I scrambled to my feet. "Thank you, Zilpah," I said, grabbing my sandals. They were sitting by the door of the tent free of mud. "And thank you for cleaning my sandals."

"It wasn't me." She shrugged.

Jacob must have done it. He'd taken time to clean my shoes? The small gesture moved me. I slipped them on my feet.

Simeon and Levi were just entering the camp. Simeon's eyes were wild, like his mass of coarse hair and beard. He was a dark image of his ruddy uncle Esau, with the temperament of the man in his youth.

Jacob motioned them to his tent. I followed. He held back the flap of the entrance for his sons and was startled to see me behind them. Women were not normally included in talk between fathers and sons, but he nodded toward the entrance and let me pass.

Reuben was sitting on the ground, his face full of sorrow and grief. Had he and Jacob been talking? Surely not about Bilhah. I had planned to tell Jacob today that his son had defiled his bed and beg for mercy, but it would have to keep for another day. I hoped Reuben would not unburden his soul now. The weight of my children's sorrows felt like bricks in a bag across my shoulders.

As soon as the flap fell closed behind us, Simeon railed his accusation. "Our sister has been defiled, and she is not yet recovered?" he said, a sharp line cutting between his brows. "What is being done?"

Jacob raked his hand through his graying hair, seeming older by years than he did a day ago.

"Nothing yet. Reuben went—and your mother." He shook his head. They wouldn't let Dinah leave."

"You sent our mother? Instead of going yourself!" Simeon said, his large hands white at the knuckles.

"He wanted to go," I said, feeling the need to defend Jacob. "I wouldn't let him. I thought it would be better if I went alone." But I hadn't gone alone. Reuben had refused to be left behind, and although having Jacob storm the palace may have done more harm than good, I wished he had insisted that he accompany me.

Neither boy attempted to hide his disdain.

"Well, we must go now! We will take all the servants. Hire an army if we must," Simeon said, his fiery eyes directly on his father.

"That will not be necessary. Hamor and Shechem are preparing to come to us," Jacob said, losing what color remained in his face. "He's coming . . . to make an offer of marriage."

An offer of marriage? They had come while I slept and Jacob hadn't woken me?

The boys' mouths dropped in unison. "He wants to marry her?" Levi said, his lips curling as though tasting the foul flavor of the words.

I remembered Shechem's words—and mine—that I would see him dead before allowing him to marry my daughter.

Jacob nodded. "So Hamor's guards say."

"And what did you tell the guards?" Simeon asked.

"I told them I must wait on the both of you. I needed time to think.'"

He took another long breath. "Whatever we do, we must do it with caution."

"Caution for what?" Levi said, his tone matching his brother's. "Our sister has been treated like a whore in the street, and we're to be cautious? We should find this coward and cut off his manhood for what he's done!"

Jacob looked weary next to his sons, who were shaking with anger. Somewhere inside I hurt for him, wanted to comfort him with my words.

But another part of me screamed silently. *Do something! Anything but sit there with that beaten countenance.*

Jacob's eyes turned to me, sorrowful—and something else.

"I wish to speak with your mother alone for a few moments." He gestured toward the doorway.

Simeon and Levi shook their heads and stood, looking at their father with scathing eyes. "Something must be done. Now!" Simeon said as he slapped the tent flap open. Reuben left without looking up.

When had my sons come to disrespect their father so? Had I not taught them better? *God, I am a wretched wife and a worse mother.*

When they were gone, Jacob stared at his sandals for several long moments. "Leah."

The air almost crackled between us, raising the hair on my arms, tasting brittle on my tongue. I wasn't going to like this.

He looked at me with sad eyes, his brow plowed with stress.

"Leah. Maybe . . . it would be best to let Shechem marry her."

His words bounced through my head, looking in vain for a place to land. What was he saying?

"No, Jacob. It would not be best," I said, panic filling my chest.

He ran his hand through his hair again. It was strange how I had always found the motion so attractive. Now it seemed rife with cowardice.

"Think about it, Leah. What man is going to want her now that she's defiled?"

What man is going to want her? My Dinah? Beautiful and kind of heart? The desire of so many? Oh, God. How can he think such a thing?

I fell to my knees in front of my husband and looked up at him like a supplicant begging for her life. "Jacob. I know this man. He is cruel. Please. Please. Do not consign our daughter to such a life."

"I love Dinah, Leah. I only want what is best for her."

"If you love her, do not do this, Jacob. To live a life without a husband's love is bad enough, but Shechem is a dangerous man."

I saw that my words pierced him. Who knew more than I about life without love? But did he not see the evil in this man? Was rape not enough evidence of it? I held my composure by a tenuous thread. *God, show mercy to my Dinah.*

"Leah, you speak from your grief," he said without reproach, "but

I fear that grief would only increase if you saw Dinah shunned and despised. And don't think it wouldn't happen. Some people will unfairly blame *her* for what happened. She went with the guards. They will say she was informed of the prince's intentions and invited them."

He squatted in front of me, lifting my trembling chin. I know this is not what either of us wanted for our daughter . . . but what if she's pregnant?"

My heart shuddered. The thought of Dinah carrying Shechem's child wrenched my stomach into tight knots.

"At least she would be protected from reproachful tongues. I know Shechem is not a good man, but he didn't cast our daughter aside without offering to do the honorable thing."

"The honorable thing?" My brows shot up. "The only honor this man has is that which is bestowed on him by a doting father. I would wish a child of his violence dead before I'd agree to see him marry Dinah. Please, I beg you, do not allow this marriage."

Shock juddered Jacob's muscles, as it did my own heart. How could I say such a thing? From what darkness of the soul did it spring?

Jacob pulled me up by the shoulders tenderly. "I don't believe you mean that, Leah—and I must do what I feel is best for Dinah."

My heart felt as though large hands had kneaded it into a lifeless lump. I shook my head, despairing that I had not convinced my husband of what I knew for a certainty—a marriage with Shechem could never be best for Dinah. Nothing was going to sway Jacob from whatever path he chose.

The flap opened, and Simeon and Levi returned. They must have listened through the joints of the tent panels and chose this moment to intervene, before their father declared something he could not recant. But where was Reuben? My son bore the double guilt of his own sin and what he saw as his part in Dinah's troubles. How could I bear the destruction of a son and daughter in the space of a week? I wanted to accuse God, but I couldn't. I'd just wished my own grandchild dead, if such a child existed. How could I put blame on anyone but myself?

I shook the thought out of my mind. Surely Dinah wasn't pregnant. But I had become with child the first night I lay with Jacob and had suffered my husband's and my sister's hatred for it ever since.

Simeon spoke, not waiting for permission. "Levi and I have an idea. We will not allow our sister to be treated like a whore. We can tell Hamor that we have agreed to give him Dinah and form an alliance with him, if he and his son and every man in the city are circumcised."

What? My head pounded with fear and confusion. Why would Dinah's brothers even consider giving her over to Shechem? And why circumcision?

Levi raised his hand just enough for me to see it without attracting his father's attention. Was it assurance in his motion—or a warning to stay in my place?

"We will promise trade and marriage between our tribes. Then, after three days, when all of the men are sore, we will demand that they meet us just outside the gates of the city. While some of us are at the gates, others will go to the palace and remove Dinah. There will be no one there to prevent us."

I could barely catch my breath. Would it work? At the least it would stall Jacob.

Jacob shook his head. "It will surely fail. They will not leave her unguarded, and I want no blood to be shed."

"It will not be that difficult to overcome a few guards. Bloodshed will not be necessary," Simeon said, his voice sharp.

Jacob shook his head. "I don't like it. We will be deceiving Hamor."

Levi's eyes were narrow slits. "Deception is nothing new in this family."

Jacob flinched with the force of Levi's words. I could see him gather every bit of his strength to answer.

"And what do you think they will do when they discover we have taken Dinah and they have been circumcised for nothing?"

Levi jerked his chin. "What can they do? They have no rightful claim on Dinah. They will be angry, but they will not risk retribution."

"We will stink in their eyes. We have prospered in this land. They will despise us. All that we have built here would be lost."

Jacob's words shot through me like an arrow. "What does it matter if we lose what we've built here, Jacob? We should never have come!" I was trembling, my voice clanging in my ears. "Why didn't you follow Esau home like you said you would? All these years, and you still haven't seen your father!"

Simeon and Levi looked shocked, their eyes so wide it appeared they might pop out of their sockets. They had never heard me raise my voice to my husband. To anyone. Anger and fear were rampaging through my mind, ripping up my reserve.

"Were you so afraid that Esau might renege and cause you harm? You should have feared for our children, Jacob! You put our children at risk by coming here!"

Jacob pressed his lips together for a long moment. But he didn't seem angry at my outburst. His watery black eyes were sorrowful.

"And if this plan fails, Leah?"

A spasm of panic juddered in my chest. It couldn't fail. The consequence was too terrible to consider.

Jacob turned to his sons. "We will try it. But no blood will be spilled."

Simeon looked at his father, the bones of his face set into hard lines. "Blood has already been spilled. On Shechem's sheets."

The thought of that sheet, soiled with my daughter's innocence, sent my emotions flying in all directions again. The sheet that should have been testament to her purity, displayed and celebrated with song and joyous dance at her wedding feast, was now a filthy rag, screaming profane desecration of what was good. *My lovely Dinah. Oh, God. Why?*

"You know what I mean," Jacob said to Simeon.

The boys left the tent, and Jacob turned to me. "I'm sorry, Leah. But if this doesn't work, I will be forced to allow the marriage, if Shechem even wants it after being duped. I don't know what else to do."

I didn't reply. There was nothing more to say.

CHAPTER THIRTY-THREE

Leah

It was less than an hour when Hamor and Shechem dismounted their scarlet-draped camels in front of our tents, flanked by several palace guards with swords strapped at their sides. I wondered if the men who took Dinah from the streets of the city were among them, and if they cared at all for the sorrow that had followed.

Shechem's dark good looks mirrored his father's but for the touch of gray in Hamor's beard. The silver and gold threads of their garments caught the sun, bright after the morning rains.

Shechem's gaze skirted mine, then jerked away. It was all I could do to keep from throwing myself on him—tearing his black eyes out of his head, but I held myself.

"Greetings, Lord Jacob." Hamor bowed low, meant to be a sign of humility in the face of a man of wealth and power. He paused for a few long moments, giving opportunity for Jacob to extend hospitality, which did not come. Good.

The governor seemed rankled but apparently decided not to address the slight.

Surely, he couldn't expect a cordial greeting from the man whose daughter his son had raped, although I was certain Hamor held the same sense of entitlement as Shechem.

"I have come to speak to you about your daughter, Dinah."

Jacob crossed his arms over his chest. "And of what did you wish to speak?"

Jacob was not going to make it easy for Hamor. I hoped he would demand that his daughter be returned immediately. Maybe an appeal to Shechem's father might be more fruitful than had my appeal to his son.

I watched Shechem, hoping he would look at me again, but he positioned his head to avoid even an accidental glance. For some reason, the prince was afraid of me. The knowledge filled me with satisfaction.

Hamor straightened his back and squared his shoulders. "We are both men of influence, Jacob. You have prospered a great deal since I allowed you to pitch your tents outside our city."

"You forget—I purchased the land on which we stand. The land is mine. I do not need your permission to pitch my tents."

Irritation flitted through Hamor's eyes, but he bowed again. "Forgive me, Lord Jacob. You are correct. We have been partners in business and have both been the better for it. How much more good would come if our houses were united. You may live in the shadow of our city for as long as you desire, and our daughters can marry your sons and your daughters can marry our sons. We will be a powerful people, made safe by our alliance."

Hamor touched his son's shoulder. "Your daughter has found favor in my son's eyes. He wishes to take her as his wife."

My stomach sickened. Favor? That is what he calls it?

The prince stepped forward, his neatly bearded chin high. "Ask whatever bride price you desire. I will pay it. I have come to love your daughter. I promise that I will care for her."

Care for her? I couldn't help myself. The anger frothed in me. I knew it was not considered proper for me to speak, but I would not be quieted. "As you care for your pregnant wife?" I fairly screamed. "Taking her by brutal force as surely as you have taken my daughter?" My thought went to the sounds I had heard in the palace. Sounds of violent intercourse with a pregnant woman. This man was a beast, and he would not marry my Dinah! Not as long as I breathed a breath!

"Leah." Jacob was trying to quiet me. Angry tears soaked my cheeks. I looked my husband in the eyes. "Do not think to keep me quiet! I have seen what this man does to the women he claims to love. He is the devil himself! Our daughter will not marry such a man, Jacob!"

I expected Jacob to strike me down, at least with his words, but he didn't. He took me by the shoulders and spoke in my ear. "Trust me, Leah. Please."

Trust him? Could I? My body was shaking, and I thought my heart would explode with grief. *Dinah! Dinah!*

Simeon and Levi presented the proposition they had devised to Hamor and his son. Hamor blanched, but Shechem spoke boldly.

"We will speak with the men of the city. They will agree, I am certain, and I will be the first to submit to this rite," he said with another haughty lift of his chin.

The prince was trying to show his intentions honorable. But there was no honor in him. Being his father's favorite did not make him an honorable man, and no amount of pretended nobility would make him fit for my only daughter.

When the prince and his father had mounted their camels and turned toward the city, I turned toward my tent without a look toward Jacob. He had asked me to trust him, but my daughter was still in the palace, and she would stay there for at least another three days. I didn't think I could live that long.

Jacob

I stood at the door of Bilhah's tent, still uncertain if I should enter. The past two days had been full of worry and constant speculation. I had gone from one thought to another with regularity, and I had never felt more alone. The night had come, and I needed comfort. Comfort I could not ask of Rachel, large with child. Or of Leah, filled with grief. Zilpah? I had not lain with Zilpah in years, and I feared her discomfort would make it impossible to find relief. I had lain with Bilhah only a few times since the last of our sons was born. Sometimes in secret, but more than once when Rachel and I were angry. I'd told Rachel she would rue the day she'd forced me into another woman's bed, and in anger I'd tried to prove it. But I wasn't angry now. I was broken and in need of mending.

I feared my son's plan would fail, and I feared it would succeed. Neither option offered a satisfactory solution. Its failure would bring scorn upon us all and perhaps put Dinah in a worse position than she was now. The advantage would be turned in a marriage negotiation. And Hamor might not even consider one after being deprived of his foreskin.

And if my sons succeeded in fetching Dinah from Shechem's bed? What would her life be? Leah thought I didn't care, and I gave no blame for that, but I did care. I cared very much. Dinah had won my heart from the first time I saw her with her curly head of black hair, looking so much like I imagined my mother must have looked as a newborn, and my imagination had proven true. As a young woman, Dinah was a mix of my mother and my grandmother: two of the most beautiful women who ever lived.

And Dinah's heart was gentle and loving, thanks to her mother's will to see it so. I regretted that I'd spent so little time with my daughter. Like most men, I'd left her raising to her mother. No matter what other men did, I should have been a better father to all my children, but especially to my little girl.

My thoughts made me want to mount a beast and head toward Shechem, returning only with my daughter or dead, on the back of my donkey. But I had been the one to caution against such actions. Was I right? I had no idea anymore.

I raked my hands through my hair at the door of Bilhah's tent. Why should I feel this a betrayal—to Rachel, to Leah? She was my concubine. She had borne me two sons. I had every right to go in to her. I heaved a deep breath.

The tent was small. Bilhah turned at the sound, and her face became that of a dead woman.

I started at the fear so evident on her visage. Why would Bilhah fear me? Surprise I could well understand, but what she wore was terror. I hesitated, the tension in my forehead pulling my brows together.

"Bilhah? What is it? Are you that surprised to see me come into your tent?"

Her face was white.

"You didn't think you still had an obligation to me?" If it were possible, her face grew paler yet.

I began to feel a flush of anger edging up my body. I had come for comfort, not to be greeted by unwarranted fear. Then Bilhah collapsed on the dirt mumbling incoherently. I could make out only that it was a plea for her life. She thought I was here to kill her? Anger was replaced by complete confusion—then cold comprehension.

Leah

It seemed our whole camp had gathered outside the city gates, anxious lest they miss the excitement. Who had asked the servants, the metalworkers, and herdsmen? And children? Women talked in tight circles, their children at their skirts! These women would call themselves my friends. Why was everyone here to see this farce? Men I did not recognize milled through the crowd, as though trying to blend in. Who were they? Spies sent by Hamor to harm us?

Streaks of sunlight striped the cold gray wall that surrounded the city. I'd always thought walls were to keep people from getting in: opposing sovereigns with their armies at their backs. But now I saw the palace walls as stony-faced prison guards, keeping my daughter from getting out.

Never had there been a longer three days. I could only imagine what Dinah thought, how she felt when no one came to rescue her. Surely, she knew that I had tried. That I had done all I could.

Zilpah stood beside me. Rachel was in her tent. I'd sent word for her to stay there. She shouldn't be standing for long periods in her condition. But truth be told, I didn't want her here. I didn't want another thing to worry about. Zilpah took my hand and squeezed it. Her mouth opened and closed again, as if she wanted to say something and didn't have the courage.

"Leah. Your God is good, is He not?"

The question took me aback. Was He good? Did I doubt it, now in this time of adversity? No. I didn't think I did, but I didn't understand either. I presumed God was good by His very nature, but He must withhold favor from the undeserving, must He not? I had done so much wrong. Maybe even a good God could not hear the prayers of such a wicked woman.

"If He is good, then will not good come from this terrible thing?"

I didn't have an answer, and Zilpah didn't press for one. It was hard to fathom any good could come from this.

The tall metal gate scraped open. Hamor and Shechem emerged from the entrance, carried in an open conveyance by shirtless men with sunbaked shiny skin who seemed hardly able to walk. We were practically in the shadow of the city but too far for the sovereign and his son to make it on their own, it seemed. Palace guards wearing short skirts, tall boots, and pointed copper helmets followed them with stiff, stilted steps. A fan of men of all ages minced its way behind. The city was small, but it seemed too few men were gathered. Had some refused to follow the prince's directive? Or were they lying in wait by the palace door, expecting trouble?

I saw guards in the towers that flanked the gate and wondered if my sons had considered that they would be watched from above. How could this plan work? But it had to. If it didn't, my daughter would remain in the palace with Shechem, and that I could not bear.

Hamor bowed before Jacob and spoke, gesturing toward the men shifting from one leg to the other. "My son and I and every male in the city have submitted to the knife of circumcision. I have to say, I don't understand why your god would require such a rite from his worshipers, but we have done what you asked."

Shechem grimaced as he stepped forward, waving to servants on either side of him. Each laid treasure at the feet of my husband and my sons: robes, armor, silver goblets, jewels, fine fabrics, and tapestries. Some I thought I had seen on the palace walls. I didn't want any of this! My sons would have to return it when Dinah was recovered!

"Lord Jacob, I offer all this as a bride price, and if it does not satisfy, I will offer more. Your daughter's worth cannot be measured in gold and garments or precious stones. Ask what you will, and I will give it."

Anger rose in me. *All I want from you is my daughter!*

Simeon stepped out from the crowd. His rugged face was unreadable, showing none of the wrath I knew raged within him. He waved an arm back at the women. "You see here our daughters who will be your daughters, our sons who will be your sons. We will be one people. We accept your bride price."

He said the words so convincingly, I worried for a moment that he spoke the truth, and I was the one who had been deceived into believing this was a hoax.

Reuben stood behind his father and his brothers. He should have been beside Jacob, but I knew his own mountain of guilt held him back. Behind Reuben were Issachar and Zebulun, watching wide-eyed. I wished for Judah to be here, but he was almost always gone. My heart was grieved over the state of my family.

Shechem glanced at me as the servants bore the gifts toward our camp. There was a glint of triumph in his heavily lashed eyes. I had told him to his face he would never marry my daughter, and now he gloated over his perceived victory. I hoped that I could see him face-to-face when Dinah was out of his grasp. He wouldn't be gloating then.

My eyes flitted to the guard towers. They were empty. No scarlet-clad soldiers. Where had they gone? Who was going for Dinah? Levi, Simeon, Reuben, and the younger boys were here. Had they sent servants, or were they going to run to the open gate and close it behind them? How would they get Dinah out of the city? So many questions I hadn't asked. Fear was creeping up my spine. Something wasn't right.

As I looked around, I saw an almost imperceptible stilling of my sons and the male servants and the men I had seen in the crowd who I had mistakenly thought to be Hamor's spies, as though they all paused in unison waiting on some mark. Then, as one man, they pulled knives and swords from beneath their garments and rushed toward the men of Shechem.

My skin began to prickle and hairs stood upright, as though attempting to loose themselves from the grip of my skin. Everything around me seemed to slow, like a dream. I saw my husband's mouth open around a silent *no*, but it was too late. Screams echoed like distant panicked birds as the women—supposed friends who had brought their children to see my daughter's shame—ran back toward our camp.

Swords slashed and blood spurted and flowed, as the sounds of death floated eerily on the air. Simeon strode toward the prince, who seemed too stunned to turn and run away. I saw the sword as Simeon pressed it into Shechem's chest and pulled it out again, red with the blood of my daughter's rapist.

The prince looked at me, still upright, shock in his wide eyes, his body rigid and straight, as though he had turned suddenly to stone. His eyes stayed on mine as the red stain widened on his fine garment. He blinked then slipped, seemingly boneless, to the ground. I had said I'd see him dead before I'd let him marry my daughter—and I had.

I waited for the sense of exultation that should have been expanding my lungs over the brutal death of the man I hated most in all the world, but it didn't come. Instead, I saw his mother's face, and I wanted to weep. Was her son's act more evil than Simeon's or Levi's? Did she love her child less than I loved my own? I fell to my knees and retched.

Suddenly, arms were around my waist, lifting me from the ground. Jacob set me on my feet and grabbed my hand. "Run, Leah."

My legs wouldn't move, but Jacob jerked me forward, and I found my feet beneath me. I kept trying to look back and stumbled several times.

When we were a good distance away, we stopped to catch a breath and looked back toward the city. Bodies lay before the gates like slaughtered kine. Dear God, what had our sons done?

Deep fear wound around me. Would word of this massacre reach the palace before Dinah could be rescued? Who was guarding her? Would they kill her in their vengeance? My heart felt like wheat crushed on the threshing floor.

Jacob turned me to him, his hands on my shoulders, trying to comfort me. I moved out of his grip, pulled myself up, and walked toward my tent. I would not look on the face of my husband or my sons until Dinah was safely home.

CHAPTER THIRTY-FOUR

Leah

Splintered bits of conversation stirred me. I had gone to my tent to pray for Dinah and had fallen asleep in my grief. I heard female voices talking in low tones, an excited murmur. I jumped up and opened the flap. The same women who were at the gate were again standing about in small groups, whispering behind their hands. Reuben was lifting Dinah off a donkey and into his arms. She was wrapped in her brother's cloak, hair loose around her pale face. I ran toward her.

Dinah! I pressed my head to her cheek. Her tears dampened my face.

"Leave," I shouted at the gawking crowd. "Bring her into my tent."

I threw the extra blankets rolled in a corner onto the pallet. Reuben gently laid his sister on the bed and took her hand in both of his. "I'm so sorry, Dinah."

He rose and looked at me, grief and guilt brimming in his eyes. "I'm sorry, Mother."

I knew he was speaking of more than his pleading Dinah's cause about the festival. He was sorry for adding to my grief. My son was a good man. But he had been foolish, and I knew not what price we both would pay for it.

When the flap of the tent fell behind him, I knelt beside the broken bundle lying on the pallet.

"Dinah." I smoothed her hair off her brow. "My daughter, my daughter."

Her eyes met mine, and in them I saw all that had happened to her. Pain as I had never known pierced my soul.

I stayed in the tent, allowing no one but Zilpah, who brought tea, which I forced Dinah to drink. When she would not be comforted, I lay beside her, pulling her into my arms as she mourned her virginity with gasps and deep moans.

"I'm sorry, Mother," she said between racking sobs. "I should have done what you told me. I should have stayed with Timnah."

"Shhh." I stroked her hair and whispered softly. "This is not your fault, Dinah. Rest now. Rest, my dearest." I held her close and rubbed small circles on her back as she lay tucked into my side, her head on my chest, her breath catching in little spasms as it had when she was a child, crying herself to sleep.

It isn't your fault, my love. It's mine. Where was I when my daughter needed me? Putting someone else's child before my own.

Dinah was in an exhausted sleep. I heard a cacophony of sounds in the camp. Sheep? Women crying? I threw back the tent flap. The glare of the sun stung my tear-swollen eyelids.

I had thought no more evil could come of this, but I was wrong. Sheep and goats and all manner of livestock were being driven into our pens, bleating and bawling in protest as the men forced them into the too-small enclosures. But the animals were lost to me next to the sight of women and children herded by Levi and Simeon and my younger sons, Issachar and Zebulon, the handmaiden's sons, servants, and strangers. The terror and grief on the captives' faces stole my breath, like a hand at my throat, choking me until I was dizzy.

I saw Zilpah standing close by, her mouth hanging open in shock, and shouted at her to look after Dinah. I ran toward Simeon. A long red trail stained the front of his garment where he had wiped his bloody hand across his chest. Flecks of blood dotted his face and beard, his clothes. Blood had dried and caked on his arms. The sharp smell of him sickened me. Who was this bloody man? Not my son!

"What have you done? Why are these women and children in our camp? Why have you done such evil?"

Simeon looked at me with what could only be judged as madness. "I have avenged my sister—your daughter. I have dealt the blow that sets the matter right in the sight of God and man, and I would think in your sight most of all."

God surely saw no right in this horror. How different were my sons from the man who had defiled my daughter? These were the boys I had held to my breast? These were the children I had counted as blessings from the Most High God? *God have mercy.*

"You have set nothing right, Simeon. These women and children did not defile your sister, and you have defiled her honor—not defended it—by laying a hand to them!"

Simeon stood still for several long moments, like an image carved in stone, his eyes dead. I thought, perhaps, he'd heard my words, but he moved on, yelling at a servant to keep his charges in line. I turned and vomited on the ground. I wiped my mouth with my sleeve, the bitter taste of bile and grief on my tongue.

I scanned the group of mourning souls for Sepha, but I didn't see her. Had she been hurt in the melee? What about the baby? Then I saw a face I never thought to see. Kishara, her emerald gown soiled at the knees where she'd fallen in the dirt. Her neck and arms and fingers bare, absent of the treasure she usually wore. Levi was pushing her along with a group of weeping women.

I ran toward them. "Levi! Stop!" The boy stopped and looked at me as I approached, as though he wasn't sure if he should listen to his mother's voice anymore. "Stop! Now!" He stopped in his place.

Kishara's elaborate hairdo was undone and in disarray. Streaks of kohl made dark, damp trails down her face. It was a moment before recognition reached her tortured eyes.

I pulled her out of the group. Levi gave me a look that said I had no say in this matter, but I would have beat upon him with my own fists if he'd tried to stop me. I supposed he sensed it and stepped aside, sending the other women along with one of the servants.

"Kishara." It was the only word that would come out of my mouth. What could I say to this woman whom my sons had rousted out of the palace as if she were one of the animals?

"Leah," she said, her voice thin and trembling.

"Where is Sepha? Is she here?" I asked.

She shook her head. "No. No pregnant women, they said."

Sepha. Would she be all right? Then the thought settled hard on me. Shechem was dead. Hamor was dead. Sepha's child might be in more danger than ever. But what could I do about it now? Nothing. I could only pray God would protect mother and child.

"I wish I had never met you," Kishara said, her lip trembling, tears spilling over the dark trail on her cheeks. The words slapped me as hard as her hand would have.

She didn't rail. She spoke calmly, as though reciting an observation. "If I'd never met you, my son would not be dead. My husband would not be dead. I rue the day you stepped into the palace."

Was she right? I had told Shechem I would see him dead before I let him marry my daughter. My heart shuddered in its cage. I had wished this woman's child dead, and he had died.

But Kishara had stood by while her son abused his wives. And Dinah probably wasn't the first woman he had raped. Hamor had tried to cover his son's crime by legitimizing it with an offer of marriage, and he'd sought to profit from his son's bad behavior with a trade alliance.

I wished I'd never met Kishara, as well.

"Mother." Levi was at my side. "I need to take her, now."

I looked at my son. He was as dead-eyed as Shechem had been before he fell.

"No! You will take your younger brothers and accompany the queen back to the palace after you have returned her jewelry and any item of hers you took. You will let her point out her servants and take them as well. You will do this now!"

Levi stood for a moment, then nodded. He took Kishara by the arm. She didn't look back, and I was glad.

PART SIX

The Homecoming

CHAPTER THIRTY-FIVE

Leah

The entire camp was standing in a field, which, after the early spring rains, had begun to bloom with small blue and yellow flowers. Lovely blooms, trampled by the multitude. Was everything lovely doomed to be trodden underfoot?

I'd left Dinah in the tent, telling Jacob she was too weak, both physically and emotionally, to stand for such a time. The odor of the crushed flowers sweetened the air. My heart twisted, and I put thumb and forefinger to my eyes to press back the tears. How could such sweetness come from destruction? I hoped it was true of more than flowers.

Jacob stood beneath a large sprawling oak that spread its budding limbs toward the sky as if in supplication.

He had called the people together to tell them that we were leaving, going to Bethel and then to his father's home in Hebron. He said the city's neighbors, Canaanites and Perrizites—tribes that had sought our favor only a short time ago, postured for it—must now consider us barbarians. He feared they would join together to drive us out of this land.

A thick-waisted woman standing in front of me leaned to her husband. "Moving? Again? What about our booths in the city? Our vegetables and wool cloth? Does Jacob care nothing for that?" Her husband put a gentle elbow to her side and discreetly nodded toward me. She turned her head and saw me looking at her. Her eyes went wide, and she quickly faced forward. I could see the scarlet moving up her neck.

She wasn't the only one complaining. Snatches of discontent rode on murmurs through the crowd. What were these people thinking? That life could just continue in Shechem as it was before the massacre? Jacob had made Simeon and Levi and all who had participated return the survivors to the city with their animals and goods, but they couldn't return to them their husbands, their sons and brothers. Did the woman in front of me really think they would welcome our vegetables?

Jacob's visage had changed. His face was drawn with grief. He was telling the people he'd sinned by allowing them their gods. Every idol, every earring forged from amulets dedicated to false deities, incense and the clay pots in which it had burned, must all be brought to the foot of the oak where he stood. Those who wanted to leave now were welcome to, but any found hiding such abominations would face expulsion with nothing but the clothes on their backs, and, most importantly, they risked the wrath of God.

Rachel's face was ashen, and she averted my gaze. Why? Why would Rachel be disturbed by Jacob's remarks? A prickle of understanding began to bud in my mind, and I thought I might be sick. It was Rachel. She was the one who had stolen Father's household gods!

Why hadn't I realized it before? She'd gone to her tent as soon as Jacob had announced the person found with my father's gods would die. I remembered considering it might be her, but I didn't truly believe she would do such a foolish thing. It would have assured that Father would follow us. Which he did! And now Jacob had given another threat of reprisal. *Rachel!*

I followed my sister to her tent. "You took Father's gods! Do you still have them?"

Of course she did. The look on her face when Jacob spoke was proof enough of that. "Where are they?" I looked around. Foolish. She wouldn't have left them in plain view. "You have to take them to Jacob, Rachel. You have to leave them beneath the tree. You heard what he said."

"I can't do that, Leah," she said, her face pleading. "What will the people think of me? What will Jacob think?"

Fury rose in my chest. "You foolish woman! You have brought evil into the camp and upon your own soul! What does *God* think, Rachel?

272

Have you considered that? Where have you hidden them?" I picked up her saddlebags and pulled them open. Nothing.

Rachel shook her head, her eyes wide and frightened. "Don't, Leah. I'll take care of it."

"As you did before? You must have hidden them while Father searched! Why didn't you leave them behind? If you won't get them, I will tear your tent to shreds until every possible place has been searched. You will not keep those abominations in this camp!"

I walked to a tall pot on the floor filled with grain and turned it over. Barley spread across the ground in a brown wave; a plume of fine chaff filled the air. I put my hand over my nose and closed my eyes. My eyes would be red-veined and miserable within minutes.

Rachel wrung her hands. "Please, Leah. Look what you've done. Jacob will ask what happened!"

"Jacob will know what happened!" I wiped my eyes with my sleeve, then upturned every pot and pulled out every basket, emptying them on the rug. Would she have hidden them somewhere outside? No. She wouldn't chance someone coming upon them, and she would want them accessible if she were making offerings to them. The thought lanced my heart. Surely, she would not. But of course she would! I had to find them.

I pulled up a corner of rug covering the dirt floor and saw where the earth was not hard-packed. Loose soil covered something. I dusted it off with a sweep of my hand and saw a wooden box. I pried open the lid. Stone eyes looked up at me.

"Please, Leah, don't break them."

Don't break them? She didn't want me to destroy them? That's all that mattered to her?

I gathered the idols in my arms and stormed past Rachel—who was weeping and begging me not to do this—toward the oak tree where my husband stood. The closer I came, the thicker the air felt, until I resisted breathing it in. It slipped through my mouth and nostrils like a snake, and I felt my lungs heavy with it. On the pile of idols and earrings and amulets, I saw a glint of orange and remembered the carnelian that had cost me Anasa and knew I had been right to reject it. I tossed the lifeless images onto the pile without reverence and stared at my husband, who was staring back at me, his face in shock.

"Leah?"

"My father's household gods."

"But where? Surely, you . . ."

His face paled with understanding.

"Rachel?"

"Yes. Rachel."

"But . . . your father searched the camp. He searched your tents." He scrubbed a hand over his face. The color had drained from it and left him looking suddenly older by years.

"I cursed my own wife. If Laban had found them in her tent . . ." He shook his head.

Anger stirred within me. At this moment, I was filled with a deep loathing for the man I had so longed for.

"You got what you wanted, Jacob. What you deserved. But I didn't blame you for choosing Rachel over me," I said, tears filling my eyes. "I didn't hold it against you. Everyone had always chosen Rachel. Why would you have been any different? I could have lived with it, even though I loved you the first moment I saw you, just as you loved Rachel."

He seemed surprised by my words. He opened his mouth as if to speak, then closed it, sorrow slipping over his features.

I felt all the rejection, the ache of heart, the loneliness rise up from the depths of me. Every bit of hurt pushing past all that had kept it hidden. It lay like half-devoured prey, with muscle and sinew torn to shreds and blood congealing over jagged rips of flesh. The sting of salt rubbed into wounds without thought for the pain that it would cause.

I was trembling now. "You made me pay a high price for what I did; I paid with my self-respect, my hope of finding love. Even ugly girls need love, Jacob."

His head came up, a frown forming between his furrowed brows. "I never thought you ugly, Leah. Never! You were beautiful to me until—"

"Until I did what I had no choice but to do."

He shook his head. "I know that. I always knew it. I—"

"Please. Just let me speak, Jacob." I wanted no half-measured apology from my husband. "I didn't expect you to love me more than Rachel, or love me the way you love her. I would have settled for the slightest show of affection. I thought providing you with sons would render me worthy of some consideration in your eyes, but it didn't," I said, tears now flowing freely down my face. I was letting it all out, searching for every bit of pain I'd ever felt at my husband's hand, forcing him to look at it. To leave one word unsaid would be to let it all begin again.

"And even my children felt the resentment you held for me. Especially Reuben, who did nothing but try to please you. But you were too afraid of Rachel to love your own son."

I saw the truth of it in the furrow of his brow—and in his eyes, dark and troubled. He had sacrificed his son to Rachel's jealousy.

A painful tightness in my throat choked the words as they worked their way to my tongue. Words that could wait no longer. My lips were trembling.

"And now you have a reason to hate him—he has lain with your concubine. I caught him in the act."

I waited to see the shock and the eruption of anger on Jacob's face, but it didn't come. His arms hung limp at his sides.

"I know, Leah."

I couldn't speak. He knew? But how? I knew Reuben hadn't told him.

"I went to Bilhah."

"She told you?"

He shook his head. "She didn't have to."

I was trembling now. All the anger that had driven me a moment ago transformed into a mountain of fear. "What are you going to do?"

He shook his head. "I don't know. I don't know."

I heard my heart as it cracked open, the sound like the snap of a twig under a heavy foot. What would Jacob do? Would he stone them or drown them? Would he banish Reuben so I would never see his face again?

My God. My God.

Who was I to blame Jacob for anything? I had done so much wrong myself. I'd laid my son's wickedness at Jacob's feet, but it was as much my fault as his.

Everything drained from me. I turned and walked away from my husband. Empty of anger. Empty of hatred. Full of nothing.

275

Leah

The tents had been dismantled, folded tight and smooth, and laid on the backs of braying donkeys.

Herdsmen had already begun to move the oxen and cattle, and shepherds were guiding the speckled flocks across the valley. We were going back to Jacob's home. Finally.

Dinah walked beside me looking small and tired. This was the first time she'd been seen in public since Reuben had lifted her off the donkey and carried her to my tent.

I could see it in their eyes, the women with their curious looks, averted quickly when they saw me looking back at them. Their conversations stopping short when we came within hearing distance. They were wondering if Dinah was carrying Shechem's child. My beautiful daughter, who had been admired by all, now the subject of cruel gossip and speculation. I took her hand and held it as we walked. My sweet Dinah. How had our lives changed so much in such a short time?

Was she pregnant? I tried not to think about the possibility; it was too painful.

I thought about the prince, eyes locked with mine as he slipped like an empty garment to the ground, glad that he could never hurt another woman's daughter.

I looked back at the city, shrinking in the distance, and wished I'd never seen the stone walls of Shechem. And hoped I never would again.

CHAPTER THIRTY-SIX

Leah

I was bending over the cook fire, feeding small twigs and dried leaves into the fledgling flame, when Zilpah came toward me, her face in an angry knot. I stood. What could have my friend in such a state?

"What is it, Zilpah?"

She could barely speak.

"It's Timnah," she said. "I heard her talking with some women." Her lips pressed into a tight line. "She said Dinah left her care without permission. That she flaunted herself before the men in the city. She said she probably went to Shechem's bed willingly, and she's carrying his bastard child."

Shock tore through my body. Jacob had said Timnah allowed Dinah to go with the guards, even touting it as a great honor. She'd left my daughter in the city alone and returned bragging that Dinah was dining with the queen. I couldn't catch my breath.

"Thank you, Zilpah. Please watch the fire." Zilpah nodded, her eyes still burning.

It didn't take long to find Timnah among the black tents. She was still standing in a cluster of women, talking in hushed tones. One of the women saw me coming. Her eyes opened wide, and she looked back at Timnah and nodded at me. When Timnah saw me, her face turned white. I had been so angry when Zilpah told me of the woman's betrayal, I thought I might slap her when I saw her, but I contained the urge.

"Leah," Timnah said, as though she was going to offer a greeting—but she knew I had not come to visit.

I stopped in front of her. I could see the tremor in her hands.

"I entrusted you with my most precious possession, Timnah, and you failed to keep her safe. You promised me you would not let Dinah out of your sight, and you left her in the hands of a fiend. We will be in Bethlehem in two days. You and your family are to separate yourself from the group when we get there. You will be given provisions enough to last until you can find employment. But if I hear you have spoken another word against my daughter, you will be put off on the side of the road with nothing. Do you understand?"

"Leah, I, I didn't mean . . . I'll never do it again. I promise. I only said . . . please don't make us leave."

"Do you understand!"

She bowed her head. "Yes."

I looked at the other women. They turned away and scurried off to their own fires.

∞∞∞∞∞∞∞∞∞∞∞

I walked by Zilpah, who had water boiling for stew, and into her tent, where I kept the bags and baskets of herbs I used to make medicines. I pulled out the small bag of Cyrenic balm and other herbs that were necessary for my purpose. The flap opened behind me. Zilpah stood at the door, silent for several long moments.

"What are you doing, Leah?"

"Where's the rue seed? I know I brought it."

"Rue seed? Why do you need rue seed?"

I continued searching through the baskets, not stopping to answer Zilpah.

"Leah, you know combined with . . ." She looked at the herbs in my hand. "It will cause a woman to cast off the child in her womb."

"Yes. I know that, Zilpah. Where is it?"

I'd never used the herbs in the combination required to end a pregnancy, though I'd been asked many times. But I would do it to save my daughter the shame she would face if she bore a child unwed. If I did it now, it would take care of it before she missed her blood. I picked up another basket and searched through it.

"I found it," I said, starting for the door.

"Leah."

I stopped, not wanting to look back at my handmaid. But when I turned, her face was drawn with sadness and concern.

"You've never done this before, Leah. You said—"

"I know what I said, Zilpah, but this is my daughter."

"You know sometimes things don't go well. There can be problems."

"There are already problems, Zilpah. I can't see Dinah shamed like this."

"What do you think your God would think about this, Leah?"

"I doubt He'd even notice—since He didn't notice Dinah when she was being raped!" My conscience smarted for the words I'd spoken, but I hardened my heart against it.

Zilpah put her hand on my shoulder. "I know you're in pain. But this is not something the woman I know and love would do."

I looked at her, tears welling in my eyes. "I don't know that woman anymore, Zilpah," I said and walked into the warm sun.

Jacob

The journey from Shechem to Luz, the city I called Bethel, was only a few short days, then another two or three to Hebron. I'd lived in the shadow of my father's home for over three years and hadn't gone to see him. Why? What excuse was there for such behavior?

Why had I not come directly here, to the place where God had spoken to me when I fled Esau's wrath? I'd heard the voice from the stairway, saying He wouldn't leave me and He would bring me again to this place. And yet I'd chosen to settle in Shechem, the city from which so much heartache had come.

God had said all the families of the earth would be blessed from my seed, but my household was in disarray. How could anything good come from men who took the sword to innocents or chose to dwell with foreign women? Did I fear my father's rejection? Or that he would see what a terrible father I was?

I could see the stone pillar on the side of the hill where I had slept my first night away from home. I was surprised it still stood, as hastily as I had raised it. Perhaps God had watched over it, knowing that I would come again, just as He had watched over me while I lived apart from it.

The pillar was nothing more than a long piece of rock on which I'd spread my cloak and laid my head that night, weary from my journey. I'd struggled to right it and had gathered stones and piled them at the base of it to keep it standing as a memorial of the visitation I'd had from God.

And now I had returned. To what end? Could God restore all that had been spoiled by my choices? I knelt before the stone wondering why God could even look upon me, as filthy as I was. I spread myself on the ground, my face in the dirt, my tears turning it to mud.

"O God of my fathers. Forgive me. I've returned a sinner just as I left. I'm a weak man. My heart yearns for you, but I continue to follow my own path. To wander from your way. How can you bear the sight of me? I am a stench in my own nostrils. Strengthen me, God, that I might be a man after your heart. Forgive me. Forgive my children. Forgive my wives. Forgive my servants and my herdsmen. Forgive every soul you have put in my charge. Let us not forget the God who spoke and the waters separated. Who said, 'Let there be light,' and the light drove away the darkness. Let us remember who created the kine and the ass and sparrow that does not fall to the ground without your notice. Let our hearts be turned toward you and your gracious mercy. Let us come to the end of our lives full of days, having finished our course with honor."

I lay on my belly for a long while, weeping, repenting, wondering what I should do about Reuben. How I could make up for all I'd done to Leah. What would become of Dinah.

Jacob.

I wasn't certain if I dreamed or was awake, but I heard a voice like a gentle rippling of grass by an unseen hand. It was calling my name.

I kept my face in the dirt, fearing to look up.

You have called yourself Jacob. Others have called you Jacob. But I have called you Israel, he who will rule with God.

I remembered the man who had called me Israel after I'd wrestled him for a blessing. The hair rose on my arms.

280

I am God Almighty. From you, from your sons, a nation, a company of nations, will proceed. Kings shall come from your body. The land that I gave Abraham and Isaac I give to you. And to your descendants after you, I give this land.

Sobs surged from deep within me, like the gush of water trapped beneath the ground that is suddenly let loose. God had spoken to me once again, despite all my failings. I could feel His presence like a swath of sunshine swallowing up the darkness.

Thank you! Thank you! Help me to remember and wrap myself in this warmth when trouble comes again.

<hr />

I brought men from the camp and built a tall mound of stone on which we anchored the rock I'd erected so many years ago. I poured a drink offering and oil upon it and watched as the liquid ran down the gray slab into the rocks below. Again, I called the name of the place where God had met me Bethel, House of God, and instructed the others that, from this time on, it would be so called. I looked out over the camp and said to myself, *Now we will go home.*

CHAPTER THIRTY-SEVEN

Leah

The curtain of Rachel's tent was open. She was kneeling on the ground kneading dough on the stone before her, her stomach hanging heavy from her thin frame. She looked pale. I hadn't checked on her since the day of the oak tree. I was sorry for that. I'd been so angry at her, and with all that had happened, I'd just put Rachel out of my mind. It was my responsibility to see to her health, and I'd let her go unattended too long. And here she was on the ground kneading dough.

"You shouldn't be doing that, Rachel."

Bilhah didn't serve Rachel anymore, but there were other servants. There was a sheen of sweat on her forehead. She wiped it with the back of her hand, leaving a white trail across her forehead. I knelt beside her and turned the stone toward me. I should have seen to it that someone was attending Rachel.

I floured my hands and pressed the sticky dough with my palms, added flour, turned and kneaded until it was a smooth lump. The scent of fresh grain jarred me. I remembered the days of our youth when baking bread together had been a time of laughter and comradery. My heart was suddenly heavy with the loss of it.

I picked up the bowl and placed it on the upturned basket in the corner. We had left Shechem in haste, leaving furnishings like tables and stools behind. We used only a portion of our tent curtains, making the setting up and taking down an easier and quicker task. When we settled again, we would build what we needed. My life felt stripped like my tent.

I left the bowl on the basket. I would roll it into balls and bake the bread before I left. But now I needed to see to Rachel. I took her by the arm and helped her up from the ground, guided her to a pile of cushions, and insisted that she sit. I pulled out the one small stool that stood in a corner of the tent and sat before her. Looking at her straight in the face, I could see the shadows beneath her eyes, like a swish of smudged kohl. Her lips were dry and colorless. She did not look well at all. Why hadn't I looked in on her earlier?

"How have you been feeling? You look tired." There was no quick retort saying she was fine. Rachel hated to be thought less able than other women and usually let me know, in no uncertain terms, that she could do anything any other woman could do, and I should not think otherwise. But she seemed subdued. Sad. My heart went out to her.

"I am tired," she said in a thin voice. "But mostly . . . I'm ashamed."

Ashamed? I had never heard such a confession from my sister. She looked at me for a long moment, her beautiful eyes filling with tears. What could be causing this? Her bottom lip began to tremble.

"I'm sorry, Leah. I'm sorry for . . . everything. I've treated you so . . ." Her voice caught, and tears spilled over her lashes. "You didn't deserve any of it."

What was Rachel saying? Tears began to prick at the back of my eyelids.

"I know Father forced you to do what you did, Leah. I knew from the beginning. I knew something awful could have happened to you if you'd refused. But I didn't care. All I thought was that . . . you'd taken something from me. No one had ever done that. And when you were pregnant, I was consumed with jealousy." She shook her head. "But I was jealous of you long before Jacob came."

"Jealous of me?" The very thought was incomprehensible.

"You were so strong and so capable. I felt stupid and useless around you."

What? I had never suspected such a thing. Had I blinded myself to it?

"Rachel, I never meant to make you feel that way."

"You didn't." She shook her head. "All you ever did was care for me and love me, and I rewarded you with my haughty attitude and my sharp tongue. You were a mother to me." Her voice quavered. "But most of all, you were my sister. Sisters aren't supposed to treat each other that way. I wasn't a sister to you when Dinah got . . . hurt. I should have been there for you. I should have been the one to comfort you. I went to you, and Zilpah turned me away. I didn't blame her. I had given up my right to be the one you turned to in your trouble.

"I'm so sorry, Leah. I know you can't forgive me, but I wanted you to know." She bowed her head and looked at her folded hands, plump tears dripping onto her chest.

Was she saying she wanted to end this grief between us? Could all the years of pain and rivalry really be over?

I slid off the stool to my knees and took my sister's hands in mine. "Rachel, I forgive you. But I need your forgiveness as much you need mine." My voice cracked, and I wasn't certain I could continue. "I let anger poison me. I'm the older. I should have been a better example to you. I should have loved you more so you would have had no cause to feel this way. I allowed bitterness to take root and choke out compassion for you. I blamed you for it all, but I played my part." Tears exploded from my eyes as I took Rachel in my arms. "Forgive me. I love you."

Rachel clung to me and I to her. I couldn't believe what my ears had heard. I had longed for reconciliation but thought the day would never come.

We wept in each other's arms for a long time. We wept for the years wasted in petty quarrels and competition. We wept for the words we'd spoken and the wounds that had festered from them. We wept for the hope of years to come, walking side by side as sisters should.

Thank you, God. Thank you.

CHAPTER THIRTY-EIGHT

Jacob

I hesitated at the door of Leah's tent. I didn't want to be the bearer of bad news, to add to the burdens she already carried. But I needed to tell her my decision concerning Reuben. How could I ask a mother to watch her son suffer? She would suffer with him. To sentence Reuben would be to sentence his mother as well, and I had already brought Leah so much pain.

But Reuben's sin could not go unanswered. To allow it would be to open the door to rebellion in the entire camp. How could I lead a people who knew my son had lain with my concubine?

I pulled a breath and pushed back the flap. Leah looked up from a cushion on the floor, where she was grinding herbs with the mortar and pestle in her lap. The air was heavy with the scent of cumin. I wished there was an herb that would soothe the pain of what I was about to tell her.

The state of my mind must have shown on my face for Leah laid down the mortar and pestle and stood like the condemned awaiting sentence, her hands gripping her elbows, pulling them to her, as if her soul might slip out of her body if not restrained.

"Leah." I struggled to swallow the sour taste in my mouth. "I've come to a decision concerning Reuben." Leah knew I had to render a judgment and was within my rights to have Reuben and Bilhah put to death. In such a case, the locals would bind the couple together and throw them in the river. I had no obligation to their laws. But I couldn't forego judgment.

Abraham had sat in the door of his tent and judged in all matters concerning his people. My father had judged my mother and me in the same way. I would call Reuben to my own tent to deliver his sentence, as much as I didn't want to do it.

"I won't require his life for his sin," I said, wishing to put Leah's heart at ease. She let out a small breath and closed her eyes for a moment.

"But his punishment may seem more bitter to him than death."

She raised her honey-brown eyes to me, and I saw acceptance in them. She understood the depravity of Reuben's sin and knew it must be addressed.

I swallowed again. My throat was dry and tight. "Leah, when you told me you were pregnant the first time I . . . I was so angry . . . that it was you, and not Rachel, who would bear my firstborn. Your child would be the heir. I resented the swell of your belly every time I saw it."

Leah caught her lip between her teeth to stem the tremble, but I saw it and my eyes began to fill with tears. "I know you sensed it. I didn't try to hide it, even though I knew it was wrong. But when Reuben was born, I loved him. How could I help it? Yet I let my bitterness toward you keep me from rejoicing at the gift God had given me. And later, when my heart began to soften toward you, and I faced what I always knew was true—that you did what you had to do, for my sake as well as your own—I let Rachel's jealousy keep me from giving Reuben and the other boys the attention they needed."

I shook my head. "How could I do that, when I'd felt the pain of my own father's blindness toward me?" Were fathers destined to repeat their own fathers' wrongs?

"I didn't want your son to be the heir, Leah—and now I'd do anything if it could be so. I've decided Reuben will lose his birthright." A resigned sadness swept over Leah's features. Reuben would be shamed. It would be a blow from which he would not soon recover. But he had defiled his father's bed, and at least he would live.

I saw the question in Leah's mind. If not Reuben, then who would the birthright fall to?

"It would fall to Simeon in the normal course of things. But he and Levi have too much blood on their hands." Leah's face paled at the mention of the bloody massacre. I knew she must have had the same sickness of soul that overwhelmed me when my mind rehearsed the spectacle of my sons pushing their swords through the hearts of the unwary men of Shechem.

"So it will be Judah." It saddened me because Reuben showed more care to be among his people than Judah.

"And he will come home?" Leah asked.

"Yes. I've already sent for him." I'd sent a messenger to Abdulla this morning to tell Judah we've left Shechem and he is to meet us in Hebron. It was time for him to come home. Would he be a better heir than Reuben? Were any of my sons fit to follow in Abraham's footsteps? Was I? How God hoped to bring blessing to all the world through this family He had chosen was beyond my comprehension.

Leah nodded, sadness draping her like a garment.

"I'm sorry, Leah. I would spare you the pain if I could." I wanted to go to her, take her in my arms, and comfort her, but she had made it clear at the oak tree that she didn't want my comfort. I had sensed the distance she had placed between us for a long time now, and I wouldn't breach it until invited. I would respect the boundaries she'd placed around her heart until she pulled them down, no matter how much I wanted to comfort myself in her arms.

I turned and walked out of my wife's tent, sadder than I had ever been.

Leah

The camp had risen sleepily and was readying for the day's journey. Tents had been disassembled and loaded on the backs of the donkeys. The warm scent of bread, baked on cooking stones for the day's journey, filled the air.

I had loaded my baskets of herbs and tinctures onto Lily, who was too old to protest much anymore, and left her with Zilpah as I searched the camp for Reuben.

I found him not far away, cinching his saddlebags to his beast. The stoop of his shoulders told me his father had spoken to him. He saw me approaching and averted his gaze to the strap he was tightening.

"Reuben."

His throat moved.

"I'm sorry, Son."

"I would rather he had dumped me in the river," he said, looking at me. His eyes were red-rimmed, his face flushing from humiliation and anger. "I'm sure that's what he wanted to do."

"That's not true. It hurt your father a great deal to strip you of your birthright."

He shook his head and pulled at another strap. "I doubt that. He's never cared much what happened to me. All he cares about is Rachel and Joseph."

That was not true at all. Yes, Jacob had neglected to build a relationship with his sons, but he loved them. I had never doubted that. And I had seen his anguish when he told me the birthright would be stripped from Reuben. As much as Jacob had sought the honor himself, he would feel Reuben's deep disappointment even more keenly.

"Your father loves you, Son. He didn't want to hurt you. But he was right to remove you from your place. What you did was a grievous thing. It could not go unrequited."

"I know that, but it doesn't make him less a hypocrite."

His words dug deep into my soul. This was my fault. I'd let my hurt and bitterness toward Jacob spill over to my children. How could it not? Children were not deaf and blind to their parents' feelings.

"What will he do to Bilhah, Mother?" he said, the lines of his face deep with worry.

I hadn't asked Jacob that question, hadn't given a thought to my husband's concubine. "I don't know, Son. But I don't believe he'll require her life since he didn't require yours. I imagine the worst of it will be that she'll remain his concubine, and he will never touch her again."

Tears pooled in the corners of Reuben's eyes. Perhaps this tryst was more than spent passion. Maybe Reuben truly loved Bilhah—which would make the consequences even harder to bear.

I put my hand on my son's shoulder. "Reuben, you have to give up this bitterness toward your father. It's you it hurts. You've seen what it's done to your brothers. You are a good man. You've done a terrible thing, deserving of the judgment your father rendered, but I see your heart. I know beneath this anger is a gentle soul. But to loose it, you must forgive those who have wronged you."

Reuben turned to me, his eyes sad and steady on mine. "And what about you? Can you forgive Father for all the pain he's caused you? Can you really let it all go and act as though it never happened?"

Reuben's words struck me hard. Could I? Perhaps I could forgive Jacob. I wanted to. But could I let go of the pain that cut at me every time I thought of his words the morning he discovered I was not my sister? *"I will be a husband to you, Leah. But you will never have my love. Never."* Could I stop hurting when I thought of the night he came to do his duty to me and found I was pregnant and said, *"If you think this changes anything, you are mistaken"*? Is forgiveness really forgiveness if you rehearse the pain of the offense over and over in your mind?

"I don't know, Reuben. I don't know. But I want to."

"Well, I don't want to, Mother. I'm sorry if that hurts you. I love you, but Father doesn't deserve forgiveness—yours or mine."

Reuben turned back to his donkey.

As I walked toward the place where Zilpah and Lily waited, I grieved my part in my sons' disrespect for their father. Jacob had his own guilt to bear, and he had told me how much he regretted his actions. But what was regret—mine *or* Jacob's? Did regret repair the damage done?

I feared I'd put God's promise to Abraham in jeopardy by my own wickedness.

God, forgive me. Help me. I'm not worthy of your love. My family is not worthy of your love. Be merciful, dear God.

CHAPTER THIRTY-NINE

Leah

Zilpah walked beside Rachel as the camp moved toward Bethlehem. Joseph proudly led Lily. It was only a short distance from Bethlehem to Hebron, where Jacob's father lived.

I had wondered if Zilpah would feel displaced by my reconciliation with Rachel, but Rachel had spoken kindly to Zilpah, and the handmaid saw my joy and rejoiced with me, though I was certain it was difficult for her. She had been my sister in Rachel's absence. But she would always be my sister. Nothing would change that.

Rachel's countenance had lightened, free of the angry lines that marred the beauty of her face. My heart was still heavy for Reuben, but I drew strength from knowing that after all these years, Rachel and I were walking the same path, as loving sisters, without jealousy ripping us apart.

I walked a short way behind with Dinah, trying to shield her from curious onlookers who looked pointedly at her stomach, searching for some change that might indicate she was with child. Did they think it would show beneath her robe in just a few days?

She wasn't pregnant. I hadn't been able to bring myself to give her the herbs, and her blood had come this morning. A great weight had lifted off me. Not just that she wasn't with child but that I hadn't followed through with my plan. If I had given the herbs to her, she would have wondered if the blood was the result of the mixture or if it was her natural courses. I would have laid a lifetime of guilt upon my daughter's back for no reason.

A sour-faced woman walking beside a girl Dinah's age pulled her daughter to the side to give us a wide berth, her lip curled as if she smelled spoiled meat. I was angry, but mostly I was hurt for my daughter. Was she going to live beneath the turned-up noses of women like this the rest of her life? It was so unfair. I pulled Dinah closer to me. *God, help her.*

My gaze fell on Rachel walking beside her donkey. Something wasn't right. Her robe seemed heavy upon her back. Her sandals dragged to a stop. She reached out a hand, grasping for the donkey's rigging, then staggered to her knees. Zilpah knelt beside her.

I raced toward them, pushing at a short, broad-backed man who filled the path before me.

"Rachel!"

Her mouth was open, a pale circle of surprise on her lips.

My heart stopped then started with a lurch. *Not here, Rachel. Not now!*

The broad-backed man stopped, as well as two women with a speckled goat and a little girl in tow, watching with wide eyes. The number of gawkers began to grow, and murmured conversations floated around me. Joseph was crying.

From the periphery of my sight, Jacob surged forward and lifted Rachel into his arms, the lines in his brow deeply creased.

I shouted to the servants leading tent-laden beasts. In moments the center shafts of my tent were dropped in hastily-dug holes and secured with bags of grain. Dark goat-hair panels were stretched over peeled poles and staked into the ground with taut cords. Zilpah threw back the flap and unrolled an old sun-bleached section of tent, a barrier against scrub brush and dirt, and spread a pallet on it.

Jacob laid Rachel on the mat and stepped aside as I knelt over my sister. Her eyes were wide and her skin clammy when I took her hand. My heart was racing.

"Has her time come?" Jacob's voice was thin with restraint.

"I'm not certain. I need to examine her." I looked up, silently asking him to leave.

Worry pulled at the lines around his eyes. "We will camp here . . . I'll give the order."

His knelt and kissed Rachel's forehead. His fingers brushed my shoulder as he left.

"Can you raise yourself, Rachel?"

She nodded, and I put my hand under her back, steadying her enough to pull the outer robe off her shoulders. I lowered her again and tugged the wool garment from under her slender frame. My breath caught. The garment was bloodstained, with bright red blood, fresh and telling of something ominous.

"What happened, Rachel?"

"A pain . . . sharp," she rasped.

"A birth pang?"

"I don't know . . . maybe. It came without warning." She grasped my hand and held on to it.

"How do you feel now?" I asked as I smoothed the hair from her face.

"Weak."

I took her small hand in mine and looked at the pale, whitish beds of her fingernails. I ran my thumb over the middle nail and felt the texture of it—rough, with small ridges raised against my touch. She had bled, nearly to the point of death, when Joseph was born. And her monthly flow was often long and heavy. I had always suspected her blood was not vigorous enough to keep her body strong.

A waft of air tickled my neck as the tent flap opened. Zilpah set my bag beside me.

"What do you need?" She spoke in a soft, calm voice.

"Warm oil and some woolen cloths."

"I already have Jacob building the fire. Anything else?"

"Help me remove her tunic."

With Zilpah on one side and me on the other, we tugged Rachel's tunic over her head. Zilpah's eyes widened for an unguarded moment at the sight of the bright-red stain.

Rachel was so thin. She had long since lost the softness of her youth. Her slender neck stretched out of a deep hollow created by the sharp edges of her collarbones. It looked like a limbless tree whose roots lay exposed above the ground.

Zilpah laid a cover over Rachel's chest, to ward off the chill, and together we raised her legs. She reached into the bag and found a vial of olive oil and poured some into a clay bowl. I dipped my hand into the slick substance and looked at my sister.

"I'm just checking to see if you have begun to open, dearest. It will be uncomfortable, but if you relax, it will not hurt."

Rachel nodded and closed her eyes. She winced as my fingers probed the entrance to her womb. I pulled my hand out and wiped the oil and my sister's blood on the rag Zilpah handed to me, my heart moving to my throat.

Rachel made a small noise and bit her lip. The tension in her face confirmed what I had only just discovered for certain. This babe would not be born in Bethlehem, or in the tents of his grandfather, but here in a tent pitched at the side of the road.

Zilpah brought the warm oil and dipped the woolen cloth into it. I pressed out the excess and spread the cloth across Rachel's stomach. The tension eased out of her body, and she was able to relax for a moment. I held her hand. It would be all right. She could do this.

The cramps began slowly, but after some time, my hope for an uneventful delivery lay soaked in a widening circle of blood. A servant brought the watery spelt I had requested. I spooned it into Rachel's mouth, hoping to give her an extra measure of strength with which to labor.

Zilpah went to fill the cow bladders with the warmed grain. I would try to get ahead of the pain, to make Rachel as comfortable as possible, as I had when she was young and suffered a painful flux. When Zilpah returned, I settled the warm bladders against Rachel's sides, soaked the cloth again in freshly warmed oil, and spread it over the bulge that seemed to sink too far into the recess of her abdomen.

She clutched my hand until it felt strangely detached from my body. Her pains lengthened and deepened, and her thin body shuddered. And with the pangs came sudden secretions of that bright-red fluid that worried me so.

"It hurts, Leah." Rachel fought each grip of labor.

"I know. Try to rest in between. Don't fight against it. It only makes the pain worse." I smoothed her hair back and dabbed at her forehead with a damp cloth. *Oh, Rachel. You can do this, dearest. Don't give up. I need you.*

I sat beside Rachel for a long time. There was nothing to do now but speak encouragement in soft tones and pray.

I was accustomed to the fouled air of the birthing tent, but suddenly the air was too heavy to pull into my lungs. I rose from my sister's side and nodded at Zilpah, who moved in to replace me.

Outside, I pulled a refreshing gulp of cool air and let it out slowly. Shadows dappled the sun-soaked hills, mirroring the white fluffs in the blue sky above. The sprawl of black tents had sprung up like a horde of insects.

Jacob walked toward me, his mouth tugging down at the corners. "Is it well? The birth?"

"Not as well as I would wish. The pains don't seem to bring the child closer."

I could see the lines of his jaw tighten with the effort to maintain control. "I've killed her, Leah. I've killed my own wife and probably my child as well. I shouldn't have . . ."

Without thinking, I reached out and touched his shoulder. I didn't want Jacob to suffer such guilt. He gripped my hand and held it to his mouth. I wanted to comfort him, but I couldn't risk losing the tenuous control I had on my own emotions. I was trying to forgive Jacob, but I couldn't lay myself bare of my defenses. Not now, when Rachel needed me.

I pulled my hand back and turned and ducked through the open flap, pulling it down behind me.

My heart shrank as Rachel labored by lamplight and more so with the morning sun that peeked through the gaps where sections of goat hair joined and through the tiny holes in the weave that looked like stars flickering against the dark roof.

"I'm going to die, Leah. My baby's going to die in my womb."

"No, Rachel. This child will be born. You will give your son life." I started to recall *son* and say *child* but let it stay in the air. It would be a son, and that son would live. Somehow I knew that.

"You have to give yourself to it, Rachel, to bringing your child into the world. You will do it." The assurance of my words came from someplace outside me, but I knew it was true.

Something seemed to change in Rachel's labor. The pains were moving the child as they should.

"Push, Rachel." She labored with renewed strength. A few long, hard pushes, and the babe slipped into my waiting hands. The child let out a lusty cry, and I wept with joy. Rachel had given birth to another son. He was too thin, but his color was good, and he would gain weight soon at his mother's breast.

I turned to her. The wide smile on my face fell into a gaping hole. Rachel's eyes were fluttering closed. I handed the boy to Zilpah and touched my fingers to Rachel's neck. Her heartbeat was weak and spotty. I spoke loudly into her face. "Rachel! Wake up!" Her eyes opened, then closed again.

Zilpah and I had changed the bloody blanket beneath her earlier, but a fresh pool of red was widening, soaking into the straw-filled pallet. I had to move quickly. Zilpah deftly cut the sinewy cord and tied the end with a piece of wool string. She laid the child on the small pallet she had prepared beforehand to cleanse him and called out the tent for one of the servants.

"Would you please see to the baby?" she asked the woman who poked her gray head into the tent.

"Salt and oil," Zilpah said, her voice tense.

I did all the things I had done when Joseph was born. Rachel had escaped death that time. Surely she would do it again. But my hope was beginning to fade with the passing of time. Was there anything else? Something I'd forgotten in the panic of the moment?

When we were certain we had done all we knew to do, Zilpah touched my hand. "I'll be near if you need me."

I pulled my cloak around me and lay down beside my sister. I could feel the damp warmth of fever radiating from her body. How many nights had I shared a narrow space with my younger sibling? She had slept all over the pallet, except when the sadness overcame her and she wept for her dead mother, or when a dream sent her into my arms, curling safely against my chest.

A pain so deep, it seemed to split my soul, pulsed within me. I couldn't lose Rachel. I had just found her again.

I must have slept, I concluded, by the fog in my head as I wakened. I sat up with a start when I saw Rachel's open eyes, looking at me.

"Rachel!"

I felt her head; the damp clung to my fingers. "I'm here, Rachel."

Her eyes had some distant essence to them as she looked at me, two lonely tears clinging to her lower lashes. "I'm tired. I'm going to leave you now. I love you, Leah."

"No, my love. Stay with me. Be patient, dearest." I swallowed frantically, trying to choke back the panic. I begged her to give us a little more time to make up for all the time we'd lost. We'd go together, when we were too old to bake bread or hold our grandchildren in our arms.

But I knew that was not to be. My sister was going to pass from this life, and there was nothing I could do about it.

Grief swelled in my chest until I thought it would crack open. I pressed Rachel's face between my hands. I kissed her forehead and her cheeks, tears flooding my eyes and dripping onto her face. "It's all right. Go rest, my dearest. I love you."

Her lips curved into a weak smile. How few smiles we had shared these last years. I pressed it into my mind, like a flower pressed and dried and put away to retrieve another time and remember with fondness.

Her eyes fluttered closed, and she was gone.

CHAPTER FORTY

Leah

Jacob had come, a broken man, to mourn his wife. I'd left them alone, wanting him to have privacy. I'd gone to Joseph and held him while he wept for his mother. My own heart wept with him, for he would feel the loss for the rest of his life, as I had felt the loss of my own mother.

But I would do my best to be a comfort to Joseph. To keep his mother alive in his memory with stories of our childhood, when Rachel was happy and vibrant and not burdened with bitterness. I'd tell him how we'd kept secrets and giggled in our beds. How his mother used to run across the meadows, chasing rabbits, her long black hair floating behind her. I'd tell him how much she loved him. And how much I loved her.

It was I who prepared Rachel's body for burial. I would leave it to no other. Zilpah brought fresh scented water in a basin and clean woolen cloths, then left me alone to my final ministrations. The undulating sound of women mourning throughout the camp sifted through the weave of the goat-hair curtains, but I closed my ears to it. It was only Rachel and I within the black tent.

I stripped my sister of the blanket that Zilpah had laid over her thin body. I sucked a deep breath and pushed a strand of dark hair from her face. It was I who had seen to Rachel's care since she was young. It was fitting I should be the one to see to it for the last time.

I dipped the cloth in the warm water and gently began to wash her face. Her lashes cast long shadows on her cheeks. "You are still beautiful, my dearest."

I wiped her forehead and her cheeks, the corners of her mouth. I removed the unseemly secretions from her nose and rinsed the rag in the basin. Milk had crusted on her breasts. I cleaned them carefully, remembering how much she had wanted to suckle Joseph and how sad she had been to give him to another. If only things had been settled between us then. I would have nursed him myself. We could have shared those precious moments.

I lifted her limp arms to clean the sweat of labor from them and washed the bloody private parts and emptied the basin at the edge of the tent, not wanting to carry it outside. I poured clean water from the pitcher and took another cloth, and turned her on her stomach, as gently as if she were a sleeping child. Her shoulder blades were sharp. "Rachel. How did you get so thin?"

Her thick hair lay heavy in my hand as I lifted it off her neck and cleaned her shoulders, her back, and her buttocks—moved the damp cloth over her firm legs and turned her again with care and started on her feet. Tears stung behind my eyelids, I forced them to stay in their place. Her feet were soiled from the journey. I had never let Rachel go to bed with dirty feet. I held each foot in my hand and bathed it gently until there was not a spot of dust or grime and dried them with a clean cloth.

Only one thing remained.

My hand trembled as I picked up the bone comb Zilpah had set beside the basin. I'd brushed Rachel's hair every day after our mother died, until she married and had a servant to do it for her. I wouldn't hurry to unsnarl the tangled mane that framed Rachel's colorless face. This would be the last time. I scored a section and started at the bottom as I always had, working slowly until the comb slipped through the smooth locks with ease.

When I had combed through the last section, I spread her hair like a dark fan around her face.

Rachel.

A long wail pushed its way out of my lungs. I lay prostrate over my sister's body and wept.

⊂⊃⊂⊃⊂⊃⊂⊃⊂⊃⊂⊃⊂⊃⊂⊃

I stood at Rachel's grave cradling little Benjamin in the crook of one arm and holding Joseph against my side. Joseph's brave expression was crumbling around the edges. He sniffed and wiped his nose and eyes with the sleeve of his clean robe.

The day was not unlike the day of my mother's burial. The breeze was warm today instead of cold, but it blew its strong breath through the mourners' hair, keeping the women occupied with holding scarves tightly around their chins. Mine escaped, and I made no move to recover it. Had the wind been called to wail at the laying down of all the dead?

Jacob and three of my sons lifted the reed-wrapped body and placed it in the grave they had dug and lined with stones.

An ominous pile of smooth rocks lay in a heap close to the grave. They would be laid on my sister's body until she was buried beneath so many that no beast could feed upon her. My eyes drooped. It was all I could do to hold them open. Every movement seemed hindered by a vast unseen weight.

As Joseph leaned closer to me, I remembered the day I'd slammed the herbs on the table and told Rachel if she didn't use them she would die, and I would be Joseph's mother and Jacob's only wife. I hadn't wanted to be right—but I had been—and I wished that I could snatch the words back from the past and soften them. Maybe she would have listened.

We stayed in the camp beside the road to Bethlehem for another day, while Jacob and my sons pulled a large pillar of stone from a nearby outcropping of rock and set it in the earth at the head of Rachel's resting place. They laid small stones around it to half its height, to keep the pillar steady and firmly placed. I saw Jacob carving something in the stone with a tool.

⊂⊃⊂⊃⊂⊃⊂⊃⊂⊃⊂⊃⊂⊃⊂⊃

Soon the donkeys were laden with the dark tents and foodstuffs. I could hear the *thwack* of the herdsmen's sticks as they prodded the beasts into motion.

Zilpah handed me a piece of barley bread spread with cheese. "You have to eat something before we set out."

I looked at her tender expression and was overwhelmed with thankfulness. How blessed I was to have Zilpah as my friend. Her long fingers ran up and down my back in a comforting gesture, but I wouldn't allow it to comfort me. I didn't want comfort. I wanted my sister.

"You did all you could for Rachel. Always. She could have asked for no better sister."

Tears threatened, but I blinked them back. It wasn't true, and I knew it.

I approached the place where my sister lay and read the inscription. "Rachel, wife of Jacob, mother of Joseph and Benjamin, beloved sister of Leah." I let the tears flow.

"I love you, Rachel. Forgive me. I will miss you so much."

A hand touched my shoulder. "It's time, Leah." Jacob's voice was ragged, his eyelids swollen.

"I can't leave her here alone," I said in a broken voice. "She always hated sleeping alone."

"We have to go." His voice was soft and tender and full of sorrow.

Men with staffs and women with children at their skirts and on their hips were moving in concert with the plodding pace of the animals.

I allowed Jacob to lead me to the road. I took a few steps, then turned back toward my sister's grave, letting the crowd move around me, the way water flows around a rock too stuck in mire to move down the stream. I memorized the place where my sister lay, the pillar that marked her existence to those who would travel this road. "I won't forget you, Rachel. You'll always be in my heart."

I looked back every so often, the monument growing smaller each time, until it vanished beneath the rise of a rolling hill.

CHAPTER FORTY-ONE

Leah

Isaac's tents were pitched between two mountain ridges, in the plains of Mamre, just outside of Hebron. Soft shadows on the grass mimicked the great sprawling oaks spreading their green canopies over the slopes of the hills. I searched for the cave in the side of the mountain where Abraham lay buried with Sarah, but I couldn't see the entrance from where we stood.

Jacob's eyes were misted. I imagined his thoughts were of his mother, who had, no doubt, waved good-bye to him from the road and watched as he traveled past where we stood now. I felt the pain in Jacob's heart. He had returned home. But to a home without his mother.

Dinah held Benjamin in her arms. She had taken to caring for him most of time, giving him up reluctantly when the wet nurse took him from her. The child seemed to sooth her. I prayed someday she would have a child of her own. But that was up to God.

Joseph clung to my hand. He stayed as close to me as he could. I hoped he would soon remember his mother with joy rather than sorrow. I hoped the same for myself, but for now I thought my heart would always grieve for my sister.

The lines deepened in Jacob's face as we drew closer to the camp—no doubt from the apprehension of seeing his father and the accusation he was sure to see on Esau's face. If he dreaded the meeting, he did not have long to do so, for a large hairy form was coming to greet us.

Esau was a formidable man, intimidating with his rugged looks and brash demeanor. His very presence made the air spark with the thought that anything could happen.

"Well, Brother, you have come at last. A long few days."

"My apologies, Esau. It was my intention to come before this, but other opportunities presented themselves."

Esau's eyes and the tiny curl of his lips said that he knew his brother had never intended to come home. At least not immediately. If only we had.

"Well, you are here now, and you are welcome."

Esau greeted me warmly. "We heard of your sister's death. Your sorrow is mine." The words moved painfully across my heart. His eyes were tender on mine, and I was touched by them.

"I'm sorry, Brother," he said, touching Jacob's shoulder.

Jacob nodded. I could see him grappling with tears.

"Where is Father's tent? I want to see him."

"Where it has always been. I tried to get him to move into our mother's tent, but he wouldn't hear of it."

Jacob nodded again, his countenance strained and sad as he walked toward his reckoning.

***

A servant, an old woman, plump and tender-eyed, came to take me to the place that had been prepared for me. The tent was large and beautifully furnished with colorful pillows and draperies, and an intricately woven rug lay over the hard-packed dirt floor.

"The master must wish to honor you," she said with a wistful exhale. "This was Rebekah's tent, and Sarah's before her."

Rebekah's tent? I felt suddenly uncomfortable, as though I was treading where I had no right.

"When Abraham's servant took a wife for Isaac from your home, Isaac brought her to this tent. He had not seen her face. He did not know what a beautiful woman she was, but he loved her immediately."

The woman wiped a fleshy hand across one eye and then the other. "She was beautiful in form and face, for certain, but Rebekah was beautiful in spirit as well. I have missed her greatly, these years since she's been gone."

She looked up at me, taking me in for several long moments. "I see that same beauty in you."

I blinked in shock that any comparison could be made between my aunt and me.

The woman patted my hand. "I will send water for you to wash with."

Jacob

Father was sitting up in the raised bed I'd built for him when I was a young man, propped against several pillows. I was filled with dread, much as I had been when I'd come garbed in the skin of a kid to deceive him so many years ago. He turned toward the tent door, his sightless eyes—almost hidden under folds of waxen flesh—searching. The sound of my heart was loud in my ears.

"Jacob?"

I couldn't answer for a moment, remembering how he'd called me by my name, and I'd told him I was my brother Esau. I scratched my arm, dug at it. I could feel the phantom itch of the coverings my mother had made for my hands and arms and neck, like lice feeding on my flesh. The panic as my father had felt my hand and said, "The voice is Jacob's voice, but the hands are the hands of Esau."

I wanted to turn and leave, just as I had wanted to back then—but my father spoke, and it was too late. I had to face whatever was coming.

"Jacob, is it you?"

I swallowed the spittle pooled in my throat.

"It's me, Father."

I waited for him to speak again. What would he say? Would he reprove me for not coming earlier? Would he remind me of my past? Would he say I should give the birthright back to Esau, since I'd not taken my responsibility?

But there was none of that. Tears trailed through the deep crevices of his face, and he opened up his arms. They were trembling, his gnarled hands outstretched.

It was only as the bands that had bound my heart so long loosened that I realized how they had constrained me. Kept me from opening my heart to my children. To Leah. To anyone.

I rushed to my father's bed. He held me to his chest, weeping. "Forgive me, Son. Forgive me. I was so wrong. I've missed you so much. Oh, thank God you've come home. Thank God."

I wept in my father's arms, my head on his chest, taking in the warmth of him, the scent of his aged body like an old familiar garment—musty, but too comfortable to discard.

"Forgive me" I said, my voice cracking with emotion. "I should have come earlier."

I should have come home with Esau when he came out to greet me. I should have let nothing keep me from reuniting with my father. I'd lived within a few days' distance from him for years and never as much as made a visit. What kind of son was I?

"You're here now, Son. That's all that matters."

I pulled up a stool and sat by my father's bedside, holding his rough hand, surprised at the strength of his grip. His hair was whiter than it had been when I left. The lines carved a little deeper in his face, but he looked much as he had when I'd kissed him good-bye and ridden out of the camp in haste.

Tears pooled in his milky eyes. "If only your mother were here to see your homecoming. She missed you every day of her life."

My vision blurred with fresh tears. A crush of sorrow had lain on my heart since I first caught sight of the valley of black tents, knowing my mother would not be here to greet me. I knew how much my father loved her and how difficult it must have been for him to live without her all these years.

"But I believe she knew from the day you left that she would not see your face again. She loved you so much; it was a sacrifice she was willing to make to see you safe."

My throat thickened, swelled, until I could barely swallow. I had always blamed myself for my mother's death. If I hadn't coveted what wasn't mine, she might have been in her tent cooking my favorite stew. I would give it all back to see her one more time.

"I know what you're thinking, Son. But it's not your fault. I'm the one," he said, his voice raw. "I was foolish to think that the order of my sons' births determined their destiny. You were chosen while still in the womb, and thus your heart yearned toward your calling. Esau couldn't have been the chosen seed, no matter how hard he tried to conform. God had purposed it be you before either of you had done a deed. It wasn't a matter of reward but of His own plan. Your mother knew it. If I'd realized it earlier, I could have saved us all so much pain."

I took my father's hand with both of mine. I had judged him so harshly through the years. Yes, he had favored my brother, but he had always loved me. And I wondered if I'd closed myself off to him—to protect myself—and turned to my mother for comfort and counsel, leaving no room for my father. We all had blame enough: Father, me, and my mother. But assigning blame would change nothing. It was time to give it up.

"It doesn't matter now, Father."

He squeezed my hand. "You're right, Son. It doesn't matter anymore. God had His way in the end. As He always does. You are home, and God will make of you a great nation, just as He promised."

I was here, but I didn't yet feel that I was home. Home was more than the ground we walked on. I was thankful to be reconciled with my father, my brother. But until things were right with Leah, I wouldn't feel at home anywhere.

We talked for a while longer, then I told him I needed to see that the herds were cared for and that I'd come back in the morning. He nodded and squeezed my hand. I kissed him and told him I loved him. He smiled and tears filled his eyes again.

I looked back at my father as I opened the tent flap. He was still smiling, peace resting on his face.

Leah

I had barely settled in Rebekah's tent, when the kindly woman who had greeted me came again.

"Sorry to bother you, mistress, but Isaac has sent me with word he wants to see you."

"Now?" I said, then regretted it. I didn't want her to think me ungrateful, but we had just arrived a short time ago, and Jacob had gone straightway to see him. Wouldn't Isaac be tired? Why not wait until tomorrow?

"I'm sorry. I didn't mean . . . I just wondered if he wouldn't rather wait until morning."

"I thought the same thing, suggested that he give you a chance to rest, but it was him I was really worried for. But he said if you would please come now, he would appreciate it."

"Yes, of course. Just give me a moment."

The servant took me to Isaac's tent and announced that Jacob's wife had come as he requested, then whispered in my ear to try not to stay so long as to wear the poor man out.

I hadn't seen Jacob since we arrived and had no idea how things were between his father and him and no idea what to expect.

The tent was much smaller than the one I had been given. The sharp scent of urine hung in the air. Isaac sat on a raised bed, several pillows at his back, his shoeless feet swollen to twice their size.

Wisps of white floated over his naked age-spotted scalp, in sharp contrast to the shock of hair that fell to his shoulders and the thick white beard from which peeked thin, cracked lips.

"I'm sure I must be a sight, old decrepit beast that I am."

"No . . . I . . . I'm sorry . . . I . . ." Had he taken my silence as distress at the sight of him?

"You needn't worry about offending me, Daughter. I am much too old to care about such things." His voice was surprisingly strong for one who thought himself at death's door twenty years ago.

"I'm sorry to make you rush. I so seldom have company other than Esau's occasional visit, or that of his sons and daughters. I have been waiting for your visit with great anticipation."

He reached out a hand. I took it in my own. It was blue-veined and weathered, with cracked yellowed nails and fingers that bent oddly at the knuckles, but there was a strange comfort in holding it.

"Sit, please," he said, gesturing widely. I found a stool close by and pulled it to his bedside. Isaac wasn't at all what I'd expected. He seemed affable, even jovial in his demeanor. I supposed I'd expected a stern, stiff-lipped man, though Jacob had never described him as such.

"I'm sorry for the loss of your sister. A trader delivered the news. And the child?"

"He is well." I swallowed the sorrow that threatened to pull me under again. I needed to keep myself from breaking down in Isaac's presence.

"I have only one brother. His name is Ishmael. We have not seen each other often since we buried our father. We never got along well, but I do miss his occasional company. The ties of blood increase with age, as the importance of the things that separate us decrease."

Isaac coughed a thick gurgling cough that brought up something from his lungs. He reached for a rag that lay close at hand and spat into it. The cough did not sound good. I would prepare a poultice for him and ask a servant to apply it. He might feel uncomfortable if I were to do it.

"Forgive me. Sometimes I think I'm going to cough up my insides, but they refuse to let go. Want to stay around to torment me, I guess." His face sobered. "You must miss your sister very much."

I nodded, fighting back the tears. Then, remembering he couldn't see me, I told him that I did miss her, very much indeed.

"I was lost when my Rebekah died," he said, his milky eyes staring at the air in front of him. "I will pray for your comfort."

"Thank you. I would be most grateful for your prayers."

Isaac tried to scoot himself up on his pillows, then gave up the effort.

"May I help you?" I said, already at his side.

"Yes, yes, thank you." I slipped one arm under his back and with both hands under his damp arms tugged as he scooted further onto the pillows.

I sat on my chair, wanting to wipe my hands on my skirt, but I didn't, afraid he would hear it. I didn't know who was charged with his care, but if allowed, I'd help them. I had salves that would protect his skin from sores and herbs that could give him some added strength. And I'd get him out of this tent into the sunshine.

He reached out his hand, and I took it again.

"I have prayed for you, Leah. Often," he said, squeezing my hand. "I first prayed for you before Jacob ever reached Haran."

Isaac had prayed for me? Before Jacob came to Haran? I didn't understand.

"I prayed my son would find a wife who was faithful to the God of my father. I believe that is true of you."

I was afraid Isaac didn't see the truth at all. He hadn't seen my struggle to keep my faith when my mother died, to keep it through the long years of Jacob's rejection and Rachel's, through my daughter's rape, my sons' savagery—and even now, through the loss of my sister. I had failed on every front to trust in God. I didn't feel faithful at all.

"I want to be faithful to the God of Abraham, but I fear I have not succeeded."

"I think you do not see yourself as others see you, Leah. Or as God sees you. You were in God's mind before the world was formed. He loved you before you existed. He chose you for His own purpose before He separated the light from the darkness or divided the waters. He has been watching you from the heavens, guiding the circumstances of your life, so you could fulfill the purpose He has for you."

A shiver rippled down my arms. I remembered the night I first believed in the God of Abraham. I had felt Him watching me from beyond the stars. But I struggled now to understand why, if He was watching and guiding me, He had led me through such great sorrows in my life.

Isaac coughed again and spat into the rag. I reached for the flask of water and poured some into a clay cup sitting on the table at his side. "Would you like a drink?"

"Yes, please." I placed the cup in his hand, and he took several sips and handed it back to me. "You are very kind. My son did well when he married you."

I wasn't certain Jacob would agree. Isaac leaned back a moment, getting another wind.

"I know the story of your marriage, but all is not as it seems, Leah. Jacob might not have chosen you, but *God* chose you for my son."

I was thankful Isaac couldn't see me. I was certain the shame showed on my face. I hadn't thought that Isaac knew just how his son had come to have two wives. *What must he think of me?*

"God works beyond the choices that we make, Daughter. He brings His own purpose to pass in spite of our wanderings. Jacob needed you because, as deceitful as he has been, his heart is toward God, and God has chosen him. That does not make him a perfect man. Not even

308

necessarily a good man, although he is that. It just makes him a chosen man, and a chosen man needs a chosen wife."

God chose me? For Jacob? If that was so, I could add another failure to my list. I had not acted like a chosen wife, or a wife at all, much of the time.

"I sense that there has been great pain in these years of your marriage. You have struggled with your sister for the love of your husband, but take comfort—a great nation will come from your progeny that will bless all generations. What pain you suffer now is a small thing in comparison to the joy that will come."

A great nation would come from my sons? Thus far they had shown themselves to be murderers, adulterers, and lovers of foreign women.

"But my sons . . ." I choked on the words. "My sons have done terrible things. Their deeds grieve my heart and make me doubt that they will achieve anything to honor God. Why would God choose such a family?"

He squeezed my hand again. "I understand, Daughter. I have felt the same about my own sons, and I'm certain my father felt the same about me. But God's purpose cannot be forfeit due to the acts of men, or the world would lie in chaos. Sometimes I think God chooses the weakest of us for his purposes so the praise goes to Him."

The weakest? Now that was a role I could fulfill. I hoped my father-in-law was right.

Isaac's sightless eyes met mine. "They are God's sons before they are your sons. He sees deep within their hearts, and He will take them through whatever is necessary, but in the end they will be a great nation."

My heart pounded as I listened to the old man's words. I remembered the dream of the line of women. Of the man on the wooden pole. I had thought Judah had some special place because he'd been conceived that night. And now Judah would have the birthright. But Judah's eyes were on things of this earth. He didn't deserve the honor. But neither did Jacob. And Abraham himself had lacked courage concerning his wife and the pharaoh.

And what about me? Did I deserve such an honor?

"But, Father Isaac, how can God bless people so undeserving? I love God, but I've allowed a root of bitterness to strangle joy in my life. And I've allowed my children to disrespect their father, to their detriment."

"Leah, there is no perfect mother—or father, for that matter. If by being a good parent you could save your children from their iniquities, they wouldn't need God.

"God sees you with different eyes than you see yourself. And He's not disappointed in you. He sees the end from the beginning. You are a woman of faith and courage, and He loves you, regardless of your works or your thoughts. You think ill of yourself, but God thinks good about you.

"Rest in Him, Daughter. You have struggled for the love of your husband, but you need not struggle for the love of your God. He gives it freely. Without condition. Nothing you could do would make Him love you more, and nothing you could do would make Him love you less. When He watches you from the heavens, He sees His beloved daughter."

Tears filled my eyes. *Oh, God. Is this true? That you love me that much?* Could it be that God accepted me after all of the bitterness I'd held? All the struggling with my sister? Could my sons still fulfill the purpose of God in their lives after having done so much evil? Could Dinah be whole and happy after all that had happened to her? Could Jacob forgive me and I him?

I began to weep, my body trembling, my hand clenching Isaac's. He grasped it with both of his hands, holding it tightly.

Isaac had touched a place in my heart that had been mauled by the circumstances of my life, and I could feel the pain of cleansing, like debriding a wound to rid it of all that is dead and rotten and a threat to the living flesh. Jacob's promise that he would never love me. Rachel's declaration that she didn't have a sister. My brother's attempt to kill me. My father's betrayal. And most of all, the mistaken idea that God didn't care about my pain.

I felt Isaac's words scraping at the putrid flesh until it bled anew and was washed away with blood and tears. The gash in my heart lay open, raw and pulsing but free from corruption, cleansed by the truth of God's unreserved love. I would have to tend it watchfully, pour in wine to kill the seeds of bitterness that would infect me again if I let them. Anoint it with the oil of gladness and forgiveness. It would take time and careful attention, but I saw the hope of wholeness before me.

Isaac let go of my hand and lay back upon the pillows with a long exhale. "Now I must ask you to leave me, Daughter. I tire easily these days. My heart has been lifted by your visit. I hope you will come again soon."

I stood and looked at the frail man that lay before me, thanking God for Him and praying that God would give him comfort. I kissed him on the forehead. "Thank you, Father Isaac." But he had already drifted off to sleep, a gentle snore emanating from the back of his throat.

"Sleep well."

CHAPTER FORTY-TWO

Leah

Dinah and Joseph and I sat on the hillside in the shade of one of the large oak trees that spread over the slopes defining the field of Machpelah. The valley was awash with the warm midafternoon sun. On the other side, the grass gave way to the rocky path leading to the cave where Abraham and Sarah were buried. Where Jacob's mother lay awaiting Isaac.

The opening was covered with a large round stone, sheltering the beloved bones from wild beasts and the elements. I thought of Rachel's grave, a simple rock marking where she lay. Rachel should have been buried here, where Jacob could join her. She was the wife he'd loved, and it was fitting she should lie beside him. I hated the thought of her being buried alongside the road, alone, with no family to share her tomb.

Even though I'd found a great measure of peace in Isaac's tent, my heart still ached for my sister. It seemed peace and pain lived side by side, in the memories of loved ones. Perhaps, one day, peace would outweigh the pain, but not soon, I feared.

Joseph wandered down the slope a short way, using a long stick to hit at loose rocks in the places where grass was sparse. He had hardly moved from my side since his mother's death. Perhaps his grandfather's home would be a place of healing for him as well. I hoped so. I leaned against the ancient oak, the solid strength of it a comfort.

Dinah was quiet, as she had been since we left Shechem, a distant stare behind her lovely eyes. Her shoulders had taken to drooping beneath her robe, as though the weight of it was more than they could bear.

"Dinah."

She broke her contemplation and looked up at me.

"Do you want to talk about it—what happened to you in the palace?"

She bit her lip, found a broken thread in the tight weave of her tunic and picked at it absently.

"It might help, my dearest. You can talk to me. You know that, don't you? This was not your fault, Dinah. None of it."

She exhaled. "What will become of me, Mother?"

My heart constricted. I wanted to assure her that everything would be well, that people would forget, and her life would be as it was before, but something within me would not let me comfort her with hope of normalcy. To place her recovery at the mercy of circumstances would be to place it in someone's hands other than her own—and God's. She was going to have to find healing for herself.

"I wish I could tell you that all will be well and someday you will not even remember the name of Shechem."

I touched her shoulder, feeling the delicate bones beneath my hands. "Life does not always follow the path we hoped, but you are strong, my Dinah. You will find your way . . . and God will guide you."

She picked at her garment again. "After . . ." Her face paled, and she swallowed hard. "He seemed sorry for what he had done. He begged me not to cry so. He said he would marry me and be happy to do it, that he . . . that he loved me."

In my mind, I saw Shechem's face, eyes locked on mine, as he fell to the ground. The thought of him telling Dinah he loved her sickened me. But perhaps he'd felt something for Dinah that he would have considered love. Shechem was the product of a father who held him to no account and a mother who thought little of his treatment of his wives. But perhaps there was some seed of good in the boy that made his heart hurt for what he had stolen from my daughter. I hoped so.

"He wanted to marry you, Dinah. But I fear Shechem didn't have the capability to love as a woman should be loved. But he cared for you in the measure he could care for anyone but himself."

I pulled a long breath. The fresh air turned heavy in my lungs.

"When you were born, I rejoiced that you were such a comely child. I thought that because you were beautiful, you would not suffer as I had suffered. But I've learned that beauty does not preclude suffering, my dearest. It is suffering that makes you beautiful. You have suffered, Dinah." I swallowed, trying to keep the hint of sorrow from my voice. "But God will bring beauty from the ashes of your life, and you will live the life God has planned for you." I took her chin in my hand and kissed her forehead, tears pooling in my eyes. "I promise."

Dinah leaned against my side, and as we looked out over the field, I thought of Jacob. My husband might never love me, and I would accept that and live in peace, but I had wronged him, and I had to make it right. I would face my own reckoning, as he had faced his.

<hr>

I hadn't seen Jacob since we'd arrived yesterday. He wasn't in his tent. I wondered if he had found a favorite hiding place from his childhood to steal away to in order to spend some time alone.

I asked the servant who was tasked with taking food to Isaac if I could take it in her stead. I had medicine for his cough and balm for the eruptions on his skin. I wanted to tell him of the peace I'd garnered from our talk the day before and ask him to pray for Dinah and Joseph.

I smelled the release of Isaac's bowels when I opened the flap of the tent. He was lying still upon his bed, and I knew that he was gone.

I set the tray on a small table near the doorway and, closing my mouth against the reek of excrement, walked to where Isaac lay. His eyes were open, staring at the pinpricks of light in the roof of the tent, as though he had been looking for someone at the moment of his death.

My eyes blurred with tears. With the strength of life gone, his body seemed an ancient thing, lying on the narrow bed, his eyes blank, his mouth slack. I touched his hand, already cold, and wondered if there was not life beyond his death. Did all end in the darkness of the grave? Where was hope if it was so? I wanted to believe that Isaac was somewhere with Rebekah now, and my mother, and Rachel, and that I would meet them there someday. Life was too short if this time was all we had.

I grieved for every moment wasted on jealousy and anger and bitterness. That Rachel and I had squandered so many years. That Jacob and Isaac had done the same. Time was illusory, telling lies, suggesting that it would be around forever, when it was all but gone before it had even begun.

I wished for more time with Isaac. To learn wisdom from his years. I touched his bearded cheek with the back of my hand. "Thank you, Father Isaac. Thank you."

Jacob

A quiet breeze stirred about me as I sat on a large rock near the cave where Esau and I had buried our father yesterday. I wanted to be close to the place where his body lay. And close to my mother, whose presence I had so sorely missed upon my return.

Yesterday, throngs of mourners had walked the rocky slopes leading from the valley dotted with black tents to the entrance of the cave, to pay homage to my father. Their undulating keening had rolled over the hillside, as though it were the ground itself that mourned. I was moved at the way the people honored him. Their devotion made me ashamed. I had forfeited so much because of my pride—my fear. But I was thankful that I had seen him one last time before he died. I knew he had waited all these years, refused to give up the ghost until we made things right between us.

After the burial, Esau told me he was moving to Seir, a mountainous region to the north, with the remainder of his flocks. Most of them were already there.

"There's not enough room for both of us in this valley," he'd said, a touch of acrimony beneath his calm demeanor. But I could cast no blame upon him. We embraced, and I told him I wished him well, and I truly did. Esau had been the better man in our dealings since I'd met him on the road from Haran.

So now I had what I'd always wanted—the birthright and the blessing—and I didn't understand why I had wanted them so badly. There was no euphoric pleasure in being the heir of Abraham. Only a weight of responsibility I felt too weak to bear. Judah would be home soon, but he wasn't yet fit to help carry the load.

I grieved for Reuben. I could see the anger on his face when our paths crossed, which was not often. I was certain he made it a point to stay clear of me. God had restored me to my father. Maybe, in the end, he would do the same for my own sons. I prayed it would be so. It seemed unlikely with the older boys, but who knew what might happen in the future to bring them to that place.

I prayed I would not make the same mistakes with Joseph and little Benjamin. That I would be a better father to them than I had been to the others. Joseph had clung to Leah since Rachel's death. She loved him, and she would be a good mother to him. But the sorrow in his young face hurt my heart. I knew what it was to lose a mother.

I'd first held Benjamin in my arms the day after we buried Rachel. I hadn't wanted to see him at first. I didn't know why. I didn't blame him for his mother's death. Rachel had chosen her own path. Whether she'd risked another pregnancy for jealousy's sake or because she just longed for another child made no difference now.

But Benjamin won my heart at the first sight of his puckered face crowned with the thickest shock of black hair I'd ever seen. Before she died, Rachel had named him Benoni, *son of my sorrow*, but I'd refused to call him that. He was Benjamin, *son of my right hand*. We'd had enough sorrow in this family. I missed Rachel. I would always miss her. I had been so grateful when she reconciled with Leah. It had brought peace and made her death easier to bear.

I prayed for Dinah. I had grieved for the girl as I'd seen her walking by her mother, head down, shamed, as though she had gone willingly to Shechem's bed. She had not. She was guilty only of not heeding her mother's words when Timnah told the palace guards Dinah could go with them. A child's mistake. When Timnah came to me, pleading I annul Leah's order that she and her family be put out in Bethlehem, I told her she was fortunate that my wife was gracious enough to offer provisions. If I'd heard her talking with the women, I'd have put her out without a crumb.

I prayed that, some way, Leah could come to forgive me. I wanted to go to her and beg that she give me an opportunity to show her how much I cared for her. How much I loved her. But I feared that she would think it was only a matter of convenience, now that Rachel was gone. Since I had no one else, she would do.

Oh, God. Show mercy on me and on my family for Abraham's sake. May my sons be lights, like the stars that rule the world by night. May their seed be righteous in their generations. May they bring forth kings, as you have said, and rulers of righteousness. If they stray from your paths, draw them as a shepherd draws his wandering sheep back to the fold. Heal their unrighteousness. Heal the hearts of my wife and my daughter. Let me live a life of honor. I don't know how to be a proper heir, a father, a husband. Teach me, God.

When I opened my eyes, I was surprised to see Leah making her way up the hillside, her straight hair lifting off her neck in the warm breeze. I hoped nothing was wrong.

Leah was not the young girl I'd met so many years ago, but age had favored her, brought the beauty of wisdom and grace. She was lovely in a way impossible to define. My heart moved within me as she picked her way over stones embedded in the ground, holding to her shawl, wiping the wayward strands of hair from her face.

I thought of when we first met. The stories she told of my grandfather. The faith I saw in her despite her confession that she had struggled to understand why God had taken her mother. I remembered the days after, when we laughed together over simple things, and she told me more of how she had come to believe in the Living God, and her sorrow that her family still held to dead gods that couldn't help them in their time of need. And I remembered the day I went to Laban to ask for Rachel—knowing that I was going to break Leah's heart.

I stood as she came to the place where the hill leveled off, my shoulders and my heart weighed down with regret. I loved this woman with everything in me. How could I have been so foolish to go all these years denying what was really in my heart?

She stopped several paces from me. The air between us stilled as though it didn't want to interrupt. She looked at me for a long moment, then bowed her head towards the ground. "Jacob, I'm . . . I'm so sorry."

Sorry?

She shook her head. "I have wronged you in so many ways."

She had wronged *me*? How could she think that? I could feel my brow pull into a deep crease. I had ravished her heart, held her guilty for her father's deeds. Dear God—I had told her I would never love her!

A knife turned in my chest. How could a woman hold up against such cruelty? It was I who should be on my knees, begging her forgiveness.

"Leah—"

"Please. Let me finish, Jacob. I need to say this."

Her lips quivered. "I have failed to honor you, and because of it our children have done the same. I allowed hurt to turn to anger, and anger to a root of bitterness. I've blamed you for all that's passed between us, never looking at my own fault." She laid her hand over her heart.

"Jacob. I haven't trusted you as a wife should trust her husband. Please, forgive me."

How could she have trusted me? I'd never given her a reason to.

I thought I might drown in the sorrow that filled my heart. I hadn't given Leah anything. I wanted to go to her, take her in my arms and tell her that I loved her, and that I had wronged her in every possible way. But I couldn't do that. She would not want it. How could I make her understand how I felt?

"Leah . . . how could you have trusted me?" I scrubbed my hand down my face, ashamed as the memories flooded over me. "I blamed you when you were clearly not to blame. And when I realized it, I let Rachel manipulate me into keeping up the sham. It is I who bears the blame. I have razed your self-esteem and ripped open your heart without a thought for your feelings. I'm sorry. So very sorry for all I've done to you."

Leah's lips parted in surprise. She didn't speak for several long moments.

"Your words ease my heart, Jacob." A small uncertain smile wavered at the edges of her mouth. "Thank you. Thank you."

And then she turned and started back the way she'd come.

No. No! She was walking away—and my heart was screaming for her to stop.

Don't leave, Leah. Turn around and look at me!

But she didn't. She kept walking. She wanted to make things right, but she didn't want *me.* I had no right to expect more. But I couldn't let her go.

"Leah."

She turned. Her damp eyes were cautious, as they had been when she'd stood in her thin shift and told me she was pregnant with Reuben, waiting to see if I would be glad or turn away. And I had turned away.

As they had been so many nights when she'd stood at the curtain of her sleeping chamber, waiting to see if I would come to her in love instead of obligation. I had not come in love, even after my heart had softened towards her, because I knew Rachel wouldn't let me love them both.

"I love you, Leah."

She didn't move. Didn't seem to breathe.

I walked toward her slowly, watching the uncertainty in her damp eyes. The question clear in the depths of honeyed brown: Was I coming to her because I wanted her? For herself? Or because Rachel was dead, and I had no other?

I took both of her hands in mine and knelt on the rocky soil, the small stones biting my knees. I kissed one hand and then the other and laid my forehead on the two. The soft warmth of them felt like healing balm.

"I love you more than you could ever know, Leah. Forgive me."

She didn't speak for what seemed like an eternity. Then knelt in front of me, tears spilling over her lashes and running down her cheeks. "It's about time," she said, a smile slipping over her lovely face. "I love you, too, Jacob."

My heart flooded with the most glorious joy. I laughed with relief and pulled her to her feet. Her face glowed with love. She was so beautiful. "How have you managed to put up with me all these years?"

"It wasn't easy," she said, laughing, her eyes bright with happiness and peace.

I took her in my arms. Her arms tightened around me, and my heart filled with gratitude and the very deepest love. I lifted her chin and kissed her forehead, her eyelids, her damp cheeks. I kissed her mouth with all the tenderness and love that was in me. I soaked up the warmth of her against me. It seeped through my robe and tunic and slipped through the pores of my skin until the cold fear that had gripped me melted and my heart was awash with peace. I had always loved Leah. She was a part of me, and I'd been only half a man without her.

As I held Leah in my arms, looking out at the sprawling oaks casting shadows on the verdant grass, at the valley of tents and cook fires and precious souls, I knew that I was finally home.

EPILOGUE

Jacob

The night of our reconciliation, I took Leah to my mother's tent and made love to her slowly, tenderly, pouring into her not just the seed of Abraham but all my love and affection. I continued to use my own tent as my grandfather had, a place to judge among my servants, to welcome strangers and sojourners, but every night I returned to Leah's bed and slept with her tucked into my chest, my arms around her, holding her close to my heart where she had always belonged.

The years were mostly peaceful as our hair turned more light than dark and our joints began to complain of the damp. Judah had returned, but he was restless, his heart in another place. But I turned him to God, knowing that He was abler than I to make Judah what he was destined to be.

Dinah studied herbs and plants with her mother and helped in the birthing tents in the valley and beyond, taking more and more of her mother's work on herself and most of the care of Benjamin, who never stood still for a moment.

Men came to offer for my only daughter, despite the circumstances of her lost virginity. But Dinah told Leah she didn't want to marry yet, and I didn't force her. She found fulfillment in her mother's work, which soon became her own. She said that someday she would accept one of the offers of marriage if the man was like her father, but for now she was content with her chosen path. I beamed at her words and kissed her forehead, thankful for such a treasure.

Levi and Simeon and the younger boys took wives and gave us grandchildren that played around our feet. Our sons lived more settled lives, though the scars of Shechem still lay raw on their souls, and jealousy still reigned in their hearts. Especially toward Joseph, who was beginning to trouble us all with his dreams of sheaves of grain, and the moon and sun and stars bowing down to him.

Then one day Leah didn't rise from her bed. Dinah stayed by her side, trying every remedy her mother had taught her. But Leah didn't respond—she became weaker. I knelt by her bed day after day and begged her not to leave me, but one morning her eyes closed, and she slipped away.

The next day, Reuben walked with me up the path that led to the burial cave. Things had not gotten better between us. But he did his duty as Leah's oldest son and accompanied me to the cave.

Somber light from torches secured in niches in the rock illuminated the large recess where three stone crypts lay. Two sheltered the bones of my grandparents and my parents, but my eyes were on the empty crypt where I would one day lie with Leah.

It was fitting that Leah be buried here instead of Rachel. The woman I had not chosen, chosen of God. What a foolish man I had been.

I moved toward the shelf carved out of the wall of the cave. Grief snatched my breath as I saw her there, taking her turn on the hard slab, waiting for the flesh to fall away from her narrow frame, leaving dry, brittle bones that her sons would gather and lay to rest in the empty crypt.

My fingers trembled as I touched the hollow of my wife's cold cheek. "I'm sorry, Leah, for all the time I wasted. I love you. I will miss you so very much." I kissed her forehead and laid my head on her still chest and wept.

I stepped out into the brightness of the day and looked out over the valley dotted with dark tents and wondered what the future held for the descendants of Abraham.

I didn't know if Reuben would ever forgive me for refusing him his birthright or keeping Bilhah from him. I didn't know what path my sons would take or what would become of Dinah. But I knew that God had said that from this family the whole world would be blessed. So I would leave it up to Him.

And I would wait—perhaps not so patiently—for my sons to walk the path to the cave, bringing me back to my beloved Leah.

A NOTE FROM THE AUTHOR

Many years ago, when I was reading through the Old Testament, I became enthralled with Leah's story, especially the picture painted in Genesis that God was watching Leah. He *saw* that she was unloved by her husband, and His heart was moved to open her womb and give her what her sister didn't have—children.

Genesis 29:31 When the LORD saw that Leah was not loved, he enabled her to conceive, but Rachel remained childless. (ESV)

Leah's journey through years of rejection was not an easy one. That God "saw" and cared about her situation was comforting to me, since I felt much of the same pain Leah did in my own marriage. Which—of course—informed my rendering of Leah's character. My prayer in writing the story of this extraordinary woman is that other women in pain will be aware that their Father watches over them carefully. He sees every tear, and He is working for their good.

Much has been made of Jacob and Rachel's love affair, but the Bible hints that all was not well with the couple. The scene where Rachel accuses Jacob of withholding children from her follows the biblical narrative very closely. Genesis 30:1 When Rachel saw that she bore Jacob no children, she envied her sister. She said to Jacob, "Give me children, or I shall die!" ESV

The next verse reveals Jacob's frustration with Rachel. (verse 2)

Jacob's anger was kindled against Rachel, and he said, "Am I in the place of God, who has withheld from you the fruit of the womb?" (ESV)

We see in Genesis 31:34 Rachel's inclination to mixed loyalties when she steals her father's household gods. Her dedication to the God of Abraham can easily be questioned. But in the end, God remembers Rachel, hears her cry, and gives her two sons, but she dies in childbirth.

In my reading of the scripture, I found it significant that Leah was buried in the family tomb. Family burial places were an important element in ancient societies. To me, it seemed it was God's way of honoring Leah. Rachel was buried alongside the road in the place where she died.

The challenge of writing biblical fiction lies in filling the 300 plus pages of a novel with gripping drama and emotion while being true to a few short scriptures. I've tried to do that, but it's possible I've overlooked something. If so, I apologize. It was not my intention. In my story-building I flesh out characters and events, but I do not deliberately contradict the scripture, either in word or in spirit.

I have, however, taken a few liberties. Covering most of a character's lifetime in one novel is not an easy task. Because of that, I've ignored the passing of time here and there. I haven't called attention to the exact number of years Jacob spent in his uncle's service. I've also written some scenes out of the order that they happened in the Bible. One being Reuben's affair with Bilhah. It actually happened sometime after Dinah's rape. I didn't feel that the scripture was violated by rearranging these scenes, and they better fit the proper structure of a novel in the order I wrote them.

Laban's sons are unnamed in the Bible, but their animosity towards Jacob *is* recorded in the scripture. Beor's attempted drowning of Leah, and his place as her primary antagonist are creations of my imagination, as are several of the scenes and secondary characters. If you'd like to read the account in the scriptures, it can be found in Genesis chapters 27-35.

Finishing this book was bittersweet. Leaving Leah and Jacob and the rest of the cast behind to create new characters in a new story gave me separation anxiety. I love them all. I hope you do too!

REFERENCES

Shechem, Wright, G. Ernest, McGraw Hill, New York and Toronto, 1963

The Oldest Cuisine in the World: Cooking in Mesopotamia, Bottero, Jean, The University of Chicago, Chicago and London, 2004

Life in Ancient Mesopotamia, Bertman, Stephen, Oxford University Press, New York, 2003

History Begins at Sumer, Kramer, Samuel Noah, Philadelphia, 1981

Soranus Gynecology, translated by Temkin, Owset, The Johns Hopkins University Press, Baltimore and London, 1991

Halley's Bible Handbook, Halley, Henry Hampton, Zondervan, Michigan 2000, 2007

DISCUSSION QUESTIONS

1. What do you think of Leah's refusal to accept Anasa's gift? Do you think she over-reacted? Do you think modern believers should wear talismans that are associated with sorcery or false gods? Why or why not?

2. Do you think Jacob's mother was right in helping Jacob deceive his father—even if Jacob's destiny to be the heir of Abraham seemed threatened? Does the end ever justify the means? Are you certain? What do you base your opinion on?

3. Throughout the book, both Leah and Jacob are conscious that God is watching them from above. Do you ever have the sense that God is watching you? Does that comfort you or disturb you? In what ways?

4. Do you think Laban and Jacob were alike in some ways? What specific actions described in the book support your theory? In what ways do you think they were different? Can God bless someone who has a tendency to be deceptive? What examples in this book support your theory?

5. What do you feel about the practice of plural marriage in the Bible? Do you think it was in God's original plan for man and

woman? Why or why not? How does it compare with marriage and divorce in our age? Can God work through people who are living in less than ideal marriage arrangements?

6. What do you feel about Rachel and Leah giving their handmaidens to Jacob to bear children by? What problems did this practice cause? What problems did it solve? How does it relate to modern day surrogacy?

7. What do you feel about Timnah and the other women's condemnation of Dinah after she was raped? Do you think the modern tendency is still to blame the victim? Do you know someone who has gone through a similar circumstance? Have people tended to put some blame on that person? Do you think it was justified?

8. What do you feel about Leah's fear that her sons couldn't be the blessing to the world that God said they would be because of their sin at Shechem? Have you ever worried that your children's actions (divorce, drugs, etc.) will keep them from fulfilling their destinies? Do you think God's plan includes our mistakes?

9. How do you feel about Leah and Rachel's ultimate reconciliation? Do you have an estranged family member? Do you believe God can restore that relationship? Is there anything you think God wants you to do help that happen?

10. What other Bible stories would you like to see Marilyn write about? Please let her know at marilyn@marilyntparker.com.

FREE AUDIO CHAPTERS!

Thank you for choosing *The Struggle for Love*! Please sign-up for my newsletter and you'll receive an audio recording of the first three chapters, read by me (I hope you can hear Leah's heart through my words) as well as access to updates about my upcoming novel, contests and other great stuff. Thank you!

HOW TO HELP THE AUTHOR

Thank you for reading *The Struggle for Love: The Story of Leah*. I hope you enjoyed it. If you would like to help, I'd appreciate it if you would leave a review on Amazon. More than anything other thing, reviews help authors to spread the word about their books. And they help readers to find the books they love. It doesn't have to be long or fancy. Just an honest expression of how the book made you feel. Please create your review for *The Struggle for Love: The Story of Leah* here.

Please create your review by scanning the QR code with your phone camera. It will take you directly to the product page.

ABOUT THE AUTHOR

Marilyn has worn many hats: pastor's wife, mother of four God-loving children, school teacher, singer/songwriter, author and blogger—to name a few. Four years after becoming a widow, she married Peter Parker. She thinks being Mrs. Spiderman is pretty cool! When Marilyn and her superhero husband are not out RVing they reside in Arizona with their monster dog, Mimi (don't let the cute name fool you!). Marilyn's greatest desire is that her work reflect the glory and goodness of God.

Made in the USA
Middletown, DE
27 August 2024

59891913R00196